My Name Is Ophelia

ELLE BOR

FIRST EDITION

www.green-cat.co

CONTENTS

Acknowledgments

This novel was written in a span of 4 years, following A Thousand Steps Home, as a bolder, more valiant, and sharpened version of Elle Bor. It was never meant to be a journey void of mental, emotional, and spiritual battles. I thank every single person who played a part in keeping me going, nudged me back to the right path in moments when I went astray, and propped me up each time a new agent or publication query response comes to deliver a cold hard blow of reality, a.k.a. rejections. There were 17 of them to be exact. In retrospect, I now understand that all the previous "no's" were not meant to deny me of my dream. They were essential so I could look back at my work and polish it to be deserving of the right editor, agent, or publishing house. More importantly, I lost myself in my blind objective, limiting my goal to simply write great novels and be recognized for them. I have forgotten that I do what I do to inspire, to put into words thoughts and feelings so that others will learn to understand and be understood. Once I recognized that, Lisa Greener came into my life and although their publishing house was not open to any new authors, she saw something in my work that others didn't and made an exception. My Name is Ophelia hardly conforms to the traditional mold when it comes to commercial impact and it speaks volumes of her faith in this story, as well as my ability to tell it. My gratitude goes a thousand folds to Lisa and Green Cat Books for taking a chance on me. Of course, this wouldn't be possible if not for the warm encouragement of this author I met on Instagram. Jennifer L. Rothwell, thank you for the life-changing connection. Special mention to Reina de Jesus and Co. for not only being a great friend all these years, but for her innate ability to wield my vision into this beautiful book cover before you. I am in awe of your talent, always. In collaboration with the latter, I'd like to recognize Maria Cassandra and Maria Enad for their contributions as well. Adopting Ophelia's persona in your image was key to binding my narrative to its ocular construct.

To my husband, Hector Armando, I thank you for your boundless love and for allowing the beginnings of this novel to rob us of our time together. Your sacrifices will never be in vain. I am so grateful for my parents and family from both sides. They have been my greatest supporters and have always cheered me on, even when my dreams are in line with great impossibility. My LOCAS, BATCHES, BERKS, ATIL Design, and CNU crew, I've seen you root for me while understanding that this may be a penniless endeavor. Thank you to my old writing mentors from grade school to college. I want to take this moment to honor my BSF English teachers for igniting my literary passion and for believing in my abilities before I could discern them myself. All those years of writing competitions and contributing to the school papers were worthwhile.

I refuse to conclude this while neglecting the multitude of people who have been my first avid readers and supporters. I regret that I cannot mention everyone. To my friends from Bato and Cebu, I will always remember being so excited to write new poems every day because you wanted to read them. It was our free and unconventional subscription system. It provokes a certain thrill down my core to reminiscence those days when you asked me for poetry dedications or love letters, even as a young and undeveloped writer back in the Philippines. My very first novel was handwritten on a thin notebook when I was 14, that ended up being passed around school without my knowledge. It was lost during a typhoon but was somehow recovered by my friend, as it drifted in flood waters. I always return to that moment when things feel so unattainable, when my spirits are broken by countless disappointments. It reminds me that whatever is meant for me will always find me.

Thank you again for the love and candor. All I ever wanted was to inspire people, to help give meaning to their lives through my writing. And if I induced that same sense of healing in one person, then I did my job. At the same time, I hope to blaze the trail for those who look like me, who came from where I started, and share similar hardships as I did. Anything is possible as long as we never give up. To God be the glory!

Dedication

To those who feel broken,

writhing in silence from aches that nobody sees

lost in a reality that others don't understand

and the ones who love them in spite of

this book is for you.

Some pains
Some wounds
Take kind hostage of souls
From the freedom
they believe
they don't deserve

A few return to the world with healed parts
while the rest lay adrift in ruins

The catacombs of the living,
that's where they go
For some of us,
who may not yet be dead
but might as well be.

Elle Bor

HENRY

"Where the hell is she?" Marcus hisses, cracking his knuckles in the dark. "I said 8:30. If anything happened. I swear—"

"Shhhh," I intrude his brewing anxiety, gripping his wrist to silence the disorder beneath it.

"What?" he asks with restraint, mouth pressed, and eyes shooting with temper.

He forces his hand out of my hold. Alarm is drumming loudly in his chest, akin to mine. I can hear them acclimatizing to the possibility of failure. The failure of our plans. The danger it levies against Ophelia. His sister. My friend. My...everything.

"It's her!" I toss a gasp of relief against the cold night air.

Marcus mimics my reprieve. "Thank God," he says quietly. I know he would have screamed, if only he could.

The grass rustles more urgently, as her feet skate through them in distress. Even from a distance, I can hear her battered lungs thirst for air. The moonlight gathers along the coarse path ahead of us, just in time for her racing silhouette to emerge.

"Here she comes. Atta girl!" Marcus whispers, voice stretching against his throat. He hides the trembles that are marshalling over his words. We both know we're not out of the woods just yet. Literally. Figuratively.

I turn around with a grave purpose, letting loose a commanding whistle. The headlights from the awaiting vehicle flicker twice in response. It's been parked on the side of Highway 61 as we waited here inconspicuously for Ophelia to reach the edge of the forest. Its hoary engine snarls at the turn of the key. I owe Anson big time for this one and practically my whole life to his wife, Adelpha.

1

The next time I look ahead, Ophelia's pale face cowers in the loss of adrenaline, as it lands on Marcus' chest. The light from the lamp post floods over them. I could feel all the oxygen within the margins congregate inside my lungs. It hurts, even this small relief.

"Marcus!" she cries, still visibly shaken.

A small flashlight leaves her grip. It tumbles over the trodden bed of wildflowers, plowed by the rush of tennis shoes at her arrival.

"Did anyone see you?" he questions her with authority.

She doesn't answer. The anticipation wrings a knot inside my stomach. Minutes pass before Ophelia shakes her head, sniffling and dry heaving.

Thank God!

He pulls away from her to inspect her feeble shape, touching her shoulders, arms, and down to her toes, as if the slim glint of light would be truthful to any of her wounds. Marcus' expression is unabashed of all the horrors that he imagined his sister endured, mostly in the few months that we left her here. But we had good reason. All of the crippling sacrifices we had to do was for this cause. How could we stomach the thought of leaving her?

"Are you hurt?" I inquire. It was almost a loud and critical demand for reply.

Her eyes widen, as if it's the first time she's becoming aware of my company. "No," she reconciles with a modest answer, even when there's a lot more to tell.

"My Ophie," Marcus whimpers, trapping her in his firm embrace once again.

The plan was to have her sneak out, once the girls head back to their tents. She used the same route we did when we ran away months ago. Thanks to Adelpha's inconspicuous access to the camp, she brought

Ophelia the message after posing as someone who delivered their food. The kids had their movie and pizza night earlier. It was their Friday thing. If only the world knew what goes on beyond that tall fence of aspen trees. It'd be hard for a couple of teenage boys to prove it, particularly because of the ordinary lives they lead. It's nothing like what you read about and see in the movies. Yet at the same time, it's every bit of horror meant to lance beyond skin deep. The home, our normal family unit- all but a smokescreen.

And I hate my parents for dying, for leaving me here to rot. I hate that the only person they trust to care for me, is a monster crouched inside a magnanimous fortress. In a few years I would become one of the richest eighteen-year olds in all of America. I'd be sleeping with money and its surplus, but at a cost. I'm certain of what that price looks like.

They'll find out what we did soon enough and I hope we're already miles away from this god-forsaken place by then. The next phase of our escape is in Marcus' hands now. My part is over. But we can't stay here anymore. What if they finally realized she's gone? What if he already sent his subordinates to search for her? They're not that far from our tails.

"It's time to go!" I disrupt Marcus' wretched gape, as alarm returns to my already edgy bearings. He flinches but is quick to recoil. He's been fraught enough to clue us in of this putrid alarm coursing in his blood, even as he toils firmly against it. I could tell that this is the last thing he wants her to see. He must be strong for her. Marcus has been good at this, the part where he forges his fear into bravery. That's something I must learn from him. But I completely understand this emotional lapse. We're all jumpy these days. *Fuck whoever thinks we have no reason to!* They don't understand. This is his baby sister we're talking about. This is Ophelia.

"Kids! Let's go," Anson reiterates my request. The brown, burly man releases his weight into his loud strides. His boots make thudding sounds against the asphalt road. He doesn't say much as he leans one side of his body on the driver's door, awaiting our compliance.

"Shit! He can't just sneak up on us like that," he drones, spitting a ball of gum right after. The quick jerk on Marcus' shoulders at the recognition of Anson's footsteps is another failure to hide his rebuttal of fear.

Ophelia is surprisingly not as startled as him. She nods at Marcus after he tells her something subdued. She hints some kind of understanding, before sweeping a quick glance in my direction. A weak smile forms across her mouth when our eyes meet. And I'm instantly threatened by the torrent of emotions cleaving the pit of my chest. I see misery underneath her forced respite, shouting a tongue-tied message only I could decipher. It bellows in a decibel that draws blood out of my heart, rather than my hearing. I don't think I've ever seen anything as strong and delicate as her spirit. And then, something latches deep, gripping the tendrils of my soul. It robs something out of me, this ache of caring for her across the wide space between us.

"Let's roll," Marcus remarks, hardly excited but simply resigned to the necessity.

The next thing I see is the sunrise. I'm numb to the passing of time now. If not for the adjustment of scenery, it feels like I'm trapped in a cyclone. Everything is at a standstill even in the midst of disarray, as Ophelia rests her weary head on my shoulder. Five hours have keenly stretched far behind us, spoiling only the truck's fuel but not the unsettling reality we must face when we reach our destination. If we make it.

"I'm gassing up," Anson slurs, busting the sacred quiet that has rendered some likeness of sleep on Marcus and Ophelia.

He adjusts his position on the front seat as our driver pulls up to a highway gas station. I don't know where we are, nor would I pretend to care. The last road sign I recognized was of Eden Prairie. Its only significance is the fact that we are far away from them now. I hope.

"Here's for the gas," Marcus says, noting the dollar bills in his hand. Took us a whole year to save those for this escape.

"No, son," Anson declines, wagging a finger at him. "Keep it. For the rainy days." His voice is stern but also caring. There's worry in them, almost a certainty of a longer, far more ghastly journey to tread when we get to Washington. I pray he's wrong but we all know the possibility of an ordinary life after what we just escaped from, is slim to none.

The next thing we hear is the driver's car door slamming shut while Anson heads for the small and almost run-down convenience store.

Marcus shifts to face me, trying not to make something out of the fact that his sister is nestled comfortably in my arms. "You can rest up here, man. I'll trade places with you," he finally says, the croak of slumber still stuck in his voice.

Is he not okay with me being this close to Ophelia? It's not the first time.

"I'm good. Maybe in the next state," I reply.

He chuckles while shaking his head. "You're gonna pop your head off by then."

"Ha! You noticed that."

It looks silly on the surface. But this is my duty, to make sure that we're not being followed. I didn't think he saw my constant stirring, making certain that every car coming behind us is not them.

He laughs again, while running his eyes down Ophelia's serene state. I don't think she slept this sound in a while. "We're gonna tell my dad everything. We have to," he adds, now looking to the meadows across the road.

"You sure?" I ask, almost lost for words. I don't know how Mr. Davis would take it, learning about everything we've been through. More importantly, I'm afraid of what he might do. If he decides to avenge his children, it'll cost him his life.

He only nods, feeling the weight of that responsibility as the oldest of us three. "How's your chest though? Been getting sick lately, huh?" he asks, trying to deflect.

"Okay," arrives my reply. I'll be fine now that I'm no longer in that filthy place. None of us are.

"Good!" he smiles, eyes falling back to his sister.

A long stretch of quiet invades us once again, while Anson maneuvers the fuel cap outside. I can tell something dark is approaching his thoughts, something that employs fear and desperation.

"Listen, man," he sighs before continuing. "We're gonna be fine. You. Me. Ophelia. We're gonna move on from this. It's gonna get better." And though he's pulling his tone to what sounds like a notion of hope, the lump in his throat is a small giveaway that he doubts the words coming out of his mouth. "But I... I worry for her. I don't wanna think about what her future looks like." His calm expression quickly dissolves into rage. "What she's been reduced to, I don't know how I could bring her back."

"Yeah," I nod and he acknowledges it. We both know what he means. I glance at the young woman leaning against my chest. I've seen broken things that are beyond repair. The last time was in her eyes, a soul burning in wounds. There are days that I just want to make it all go away. This pain never belonged to her and I hate how she made herself believe that this is all she deserves.

"And if anything happens to me, I need you to—" he adds, before I halt his momentum.

"Fuck off, man! Stop!" My loud reply forces Ophelia to shift her position, while still half asleep.

"Just let me finish!" Marcus mimics my temper, throwing his hands up.

"Hmmm," she groans before finding a pillow and leaning it against the window, away from me. She resumes her slumber, unsuspecting of the looming argument that has everything to do with her.

The fuel tank should be filled by now but I find Anson across the parking lot smoking a cigarette. It's better that he doesn't hear. Although, it wouldn't matter. He usually keeps to himself.

"I'm just being realistic here," Marcus continues, biting his lower lip. "We'd be lucky if she finishes school without thinking everybody's trying to hurt her. Will she have friends? A career? Will she fall in love? Will someone love her? You know, normal things."

I'm taken back by what he said, almost insulting my ability to see through all the brokenness and find something to love in his sister. *What about me, Marcus? Are you fucking blind?*

"She'll be fine!" And by God, I shove all my prayers into that thought, demanding it to come true. "She will be okay. She has us."

He forces a smirk, unmoved by my reassurance.

"But if anything happens to me, you're it. You have to make sure she's safe, no matter what," he whispers, aware that Ophelia could be listening.

Of course! Isn't it obvious? I'd die first before I let anyone lay a hand on her. But I dread the possibility this conversation draws. I just can't think about it.

"Man, I'm not even gonna apologize for this job I'm about to put on you. It has to be you. You hear me?" His voice resumes in subtle gasps, chest labored by the emotions he's trying to keep at bay.

I feel my heart drop to the bottom of my feet, carving out a hollow path through my gut. I know what that looks like. I'd lose my friend and the future I dreamed with this girl next to me. My fury is breaking my bones and scorching them without delay. It's the same chaos I go through in moments when she's right there but I couldn't touch her. There's just no way I could love Ophelia and protect her at the same time.

I drop a gape to her tranquil form, body already returning to the cradle of sleep. If only she knows that she's worth every sacrifice I made before today. And I will not hesitate to do the same thing tomorrow. Marcus' desolate expression reels me back to him. I know he's waiting for me to put to words our unspoken pact.

"You got it, bro," I finally tell him. And nothing feels as heavy and hollow at the same time. It draws blood out of my skin in the absence of a knife.

"Thanks, brother," he whispers. His eyes are cupping a well of tears, red and weary. He turns around the second he recognizes what I discern in them.

Ophelia's hand brushes over mine, and somehow, the burden of this promise feels a little lighter.

CHAPTER ONE

Some Monsters Don't Live Under the Bed

"Don't look at me like that!" I tell it, as desperation continues to lord over my frail silhouette.

The bald eagle perches tall on a Douglas fir branch, stalking its next meal. At the same time, it grimaces at me in disappointment. We capture each other's ogles from time to time. I'm certain of its scrutiny towards the rich variation of my wounds, even from the far distance. These injuries are seemingly the only ones capable of chronicling the passage of time, from infliction to the birth of scabs.

"Why don't you come down here and help me then," I implore the naïve beast once more.

Down below, the Puget Sound crashes into the boulders. Its graceful course is an invitation to the sea's imminent hunger. But the starvation it exudes is no match to mine, as I see no end to this fierce pursuit of liberty- in whatever form I could seize it.

The water's careless music and the carcasses it traps afloat, are almost inescapable upon their deathly calling. It's true. The waves chant my name every day, pitching an enticing message to end my life. But an anchor keeps me here, more than the physical ropes around parts of my body. It's always been Henry. Without him I would have already fled to that bluff.

The stinging pain on my wrist pulls me back from the fleeting distraction. Nothing I tried has been effective at unbinding my hands. I use another trick that was successful before. However, my teeth arrive at their pain limits, about to be pulverized by the grinding motion. It's not going to work this time.

Damn it!

Within these four walls and where the sunlight has been eager to evade, is my hell on earth.

Shall I give up now? What's the use in trying? Suppose I escape, where will I go then?

The same questions brought me back here inside this wooden cabin not so long ago, unappreciative of the outside world's grandeur, while nursing the many blows met by my diaphragm from last night's beating.

The door creaks, only revealing a pair of round eyes. They're illuminating from the dark hallway.

It's her.

I try to ignore the body walking into the skeleton room. Instead, I pull my attention back down to my bare foot, scanning over my unkempt French pedicure. It was a celebratory gesture for my impending liberty. Henry never showed. He was never planning to leave Landree for me.

Footsteps draw closer but her presence is not welcomed by my aching body. The remarkably glossy loafers she wears, along with her white buttoned up shirt, tucked inside a pair of waist high trousers, almost never give away the horror she witnesses night by night. She brings herself down to my level and clutches my shoulders with tenderness. I respond by shrugging them off, condoning her warm stare. She doesn't seem to be too surprised by my reaction.

"What do you want?" I ask in a muted scream.

She takes a deep breath, and pauses for a second before responding. "I just want to see how you're doing and I thought you might be hungry".

She waits for an answer while focusing on the purple patch of skin around my neck. A wince surfaces on her ceramic-like face. Maybe because she knows exactly how it got there. She looks away to blink back tears. They've been pooling in her eyes since the moment she saw my disfigured self. Rays of sunlight penetrate through the window behind her, taking with it the breeze. Her brown hair dances in it like a golden ocean. Light eyes assert innocence, even when they've been a slave to the tortures I happen to be the recipient of. She can do so much better somewhere else, but her decision to become Andrew's chambermaid is baffling. How far she'll go for this sick and sadistic loyalty, remains to be seen.

"Where were you last night?" I ask, armed with an unspoken message that's meant to guilt her. "Where were you when he was beating me?"

She looks my way, shaking her head and smirking at the same time. She crosses her arms and paces back and forth, probably to find the words to say. She seems riddled with discomfort.

"Why did you come back?" she replies with a useless inquiry, while moving about. A genuine care breaks out of her steel bearing. "I mean, you were out there, free from all these. You were out there. I gave you a head start to run to wherever you need to go. But you came back. Anywhere else would have been safe."

"I don't know!" I shout at her. "I don't know, okay." That's the truth.

She returns and sits next to my huddled form. An expression of concern brushes her face, the way someone in my past did. Her arms are draped tight around me now.

"I'm sorry. We'll find another way to get you out soon," she whispers to my ear, changing the course of her emotions.

If I'll ever make it.

"I was rooting for you. Rooting for Henry to come save the day. I see it. The way he looks at you. He'd die for your cause. That's how much he loves you."

He loves me? I test the words in my mouth but they're stale. I still have residuals of the same thing, left-over from when he last said it himself. Now, they're merely regurgitations of a lie that was forced down my throat. Henry's actions tell otherwise.

She gets up at once, and claps away the dust off her hands. I remain crouched on the filthy floor because I cannot bring my body to get up and lay on the bareboned cot.

"He'll be home soon. If you wanna eat, now is the time," is her subtle warning.

I only shake my head, while wrapping my arms around my knees.

She leaves me alone in silence. All I could hear is the sound of fragments from what used to be a living room décor, as she gathers them in her hands. Yes, that vase of course also left a number on my skull last night.

It is just me once again, trapped inside the four corners of this naked room, where the floorboards creak with each movement and body weight they cannot sustain. Insulation panels splay out from the sidings opposite me, exposing the busy spiders that have been my detached allies while in captivity. The ceiling is non-existent and has left the intersecting wooden beams orphan for what seems like a hundred years. The whole cabin reeks of abandonment and the notable wood odor declares a constant innuendo that it has gone through many Pacific Northwest storms.

This horrid space has witnessed enough vehemence in the form of Andrew, and his always innovative ways of making me watch myself crawl out of the brink of death. This is how he satisfies his perverse mind, while I endure this unimaginable pain that could coax even the wildlife outside to come crashing in and console me.

Yet, even as I howl my loudest, no one seems to hear me. They just know that nothing in me is salvageable. My insides, just like my once delicate and striking façade, are long gone. Maybe Henry feels the same, so strongly that he still couldn't go through it. Leaving with me a second time was just as bad of an idea as the first.

At the corner of my eye a flock of birds emerges from hiding, as if disturbed from their afternoon nap on the paper birch trees. I feel compelled to get up and watch the glorious spectacle closely. The bright yellow leaves are what's visible from up here. They border along a muddy trail, which leads to the back of this cabin. The window's security bars do little to impede my field of vision, as I see more grey birds fly out toward the Sound. With suspense impounding the air, an olive Jeep turns in from the blind curve. My heart falls.

Speaking of the devil.

I watch the car drive closer to the back entrance. It stops. He looks up, through the bird dropping-stained windshield, and catches a glimpse of me. The sight elicits no reaction from him. No surprise there. I sit back on the floor where he left me this morning, still bound at the hands. My bladder has been protesting for hours at this point.

Meanwhile, the engine dies and I can hear the slamming of the car door shortly after. I imagine him find the right key to insert into the keyhole. They're making jangling noises in his hands as we speak. Finally, the back door opens and his footsteps lead him to the kitchen, just a floor beneath me. I know he'll be grabbing a can of beer and he does just that.

Heavy footwork begins to make its way up the stairs, in the moments after the short pause of sizzling sounds.

One. Two. Three. Four. Five.

Then he moves around a stair landing.

One. Two. Three. Four. Five. Six.

Silence.

I choke from all the dust that blew into my nostrils. I can hear him clear his throat at the same time. The door pushes open, crashing into the wall behind it. More dust bunnies swirl downwards from the framework above him, but not remarkable enough to be noticed by his laser focused eyes. Their only subject is me.

"Hey!" he announces with a dreadful glee.

He doesn't hear a word from me but I hold my hands up to him, asking permission to be unbound. My bladder is about to explode in its internal pressure. Yet somehow, the request ignites a devious plan in his mind. I can see his eyes submit to the ruthless commands being concocted by the voices lingering in the shadows. His cheeks turn red, concealing the innocent freckles as he shuffles closer to my direction. I watch while his rubber boots leave behind a trail of desiccated dirt on the floor. He breaks in front of me. The stench of fish and saltwater plugs up my nostrils. He yanks my shoulders. I'm standing now, his face just a few inches from mine.

I examine him quietly while he scans me from head to toe. His brown hair has been drenched underneath his Mariners baseball cap. The waterproof jacket smells worse than it looks. Long lashes curl up just at the edge of his eyelids, highlighting a pair of deep-set eyes that brightens from time to time. He still looks flushed as I stare at his cheekbones, which has been contoured to almost perfection by God himself. He could have been an angel, one would think. But to hail him as such, is a betrayal to the carnage looming in his path. Because watching him is staring at my mortality in the eye.

His lips move, willing himself to speak through rancid breath. The smell of beer and barbecue sauce triggers my gastric juices to rise up my throat.

"You want me to untie you now? So you can pee?" mocks his deep and gruff voice.

"Andrew, please. I need to go," I plea, holding my hands up again at his mercy.

Tears roll down from my eyes. More than the fear, my body's internal dispute is getting harder to escape. I need to urinate. I've been urged to since he left this morning, and the burning pressure in my privates is intensifying by the minute. I continue to heave while begging him, both thighs clenched together to control the imminent leakage.

For a second, I become hopeful that my wails are breaking through his conscienceless bearings. He untangles the tight knot from my hands. I can already feel the relief as I ready myself to sprint to the bathroom, once this task is over. The rope descends to the floor but my hands are still held together by his strong grip.

What now?

I look back up to his angelic face and notice a smirk forming at his mouth. I should have known better.

In a swift motion, he turns me around and pushes my body against the wall. I can feel my lip splitting open on impact. My head bounces off. He reaches for a string to pull the blinds closed. The room becomes dark.

"Not so fast, Ophie," he tells me, in a murmur so sinister.

He works himself up as he moves to kiss my neck. The hairs on my nape stiffen in response. He continues to lather my skin with his wet tongue, while I'm listening to him throw pieces of clothing in all directions, including his boots. He glues his body again to my back, and his pitiful erection is felt on my unwelcoming form. His warm breath pinches my ear, as he gropes my breasts over my clothes.

He expects me to submit to this act but my body just recoils, still reminded of its angry bladder. Next, his cold hands touch my shoulders, stroking and taking both my sleeves down with the motion. My nightshirt falls, revealing no undergarments to protect my vulnerability. I am now exposed for this monster's voracious taking.

"Andrew, please! Let me go for a minute and you can do whatever you want afterwards," I cry out again, hoping for a different response.

"No, not yet!" he cautions.

His voice reverberates across the room, before I meet the wall once more. This time though, I prepare myself and use my hands to absorb the blow. The effort protects my face from another impact. But now the pain is irrefutable, so convincing I can feel it trailing in my bones. Never mind the splinters lodging inside my face, as he scrapes me toward him by my hair.

My back to him, his sex invades between my legs with hands securing mine to the wall. I resist, imagining my vaginal muscles clamp to deny him of the pleasure. It angers him into a bestial state. He releases a rumbling sound but I cannot decipher a word. Who knows what he'll do next. He tries penetrating through my anatomical barricade once more, prompting the same response from me. I lock my thighs together. Perhaps he'll stop. I'm hoping this torture will cease, even just for a moment, while I comfort my bladder. I hear him mutter something under his breath, while deciding to remove his grip off my wrists.

A tiny voice in my head dares for my escape but it will be in vain.

It plows through my body, a volley of agony. I can feel my throat constricting as another part is being smarted by his brutal force. The air in my lungs seems unable to sustain the massive blow, as I enter a dark phase that is now unavoidable. The pain is blinding and suffocating, muffling my violent screams out from my own ears. I can't tell anymore where it's coming from.

"You! Will! Let! Me! In!" he demands, fingers digging deeper into my arm, as he utters each word.

My pelvis endures the departure of bravery and the subsequent arrival of utter damage. Resilience waves its white flag as I drop down feeling spent and hopeless. I plant my body to the floor, as if by doing so will make this all stop. Not a moment too soon, I get an answer denying me of such naïve request.

I keep my eyes open, long enough before the pull of unconsciousness stakes its claim. Andrew rolls me over to face him, as the blur of his silhouette imposes both power and frustration. "Don't make me do that again, Ophie," he warns, voice now certain of his triumph.

He eases inside me while I lay there, allowing this assault to take place in its natural order. I don't have the energy to stop him anymore. His thrusts are slow in the beginning, but violent enough as it scrapes my raw insides. He continues on until his pace wages a taunting game against my bladder. He sees me wince and his smile right after proves his satisfaction. The shoving becomes faster and faster, until the last sign of my defeat streams out of my ureter.

The urine and his erection are taking turns stinging and grinding against my sore and extremely bruised interiors. He moans and groans before his steel expression replaces the exhilaration and gratification. He knows it's coming to an end and he can't accept that the short drive is more than enough to max out his potency. It emasculates him and his eyes blame me for it.

His shoves slow down to a halt and he collapses on top of me, right after his ejaculation becomes one with the rest of the lethal mixture, already steeping inside my vaginal walls. It's over for now and that realization leaves me with no purpose but to lay there.

I see him regard me with tenderness, an action that is both natural and peculiar. Whoever that monster was, it's gone. He touches my hair but I do not react. I want to cry, kick, and scream but there's no strength left to. It's already difficult to decide how I could possibly bring myself up from the flat surface, after all the beating my body has amassed these past few days. The only thing I know for sure is that I don't want to remain in this filthy state, while I am reminded of the poisons I must immediately eradicate from within me. Somehow that seems enough, as I find myself readying to leave the room.

I am bare from head to toe, walking down the hall towards the bathroom. Semen, blood, and urine stream down my inner thighs, creating a track of horror behind me. It's futile, to cover myself with any clothing article. There's nothing to preserve here.

I pull the brick-colored curtain. It makes a weird clattering sound against the metal rod. The shower is already running as steam soars listlessly from the tub, like hostile spirits being exorcised from my body. I step into the temporary relief, letting the water sooth me, every bone and muscle that needs a tender touch. This will be the next best thing to a human consolation I will get in a while.

Then I cry, loud and quaking. But it comes out hollow, wrung out of purpose. There's just a blank space in front of me, silent but hardly peaceful. Tears have always been a false sign of defeat, I now gather. Something worse is looming. This utter emptiness is a place I've never been to before. And I am terrified. At least in pain, there is something real to hold on to. There is an ache that accompanies me in the dark and deceitful road, a feeling at the very least. Right now, I feel nothing, as if I am not here.

I am not here.

CHAPTER TWO

Just As Nightmares Go, We Don't Lose Them In Waking.

It's over, the weekend. Everything but the terror on my skin.

"Ready?" Andrew asks, walking into the living area from the back door. His luminous glance is warring against my apprehensive shape.

Today, we return to Seattle. At least there, the proximity between neighbors makes it difficult for him to execute the degree of abuse he is accustomed to. There, my life is some semblance of ordinary.

I nod as I finish zipping up my duffel and purse. He looks decent today without his fishing garb. His plaid shirt compliments the faded jeans he has on. He is hunched down to the floor, tying his shoelaces.

My sharp gape lands at the corner of his eye. He notices my stare.

Shit!

I look away before our eyes could meet again. Will he be irritated or amused? With him, there's just no telling.

"Gonna go put the bags in the Jeep now," I announce, my voice quaking.

Getting up from a sitting position is more difficult than I had thought. I purse my lips to stop myself from whimpering and just then, the lower part of my body, particularly in-between my legs, screams in agony. I feel faint, my body weak. I see him rushing to my rescue, before the world spins.

"Easy now." He holds my shoulders to keep me from falling.

And even though Henry did not make good with his words, I still wish his arms are free to hold me right now. That child in Landree's womb should have been ours.

We were meant to be together. He was mine first. Then I realize, the year's long wait is probably enough of a statement for Henry to make, that I am not worth fighting for. In the same amount of time, I have been playing a fool. I subscribed to my own detriment- this godforsaken life that nobody would ever choose, not even for their mortal enemies. Yet here I am, making this relationship a launching pad, while I wait for him to come to his senses and pick me.

"Let's get you in the car now. I'll load up everything myself."

"I'm okay. I can do it," I lie, mentally assessing what threw me off balance. Nothing comes. Nothing beyond my cruel-stricken form.

"Hey..." His suave voice spoils my apprehension. "...I got this. Told you. This is what happens when you skip meals." He moves to face me and refuses to let my shoulders go. "I need you to make it to brunch. Heard about this place in Maltby."

I know better than to defy.

The outside air is just at the cusp of growing brittle. I forget how lovely the sunrise could be, just gazing at it. I spent the last few years discounting its beauty, only using it to flip the pages and look for something that may never be found.

We reach the passenger side of the Jeep and Andrew, in his atypical chivalrous deportment, opens the door for me. There is still that step-up I need to get to before sliding in the seat.

This is gonna hurt.

"Here, let me get you up." As if listening to my mental dialogue, he slides his arms on my back and carries me in a sweeping motion. I am now tucked into the safety of the passenger seat.

"Thanks," my voice escapes as a croak.

Even with the cushion absorbing my weight, the subtle impact and contact between my bottom and the seat doesn't spare me of the pain. I have neglected how much this hurts every time. Experience still hasn't prepared me for the next episode of torture.

"Heard they got huge cinnamon buns for five bucks," he yells from the back of the Jeep. "Crazy."

I watch him from the rear-view mirror load up our bags, grinning and shaking his head at the same time.

"Oh yeah? Can't wait to try it then," I respond with a forceful cheer, as I snap my seatbelt into place.

I hear him close the back of the vehicle. Soon enough, he hops right into the driver's seat. He looks at me one last time and winks before his turn to buckle up.

What a fucking psychopath!

He shifts the gear to reverse until the hood of the car is facing south. We move down the hill, on the mud-covered, semi-paved trail towards the public campground. We pass by the same rich-colored trees, until a curve slows us down. Two females on foot wave at us from the right side of the road. It is uncommon for hikers to make it up this way. This part of the Swinomish Reservation is off limits to them. The few cabins up here are only residential to the tribe members, like in Andrew's case.

Our vehicle comes to a halt.

"Hello. How you guys doing?" he greets them but the somberness remains a cord around his voice.

The women look distressed.

"Hi, sir! My name is Mabel and this is my daughter Harlow," the middle-aged lady replies.

"Hello," the daughter waves. I notice her inspecting the inside of our car before making an eye gesture to her mother.

"Hi," Andrew and I say in unison.

"We can't find our dog, Charlie. We saw him run up the hill two hours ago. Been looking for him since," Mabel explains.

The daughter examines me, probably wondering why I'm sitting here mute. Andrew is oddly calm in their presence. There is a silent exchange of pleasantries from them three. I feel weird. It's hard to explain.

"We haven't seen a dog wandering in these parts. I'm sorry," Andrew replies with concern, draping his free arm over the open car window.

"I don't know what to do," Mabel adds, shaking her head. She straightens her hiking pole and leans on it for support. But it's all hollow beneath her worry. I'm not convinced. Meanwhile, the daughter is yet to abandon her stare from me.

"I'd give you a lift to find Charlie but if he headed for the deep woods, we got hunters right now. It's not safe," he explains.

Liar.

"Is that so?" Harlow sounds hopeless and disappointed. She begins to play with her curly locks.

"But there are rangers down by your campground office. They can help," Andrew assures them. "I'll drive you."

"That sounds wonderful! Thank you so much!" says Mabel, expressing her immediate gratitude to him. The quick change in mood is almost suspect.

The two hop in the back seat without hesitation. I could sense caution from their body language, a forewarning of some unknown danger.

They should. It is Andrew we're talking about here.

It's a five-minute drive down the ranger's station. The ambiance seems quiet and eerie now inside the Jeep, but I don't have the ability to break that by any means of a small talk. I got better things to worry about.

When we finally reach the campground premises, I notice that Harlow is still watching me through the rear-view mirror. She is startled by Andrew's announcement of their arrival, and my eye contact.

What the fuck is her problem?

The three of them leave the Jeep after Mabel thanks me. Harlow, meanwhile, has not stopped scrutinizing.

Do I know her?

The dream ends.

****

I'm awake now, eyes still shut while wondering why my sleep always reaches out to that memory. The cabin torture and those strange women, none of them seem easy to forget. I repeat this scene every day as though Andrew's last morning was something to be honored in memory.

"Seven thirty-three," the small bedside clock heckles as I turn over. Teeth-grinding, jitter-inducing coffee is already permeating inside the room. It's a noose to my wits, this waking up every morning. The calm feels unnatural and the sense of an approaching danger is hard to disprove. But he's not here anymore. We've settled for that relief. The tapping of his tan brogues are merely ghosts, revived by no other than Adelpha's similar commotion on the kitchen floor. Although she provokes this trademark fear, each time she hands me a collection of pills for immediate and definite consumption, she never stays long enough to watch me swallow them. Andrew would have not allowed even a thin pill coating to melt in my palm. I'd have to take them in front of him, the same medications that sever my abysmal yearning for

23

Henry. He sure liked that, having this so-called power to rehabilitate me from this lifelong addiction.

"Aren't you getting up soon?" Her voice startles me. I nearly break the lamp on my side table.

It's not Andrew. Thank all the gods for that.

I open my eyes to a blurry apparition of her.

"What are you up to today?" she asks, picking up Andrew's overused question along with the throw pillows littered on the floor. "Adelpha opening up a Starbucks upstairs or what?"

I laugh hard. It feels too foreign and ancient. I didn't want to but it was a funny thought.

She looks more casual than the last time I saw her – just a pair of sweats and chestnut plaids. She seems tired too. Dark lines border around her eyes. Not sure where she's been since the impromptu visit at the hospital. She must have gone somewhere fun for the holiday.

"So?" she tries to remind me of her annoyance.

"So, what?" I reply, pouting my lips before hearing her inquiry a second time. "What are you up to?"

"I don't know. Stop asking me questions right now!" I snap back.

"Oh-kay..." rolling her eyes, she settles for an answer. Her sarcasm is now tucked inside her crossed arms.

I see her drag her bare feet to the corner of the room, collapsing on the sofa by the window.

"I'm sure you'll find out when you check her Instagram post," she teases.

"What do you mean?" I become intrigued.

"See for yourself!" She clowns, promising some interesting details.

In no time, I run my hand to the side table, pull the drawer open, and retrieve my phone. I can hear her chuckling from where she's seated, already aware of what I will find.

The application comes to view and I angrily tap at it until I get to her profile. Landree posted a photo ten minutes ago of her having breakfast with Henry. She wraps her arms around his neck, smiling from ear to ear. Henry holds an arm out, obviously the one taking the picture. Of course, he goes back to her as expected. This is the same storyline that is running its track once again. I saw it coming. I knew it was bound to happen, but I still happily slid back into the trap like the love-scorned, foolish girl that I am.

That's it? I imagine me giving up. There's a clear picture in my head of what that's like and it does not involve me crying in this room. It's more monumental than this. I need it to feel like the big bang theory, everything stops around me, Ellie Goulding playing in the background with her glass-breaking, light lyric soprano voice, and a convincing goodbye from Henry of some sort. I don't know, maybe I need to see it in his eyes. This doesn't feel like it and neither does that text from the other night, asking me how I'm doing.

"What are you gonna do about it?" she inquires, feet still dangling from the sofa's arm rest.

"Get answers," becomes my firm undertaking.

"No you're not! Are you trying to get yourself in trouble with Henry again?" she reasons, getting up from the sofa to move towards me.

She continues to nag her way forward, arms dangling on each side, and temper piping hot. Yet I have a way of phasing her out, much like her façade is completely exiled to disregard. I don't get her at times. She tempts me with information but tells me not to act on it. She fans the flames and abruptly puts it off when I'm finally provoked. Some friend she is. But I'm sure of it now. A simple response to "why" would do. Why, as if I'm going to hear a different answer than what he always pulls up from the recycle bin, break up after break up. No matter, there's still conversations to be had. I deserve the very least of that.

Hope barges in. My chest feels a slight tingle of excitement. All I can say is, thank God for technology.

CHAPTER THREE

The Phantom At Broad Daylight

"Just drop me off here," she orders, as the breeze rolls in from her side of the car. The restaurant is just around the corner. This is a good stop for both of us. "You're gonna be okay?" she asks quietly, even when the answer is too obvious.

I nod.

Perhaps the black hoodie will make me unrecognizable to them. Everything else is a product of a valiant stalking impulse and an addiction to torture. I only wish I have a decent hairdo than this bun held together by my natural hair oils.

"Goodbye," I bid. My subtle urging for her exit is welcomed by her similar goal to leave in haste.

"See ya!" She hops out. I watch her reflection until she becomes a mere dot, drifting on the side mirror.

What are you doing here, Ophelia? I ask myself, as the wind rushes in and knocks some sense into me. Right! I wanted answers, as if Henry leaving me was not enough of an assertion. I just can't let go. I want to see them and find the cracks where I can somehow lodge in, until I'm allowed to enter. Landree is the only pest I can't seem to eradicate. She is the Goliath among all my foes, favored to win but certainly not undefeatable.

I pull the hand brake up and ready myself to exit the vehicle. But first, I examine my facial features in the rear-view mirror. I think of how pointless this decision could turn out, but I can also argue its significance to where I stand in Henry's life.

"Welcome to Green Lake Bar and Grill! How many?"

I hold out a "sshhh" index finger to my lips and her face becomes apologetic.

"I'm sorry. I didn't mean to be rude, just that I'm trying to surprise someone. Wanna make sure they don't see me coming," I reason.

"Ok. Sure. Check to see if he's already here. If not, the bar and patio have open seating," she whispers back, assuming I'm meeting a man. Well, she's almost right.

The patio's side entrance seems like a good idea to go through without attracting their attention. I sneak in between the slew of brunch eaters, until I find a spot near a group of giggling senior women. Behind their camouflage is the perfect seating, just against the brick wall. I slide in haste before the table gets taken by the rest of the incoming guests behind me.

And there it is, their dreadful sight, becoming front and center through my focus lens. I watch in aching amazement the connection they have, that my eyes have been trying to deny all this time. My knuckles can be heard cracking in conjunction with the tormenting process. That's all I could do to repress myself of the pain that is slowly simmering in my chest.

Or is this something else? I have watched them from a distance many times before but there is no getting used to the hurt. It could easily knock the wind out of me, if I lose composure. How incredible, even dizzying for a single human being to carry and endure this much torment. What once was a place of love, I am now here witnessing this debauchery that love itself brought to me.

"Hello there! Have you decided what you want?" The wide-eyed , dark haired waitress inquires. "Or I can give you a few more minutes."

I have been sitting in front of an open menu for God knows how long and no clue what they even serve.

"Can I have some orange juice please and do you still have the crab Benedict?"

She listens with full attention. A trace of wonder is palpable through her facial tics. "I'm fairly new here so I don't know if that was on the old brunch menu but I can check with the kitchen staff."

"Sure thing! If not, the regular eggs benedict will do. You have those, right?"

"Yes, of course," she whispers, taking the menu from my willing hands.

"Thank you," I tell her, as I am scouring for a name tag of some sort. "Ahh. Thanks, Lisa."

"You are very welcome!"

She gives me one last innocent smile before turning her heels back towards the side bar. She's fetching my beverage now.

Now, where were we?

They continue their conceited display of affection. She touches his face, he brings his hand to her thigh, and it goes on and on. She chats away as he listens closely. His lips move, showing a grin that I wish was for me. How did I become such a glutton for punishment? My world stands still as people pass me by for either exit or entry. If being here is not proof enough of my madness, then I don't know what is.

"Okay, I got your orange juice here."

Yet, I cannot even turn to face her. My eyes are incapable of detaching themselves from what is happening ahead. I read his lips say, "I love you so much." I swear it was in slow motion.

In a moment of sudden thought, I am struck with disbelief. *That is a lie. You don't love that scum of the earth. Never. You love me. That depth only belongs to us.* I feel stones being thrown my direction and the feeling as they hit my body is beyond understanding.

Today, the robust glass I kept around me has been shattered by those mere words being told, though inaudible. Now it feels cold and gloomy. And after years of being in the sidelines watching, I can no longer bear it.

"Also, we were able to get your crab benedict going, and…" she tells me before pausing in anxiety. "Oh! Your elbow. Hold on please!"

She points to my arm but I can't entertain her warning when I'm still trying to make sense of this despicable sight.

Not long enough, I look down to see orange liquid spilling on the blindingly white tablecloth. That's all it takes to give me a momentary relief from the mixture of emotions I'm feeling. I get up at once and I can hear Lisa exclaim her apologies.

"It's okay, Lisa, don't worry about it. My fault," I assure her, my hand patting her shoulder.

I just don't want to embarrass her and draw attention to our table at the same time. I scan the surroundings in panic but it is already too late for that. Everyone has either taken a glance at the ruckus here or is staring.

Shit! Fuck!

I dock down in panic, pretending to help Lisa pick up the broken glass fragments off the floor.

"Miss, you seriously don't need to help me. It's my job you know," she advises, discomfort unmistakable on her face.

"It's okay, I want to. I knocked it over, remember?" I wink.

She responds with a shy beam and carries on with her task overhead. I remain hunched on the ground, allowing the barrier of waiters to shield me as they make a new table setting.

"Okay, almost good as new!" she calls out, my cue to get me out of hiding and back to being an adult.

Another waiter comes in with a dustpan and broom to dispose the broken glass pieces scattered on the floor.

Here we go!

Carefully, I ascend back to my seat with as much grace I can put out to the world. It looks like they have carried on with what they came here to do, my incident was but a quick nuisance and have been forgotten. I look over to Landree and my Henry to make certain that they didn't notice what has happened outside of their nauseating love bubble. I almost unknowingly make a gagging face, which brings my attention back to Lisa. She's been awaiting my approval.

"I'm sorry is there something wrong with the food?" she asks.

She must have seen the repulsion on my face as my food was being set on my table. Talk about awful timing.

"No. Not at all. Don't worry about it. This looks tasty though," I respond quietly.

"Ok, enjoy your meal!"

And she is gone before I could tell her to leave.

It appears as though they are wrapping up their meal and not a sign that they are aware of my presence. Just the way I like it. The tart taste in my mouth from the orange juice is slightly distracting, but I have to start consuming something before looking outwardly suspicious. I see Henry flag their waiter. As it appears, he wants the check or probably dessert. The waiter leaves and returns with a small, black leather binder. They're getting ready to go. Henry talks to Landree a little bit more. Its indescribable how carefree he feels around her. Landree just brings out the peace in him. I hate to admit it but I guess it's true. He is different towards me, there is care but tender and delicate. It's almost like he's walking on eggshells, afraid to hit the wrong fuse. Why am I just realizing this now? Perhaps my loneliness has peeled off a layer, exposing defeat in the face of my struggle to claim him. I don't know what it means anymore to love him these days.

He grabs his wallet and slides out a credit card, tucking it inside the binder. She smiles at him and in return, he steals a kiss from her lips before getting up to leave. Should I follow him or not? But before I could decide on either, Landree looks up to my direction. Her knowledge of my presence now becoming obvious. The waiter comes back to take the credit card and Landree gives him what he needs. Her eyes don't leave mine. She gets up, throwing the cloth napkin on the table. Her sly smile is evident and I can't help but cringe. She walks my way, a walk of a winner towards a sour loser.

Bring it on bitch!

"Ophelia. Fancy meeting you here," she greets me with a conniving smile as she makes herself welcome at my table.

"Landree. What are you doing here?" comes my surprised response. I almost fooled myself there.

She finds her seat across from me, elbows on the table. The scent of confidence reeks strongly from her.

"Oh, you know, just having a nice meal with my man. I saw you walk in," she hisses. "I don't know why you think you can just waltz in here and expect not to be noticed. For what? To watch us, like the freak that you are?" She wastes no second for any peaceful introduction. Her tone is frosty. "Look at you. Have some self-respect," she adds. "It's time to be done with this!"

"Huh? I don't know what you're talking about. I'm here with someone," I lie. "I don't see a sign that says I can't come here and eat. Do you?" A giggle leaves me as I look around.

She sighs as the fleeting silence comes between us. I can see the whole thought process on her face and the exasperation turns into concern. She shifts her body posture, arms intersecting over her chest. I'm not sure what to make of it.

"Please get help." She shakes her head and continues. "You obviously need it. You're sick, very sick! I truly feel bad for you these days."

Does she mean from Andrew? Is she telling me to escape from him? Has she forgotten? It's been done. I don't need her unsolicited advice.

"Henry's a better person than me. He still cares about you after everything. If it were up to me, you wouldn't be here," she warns.

I take a sip of my orange juice before responding with indifference. "I don't know what you're talking about."

"You know exactly what I'm talking about!" Her voice is escalating now.

She makes sure we're not within earshot from Henry, who just returned to an empty table. He sits back down, somehow assuming Landree just took a quick trip to the bathroom.

"What I'm trying to say is that you could do so much better with your life. I know this breaks you. But please, leave us alone," she continues. "He will never tell you to go away. You are Marcus' little sister and that's enough of a reason to keep you around. But don't confuse that responsibility for love. Just do the right thing."

The nerve!

"Whatever it is that Henry and I have is really none of your business," I bark back. "And, if it's staying away you're talking about, you need to take that up with him. He's the one holding the leash." I push my face close to hers, with an explicit mocking expression. "You know what I'm talking about!"

She looks away before responding. "But do you even hear yourself? Of course it is my business. He is the father of this child." There's a pause to cradle her belly. "And for crying out loud, Ophelia! You have lost your damn mind."

"Hmmm... Okay," I nod, rolling my eyes.

It's not the reaction she is hoping for. In fact, it's quite evident she's holding back her rage, the one that has the potential to rip me apart. She's hormonal after all.

"You just don't get it, do you? Henry and I are moving forward. If you can't do that, leave us alone. Stop showing up to fake brunch dates in the same places we go. You're just wasting your energy," she cries out.

"But it's not going to waste at all. I told you I'm waiting on someone," is my defense.

People from the nearby tables are beginning to notice the tension in ours. I wish for a miracle, right this second. A hot and tantalizing hero wouldn't be so bad. My little patience is not going to hold me down for much longer. I am ready to just break her nose and I can see that she wants to do the same, judging from the tremor in her hands. Onlookers are increasing by the headcount now.

"Really now. I bet that if I sit and wait here all day," she brags, wagging her index finger at me. "Nobody's gonna show up."

"Oh, but I bet you a hundred dollars you're wrong about that." A man's voice busts in between our quarrel.

Who the hell is that?

We both look up to see who the husky, unfamiliar voice belongs to. This towering man, over six feet tall, comes around to leave a peck on my cheek. I regard him with so much wonder and mystery. His skin is dewy, kissed by the sun gods to perfection. I trace his neckline up to a face brimming with excitement. Those teeth could blind me. When the wayfarers come off, enviable lashes adorn a pair of mesmerizing eyes, that showcases my reflection in them. These butterflies really have their uncanny way of making me feel things in my body's lower half. *Be very careful what you wish for.*

He begins to remove his leather jacket and hangs it on the empty chair to my right. *Good Lord!* All the time spent at the gym can truly do a man justice. Half-exposed biceps allow one to catch a bitch mid-swoon.

Landree I see you!

"Sorry I'm late! Traffic was bad on I-5," he announces, turning to flash a sexy look in my direction.

Okay. I'll play along.

"I hope I didn't interrupt anything here, ladies," he says, picking up a fork and tasting the already cold meal.

"Hmm. Crab Benedict!" He mutters distractingly.

"No, not at all," is Landree's response, startled by what she is seeing.

Yeah, bitch!

"I was just leaving but nice to meet you..." She pushes the chair back and extends a hand before a thought diverts her focus. "I'm sorry, I didn't catch your name?"

"Oh, my apologies how rude of us," the man jests, mouth full while wiping his hand with the napkin, hanging off his neck like a bib. His smile continues to rule above us like a puppeteer.

"Noah, my name is Noah," he says, shaking Landree's hand.

She turns to regard me one last time and I smile back, a victorious one too. I haven't felt like this in a while. I win today. I feel the stranger's arm slide around my neck, while the other waves at her. Just the cherry on top!

And she bids goodbye, conceding to her wrong assumption. She returns to the waiting arms of Henry, who has a quizzical look on his face. He realizes where Landree's been. I know he sees me. We catch a glimpse of each other. His eyes raid the male presence sitting at my table. Noah acknowledges his attention with a nod. Somehow, it provokes disorder in Henry's bearings. He lunges forward before Landree shoves her hand on his chest. He was going to come over but stopped at her command.

In this moment, I realize that my efforts have been rendered impotent against her. Landree had already won the true prize in this duel. My strong desire for him continues to salivate as she waves that trophy in my face. They disappear into the exit, with Henry still visibly upset at something. It's over and so is this charade.

"I don't know what to say. I mean, why did you do that?" I question the stranger nervously.

"Uhmm! A thank you would be nice for starters," he responds before gulping the whole glass of water intended for me.

"Gosh! Of course! Thank you. Couldn't have been a better timing. How'd you…" I ramble on before being interrupted.

"Okay now. Too many questions. Let's take it easy. People already saw enough drama today," he says, spreading his arms to regard the surroundings. "But yeah, I was just minding my own business, looking for a table then I heard a cat fight about to break. Thought I'd step in and save you. By the way, you're not waiting for anyone, right?" He begins to worry.

I let out a laugh, short but a genuine one from amusement. I have not felt this in a while.

"No! Good thing. I was waiting for you, remember?" becomes my answer.

"No problem," he laughs. "That was fun," he adds, with a fist out to me, waiting to be reciprocated.

I oblige by tapping it with my own balled hand before inquiring, "You said your name's Noah?"

"Yup!" he nods, keeping busy with the pancakes.

Noah. It has a feel to it and incredibly natural to say.

"Nice to meet you, Noah. You know I can call Lisa, our waitress to order more. You look like a hungry beast! On me of course," I remark with a tinge of humor.

He stops, almost embarrassed by my statement. If his complexion is a bit lighter, I'm almost certain he's blushing right this second. There is a grin starting at his mouth now and he shakes his head, as if to rid of some silly thought. I don't know about this one. A cosmic and dangerous unknown seems to prowl in that head but everything about him is beautiful, even if I'm just barely touching the surface. The mystery draws me through the magnet of his gaze and I didn't even realize it earlier on.

"I'm getting the brunch steak, medium rare, Blue Moon 20, and a mimosa for the pretty lady. Also, everything will be on my tab. What about you, O?"

Huh? Didn't realize he had lured Lisa to our table in the midst of my musing. I can tell she appreciates the lovely sight, as probably every girl who lays eyes on him. Her smile tells everything of her fascination. I feel a shade of discomfort in my chest, a sense of ownership in the verge of being confiscated. The answer grazes my consciousness and I don't like the sound of it. It's shouting at me, saying that he's mine.

"Earth to Ophie," he interrupts, snapping his fingers in my face.

"Oh. Sorry. I'm good. I'm not hungry anymore," I fumble through my words, slightly turning to the waitress. "And please, Lisa, I will pay for it all, including whatever this gentleman consumes."

He scowls, somewhat tilting his head to the left, for Lisa to see his sternness. "Not a chance, Lisa. I'm the guy. You know the rules."

The waitress nods, feeling his sweet dominance over her. She's not willing to argue. "Okay, charge all to him then," she confirms, before leaving the table in a seductive manner.

"So that's settled," he announces, rubbing his palms for whatever purpose.

He acts very carefree, seemingly undisturbed by any movement outside of our space.

"You should have seen your face earlier. I mean, she was about to eat you alive and you just had that 'SOS' sign on your forehead. It was hard to miss," he jokes about my earlier confrontation with Landree.

I shift my weight to the right side of my body, preparing myself to counter his witty insults. "You didn't have to. I was handling it fine."

I am a bit irritated. Is it because of this buoyant energy that I'm not used to? Or because my body is hardly impervious against his charms? In the midst of his playful ways, Noah's expression changes. He opens his mouth to speak but holds back, cautious of his words.

He clears his throat again. This time, allowing passage for his deep thoughts. "Look, I'm sorry," he whispers, reaching for my hand. "I mean no disrespect. Saw what happened and just wanted to help."

I quickly withdraw from his hold, feeling the undeniable electric surge from his touch. It's hard to read this abrasive character. He's not like any other guy I met before, and I don't know how to act around him.

"Apology accepted," I respond quietly.

His face lights up in an instant, like he'd just won something out of the slot machine. Well, that is encouraging that my approval means something to him.

"Steak and eggs…" Lisa trails, carrying a tray of food and alcoholic drinks.

Or maybe that was just his excitement for the food coming his way. I may have expected too much.

The waitress leaves as quickly as she arrived, but not before batting her synthetic eyelashes for Noah's appreciation. I do a mental eye-roll before sipping the mimosa he ordered for me.

He starts to cut his steak into thin strips. "What were you doing getting rowdy with that Landree chick anyway? You seem like a nice girl." He asks a simple question, that to me holds some profound weight.

Silence.

How does one answer that in this point of the saga? Do I start by telling him the history, detail by detail? Or just the recent events that led me here? Does he even deserve the truth? Christ! I've only met him not even an hour ago.

He finally looks up, realizing his question yields some discomfort from my end. Regret is obvious in his eyes even though he plasters a wide smile. I gather that I must say something now before he apologizes again. It's not his fault that he unknowingly scratched the surface of a really messed up situation, for lack of a better term.

"Long story," is all I can muster.

"Okay, I got all day. There's always next time too," he quips before dropping a bite size piece of meat in his mouth.

What does he mean next time? That will never happen. I mean he's nice to look at and for a moment, the attention is a welcome distraction. That's all there is to it. My goal remains clear.

"If it's not obvious enough, I wanna do this again," he clarifies.

I laugh hard, not knowing why. Maybe I'm entertained by the idea that this guy, a really handsome one to say the least, is asking me out. Not to mention, he just saved me from a great deal of embarrassment with Landree. Men like him don't just come at my feet and see something beautiful. It just doesn't work that way.

"Hmmm?" The lines on his forehead are probing. "You're laughing now? Is that a *yes* or a *no* laugh? I'm sweating here, babe," he appeals again.

"Oh. My. God. You're serious," I reply, still giggling. It's hardly a statement. I'm uncertain of his objectives.

"So, yes to a second date then?" he asks me again, voice low and hopeful this time around.

I clear my throat before the next time I speak. "Noah, right?" There is a sudden pause to his scrutiny now. His spine collapses on the back of the chair afterwards, disheartened by the approaching rejection. It's palpable in my voice. "Listen, as wonderful as this has been, I just can't. You're a very attractive man and I'm sure there's a lot more prospects out there. But I am a married woman," I tell him, confirming his pending disappointment.

He shakes his head. A weak smile bends his lips. "Ok. But wait a minute." I dread his next words. "You admit that I'm cute then?" There is a playful arrogance to his tone, something to be expected of him. It seems like.

I shake my head while biting my lips. This guy is determined.

"Yeah sure, but you missed the point. I'm married," I say, aiming at my ring ringer.

"Spouses who are gone, they don't count. Try again," is his brass comeback, still devouring steak in-between words.

Somehow, the response lights a fire under my skin. His tone is all-knowing and it makes me feel vulnerable. My mood skates to the end of the spectrum, to the embodiment of undiluted fury.

"What do you mean?" I yell at him, grabbing the straps from my handbag off the back rest.

I wasn't prepared for the conversation to go this way but I proved my point that he's nothing but a pretty face to look at. He can't be allowed in. I set myself to leave, getting up and pushing my chair back to allow space for my departure.

He grows worried and stands up, moving quickly to my side with an appeal. "Wait! Don't go yet or at least let me walk you out."

"It's okay. I have to get going now. Thanks for the save and brunch," I address him while collecting my keys from the purse, never looking up.

Regret is overwhelming his appearance, when I finally get a glimpse of his face. That is not going to work anymore though.

"Noah, it was really fun but there's nothing else to it," is my final au revoir before turning around to leave behind this fine-looking bloke and the sore events leading up to his cameo.

I half-expect him to run after and stop me, but even that tiny hope is rejected by the universe. He doesn't press further. Noah just allows me to go back and resume my uncanny role in Henry's life. I will be returning to the bedlam brought about by the angry voices in my head and the ones from the murky eyes of Andrew.

The ground taunts me. How quickly did that stranger enter into this mess? He barely looked into the peephole and found out all there is to know about Ophelia's obsession with Henry. That has really been the entirety of what my life means now. Or is that a noble cause for which many have statues in their name? Ten, twenty years feels like a hundred when one just waits. I'm slowly beginning to question its worth.

ELLE BOR

CHAPTER FOUR

When The Dream Ends

"Ophelia! Breakfast!" Adelpha's deafening order from upstairs interrupts the subtle noise of the television. "I'm leaving now. It's late," she adds.

My breath reeks of this blend of saliva and alcohol, and my hardened tears seems to have glued my eyes shut. The wool blanket around me was the perfect accompaniment to the heavy crying session I endured on this couch last night. I wish I could just stay here forever.

"Bye, Ophelia," she yells. The framework above me wobbles at her footsteps.

"See you, Adelpha," I reply with my hoarse voice.

The door closes shut. I don't think she heard my farewell.

Yesterday's events keep replaying in my head. For the very first time, the inclination to give him up amounted to something more. I was seeing Landree and Henry from a different angle, even when they were doing the same monotonous demonstration as they always have. There's something about what happened that makes me feel so defeated.

I scour for the remote, eyes still closed. I hear her walk in.

"Well, what an eventful affair! Wasn't it?" she announces.

"You could say that," I reply, as I open my eyes to watch her pull the blinds.

The light invades my vision. An imaginary hammer pounds hard. How painful this hangover is, I'm just now realizing.

"I let myself in cuz you haven't been answering my calls." Her crinkled eyes are welcome by my emotionally battered state. "You should definitely change your hiding spot though," she remarks, as the silver key swings around her index finger. Her silence awaits my reaction but I have been stingy with my answers. "Well, tell me everything," she demands.

"Hmm, same shit different day," I lie, easing myself up to a sitting position. There's reluctance from my body to do the task and I understand why. I'm aching all over, in my chest more importantly.

"Whatever you say then." She doesn't broach this subject, diverting the tension to a more suitable source instead. "Any word from Andrew?" she solicits.

There's a zap on my spine, just hearing his name being spoken.

"Nope!" I respond, dreading the thought.

For a short time, I have forgotten of his existence, of such horrific non-human. Thanks to her, reality is now returning, swerving in. The break from his cruelty proves to be short-lived.

My phone rings but I refuse to find it, much less answer the caller. Who could it be? I hope it's not one of Henry's people from outside. They must be angry that I left yesterday, right under their noses. I stir to find a more comfortable position while getting a hold of the remote control once more. The insignificance from the television show is finally over, now that it's been powered off. It continues to ring but I go on without a care, rubbing my eyes, and tying my hair up. However, she emerges from the bathroom to retrieve it.

"It's Henry!" is her deafening confirmation, as the ringing ceases.

I'm frozen. He hasn't called in a while. Lately, middlemen have been carrying out his bidding, such as getting my house in order and paying my bills.

Five missed calls from Henry, I confirm after she hands it to me.

"Are you gonna call him back?" she asks. The pressure to do so is obvious in her tone.

"I... don't know. I have no clue," is my dazed response.

"Maybe he misses you. That you mean so much to him than that bitch Landree. Come on! Do something now," she urges.

I wish for nothing more than that future but something tells me it's not why he called. I waited to run away with him many times before, and was disillusioned just as much. I would jump at the opportunity but it feels different waking up this morning.

Yesterday, I was seduced by this new feeling of importance. I thirst for the same elation when I met Noah.

Damn! I shouldn't be thinking about that guy.

But I couldn't help it. Many have failed to exude his wild and irresistible influence. He invites himself into my waiting arms, like a new plaything.

Henry on the other hand, he's probably just calling to nag.

"It's ringing again," she brings me back from my reverie.

"Hello," without thought, I answer, my voice cold and uncaring.

"Hey, it's me..." It's Henry's soothing voice swaying in my ear.

Of course, I know its him. I have committed that name to my whole existence. This voice is unmistakable, the one I long to hear in every waking moment of everyday. Meanwhile, I see her clasping her hands in front of me, with a wide grin and a nod of approval. Then, she comes around the coffee table and listens in, one ear against the back of my phone.

"I'm outside."

And that's all it takes to disable all my bodily functions. On the other hand, she jumps up and willfully mimics the running man dance as a show of excitement.

"Okay," I answer in a low voice before the call's abrupt end.

What in the hell!? I should be ecstatic. What's happening warrants a more positive reaction other than what I'm feeling. I have been waiting for this moment when, at last, he'll come knocking at my door again.

Wait, why does he even knock? He has the spare keys. This is his house and the people manning my life are on his payroll.

"Okay, that is my cue to leave. I'll go through the back," comes her singsong voice, as she puts on her coat and disappears quietly from my sight.

I find myself pacing around after retrieving my slippers. What do I do? At least wash my face and gargle, right? I do that in the bathroom nearby. I let the faucet run. Warm water flows through, before I bring my face down to wash. Next, I grab the Listerine to dump in my mouth. The minty sensation wakes me up, before I spit the liquid out into the sink. I pat my face dry with the small towel from the drawer, and all the while, catching a reflection of my sullen face on the mirror. My deep sigh echoes within the small space, at the realization that Henry is outside waiting for me. I'm only prolonging the inevitable.

On my way up the stairs, I pull a silk robe from the hook and don it. The clock on the right side of the wall settles my disoriented state. It's 2:30 pm on this autumn Tuesday. Sunlight creeps in between the cracks of the wooden blinds, its glare is offensive to my eyes. After a few painstaking steps, the front door is before me. My body is put to a halt. The man I love at the cost of my measly life is just behind that door. I am suddenly met with indecision.

Whatever news he brings will never be in my favor. Just as the excitement warms my stomach, his presence carries a stigma I know all too well. His sweet arrival will always be punctuated by an abrupt departure. Have I become jaded and finally opened my eyes to this catastrophe of a love story? I should be, but I continue to devour this fragrant bait over and over.

I turn the knob to open the door, my mind refusing to imagine what I'll find outside, and in what form he'll be in. He stands tall, with strands of his light brown hair peeking from underneath his neon-green Seahawks beanie. These past few weeks while apart from him, I have briefly overlooked the gravity of how much injury my heart could sustain, while loving him in the same breadth. Henry's desolate gaze only adds to the emotional assault. No amount of training can ever prepare me well enough to evade it.

"Hey!" I greet him, voice sounding uninterested.

"Hi," he responds, gloom recognizable in his tone.

There's an eerie chill in the background, apart from the barren trees in my front yard. Crows line up the branches where the leaves would have been, cooing and rattling in a daunting melody. The sun hides behind the hovering gray clouds, sensing the imminent heartbreak that is about to begin.

"Is this a good time?" he asks, regarding me from head to toe.

"I guess so. I mean, Andrew's not here," I say, with apprehension.

He's noticeably shaking his head, grinning in disbelief and adds, "Of course he's not. Why would he be?"

He makes it sound like I just said something outrageous. I couldn't ignore it.

"What was that all about?" I ask, my temper elevating.

"Nothing. Forget it," he dismisses.

Henry rubs his neck, maybe to maintain his composure but his body language still lingers in doubt. I can hear him sigh, more than once in fact. His hands slide inside his jean pockets, and it seems like there are a lot of things boiling in that head of his, a lot more than I may be ready for.

"Do you think I can come inside?" he inquires in his uniquely deep and warm voice.

I hesitate for half a second for no apparent reason, but resolve not to keep him outside.

"Sure."

I make a hand gesture to usher him in. He halts at the door, brushing his muddy boots against the mat. He removes his hat. We walk a few steps to the receiving room, in front of a dead fireplace. Without command whatsoever, he brings himself to a sitting position, landing on the cream upholstered seat. Next to him is a glass-top round table, with metallic legs. A picture frame of myself in my veterinarian gear and Maddie, my old husky, catches his attention. With legs-crossed in a four-figure manner, he examines the photograph.

"Maddie was a good dog," he announces, with one hand rubbing his chin.

Really? Did you just come here to tell me that?

Deep inside, I could just lunge at him! I want to scream at the top of my lungs and ask him all the questions lagging in my brain, since he left me waiting a second time. Or was that the third? Fourth? I don't know... I lost count. It doesn't matter anymore. I'm just tired of passing my days, scrutinizing the immense heartache he left me to deal with on my own. I can't believe I'm even admitting to it. I'm finally tired. I told myself I could never get weary of him. I'm going to live to tell the story now.

I make my way to the sofa across from him, to sit down and drive this verbal and emotional exchange to the right direction.

"Yeah, she was. I miss her."

In retrospect, that was one of the best unguarded moments in my life. I had just finished veterinary school, a day after adopting Maddie from her unruly life to death row. My best friend, the apple of my eye was the one who took the photo. Henry and I finished school at the same time, planned our lives with certainty that we would spend them together until the end. We would open our own clinic, not that he needed the money. I thought that we would become a love story fitting for the books.

Yet, he had a different future in mind, one where I am merely a spectator. This life was not what I foresee but for years on end, I hoped to change the outcome of this bleak tale. I have lost everything in the process and my desperation landed me in Andrew's arms. His entrance meant nothing more than a temporary haven, to nurse my wounds until I'm ready to fight for Henry again. Much to my dismay, the shelter became a prison, a maze I can't seem to escape from to this day.

"What are you doing here, Henry?" I ask coldly. "Does Landree know you're here?"

He pulls away from his musing in response, eyes peeled to the aloofness on my very form.

He sighs before dismissing my outburst, "That's not important anymore."

"Okay, then what is?" My voice is mounting to a scream. "Why are you here now?"

"Ophie, settle down please," he begs, adding, "I have to just check up on you, make sure you're safe."

Check up on me? After all this time. Why?

"Ohhh....kay?" My pitch grows sarcastic. "Safe from what?" I let out a laugh.

This is becoming silly, the concern and visiting out of the blue, when for months, I could barely get a hold of him without choking the men outside.

He gets up, feeling endangered by my remark, or from the reaction he'll receive once he finally tells me what he came here to do. Looks like the fireplace is his obvious destination. He stands next to it and holds on to the deep molding profile of its mantle. The grass-cloth wallpaper highlights his sullen and dreary figure against its gray canvas.

He takes a deep breath before speaking. "Listen, never mind what happened before this but you need to be careful. Be sure you know who you're letting in. Nothing's changed."

What is he talking about? But I take a wild guess. "You're referring to Noah... The guy from yesterday."

He nods, "Or anyone for that matter."

I shake my head, disbelief gnawing at my ears. "I don't know why it matters. It's not like you don't already decide that for me."

Though for a short-lived moment, I feel a pinch of triumph. He's jealous. He can't stand to see me with anyone else. The adlib of Noah saving the day must have worked to my advantage, even with the slight inconvenience that's Noah himself. It is unfortunate that he didn't stand in the way between Andrew and I back then. Why, the answer of which remains to be told. For now, let me revel in the thought that this day has finally come.

I leap from my sitting position to his unsuspecting form. Even with his arms still crossed against his chest, I force an embrace. The action startles him at first, but he adjusts.

"Ophie..." I hear him say with mild retaliation.

In my ears, no sound could ever sway in an invisible dance quite like his. It tantalizes my wholeness and awakens the hair on my nape. His voice electrocutes my spine and my glands salivate excessively. Surrendering to his strong hold makes me feel weightless. We are on a blank plane, just us two in this uninhabited rendition. I feel his warm hands on my shoulders and I prepare myself to be pulled into his sweet attack. I close my eyes to focus on his mouthwatering lips, that are about to land on mine any second now.

The wait becomes excruciating, as the chill in the air passes through the growing space between us. He pushes me away and I'm realizing that I expected nothing more than a fantasy.

I open my eyes to his hardened expression. Yet, even that could not erase the tenderness in his gaze. It makes everything forgivable as I drop down to the floor, defeated. I bury my face in my own hands, is gradually soaking in tears. I didn't know I could still yield them. The pain of rejection is not new to me but the ache remains brand new, as long as Henry inflicts it.

I can feel his presence assuming the same position as my body on the ground. His arm touches my back while the other tries to remove my hands from my face.

"Come on, Ophelia. Don't do this right now," he pleads.

But I continue to heave and wail as if today is my last. It sure feels that way. Using my silk robe, I wipe my face and sniffle the last bit of moisture. Tears are pooling in Henry's eyes when I finally find the courage to look at him. The trace of disappointment is hard to miss, and he stares back at me with sadness that pales in comparison to what's escaping from my chest.

"What is it though? What do you want from me?" My voice trembles as I stare at the window ahead. "We had something. Everything you did. I know you love me. Why can't you admit it just this once?" My robe continues to sustain the tears that I can't seem to stop from falling.

"You're not a hard person to love Ophelia and—" A thought stops him.

"Because what? Why do you make this so difficult? Everything I've ever done was for you," I ask, whimpering a little.

He remains quiet, slow breaths casting away his rage. He's failing. I know. "Because that's not what I'm supposed to do!" he yells, shifting his body to face me. "Do you understand?"

"If you can't, then leave me alone. Stop doing this..." I beg him, my voice trailing in tremor. "You know what that does to me. You confuse me. I accept my fate and then you reel me back in," I continue.

"I'm sorry.. Sorry.. I'm really sorry. I just wanna protect you," he consoles as he cups my face, wiping the tears with his thumbs. Shame and guilt strangle his voice. It was easy to mistake it for love in the beginning.

"Let me go. Let me live with whatever I have left," I beg again, with a distorted expression, unable to hide the blow to my heart.

Swiftly, he brings me to an embrace. "Easy now. Sshhh. It's okay, Ophie," as I carry on with my quiet cries against his steel build.

"I hate to see you this way. I just can't bear it," he's heard muttering from behind my hair.

I pull away as an immediate reaction. I know what he's about to say and I'm not prepared to hear it.

"I have to protect you. For him. I promised him," he continues.

"Don't say it!" I warn, finding my footing to get away from him.

I can hear his tracks following me back to the sofa area, his hand catching mine. There's no choice but to face him. The sight could crush me. Henry stands motionless, molting away his tough layer to expose his most vulnerable self. He's overcome with tears. There's just no way to describe it. Words fail me.

"I miss him too, you know. Every day," he declares, under pained breath. "I'm doing this for him. I need to take care of you. He made me promise that and you know I already failed him once."

Yet in this fragile moment, I can't help but rebel against his testimony. "I don't need protection. I can take care of myself!"

"Of course you do!" He points his index finger to the door's direction. "You have no idea how grave this is, why you're here right now sitting inside as they stand guard. You have forgotten about what brought us here. We tried so hard to live a normal life but you know at what cost," he responds, appearing stern even as his cries leave no room for both of us to recover.

"I don't know what you mean. What is it, Henry?" I ask, still confused. I really don't.

"And we had a deal. You can go out but never alone. They answer to me, not you. Okay? I understand that you wanna forget. Maybe it's better that way. I want the same for me too but I can't turn it off like you did. Those were awful times for both of us. Just. Just be careful. Don't trust anyone you meet," he warns, cupping my face a second time. "And you're right. You deserve a normal life. But I'm here to make something clear to you. There's no easy way to go about it. Not for you. Not even for me. What we've been through, there's a certain method that have always allowed us to survive, far away from it all. I need to make sure of that, which is why I can't just give you the kind of freedom you're asking. I'm always gonna be looking after you, no matter what. Yes, even when my life is with Landree now. It seems selfish and I wish there's a better way to make you understand."

Possibly for moral support or just the need to feel him, I place my hands over his. My sobs escape me once more, realizing this is goodbye. Not the kind that would prevent me from seeing him again, but it is the goodbye meant to cement the fact that we will never be together. I won't need to chase him. Maybe I just needed to hear it, to give me some sort of closure. I'm being freed from the incarceration by my love for him.

"This is hard for me too but with how things have been with Landree, I can't be here all the time. They'll still be around for your protection though. That won't change." He's quiet for a moment, allowing his thoughts to form into something worthy of his words. "All this pain, you and I," as he taps his chest, "I'm gonna need to walk away from it. You deserve it. I deserve it. It's haunting me, Ophie. Everything! His memory, all of it. I don't wanna feel stuck anymore. All I'm asking is that you be careful."

My heart stops to make way for the alarm, slipping through my entirety. A loud explosion enters my senses. It could only be coming from my own artillery, deep in my chest. It hurts as if my muscles are being stretched to their limits, twisted, and finally torn into shreds in a fast forward pace. Every ounce of hope left to carry me out of this hell hole is obliterated by just these parting words. I am hurt and angry but none of my tears are outfitted to justify how I really feel.

He brings my face to his, and kisses me on the forehead, quickly but fervently.

"I'm always gonna protect you, Ophie, even when I'm not here."

And he turns around, heading for the door. I feel a massacre commencing from the many nerve-endings in my idle body. No reprisals, just screams of agony. The carnage he left of myself is unspeakable and the damage has been over a decade in the making. I stand still, with a heart stained by the bloodshed love often leaves in its wake.

CHAPTER FIVE

The Monsters Under My Bed

"Kara! Hey! Come out," I call out to her.

There's always been a prophesy of how this day will turn out. The hymn of his departure was just too wicked. I didn't expect that we would reach the end of the road this way. When he first met Landree and got together with her, I knew that our love still had a fighting chance. This time it's different. The tiny voice of hope was intoning a sad soliloquy, much like waving a white flag. All I had to do was look at him in the eye to know that I have lost him forever.

Where is she? I need her. This solitude will destroy me.

As an answer, there's a loud knocking from the front door. A sense of urgency from whoever's outside to be let in is obvious. But I'm almost certain it isn't her. She never comes announcing her arrival.

"Coming!" I yell.

I walk through the living room, towards the receiving area. I scan through the spot where Henry and I had our conversation earlier, and decide that it might be worth it to put a caution tape around here. The door is mere steps away but I am stopped in my tracks. No matter who is outside, they do not deserve my deranged form. The thickness of my eye bags almost obscures my vision and I'm dragging myself as if my body weighs a thousand pounds. My croaky voice would fail miserably at denying the fact that no sort of mayhem happened within the four corners of this room. I probably stink too. My whole self, is not a sight to be seen just yet.

Wait! What if it's Andrew?

But the person made it as far as my entrance. He must seem harmless to the people outside. I should ease up.

"Yes?" I open the door to inspect the insistent company, already forgetting Henry's stringent rule of looking through the peephole first.

Then, it raids in almost immediately, this hollow feeling from all the meals I skipped today. It could also be from the nostalgic sight of Noah looking relieved to see me. At the same time, his get-me-inside-right-now face is hard to ignore.

"Hi!" he exclaims and looks back at something he's trying to avoid.

Soon my neighbor comes running from her house across the street. As she arrives at my front door, her look of suspicion is met by Noah's alluring smile. The quite heavy set, middle-aged lady brushes by his shoulder with just a tinge of impoliteness. His appeal falls without grace against Adelpha's thick defenses. There's a swell of defeat in his shifted body language, probably realizing that some women are immune to his disarming presence. Now that we're face to face, she seems almost appalled by my unkempt appearance but decides not to mention it.

She gives Noah a sharp look before asking me, "This *andras* bothering you, Ophelia? I'm feeding the boys at the house but they come back soon. I watch you for them."

I look at him with a little bit of playfulness and his eyes widen at the realization of my mischievous plan. He shakes his head to plead his case and of course, I already know I can't bring myself to carry it out.

"Well? Do I call guards now? Police?" she presses on, in her ostensive Greek accent.

I catch Noah at the corner of my eye, resolved that I'll take Adelpha's offer. After all, we left yesterday's conversation in not so good terms. Why be courteous now?

"No, Adelpha. This is my friend, Noah. He's just visiting me," I finally respond, while patting him on the shoulder.

"Oh yes! I'm Ophelia's friend," he interrupts, the edges of his smile expanding to his ears.

I see him move around to face my neighbor and holds out a hand. "Adelpha? My name is Noah. Pleasure to meet you."

But Adelpha is less than delighted. She plants her hands on her hips and carries on with her distrustful front. Her ankle length floral dress is covered in white powder. Must be flour, I gather. She ignores his courtesy and instead, interrogates him.

"Why I see you drive too much here this morning? You're thief?"

Noah's eyes flash. "Oh no. I just can't seem to find Ophelia's house here. It's been too long since I visited," he responds, now standing next to me with a hand dangling over my left shoulder.

Wrong! I just moved here. Nobody else from my past could have known where I live now.

"You sure?" enters Adelpha's determined wariness.

This morning? How does he even know where I live? Has he been following me since yesterday? Has he been stalking me? Oh God! Insecurity explodes from my chest, giving me a taste of my own medicine.

"Not to worry, Adelpha. Noah here..." I reply, regarding him with a sense of familiarity before continuing, "...is visiting from out of town."

Adelpha becomes distracted by her cellphone, nullifying Noah's female magnet. "Mmmm... Okay." She taps on the device some more. "Whatever you say," she adds, still with suspicion, but resolves that it's not her place to question me anymore. That's Henry's job. It is possible that she's conversing with him right now through text.

She turns back around to head home without some sort of goodbye, as if some command prompted her to.

"Adelpha!" I call out. To which, she responds by turning her body halfway in our direction. "Thank you for the concern again! But nothing to worry here." I wave at her.

She dismisses my gratitude, feeling resigned but still suspicious. "Yeah! Yeah! You young people very careless," she mutters.

Even as she is crossing the street, nearing her porch, Adelpha can still be heard mumbling some sort of lecture about this generation of women. She finally disappears into her front door and it's time to deal with the task at hand.

"And you can explain inside," I whisper without looking at him.

He springs forward, closely behind me, as we cross the wide-open entrance to the receiving area. He shuts the door and locks it, then is quickly back right next to my shoulder. He seems to ignore a cardinal rule of personal bubbles. The feel of his body is electric as it was before, even with my satin robe as armor. I feel defenseless in his company but I will neither admit to that nor show it.

"Nice digs!" he announces, venerating Henry's interior design choice. He has yet to find out our odd arrangement.

Unbeknownst to him, here was a battlefield not so long ago. Of all the fights I am willing to surrender to, the one in honor of my love for Henry was my greatest fall. I can still feel remnants of the attack in my chest as I tread through land mines of pain. Residual echoes of my cries for him will now disturb this sacred space. It will be hard to see the light at the end, with this fog of uncertainties blinding my war-torn view. Henry drained all the fight left in me, the moment he begged not to be fought for any longer.

We reach the kitchen. He begins to detach from me. I observe him move around the marble island to inspect the photos held by souvenir magnets. The stainless-steel fridge with its towering height is almost to Noah's level. *What a strapping man!* I think to myself. While Adelpha was able to fight off his charms, my resistance is rendered limp by the mere sight of him. The attraction is a snake, slithering from hiding towards my unwary stance. I feel it wrapping around me. I'm breathless at every magical blink of Noah's eyes, even from the limits of his side view. Head to toe, he's every inch of a golden warrior I imagined one to be.

"Is this who I think it is?" he asks, pointing to a photo that becomes a rapid antidote to Noah's spell on me.

"Yeah. That's Andrew. My fiancée," I confirm quietly with my head down.

"Ex... Ex fiancée," he argues, moving towards me.

He's right, Ophelia. Why is that photo still there? Are you crazy?

I think he's wondering why that photo still lives and is on display inside my home. I question myself of the same thing. Just as she does. I guess I just forgot. I'm rarely in here. Perhaps Andrew left behind a chilling authority here, as if he is a god that I'm forced to worship.

"Come on, Ophie. I'm not naïve and I watch the news sometimes," he continues.

Anger plagues my blood almost immediately. My body is predisposed to it.

"You don't know what you're talking about." I become defensive, my voice escalating to a scream.

Though Noah is unaffected by my oral attack, his face softens at the sight of tears, assembling in my eyes. He is calmly absorbing the quiet rage in the air and the indecisions questioning me in my mind. In the meantime, he scans everything in the room until something catches his interest.

"And what about this?" He asks, picking up an old newspaper from the counter.

Only a few parts of the headline can be discerned but I just want it out of my sight. Apprehension abruptly fuels my mind to take the next step. I begin to walk towards him like a woman on a mission.

"Give me that!" I order, grabbing the item from his hand.

He lets it go without a fight. I see him put his hands up in surrender to my irrational and childish outburst. I can feel him stepping aside as I crumple the papers, finding their way into the kitchen trash afterwards. I sigh to find air but fail to bring any into my hungry lungs. There's just no stopping this paralyzing feeling. Andrew's reminder is capable of affecting me in two ways. I either tremble in horror or in regret at what we could have been. Right now, it's obvious which way I'm leaning towards.

Noah's warm touch reaches my arm. He appeases me but I grow even more troubled. I'm mad at myself. It's torture, the fact that my skin throbs in the area where his hand is. I like the sensation. I hate it at the same time. The surge has become stronger. His hold burns my skin and I know I have to fight it.

"Are you okay?" he inquires.

Everything becomes dark. I'm not okay. My life is a mess. I just lost my only reason to go on. What do I have to live for now if not for my love for Henry? It's Andrew's fault. It's everyone's fault. I will never be happy. Now this stranger just comes, confusing my heart even more.

His grip on me flourishes stronger, as the thermostat in my head adjusts to high. My emotions are breaking out from every exit in my body. I can feel myself quiver.

"It's okay, Ophie..."

And nothing angers me more. *I said I'm not okay!* Everyone thinks they can decide how I should feel, specially this stranger.

I turn around, marking my obvious target. Something has been stirred in me, a switch flipped. He has nothing but mercy. But I see through him. Beneath that, he thinks he's better than me. I imagine him laughing deep inside, mocking the circumstance that I'm in.

Poor Ophelia.

"You don't know what I deal with every day!" I scream at him.

He stumbles back, not from what I said but by the adrenaline rush that's powering my rigid shove. Unrelenting, he gets back up to my aid and secures me in his arms. I resist. My fists reach his chest, pounding in defiance. The voice is coaching me now. *Show him! Show him what you can do! You're no chopped liver.* She instigates. He does nothing, says no word while I continue to hit and scream at his strong barricade.

I cry and moan, my voice almost unrecognizable. Who is this person? I wish I had met her when Andrew was beating me and when I was ensnared by the monster that came before him. Not for long, I finally submit myself to Noah's warm embrace. Feeling depleted of everything, my upper body curls up to the safety and protection of this stranger.

We stand like this for a while.

It is possible that Noah has a cunning plan threatening in his head. He could harm me if he wanted to. Hell, he could even kill me. So, what if I'll perish in his hands? It was only a matter of time anyway and what better way to leave this world than in the hands of a god? *I'll die anytime.* The thought makes me chuckle, a comic relief. I'm dangling between forces of emotions, all screaming at me to be obeyed.

"What are you laughing about?" he asks, pulling away.

He heard me. Noah's grin is natural. There's nothing in his body language that tells me about any apprehension at my recent display of fury.

And I respond, staring at his warm smile, "I don't know." My voice remains unsteady. "It's just so fucked up. Everything."

"It's gonna be alright," he assures, wiping the excess tears from my face before continuing. "And I'm sorry for whatever I said to cause..." He pauses to find the right words to describe the disturbance that unfolded before him. Well, what was it anyway that started this? Andrew? The trash that is my life? "...to make you feel upset."

I find myself nodding, his sincerity nudging at me. Of course, there is always a likelihood that this is a sham but I'll take it. Nobody has been able to stand patiently against my deficiencies, except for Henry. Noah should have called for help by now. He must already think I'm crazy. Something about him though. There's a subtle indication that he's used to this, that he knows I'll act this way. What is wrong with him?

This man is an enigma, just his presence alone brings forth so many questions.

Oh no! His presence!

"Wait. How did you find me? How did you know where I live?" I ask, pulling a bar stool to sit.

Why that wasn't my first thought, is a testament to his spellbinding character.

"Well," he smirks, with one hand inside his jacket pocket.

I see him pull something out and it's not until he holds it up when I recognize my wallet. Oh Lord! How could I have forgotten that?

He sets the object on the island counter before saying, "I found it when you left and of course I have to return it."

"Oh," I respond, shaking my head. "I didn't even know. Thank you for the effort you put into getting this back to me."

"Well, it wasn't hard with your driver's license being in there, Ophelia

Noelle Anderson," he remarks with a hint of innocent mockery.

Warm blood is felt pooling in my neck and face. I have never been so embarrassed. Nowadays, I'm just Ophie. Something in the way he said my name gives a resurgence to my identity. It feels old but new. There is an awakening in my gut.

But wait! My address? I thought Henry took care of that. That's not a real one on there.

"Also," he continues, as I watch him come closer to me. "That was a good excuse to see you again."

His wonderful smell reaches my nostrils, just as he stops inches away from me. He leans over the island in a submissive and childlike manner, lips pouting. My fretful query and its consequence to my safety dies in an instant. The declaration feels nice but also prickly. Why me? What did he see through my vacant eyes in that restaurant? What did he see in my empty life that can still be salvaged? I have nothing to offer him especially after moments ago. He should flee while he can.

"I'm sorry to disappoint you then," I answer coldly.

"What do you mean? I'm serious," he reveals. "I wanna take you out. For real this time."

What he said catches me off guard. My heart could leap. Really? Why?

"After what you saw...You should be running for the hills. Are you?" I ask. Even I fear the answer.

I manage to get a hold of my wallet from across the surface and begin to play with it. He has not responded and that becomes the confirmation of what I already suspect. I don't want to see it in his eyes. There is already ample rejection to go around from the days that passed.

I can feel Noah shift, until I realize he's standing very close to me. He leans forward to close the gap between our faces.

"Hey you, lighten up!" as his hand crawls over towards mine. "Everyone has their quirks and I just so happen to see it right away." He ends his remark with a sultry wink.

I feel the rush from his touch, and through his words, spoken with so much legitimacy. It makes one dispel any doubt. Our skin together is electric as usual, resuscitating my spirits to life. There must still be something left inside this wounded heart that only he could see. I can't believe I'm even saying that.

Gazing at him, I joke, "I guess no more surprises now!"

And he laughs like a kid full of animation, an effect I have yet to be successful with virtually anyone. When I say that, I really mean Henry. That would be a first, to laugh at my unoriginal attempt at a joke. It feels unreal.

"That was a good one," he comments when he finally catches his breath, never letting go of my hand.

I find myself smiling, in a manner so relaxed. The feeling is alien. It's hard to accept that I deserve this but I ignore the mental debate between logic and emotion. I lay my head on his shoulder, with this newfound and immediate trust that I built in a matter of minutes.

Maybe it's him, a shot in the dark abyss not very many escape from. It might be too soon to tell. I am finally aware of the undeniable connection we have, though the memory of Henry and my nightmare with Andrew keeps tugging at my feet. Having known Noah in this extremely short time is dangerous but why do I feel safe? This emotion he swiftly evokes from me, even with its oddity is welcome to all my senses. That should be enough to cease the questions.

For now.

"You hungry?" he asks in the middle of the soothing silence.

A few minutes have passed while we sat there as we are. I, with the load of contrasting emotions, tucked together in their safety space. Him on the other hand, is an inscrutable presence taming my feral nature.

"Very!"

I speak for the long hours of no sustenance in my body as I hear my stomach grumble in recognition. A smile escapes my mouth. He answers with a gregarious one that momentarily hides the diamonds in his eyes.

"Ok, Ophelia! Better get dressed," he declares, while pulling away to face me.

"Sure," is my response, readying my body to go to the bedroom and change. "Give me like ten minutes."

He looks at his watch. "Ten minutes starts now," he jokes. "That's in eighteen hundred hours."

Whatever that means.

I'm giggling while I leave the kitchen in a hurry. An aching pull stops me in my tracks. I realize then, the scale of which he affects me. It feels like a metal chain is tied around my body, the other end at his command. The farther I go, the more uncomfortable it becomes to be away from him. This can't be. I've only known this person for a mere few hours and I have become a puppet to an unsuspecting puppeteer. Or is it my hesitation to move forward? It could be that my current prison is tightening the shackles, unwilling to set me free from the howls of my past. This is the same past which equates to Henry and Andrew pulling me from opposite directions.

You don't deserve this!

Oh no!

You belong here instead!

They're back, the taunting voices.

Pursue that future with Henry.

It's not over until you say so!

Don't forget what you did.

Remember?

"No!" I shout at them.

They become unrelenting, like gibberish chants that are weakening me. They're louder, this cult surrounding my thoughts. I remember vividly when they came last, with Andrew as their target. He was weak enough to consume the poison that made him who he is. Exaltations about their power is paralyzing and I feel my defeat taking over. I'm seconds away from losing until the dark blockage immobilizes me. Their white noise is now a heart pounding blast in my ear. I'm rendered into nothing but somehow, I'm able to trek back into the warmth that's calling my name. I can fight this. I know I can.

"Ophie. What's wrong?"

I open my eyes to Noah gently caressing my shoulders, worried and confused. I watch the demons slither away, dissolving back into the walls behind him. I did it. The air of victory graces my body. I won, at least today.

"There was a spider," I lie.

And more intensely than the last, he chuckles. The sound is heard all over the house as he tilts his head back in humorous disbelief. He pulls me in to an embrace.

"You're okay now," he consoles, rubbing my back while still riding in the waves of his own laughter. "I'm here to annihilate these damn spiders."

"Oh, stop it!" I push him playfully. "You have no idea." A pout disfigures my face.

"Okay. Okay. I'll stop but you should see your face. White as flour," as he points at me, still controlling his amusement inside the puffs of his cheeks.

All I can do is shake my head, hands on my waist. "You sure think everything is funny."

I watch him shrug. "Well, pretty much," he replies while touching my face. "You should really get ready now."

"Okay."

I reach to turn the knob, sensing him watching me and relishing in the thought.

"Wear something comfy and bundle up," he calls out before I shut the door behind me.

I run to the wicker hamper, placed at a corner by the window. There, I'll find my outfit of choice.

****

I wait for a click to make certain that the front door is locked before turning to the street. I don't see a car, not even Noah. I'm just with the company of cicadas, preaching an insect chorus. It's their show of solidarity at my brand-new wealth of courage. The men are nowhere to be found but I know they're around, disguised in vigilance. I half expect them to stop me but instead, I see Noah. He props up from behind the rhododendron bush, with a beam that could knock the wind out of me. This feeling is familiar but unlike how it came to me before, there's a touch of freedom this time. My emotions are natural and unprovoked.

He puts his leather jacket on as he regards me. I stand there, three steps down my front door and in utter simplicity, that is undeserving of his splendor.

"I like the view," he calls out, eyeing me from head to toe.

"Where's your car? Or should I drive?" I ask, pointing to the garage behind me.

He quips, "Nope, my lady, we are going for a ride, a real one," he teases.

I see him hold a hand out and I gladly take it when I reach the bottom of the steps. My heart is bouncing against the trampoline of my chest muscles. I am nervously inspired by the thought of going off course, no plans, just pure spontaneity. He guides me to the side of the house where I discover the ride he's referring to.

Fear runs over me, but the quiet elation that is a gift from Noah's presence bans any anxiety from entering. The Harley shines her silver metallic glow, a masterpiece waiting to be tampered with. Behind it, the auburn reign of this September dusk burns fiercely. The rain takes a needed break for now, while the sunset paints an impeccable shadow of him moving about. It casts a mesmerizing commotion ahead of nightfall. Now with a helmet on, he hands me over another one from the compartment.

"Wear this," he orders.

He places it in my keen hands but I am stopped by the idea of getting on a motorcycle. It's never been done before.

Noah senses my discomfort and comes to my assistance. He takes the item back. "What's wrong?"

"Nothing," a little white lie.

"No, tell me," he inquires again. This time he grabs my hands. "My God! They're frozen."

"Uhmm. I just... I've never done this before," I say quietly.

His forehead wrinkles upon hearing my response and certainly there are more questions he'd like to ask. But he doesn't. Noah places the helmet on the seat before seizing my hands again. He tucks them in between his palms, rubbing our skins for warmth. The friction is stimulating my every sense, more than the electricity his touch compels. Heat flourishes within our grip and I know then that there's no place I'd rather be.

He blows on our hands before speaking. "First time being on a motorcycle with a stranger?"

I shake my head.

He argues coolly, "Come on now? What is it? If I were to do you harm, I'd have done it there inside the house."

"No, it's not that. I'm just scared," becomes my near inaudible response.

"Okay. How about as a show of good faith, I would go to Adelpha's house and leave her my info. Fuck, I'd even let her take my picture," is his urging.

I smile back at him just a little bit before sarcasm spoils it from my end, "That's cute."

But he persists, "No, really! I would."

"No need. It's just that…" I trail, feeling shy about my hesitation. "I just have never been on a motorcycle before."

It would be hard to hide the surprise on his face but he doesn't even flinch. "You'll be fine. Already forgotten how to ride, huh? Just hold on to me. I got you."

I nod in response, resistance bellowing at my feet. It's hard to ignore his comment, the certainty he has that this isn't my first time being on a motorcycle. Maybe I heard it wrong. Perhaps, he just wants to distract me from my own discomfort. He takes the helmet back and gently slides it onto my head. It's a bit suffocating at first but something I could get used to.

"Perfect fit!" he declares.

After the task, he hops on the regal beast to prompt a wild sound from the motors. Or motor? I don't know. How many engines does a motorcycle have?

"You're gonna get on, right?" he inquires, turning his back to face me.

With his eyes the only visible part under the protective gear, it's enough to coax me into the mysterious world this stranger leads. I take my steps toward him, with caution guiding my feet even at my mind's objection. Before I know it, I am on this imperial ride, with an equally robust body commanding it.

Where do I hold on? How should I act? I don't wait for him to answer my mental questions. Instead, I allow my arms to dangle on each side of my body, limp and uncertain. I should grab on to him but is that coming on too strong? I haven't made sense of the last 24 hours, how much more the last three? I have to be poised and act like how a lady should, despite the craziness I've shown to him before this. Maybe if I scale back a little, he'll forget my recent breakdown.

"Put your arms around me or you won't make it by the next block," arrives his response to my odd but reasonable concern.

I do as asked, feeling the surge again as we become body to body, even while fully-clothed.

"You'll be fine!" he adds, squeezing my intertwined hands on his rigid trunk.

And I am susceptible to his promise, as if fairy dusts are blowing on my fearful form. My mind opens up uninhabited. I am in his safety and it just feels different, a sweet surrender I might say.

The streets are empty, as if silenced by our impending arrival and passage. The world belongs to us, and this feeling that I couldn't put into words. While the engine roars at each acceleration, twist, and turn,

I zero in on my heart, floating in its own tranquil waters. The memory of Henry is reduced to nothing but a mime. I see it but I am unable to hear the spiteful voice. For now, I feel strong enough to ward off the pain, and I feel protected by the hauntings of Andrew. There is a powerful bubble that shields me from everything and it is only at Noah's beck and call.

"Did you make a reservation?" I inquire.

He laughs before responding, "We don't need one."

Oh! But we've always made reservations everywhere we went, Andrew especially.

"Don't worry. Just reserve your appetite," he adds.

Then, I remember our attire. Those restaurants surely won't let us in with sweats or ripped jeans. And my face, I'm not put together at all.

"Do you think they'll let us in? I'm in sweats," comes my next question, feeling the sheer panic from this minute detail I missed.

"It's okay! Trust me." And that's all I need to hear.

I gather that Noah lives in a world apart from mine but I can say for sure that the affluence I belong to, did little for the many things I wanted but never got.

We ride in stillness while continuing to notice the ghost town that Seattle has become. Where did everyone go? Well, that doesn't matter anymore. Unlike my time before this, I learned that I don't have to weigh in on everything that happens around me.

"We're here!" he announces.

I hear the engine die but I am more interested in this place. It looks like half of a trailer, sheltering only the workers within. Two people are in line outside what appears to be a state fair stand, only longer. Tables and chairs are missing. How is one supposed to eat?

"Welcome to the best burger in town!" he brags, already holding a hand out to assist me down the motorcycle.

"We're eating here?" I question.

"Nope, just stopping by to pick up," he responds before pulling my hand to walk towards where people order. "Come on!"

"Welcome to Dick's! What can I get for you?" The teenage boy beams as he peeps out the small window.

I see Noah watching me, rather than attend to the boy. I know he's waiting for me to tell him what I want but I have no clue. I have never been here before but the thought of having a burger makes my stomach growl.

"You can just order for me," I say, with a soundless surrender that I used with the past men in my life.

"Gladly!" He turns back to the young employee, seemingly with a more knowledgeable palate. "Can I get two deluxe, 2 regular vanilla milkshakes? Oh for those, just don't stick the straw yet. Put them in the bag. And, a large fry. Two bottled waters. Uhmm..." He pauses, making way for his loving stare. I am its recipient. I smile back while taming the emotions boiling inside of me. "I think that's it!"

I find myself gawking at him, staring in wonder at his carefree nature. It's very fresh, this thing we're doing outside of galas and dinners, the napkin-on-your-lap type. I prefer this outside world, against the multitude of people I only know by name. They only regard me by association to a family prominence, usually in Andrew's side. Henry runs around this same circle of fake idolatries, although I thought he seemed more genuine than the standard.

He catches my stare, "What?"

"Oh nothing. Just new to me, all of this," my reply while my eyes stare across the surrounding infrastructures.

"Yeah this is better than reservations and what not. Not prissy. Not pinky up. No offense," he banters, leaning on the counter to look at a tiny television hanging overhead. "And something tells me you don't seem to be like those snooty rich people." By this time, his face returns to me. I watch him lift his hand to cup my left jaw, browsing on my excitable skin. It is an occurrence of only a second or two, but the world stops for longer than.

I giggle a little, trying to find a way not to show that I'm dangerously attracted to him. "Hope so. I don't like them anyway."

He looks at me again with his signature grin as he bites his lower lip, "See! I was right."

Now besieged by the happenings on that TV, he maintains a nervous glare but I can't help but put to light that fleeting action just moments ago. I'll transform into a willing bait, if only to see those lips move.

He taps his fingers on the counter, "Come on guys! Five yards!"

The rest of the Dick's crew is now focused on the screen at once. Erupting cheers and howls from the small appliance have swept us all with silence. I too feel the nerves and the anxiety from the contagious attention, domineering over virtually everyone in the city. I don't know what is supposed to happen, just that the ball must be carried someplace within the outlined field.

A furrow forms above his eyebrows to focus and I'm tormented by a sense of wonder. How come it was easy for me to trust him? It's effortless, like somehow doubting just slipped out of my mind.

"Touchdown!" he shouts minutes later. "'Seahawks! Seahawks!"

Now everyone is jumping up and down, chanting in unison with him. He turns to face me and carries me up to a swirl. The surprise morphed into exhilaration. It's very infectious. I begin to pump my fists to celebrate with him, even with the lack of football understanding. When he is finally done, we come face to face, my arms still around his neck. I feel my feet land on the ground and still, we don't let each other go. His stare makes me weak, locked in at his command. The magnetic pull reels me in closer to his face, this moment rendering me weightless.

I feel unarmed to dispute the fact of the matter that my heart craves a taste of those lips. And then, something inspires me from a short distance. In his eyes, a sign of reciprocation ignites, a desire that fuels the scorching embers from within me. The hands on my waist latches deeper into my skin, gently but hard-heartedly while his cheeks reposition just inches away from mine. Yet, the intensifying urgency to be sweetly conquered, dies in the same place it was birthed.

"Order's ready, Sir!"

The link and the mounting emotions from us two have been quickly severed in the name of burger. He pulls away and the undeniable ache from our bodies' separation makes me want to cry. I sob internally.

"Cool! Thanks, man," he mouths, grabbing the multiple paper bags on the counter.

With the other hand, he pulls me by the waist that has now become too tender to touch, all by his doing of course. The motorcycle appears to be parked farther than I originally thought, or maybe walking together in the awkward silence just makes it seem a trek to get to.

"Go Hawks!" he announces, to break the ice.

I watch as he glances quickly to his side, where I happen to be. He awaits a reaction while the bulk of me is still trapped in that moment, the obviously almost kiss that was rudely interrupted. I don't think I imagined it. Unless...

"Ophie, are you okay?" he inquires.

My discomfort is now becoming obvious. "Uhmm, yeah! Just thought of something."

"Tell me then," he probes further in his low voice.

A touch of concern can be felt in his tender hands, sweetly coaching my body to stop moving. He breezes around to face me, confirming his eagerness to know.

"Oh, it's really nothing. Just some silly thought," I respond while playing with my hair, seemingly to ward off the anxiety.

Make it stop!

"Really now. So you think this is silly?" He turns stoic, but I don't think I said anything offensive.

I realize I should defend my answer. "Nope. I don't mean this, just…" but my response is interfered by a soft touch on my wrist.

He brings it down, away from my hair. With his fingers, he brushes back the tangled strands. His eyes burn with ungenerous hunger, and I am a willing victim to his imminent tirade. In a swift motion, I feel a cloud of sweet reverence grace my lips. I do nothing because my body is unequipped to meet his obvious intentions. He is unaffected by my indifference, pulling me closer in a polished endeavor to cloak me within his masculine armor. His lips linger on mine, still unmoved for another half a second before desire makes its way into my mouth.

I become weak, fragile against my own volition. A window breaks open, releasing my own yearnings. My tongue dances back, in its own retort to his passionate manifestations. I even gather the audacity to hold him by the neck, if only to pretend that he is mine. I savor the ecstasy bit by bit, before it learns of its wings and fly away. I have no words, the wondrous exhilaration I feel will be left undefined. I am dissolute in his prison and I want him to incarcerate me so I can feel free.

But this isn't real, merely a dreamer's catch spilling over my unworthy mind. This will end like everything else. Nothing ever lasts. An antagonizing image of Andrew appears, along with Henry's displeased expression. A woman's face floats in front of my bewildered thought in the seconds after. She looks like me, sneering with an obvious plan to destroy my happy moment.

That's enough!

And the background of this romantic moment shreds off.

The tenderness and its deadly affliction skids away as Noah confiscates his grasp. I could barely feel the distance expanding between us because I was detached long before. I tried, I really did but the nagging in my head is unceasing. "I don't deserve this," it says. I left a mess behind this fresh curtain of harmony. It's almost a crime to feel happy. Let us not forget my undying love for Henry most of all. Merely a day ago, there was no way to live without him. How could a stranger just fly by and collect an emergency pass to stay, just because he hit the precise notes? It can't be that easy for me to exfoliate from my old self because Noah holds all the right answers, even while not saying anything at all.

"Was that silly to you?" he asks with obvious mischief. His smirk would have been delightful but the mood has changed. He strolls back into the unpaved alley, leaving me alone to find logic in what just happened.

I follow him, stomping my feet with anger. "Hey! You can't just do that!" I am enraged by the thought of wanting him in a reality that renders it all a fiction.

"I just did," he responds, amused but doesn't look back.

I shuffle my way faster towards him until we're both face to face, our food dangling in each of his hands. My face exudes annoyance and more than a tinge of anger, lips can be felt pouting. It must be obvious to him now as the playfulness evaporates from his form.

"It's just a kiss," he argues coyly, while loading up the paper bags in the box-like compartment of the motorcycle.

I wait for him to regard me in the eye before answering. "Well, I just met you two seconds ago. That's disrespectful."

He shakes his head.

Arms crossed on my chest, I mentally select my words because I can sense that we are drawing attention from passerby's. Streets are now flooded with people, an inundation of green and blue after the Seahawks won. The war of sounds is from fans and spectators emerging from caves like hungry bats in the darkness. A CRV just arrived along the parallel demarcation. I watch the driver roll down his window to inspect the scene of two distressed people, waiting for an escalation to follow suit. *Sorry, no not here.*

Noah regards me with a mental message after that. It's not a feat to decode his gape. It's time to leave. He moves around to get on the Harley and I walk to be near him. We both become mute.

"Just take me home. Please," I whisper before hopping on behind him.

I can't see his reaction and he doesn't say a word in reply. When I touch his body, both disappointment and tolerance dance with each other. Somehow, I feel like he understands, as if he knew his place in my life all along. I was only ever meant to chase, never to be wanted back. Everything about him is just too good to be real.

Chaos ensues in my head, as the Harley provokes the same from its engine. I feel like I'm losing it again. I feel like she's coming back. And I haven't yet found a way to stop her.

CHAPTER SIX

The She-Monster

Now enclosed in absolute isolation, I have pushed away my chance to escape from a perilous life of monotony. The unearthing of this utter mistake renders me paralyzed in this bed as the morning chirps with much gusto. Not even the break-in of sun rays could offer me a glimpse of light through the crack between the blinds.

I'm sorry to Noah, but most of all, I mope for my sorry self. Our voices denied us through the ride home last night. I shut the door to my wild bidding when it should have been welcomed. He was merely an innocent casualty to the tug of war between a new horizon and my past, that has been graciously swept under the rug at his arrival.

I need to miss Henry, especially in the moments when I feel his memory slipping away. It's the only thing that makes sense in my life. I am clueless outside of that realm, barren with no purpose. He is the true north I must steer to. The rest are just white noise, resembling some unfounded equations, floating around unsolved.

"I see you're up!"

I freeze. There is certainty in the purpose of my action. I know that voice.

Carefully, I rise to a sitting position, with my back resting against the headboard. I ready myself for the imminent danger and torture he'll pursue, once he finds out what I have been doing.

Andrew sits with his legs crossed on the upholstered chair. At the frightening nook, traced by the shadows of partial darkness, his silhouette is that of a displeased man. The thin spotlight of sunshine captures the rage in his eyes. Fear envelops my whole frame almost immediately. And like all the other occurrences of cruelty, I wonder if today will be my last. Yet we are in the city, not in the torture chamber that is his cabin far away. Somehow, a little hope blooms warmly from my chest. Maybe, just maybe, he'll spare me today.

"You...you're home," my voice trembles.

"Of course, I still live here after all," he responds, lips pursed.

He makes his way to me, with a bearing of a bull seeing red. "I also had a little chat with the neighbors. Seems like you had a slew of visitors while I was away."

His tone echoes with cynical dominance. A mounting wrath sweeps the room. I can't find the words to say anything. Telling the truth, or lying, I'll meet the same fate either way. The floor creaks at his every step, like high pitch shrieks of infinitesimal beings, warning me of my demise. But there is no need for that, my fate I see clearly. The blood-curdling chill ripples through my skin, as he stands over my side of the bed.

"What's the matter, baby? Lost your voice?" he asks with proud bearings.

I regard that face, a beauty full of deceit. A smile squeezed out of me but he becomes none too pleased. Lines begin to form above his brows. He rubs the back of his neck intensely. I know from experience that this is Andrew, the vicious beast sharpening his claws. Not a moment too soon, a force would wreck my face. I drop to my side almost immediately, cupping my cheek to soothe the pain. I feel fuzzy, with only a certainty of numbness at the point of impact. Total darkness entraps me now, but I know I'm still here.

I can sense him getting on the bed. He straddles on my limp form. Still not a word from my mouth, not even a yelp to affirm the pain. He traps my wrist, breaking-up the protection from my face. He forces me to turn so I can lay on my back.

"Look at me!" he orders, clamping my bottom half in between his legs.

But I don't open my eyes. I don't know if I couldn't or I just don't want to watch myself be wasted away. I'm afraid to know.

"Henry is one thing but some other guy? Christ, Ophelia! I give you everything so you won't have to look elsewhere. And what do you do?"

I hear him but the sounds are muffled, a lingering voice from far away. Though something he said stood out to me. Everything? He couldn't have possibly given me everything or we wouldn't be here. It's almost hilarious. Who is he kidding? And before I could even realize it, laughter gushes out of me. How dare I? It's already too late to take it back now.

My eyes burst open to somehow undo the last minute but I'm met with a fatal gaze instead. I smirk a little. The humorous relief of my heart and mind's disloyalty is not lost on me. I mean, I could have just kept my mouth shut and get this over with, but no. The more valiant part of me is willing to strike back. Who does she think she is?

"You think this is funny?"

And I just lay back, smiling as a response. I really just have to wait out for his anger to mount, high enough to reveal what form of torment will see me through. Then, he slaps me before continuing to nail my wrists to the bed. There it is, with all the power he could muster from his ire. It sends shockwaves down my neck.

"You still think it's funny now?" he asks again, still seething with rage.

I glower at him, dead in the eye like gaping at my own mortality. Another smile blows through at the corner of my mouth to challenge him. Come at me! I have nothing to lose now. My suffering, this holding cell had lost its purpose the day Henry made it clear that there is no longer any sense in waiting. He can end this now, once and for all. I have no reason to be caged by Andrew anymore but I also can't find any to live for. I wouldn't know how to tread a future with no Henry by my side. This is the only sensible way to go. I am in fact taunting Andrew to abandon his semi-tamed self and break free the primeval man to do the honors. So, this sneer won't leave me until then.

"I don't know what you're doing, Ophelia! Not here. You really don't want to tempt me. The things that I want to do to you!"

He sighs angrily before letting my wrist go. That can't be it, no way! But I just missed it by a blink or I would have found the answers in his eyes. Within the moment of my guard down, his hands slowly crawl up my torso, sliding through my breasts, before stopping at my neck. His lips are pressed together by rage, laser-focused on his goal. Second by second, I feel the pressure around my neck. It's tightening now, making its way to my windpipes and blood vessels. I allow him without objections and if he looks deep enough through my eyes, he can tell that this is a favor he's offering.

The denial of air is now felt in my chest. It won't be long now. I lie here feeling empty. I don't feel wrong or right, just somehow existing on a plane between the hollow of my life now and a desolate field. I am reaching the point of no return. All the memories run adrift into the dim corners of my vision. My mind is gradually becoming a sheet of nothing. In me, is a silent incantation.

I stare at the end. In its eyes, a thirst I just quenched. The image of Andrew and his visceral expression is fading away into scraps, to an infinite dump. In a moment, a mirage will guide me into a happy place, or an eternity of pain that mimics what I'll be leaving behind.

Easy now. The sun will soon set to sleep forever. Until then, I relish in the blank.

Yet somehow in the middle of bodily deprivation, I spot the light flicker from a distance. A fragrant breeze plunges in. It has Noah's memory swimming in its current, back to my dying heart. A warm touch of recognition graces my senses. And I remember it all - how he made me feel, and the freedom attached to his presence. There is nothing quite like it. How he affects me with the little time we spent together, is beyond logic. He overpowers me without the control that Andrew imposes. His existence, my longing for him grows apparent. A gentle whisper in my ear is a reason to go on. It was right in front of me, overshadowed by my obsession with Henry and the consuming fear for my life. There is still more to know and happiness to feel. The thought of what could have been with Noah is exhilarating, that I find my strength all of a sudden.

I decide to fight the hands that are smothering me, even while blind. Andrew's choke is strong and the more I peel his hands off my neck, he buries them deeper. I still persist.

"You're fighting back now, huh!" he shouts.

This newborn power is being fueled by a simple objective - to live. Again, I push the weight over me, and I can feel the pressure loosen up a bit. He finds his bearing once more and I'm back on the bed, trapped by his strength. Darkness is gradually pushing itself to the side. With my sight somehow regained, I pull his hair with all I got. His eyes widen at the realization because I never fought back this way before, or at all. When I gain momentum, his hold weakens. I see a small window of opportunity open up this second, and I use my knee to kick his crotch. When the pain reverberates through his scream, I kick him off the bed.

In one fell swoop, he is gone. He disappears, not just off the bed. The room is empty now. I'm left with only the signs of struggle, to remind me that his hauntings came at a high price.

Nothing. There is nothing but silence. Somehow, all the motions outside and within these walls were obtunded by the wave of truth, sweeping before me. Andrew's ghost, or whatever figment of reality he came back as, shall never be. I'm certain of that now as I look around the frenzy around me with open eyes.

I catch a glimpse of my reflection on the glossy division ahead. My hair has dropped a few more inches down my shoulder, black and brittle. God knows how long I had this white gown on. My pale face recruited a few struggles during the course of my entrapment, but my neck seems unscathed.

Andrew was never here, is what I gather. A dull ache can be felt around my wrist and in it I see the markings, where a tight hair tie would have lodged. But really, they're only identifying bracelets to somehow remind people of who I am. I try to yank them off, one at a time but their strength is no match to mine. I decide to use my teeth but I become interrupted by a sound, a creak at the door.

"I wouldn't do that," he orders calmly as he reveals himself from around the corner.

I look at him briefly before focusing on the dead television in front of me. I've seen him before but not this way, not here.

"Mrs. Anderson. We're a little behind schedule. Your ride is here," as he steps closer to my side.

"What day is it?" I ask, feeling my wrist get pulled away.

"It's been two weeks. If that's what you wanna know," he responds in a soothing manner.

His voice is cool and like summer breeze, collects his words in a song. I can see the charisma drawing people in and I would be too, if the circumstances were different.

I can feel the bracelets drop from my wrist as he maneuvers it, "There you go!"

"Thanks," I say coyly.

He collects some items from the bedside, and wheels them out on a cart across the room. He seems intent on just leaving right then and there, but not before examining me one last time. He pulls a rolling stool from underneath a metal desk and begins to scoot towards me, with him on it. A plastic clipboard is revealed from his side pocket. He studies it, carefully. I even notice his nose wrinkle doing so.

He visually examines me again, before reading the documents a few more times.

"How are you feeling today, Mrs. Anderson?"

"Okay, I guess. And it's Ophelia, please," I reply dully.

"And the side effects? The nightmares?" he continues.

"Fine," I settle for a short answer.

"Well then, I'll tell them you're getting ready. Have a great day, Mrs. Anderson," he bids, holding his hand out to me.

I shake it with nonchalance before turning away to ready myself. He shuffles out, until the door slams shut behind him.

Outside, I'm met by endless hallways, all empty. If not for the sign that points to the lobby, I'd be lost in this is silvery frost mess. I follow the arrows. I continue on and on until I reach a distinct hallway. The walls are painted differently than the rest, and I can hear some signs of life. When I turn the corner, it leads to a chilling scene. I am halted in my tracks. People of all forms walk aimlessly in fugue states. They seem unaware of my presence even as they've met my gaze. And like a bolt of lightning through my spine, a thought haunts me. They lost me again!

I seize my lungs to be able to breathe when I finally reach the check in area. Here, I see normal people, sane people like me moving about in all directions with a plan. Nonetheless, my narrow escape from the crazy crowd was a sweat-inducing one. I can feel my body melt into perspiration and disgust from recently brushing up against them on my way out. I don't belong with them and just thinking about our association by proximity, just makes me cringe.

While the disarray of movements distracts my vision, I see Henry between the gaps of bustling figures. He's the "they" being referred to earlier and my heart should skip at the sight of him. Yet all that has changed. The ache calls me from a distance but an echo from Noah's voice is more audible to my senses. I'm more focused on that now, surprisingly.

He's seen making arrangements at the front desk, signing papers, and absorbed by the words of the other person in front of him. I walk closer to grab his attention but before I could tap his shoulder, Landree emerges from behind him. Her ungenerous demeanor is obvious as she whispers something to Henry's ear. In an instant, he looks up to abandon all that he was doing. He runs up to me and his warm body around my drenched chest is the next thing I feel. Tenderness emanates from his embrace, but I feel indifferent towards it. Whatever happened to me in the days that passed has left some room for me to see beyond the endless days of hoping, of wishing that he will love me as I do. Deeper inside my heart, I have severed that one-way connection. All I really ask for right now is that it isn't yet too late for Noah and I.

I drive him away, my hands wedged between us now. It's what I should have done a long time ago. I smile, just of gratitude and nothing more. It is then that I notice something else besides his disheveled face. A trace of bruising encircles the left side of his mouth and it is obvious how it got there. But why and who? Meanwhile, a limited view of Landree behind him, is finishing up the checkout process at the front desk. A few seconds go by, and she turns around to be by Henry's side.

"Okay, time to go," she orders with a flat tone.

She barely acknowledges my presence but I watch her closely as she squeezes into Henry's side. He puts his arm around her as an automatic response. Their bodies melt into one another like puzzle pieces fitting together. In the past, I saw it without really seeing their connection but like the spectator that I was meant to be, I'm paying attention now to the bond not even my most deceitful plans could break.

Yet a lingering question continues to poke me and I just couldn't help but ask, "What happened to your face?"

It is obvious in Henry's expression that it doesn't matter now. He really isn't in the mood for talking much but I see Landree's brows raise.

She shakes her head in sarcasm before answering my question that wasn't really directed at her in the first place, "You did! You happened!"

Instantly, Henry makes a face at her, ordering her to stop but she's not having it.

"Whatever! I'm so done with this shit. Little miss thing always sucks us into her crazy," she tells him, more annoyed than angry.

I snap back at her, "I'm right here you know!"

"Urgh! Whatever! I'm getting the car," she dismisses. "I don't know why you put up with her."

We both watch her walk away towards the entrance.

"I'm sorry. She's just tired," he whispers, as a defense to her adult tantrums.

"What really happened, Henry?" I probe.

He is quiet for a moment, closing out every avenue to pursuing the truth.

"Nothing happened. It was an accident. Let's get you home."

His response only paved way for more questions but I know him well enough to stop my inquiry now. He taps my back lightly to lead the way and we begin walking out.

"There is something I do need to tell you though," he reveals, while making our way out the wide entrance.

I have no clue what he's about to say. "Okay?"

"Your dad was here."

"What?" I turn to face him.

"But, he didn't see you. I wanted to get your approval first. And you just weren't in a situation where you could make that decision."

Yet everything else he said after that doesn't make sense. I'm worried about the monster finding out about me too, much less know where I am.

I yell at him because of the betrayal I feel. "What about? You didn't! You have better not called -" but his reply barges in before I could finish.

"No! I didn't call him and Mr. Davis promised that he wouldn't tell him either. Come on, Ophelia. I would never do that. Even if you're not with me under the same roof, I'm still responsible for you. No matter what happens," he assures, hands arriving on my shoulders.

I feel a bit of relief but still lost. I thought I would never see him again. I cried, I drank. I did my due diligence to formally close the past chapter and leave him there, yet here he is.

"Do you trust me?" he asks after driving the silence towards me. "You know I would never put you in harm's way."

I nod in reply.

He smiles at my gentle agreement, looks away, and shakes his head.

The car horn honks aggressively from steps below, and Landree pops out of the driver's side window. She throws her hands up to force a sense of urgency from Henry and I, the sun descending behind her. We make our way to her, to a car ride bound for hell.

Here we go.

I find myself stuck inside the back seat of their silver Panamera, after twenty long minutes of being victimized by Landree and her vulgarity. She ran out of the car, barely shifting it to park, with Henry on her tail. She nearly crashed into the garage doors because her eyes were more adhered to my reflection in the rear-view mirror, than on the road.

I make a decision to head inside as the temperature plummets to the low 50s. All I know is that I'm supposed to stay here for a night or two after my ordeal. I'm still in this fog of utter ambiguity. I feel reinvigorated but also hollow in its purest form, like some vital organs have been extracted from my body. In my senses, something's amiss and a black-hooded woman appears, from what feels like centuries of hibernation. She leans over, right there with a confirmatory smile.

It was her.

In an abrupt pause, everything returns to me as the sum of nothing. I don't know of those memories obliterated by her. I'm only certain of her triumph, to once again use me as a medium for her sinister plans. If only I could remember. Kara's absence explains it all. She failed to warn me. This entity, she has been lurking within the minimal obscurities in my vision, calculating my weakness, and using it to propel herself back into my fragile vessel.

"No."

I scream with all that I could. The action swirls my head, driving my emaciated self into shivers. Paranoia drizzles, turning my skin to ice.

"What have you done?" I ask her with my trembling voice.

She barely smiles as a retort, with pursed lips tinted in the brightest red I have ever seen. She leaves a taunting wink before returning into hiding. She's the most menacing of them all, of us all. It makes me sick to my entrails, knowing we are linked somehow. I am repulsed that we both transpired from the same belligerence.

She disappears in an instant.

The urgency to leave the vehicle returns as a chill down my nape. I'm still tending to the ocean of haze in my mind but I try to focus anyway. I have to. It's the only way to repair myself after being halted, after she rendered my mind lifeless. It is the only way to be deserving of Noah.

My knees tremble as I leave the car but I will them to carry on until I reach the path made of grey cobblestones.

The way to the front door is lit by garden lights along each side. Two white columns stand erect, holding up the shingled canopy over the entryway. I walk two steps up until I encounter a distinctive oak door. The feeling of being followed hasn't left yet and I turn around to inspect the presence dogging at me. I get dizzy again, but not as intense as the last.

"I don't get it! You don't need this shit! Sign off on it now. If you truly love me please... let her be someone else's problem."

That's Landree's voice, understandably upset by my presence in her house. Henry's responses are imperceptible under the noise of things crashing on the floors and walls. I have never seen them fight this way and a pang of guilt bites me in the chest. I am not an evil person, just a faulty human who crossed the line for love. For the very first time, I feel sorry for her. Somehow while I was gone, the poison in my head, the one that really despised her has been bled out. I didn't realize it then when we were at the facility but maybe I have regained some understanding, the one deprived from me during the pursuit to be loved.

I can hear her cry from the other side of the door, taking turns with her exasperated screams. There's movement, Henry motioning towards her. She yelps to protest but her emotions are now demoting to quiet whimpers. The momentary truce allows me to focus on Henry's voice.

"I'm sorry. I love you so much but you know I have to help her. Because who else will? She has nobody. And I promised him. I promised that I won't leave her."

"But at what cost?" her voice is quivering. "How much more do we have to sacrifice? Now she's gonna be in the same roof as I ? What else? I can't sit here and just watch her make a pass at you. She's a delusional

—" but she cuts her tongue quickly before it builds another sore adjective against my name. She knows Henry will not approve of it. "This love shit she claims that you two have, I mean she's bat shit crazy. What else is she gonna take? Are you waiting for her to hurt me?"

"I'm sorry! Of course not, she just needs us right now. She's all alone," Henry responds with an almost sedative tone.

"I don't know! I don't feel safe around her," she reveals.

But he defends my honor instead, "She would never hurt you. She just gets upset at times."

"Upset? You call that upset? Why isn't she named a threat to society yet, huh?" she argues even more.

Henry remains calm, true to his nature before responding, "She's been through a lot. But she would never."

"Are you kidding me, Henry? Have you forgotten what happened? It kills me that you know what you know and I'm carrying this thing... This thing I know that can somehow fix all our problems," her voice escalates again. "But no! I can't do that because we have to keep her safe. Fuck it, Henry!"

It was her, not me. It was her then, the pugnacious duplicate of Ophelia who robbed me of my being once more. It was her - my gut undulates with certainty now. I felt her coming, the taunting voices of doubt as I readied myself for an earnest place in Noah's life. I fell for the misgivings, and as before, I fell back into the time capsule of oblivion. She acts like me, talks the same way as me - the more cunning fabrication of my own image. I have no proof and until then, I stay imprisoned, tucked nearby as time after time, she wreaks havoc in my name, at my expense.

"I'm sorry. I don't know what to say. Tell me what to do. I'll do it. Please…" he's heard pleading.

"You told me this was it. When we got her the house, you said that was it. She goes berserk and we sent her away, you told me today that was it. Then, you tell me she has to live with us for a little bit? That's just asking for too damn much, don't you think? What are they for? Those people you pay. Let them do their job. You won't even fucking marry me cuz of her. And I don't want to lose this baby again. God forbid!"

There was only silence from Henry. I can hear him breathing fast and then slow, fast then slow. I did this to him. It breaks me to hear him in despair. A single teardrop leaves my eye but I pay no mind. I just want to force myself in, so I can comfort him the way he did all these years for me, even with Landree's objections. Yet I feel helpless, glued to the ground as blame castigates my thoughts. I can sense his frustration of having to choose between two things he feels equally right to do. I know that despite how imperfect the circumstance may be, his heart has always been in the right place.

"Henry, please. I need you to leave now," she pleads.

But the stillness remains, no movements or any intentions from Henry to do as asked.

"I said get the fuck out of my house, Henry!" she says again, this time in her domineering anger.

Eventually, I hear shuffling and unimportant commotion moving towards me. After seconds of pause, the movements resume at the other side of the wall. The door swings open, letting out an air of turmoil. I see Henry and the mental mayhem revealed through his bloodshot eyes. Behind him is the sight of Landree at the bottom of the grand staircase, pale-faced and drenched in tears. Her hand cradles the tiny protrusion in her belly, encasing a tiny heartbeat that I despised until recently. In her mouth, the mark of unreserved betrayal wrinkles through.

She turns around, just as Henry closes the door, leaving behind all the reasons why their love is the only thing right in all our wrongs.

We take the back road. My house is the obvious destination. On here, acceleration is halted at 35 miles per hour if such rules are followed. Henry, always the virtuous human being, obeys the speed limit in absolute silence. Strangely enough, I'm in my own vehicle, which was revealed to be parked inside their garage, following their emotional spat. I ease into the safety of the front seat, windows rolled down. Besides the reflective signs on the road, darkness is the only view I can distract myself with. The wind on my face is welcome as I inhale the fresh scent of damp wood along the way. It brings back so many memories from so many moons ago. Only now, we're missing a few people in the car.

My qualms from her return have eased away in Henry's safekeeping, that today's events can easily be forgotten. I feel a pure sense of security by his side and that the world seems so far away, or deep beneath our feet. In the past, I would have been satisfied. All I need was this feeling. This was what love meant to me, as defined by what little Henry could give. Yet I crave for something else, something new.

The stars flicker in and out from behind the dense woods as we pass them by, like cartoon snaps in motion. Each radiant glimmer, gently but harshly reveals the cracks I've foolishly covered up all these years. I glance at Henry, still deep in thought as I endure in the same inexplicable crisis. I discover a freshly dug pit in my chest and the revelation is astounding.

Now that we're alone, just us two after a very long time of waiting, I realize that he isn't the answer. I lost myself, as he already lost me in the midst of fighting for this very moment to transpire. I discovered that love doesn't have to start or end in bloodshed. It can be as easy as opening your eyes to a new day, or as simple yet profound as breathing.

This acquired absence of freedom, for which I learned just of late, is begging for recognition. With Noah at the wheel of this yearning, everything seems so vibrant from where every one of my desire converges.

"I'm sorry about today. I'm sorry about Landree. I can't say it enough," I tell him quietly, as the fleeting view evolves into pitch black.

I hear nothing but the smooth rumble of the engine, and I finally turn my head to regard him. With eyes still fixed on the dark road that's merely brightened by the headlights, an internal dispute lingers in his gloomy form. Yet his awareness of my gape is obvious, a response becomes pending.

"I messed it all up," he replies, shaking his head. "I don't know how I could fix this. Your brother was a fool to think that I can handle everything. I can't do it."

His bitter submission to defeat strokes my chest. I could feel it, of having lost it all. But this one is on me. I was the one who channeled his life into destruction. I'm partially to blame and the sly monster who takes my place from time to time is the mastermind. In his face, a blend of emotions presents themselves to the light shining from the approaching traffic. We are nearing my home. I care so much for him now, more than the other selfish times from which my emotions were ruled by my pseudo-self. I just want him to be happy, even with Landree.

"What can I do, tell me what to do? I'll do it," as I stroke his steel shoulder. "I'll do anything."

"You're not responsible for anything, Ophie," he answers sternly, along with a tender glance while we wait for the green light ahead.

He reaches across his chest to clutch my hand. He removes it from his shoulder to hold within his fist. "It's not your fault."

I understand now with all certainty. I am the cracked mirror for which he felt must be repaired back to its original state. He's bound to a responsibility, a pact he made with Marcus. Somehow, he thinks that by fixing me, my fragile tendencies, will allow him to look through and see his long-lost friend. He didn't stay for love, at least not the kind that I wanted back. It has always been Landree. I was the only one who didn't see.

"I'll get your bags," he announces, as we pull in my driveway.

I look ahead, to my house where I thought I'd wake up to this morning. Suddenly, I notice movement, shadows pacing behind the white curtains. I feel immediate panic. Who's here?

"Henry!" I call out. He runs back to the passenger side with my bags, inspecting the periphery for a brief minute before opening the door. Without delay, I throw myself at him.

"What's wrong?"

Henry pulls away to see my face, gently sliding the bag handles to the fold in his arm. I glance at him, fearful. I'm like a timid animal being prepared for slaughter.

His eyes drift to the front of the house before returning his attention to me. I hear the offering of a quiet assurance the next time he speaks. "It's Adelpha and some help. They're just getting ready to leave. She wasn't expecting us tonight."

"Oh," I mutter, sliding out of the vehicle.

I guess I overreacted.

"Let's go," he orders, tilting his head to the direction of the front door.

I follow carefully behind him, watching his body take splendid steps up to the front door, where Adelpha meets him with a hug.

"She's doing well," Henry can be heard telling her, underneath the quiet hisses of conversations between the two.

I stride steady until I reach them.

"Ophelia! Welcome home, dear!" Adelpha greets warmly, with arms wide and ready to spool me in.

In no time, I'm trapped inside her embrace and a concoction of aromas from apple pies to vinegar, swirls into my nostrils. My stomach churns, A surge of nausea spills out from my throat.

"Thank you, Adelpha. That's so sweet of you," I respond almost inaudibly, while breaking away from her.

If I'd waited another few seconds, she'll get a vomit full from me instead. A younger woman emerges. She takes her place behind Adelpha, giving me a hint that she plays a subordinate role to her. She's undeniably beautiful and seemingly displaced by her plain clothes. I notice her commanding Henry's attention as well. I can sense an internal gasp of "wow" from him. He's not to blame for that though. She should be gracing the cover of a magazine, instead of my home front with cleaning supplies in both hands.

"Hi!" She greets with vigor.

I smile back and Henry waves at her. Oddly enough, Adelpha doesn't introduce her to us but then again, there are so many peculiar things about this otherwise kind woman. The lack of courtesy would be no surprise.

"Anyway, can you give me some moments? Henry. Talk please?" Adelpha requests.

The young help nods. She walks away from us and down the steps until her presence becomes invisible.

"It's okay, Ophie. I'll be right in," Henry tells me as he pulls our neighbor to the side.

Curiosity gnaws at me. I would like to know what they're going to talk about but it seems like Adelpha is waiting for me to leave.

"Okay. Sure. Goodnight, Adelpha."

I mentally count my steps in. My receiving room meets me with luster and a pure state of tidy. There are no longer streaks of darkness in here with the absence of the grey paint. The furniture has been re-arranged and surprisingly, to my liking. The space seems wider, giving me a sense of ease and freedom.

I recall entering here feeling completely different, that one night when I was too scared to let Noah in. I pushed him away, to the safest distance I could. I won't ever see him again no matter how much I wish to, that I'm certain of. Right now, all I have are pages full of blur, photographs of doubt. I lost a chunk of time and memories were robbed from the safety of my mind.

She carries the same dangerous access to myself and Noah is better off untouched by her. She truly is my greatest foe, not Landree. With that, I sink into the couch to feel what little security it offers.

"Do you like it?" Henry asks, announcing his presence at the door.

"Actually? Yeah! It's different but I like it," I respond with forced enthusiasm.

I feel his weight next to me, his focus still to the fresh interior design.

"I talked to Jessica. She was the one who told me to do this, that you need some changes when you return.

"Oh yeah?" I quip, knowing what he'll say next.

He stirs gently, until he can see the guilt on my face before he scolds me. "She told me you haven't been seeing her. In fact, it's been months she said. I saw a collection of pills in the bathroom trash too. I thought we already talked about routine."

My hand finds my chin. I begin to rub it as I look away from him. It's true, whatever he said. I have neglected our agreement. It was reckless.

"Ophie. It's okay. I'm not here to start a fight with you. You'll just do better next time. We'll work something out soon," he assures me.

He strokes my hair gently and I curl my head at the action. I am absorbed by his smile in response to mine. I see it, the protection and love that Marcus left him so that in turn, can be given to me.

But a thought reminds him of a seemingly graver matter. It straightens the curve on his mouth right away. A brush of concern annihilates the comfort between us and I sit here wondering. What now?

He breathes slow and heavy before speaking. "We need to talk about something else."

"About what?" I ask immediately.

He sniffles and begins to open his mouth but no word comes out. He resolves to bite his lower lip instead.

"Tell me," I urge, holding on to his arm to plead with maximum effect.

"It's Noah," he reveals, as he throws out a look of concern at me.

"Okay? What about him?"

"Well, I got word..." he hesitates before continuing, "He came around looking for you while you were away. Many times, they said."

The revelation sends me into a mental dance. He did? I don't know what to say. He came back looking for me?

"That's not good, Ophie. I told you. And you gave him your address? That was reckless, don't you think?" is his stern response to my apparent musing. "Never mind him but what if he was one of the other guys? I have people who are responsible to know your whereabouts at all times of the day, or did you forget?"

"But that's hardly the case. He found me. I left my wallet at the restaurant and that's how he found out where I live. I didn't give him anything," I argue calmly.

He leaves the sofa to inspect the door. Then, he makes his way to the windows, closing the blinds before turning to face me with reprimand. "Then we gotta do something about that soon! Who knows what could happen. We didn't move very far from your old place. We're still in Seattle because you asked me to, on one condition. You swore you're gonna be careful. No strangers."

But he's not! Noah seems far from a stranger.

"Why? Is that necessary?"

I'm confused by his reaction. That's really taking this whole protective thing to a new level. I mean, I'm barely getting warm here and we're back on high alert. If I didn't finally know better, I would think he's jealous. What is he afraid of?

Oh no!

"What is it, Henry? Did she get to Noah? It was her, wasn't it? Is that why I can't remember? You didn't want him in this mess with her?" I scream at him out of frustration.

"Sure, you could say that," he answers in his low voice.

I can tell he's being dismissive.

"It was her, right? She was here as me?" I seem sure of that. He just needs to confirm.

Then came out from Henry's mouth, the ratification, "Yeah, she did."

Yet I find myself defending Noah's role in my life. "Maybe he'll know the difference when it's no longer me. You do it all the time. You can teach him."

"Do you even hear yourself? Do you know how silly you sound?" he disputes, as he comes near me. "That's where you're wrong. I can barely do it myself."

"I don't know but he's not like that, he's not like anybody I met," I reason. "Plus, why are you acting like this? I mean you were okay with Andrew, left me alone with him."

He sniffles again and quips with a tiny sneer, "And look where it got you?"

I can't win with him. I vaguely remember him saying goodbye to me for good. Hearts were poured out, tears were shed. He just can't quit his ambiguous role in my life.

I feel his arm around my shoulder. The sudden clamor for reason invades me but he speaks first.

"Look. I know I said I'm walking away but I just can't seem to do that, not like this." He shakes his head. "I felt like I betrayed Marcus when I turned my back on you. Landree will come around. Even with the frustration, she cares for you too and she'll understand my responsibility. I signed those papers before I met her."

His eloquence, with words spoken softly beneath the gruff voice and steel expression, has always been the home I've come to know. It gives me the shelter I need, assuring me that everything is going to be okay. Sadly, I can't live in it forever and things must change.

"You can walk. Right now! Someone else can take that responsibility. I've ruined you enough. You knew that for years, yet you allowed me to continue." My reaction is riddled with frustration, my hand gestures waving in his face says so. "I feel sick thinking about it now. You can't keep me while you sleep with someone else. You're free now. You can go," I beg him.

Tears boil in my eyes because even if he failed to reciprocate my heart, I know that he is my lifeline and I'd have to see the world differently without him as my compass. Mourning for his impending exit doesn't get easier with this second take.

"I'm just trying to do what's best for you. We're not ordinary people and it takes someone with skill to be able to stay in our lives," he says, defending his actions.

"Someone like who? Of course, someone like you. But you can't always be that person for me. You can't give me what I want. Don't you want me to be happy too?" My pleading voice is a mark of desperation.

He pulls me into his arms. The sweet scent of his skin taunts me, screaming a message that I will never belong inside his embrace. I hear myself sob for all the emotions in my chest, both clear and undefined. I just want to get out of this darkness, of this prohibited love and unkind abduction by people pretending to be me. I'm tired of constantly being seized by my past, every time I take a step forward.

"I just... I just want nothing more for you but to be happy," he whispers. "But we have got to take extra measures to ensure your safety. That is my job. I don't think I can say that enough," he adds, his hand brushing the strands from the back of my head.

I stay quiet for a little bit, to warrant my understanding of his concerns. Yet all I can think of through these tears is Noah and what a close call that must have been to meet me as her. I won't remember anything and that is the worst of it. The chance to backpedal through my memories and right her wrongs, even that has been deprived.

He wipes the stream on my cheek with the back of his hand. His eyes fix on my forlorn rendering, and the hunger for an escape from all of this. We've been down this road before, just a few days ago in fact. We must get out of this limbo, from this broken record for which we both feel obliged to hear.

"What can I do so that you could trust me again the way you did months before? The way you trusted me alone with Andrew?"

His expression unravels nothing, just the good intention of listening to my equivocal questions. I watch him run his fingers through his hair before an answer materializes.

"You know why she came back?" he asks through the wrinkle on his forehead.

"What does that have to do with this?" I respond, with yet another probe.

"You just have no regard for anything that we worked so hard for," he reveals a bleak message.

I don't know what he means and I always hate the superficial formality in his voice when it comes to my so called safety. Is he forgetting that I'm a friend first? I'm starting to build up some displeasure towards his presence even though he means well. There's never just laying out a plan. We always go through this game of charades, keeping each other guessing.

I throw my hands up before finally expressing my frustration, "Jesus Christ, Henry! Just tell me in plain words! Why do you have to be so hard on me? I'm trying to help you help me so you can run off into the sunset with your woman."

"Don't do that, Ophie," he orders while his index finger wags at my face.

That only infuriates me more, as I abruptly shift my body to slam my fists to the table.

"Ophelia Anderson!" he calls out with authority, breaking my force without any effort whatsoever.

He traps my wrists in his hands and my strength is no match against it. My cries are like that of an injured dog as Henry gets up to regard my apparent outburst. He's angered by my actions but he will never reciprocate my violent screams with any force other than to calm me down. I continue to sob but quietly now, giving him a cue to let me go. I sink back into the couch with less dignity than I had before my flare up. I watch Henry remain standing and he shakes his head from disappointment.

"This!" he points to me and continues. "You have proven my argument, Ophie! You're not worthy of my trust, nor anyone's for that matter. Until you listen and do what you're supposed to do, this conversation is over. Do you understand me?"

I swallow the lump in my throat as I change my position on the couch. My head is draped down from my neck, embarrassed by my actions and my inability to control what my mind tells me to say or do. Henry's shadow moves closer, tainting the rare sight of this freshly polished floor. He always holds himself well and he's never angered by anything easily. To see him this way would have been a cause of fear. Yet I know I was the one who drove him to the wall and that he would have to fight me back in order to bring us both to the middle ground, where it is especially safe for me. Taunting his well-guarded fury would have been a catalyst for my own demise but Henry is nothing like Andrew.

"You should get yourself ready for bed. I'm gonna be in the guestroom. We'll sort this out later," he orders.

"What if Andrew comes back?"

The thought haunts me, just as I remember him this morning. His presence slowly creeps up to my weary emotions and I don't feel secure, even with Henry nearby.

He brings himself down to the floor, squatting in front of me so that we're face to face. I feel a warm breeze of comfort that only belongs to Henry. Even with my gentle retaliation, I know I'll always submit to his safety, one way or another.

"This is what you need to remember," he whispers as he asks for my hand and I'm inclined to do so. "Andrew is gone. I know you feel like he's here but that's not real. Listen to me when I say he's gone, gone for good. There's nothing to dispute that. Believe me."

"But...but, he keeps coming back. It feels real. He goes away but he comes back. I can touch him. It feels real when he strikes me. I'm sure of it," I reason with a shaky voice.

It's true. If he can only see what I saw through my own eyes, and endure the pain inflicted by Andrew. Maybe, just maybe he'll realize that this is far from make believe.

"Okay. I understand you need time but for now just trust me on this one. Okay?"

I nod back at him. He seems certain that I'll do as asked. His hands gently slip away with the footsteps that disappear with him into the dim hallway. And here I am, alone and vulnerable to the predators lurking close by. The girl who wants to be me, and the man who pretends to love me, just to name a few. The only weapon left for me to go with is a gentle promise that everything is going to be okay, that I am safe. I suppose there is something to look forward to in the end.

The world outside stirs in nocturnal repercussions but the only sound I welcome is absent. I cannot sit here and wait to drown the emptiness from this wave of sobriety. If I had not met Noah, I would have not realized that there's still a little life he can salvage out of me. I want to go where I might find him but I don't know where to start.

CHAPTER SEVEN

Henry, My Sworn Protector and Love's Guillotine

"Don't forget these," he reminds me, sliding a Zip Loc bag of medication bottles over to my side of the table.

The mood is better this morning. Both our bodies are starting to recover collectively, having endured some trauma from the weeks that passed. I take a tablet from each bottle and subsequently dump them into my mouth, one after the other. I couldn't protest the medications and risk marring this fresh start, even though my mind is still a residual of chaos. I have to make him believe that I'm agreeable to all that he asked, even though I couldn't stand another minute not wondering about Noah.

"Thank you for breakfast." I nod at him with a grateful smile, after the last pill makes its way to my throat.

"Anyway, let's talk about today," as he wipes the kitchen counter to dismiss my gratitude. "I called Jessica and she said she'll meet you later. I already filled your tank this morning. That should be more than enough to get you to Bellevue and back. There's cash in your wallet in case of emergency but no unnecessary stops, just there and back. There is absolutely nothing you will need that isn't in this house already."

"What about my sanity?" I call him out with sarcasm.

I do mean what I said but I mask it with a thin smile to avoid argument.

"It's for your own good," he responds, shoving away my playfulness. "I'll see the realtor today about selling this house. We'll figure out where we can move you next. Maybe a smaller place near Landree and me? I don't know. Just where I can keep an eye on you and still save my relationship." His face becomes unyielding, stern in his gaze. I know how it led him here though, by a path trodden with horror and trauma.

"Again?" I conceal my panic. Without this house, Noah will never find me. I don't know any other link to him but here.

"What? Either move to a different house or a different state. Pick your misery," he defends his decision.

"Wait up! First of all, why do I feel like you're taking away my independence?" I start to feel the walls closing in. This hasn't been the version of Henry in a while and the dangerous control he imposes on me sounds a lot like Andrew.

"Because I am," he confirms.

"But why? Since we moved to the city, you just left me be? Up until yesterday, you stayed away when I very much wanted you to be this way then."

He stands in silence, back is to me now. None of what I just said can draw enough resolve to gain any answer from him. He continues to rinse our dirty dishes under the tap. I could hear the steady stream, its sloshing sounds of busywork.

"Come on, Henry! You can't ignore me forever. I hate feeling stuck," I probe again.

And this time, I'm sensing my bothers breaking through his barriers. His shoulders are now pushed to each of his side, veins swelling in tension. Almost conceivably, porcelain platters crash into the sink as an immediate reaction to being flung by his hand's brute force.

"You wanna know why? Let me tell you why!" He shifts his body to face me, the anger in his voice still unmatched by his cool expression. There is a safety clause in our midst, one that Henry will never breach no matter how infuriated he becomes. I feel grateful for the fact that I won't ever feel his hands on my skin, other than to touch me. I trust that when he makes a fist, it is only to secure mine in it.

"Enlighten me."

"It's because I thought you were fine then. Okay? I thought I told you last night," comes his distraught argument. "You're not. You're not okay. And Andrew, stop bringing him into this. He can't even hurt a fly."

I exhale, pulling air from parts of my body that received the most betrayal.

Hearing those words from Henry becomes the dividing wall between us. He doesn't have to say it. I can see the cloud of mistrust in his eyes. He doubts me and for the first time in a while, Henry seems worlds away. He left my corner, the second his words began marshaling against my claim of innocence.

He stares at the wall behind me, recounting the events from weeks before. "When you came to my house this last time, I couldn't see you anymore. I saw her. The angry, vile one who was just waiting for a window of opportunity. She was just there, declaring her win. It's my fault. I should have done more. Marcus would be disappointed."

"But you have done enough. More than enough!" I scream, before realizing I shouldn't have done so. "Marcus this and that... He's gone. What is he gonna do to you now from his grave?" my voice low but fiery.

The thought of Marcus is unfailing in its ability to break me. His departure has been indelible despite not remembering. The eagerness to rinse his memory off my body is in constant battle against the earsplitting sirens of that night. I don't recall much. I don't want to but what little I allow myself to remember are more than plenty. There is a vision of his face that remains untampered, cradled by his palpable ire of me. My heart has been rotting in silence for years now.

As if he hears my mental dispute, a suitable reply pummels through. "You don't get it. He's gone because of me. It should have been me."

He returns to the sink, to clean up the consequence of his outburst. I watch him handle the shattered pieces. He collects them with care, just as he does for his composure. After the last fragment is thrown into the metal trash can, I hear him inhale profoundly before turning to face me again.

He is quiet for a moment as he looks at the uncertainty on my expression. I feel overpowered by the strength of his gaze and the sincerity of his care, even without touching me. Once upon a time, I mistook those for romance. Yet he never desired me that way. He was always just close enough to keep me safe while within the margins, always dreading the possibility of letting himself in.

I remember that feeling, the kind that makes my heart explode at the sight of him. I can sense it in our midst, as if in material form, swaying discreetly between us. And although this love still finds home in me, it no longer recognizes Henry. My heart, however, will remain its property in its pursuit for a rightful match. I find no fault in that, to finally be unbound from what was never right all along.

"I don't wanna argue with you anymore, Ophelia," his remorseful voice quarrels against the fleeting silence. "This doesn't make me feel good, fighting with you. Let's get you well and we'll worry about the rest later."

"Sorry. I don't like it either," is my reply.

He moves closer to stroke my shoulder, a passing action as he heads for the door. "I gotta go now. I have to stop by the house, check on Landree. Then I can see about what we should do here."

"Okay," I say, nodding in compliance.

"You know who to call when you can't reach me. No driver, just as you asked. That's my compromise. Now hold your end."

"Okay."

He clutches the knob and swings the door until he remembers something halfway through. "Call me when you get home."

"Okay. Drive safe." That is me returning his concern.

He smiles softly at my response before the outside world gets shut out again. But something snuck in, before he closed the door- Noah. I wonder how he is now. I haven't been able to keep him off my mind since I woke up yesterday. He was my first thought when I spoke to the morning sun and as I breathe in, what is otherwise this unkind reality. My memory of him is a genuine execution of the effect he brought to me during our brief encounter. He rewired my beliefs. What I need and how I see my future - all that's changed. Whatever it is, a poison of desire, lust, or attraction - my body is susceptible. There is no cure, except to bathe myself in the same disease that infected me in the first place. He cast a spell on me, just by being himself, just by being carefree.

CHAPTER EIGHT

We Feared Only The Depths, As If The Shallows Couldn't Drown Us The Same Way.

I ready myself to leave. The thought of Jessica is daunting, as getting out to the world that has robbed a chunk of my memory. The garage door cascades down. I watch it through the reflection on my rear-view mirror before stepping on the gas to the street ahead. To the mental torture I go, to the face of its paramount.

"Thank you," I wave to one of the men.

He's speaking to someone on the walkie-talkie, vigilant to any movement in our neighborhood.

The quiet drive ushers Henry into my mind. He always seems to be the take-charge kind of guy but one of these days, he'll have to choose between his responsibility to me and the life he designed with Landree.

Noah was able to resuscitate my decaying life. I don't know what kind of witchery made that possible but it was just automatic. My eyes have been open but I can finally see. I want it so much now, the incessant hunger to see him, to feel Noah underneath the shelter of his embrace. I only need to taste it once, the beauty of this unknown. It filled me up with raw anticipation, enough to keep wanting more.

I make it to Bellevue, where high-rise buildings glisten under the heavy September sunshine. The blue skyline up ahead frames their view. Vehicles begin decelerating to red brake lights, lining up towards the exit. With mindless focus, I watch a trailer truck pull up slowly next to me, as I await my turn to merge. Behind it, gusts of hay loiter around the air, escaping the bales that were once their prison. I watch them drift away, some landing on the grassy highway division that has not recovered from the wrath of this past summer. Like them, it doesn't

113

matter where I'll end up, as long as I'm free.

Jessica's office is now a mere block away and I'm instantly struck with indecision, to park on the street, or in the building garage. I go for the latter, driving towards the barricaded space beneath Colombia Tower. I approach the unmanned ticket booth and the yellow machine spits out the dashboard ticket.

I think of what an embarrassment it must feel to run into Noah this way. Where do I begin? How do I explain to him that amid the chaos surrounding my life, and monsters poisoning my mind, there's me? Outside the wounds of corruption, there is a part of my heart that was saved for moments such as that. He gave birth to the soft innocence that I didn't know I still own. Wouldn't that merit a little of his affection?

"Good morning!" I hear the receptionist greet from behind the tall wooden desk.

I approach briskly, hearing my heels make hurried sounds with the floor. Unintelligible conversations drift from the waiting people on the chairs to my left. Seems like a demanding day for the practice.

"I'm here for Jessica," I tell her, as I scribble my name on the sign in sheet.

"Great! Thank you. You can have a seat and she will be right out for you." She smiles back with her routinely bleached teeth. Her ensemble conforms to the upscale lifestyle of Bellevue as what I can observe. Dolce and Gabbana suit, Burberry watch, and a Tiffany's statement necklace are her name brands of choice. She seems new, at least to me, who hasn't really been here for months now.

I gather myself from the uncomfortable ogling, the bench is my next stop. Across from me are two women, similar looking and about middle-aged. They're probably related, judging from their physical attributes. I watch one leaning over, comforting the other who is in tears. The distressed one buries her face on the Kleenex and I overhear her quiet sobs.

A realization assaults me. I don't have that kind of support in my life, from a woman who can empathize the same way. No sister. No friend. A mother would have been the best safety net in the absence of one. Mine did everything but. Kara on the other hand, is a fleeting companion and we were only bound by Andrew and his horrific involvement in each of our lives. Ours, though seemingly convenient, is one that flourished out of necessity.

"Ophelia!" I hear my name being called by a familiar voice, crisp and cold.

I look up to find Jessica by the narrow hallway. Her hair bobs charmingly as she makes a gesture with her head, to lead me into her office.

I rise up to meet her perplexed expression and I know she's already making an accusatory remark, mentally at least.

"Ophelia! Good to see you," comes her dry greeting. "It's been a while, hasn't it?"

I glance at her with a forced smile, feeling her hand lightly tapping my shoulder. "I didn't even realize how long it's been," I comment.

We make our way into her office. There, I spot the same sofa where I would habitually sit in, unchanged and still pristine. The adjacent structures, including the bustling goings-on below us, are visible through the floor-to-ceiling glass window. I make myself comfortable in the swanky furniture while Jessica collects some items from her desk ahead. I continue to watch the activities in the city beneath me and I wonder if Noah is among them.

Will I run into him today? And if so, what will I say? I miss him and I know it's a silly, obsessive affection for someone I've only known for a couple days. I've accepted the fault in feeling the way I do. Tiny voices of myself have been disapproving. I hear them from the back of my head, begging me to relish in this brand-new Henry instead. However, it's already too late to turn around and be a slave all over again, to my unreciprocated love for him. Noah made me realize what I really wanted.

"So, tell me what has been going on with you? I spoke with Henry," she asks, breaking my abrupt pondering. She sits in front of me on a swivel chair, a notebook and pen in her hands. "I was told what happened but I want to hear it from you."

I purse my lips. I really didn't want to open up to her. If not for Henry, I'd be out of here in a second. I glance at her as she regards me, awaiting any word to fall from my lips. She crosses her legs and begins to shake them. That's what people usually do to relieve themselves of the tension some silence brings.

"I don't know what to tell you," comes my reply at last.

I watch the voluntary wrinkle on her nose as she thinks of what to say next. "Well, how about I ask you questions and then we can see if things will flow as they should?" Her encouraging voice sprouts some irritation from me but I'd have to just endure this full hour of discourse, for Henry's sake.

"Sure," I answer coldly.

"So," she pauses, perhaps to find the right way to ask before continuing, "This person is back, the one from before. Do you remember how it happened this time?"

"I don't think so." I have not been awake for it.

"Okay, why do you think she's here again?"

"I don't know," is my answer again.

How am I supposed to know that? She's the expert, not me!

Jessica remains calm, even when I haven't been generous with my answers. "Okay, is this the woman who told you that Andrew was bad then?"

"Yeah. But how is this relevant? Is this supposed to help me?" I snap. She's spinning the wheels again and I just can't handle it this time.

Her face is still composed, despite my sudden outburst. She smiles and nods back at me, as if she understands what I'm going through. "I'm sorry that you feel that way, Ophelia. I can only help you if you let me."

As a response, I scrutinize my emotions, fiber after fiber. I realize that this is what the other woman wants, to drive me to the edge so she can slide her way in again. I can't allow that anymore.

"I'm sorry. I just feel like everything is slipping out of my grasp," I tell her as she nods and smiles at the same time. "I have no clue where to even find myself." My apologetic voice is flawed by a steel expression but I can sense that we're going somewhere from here now.

"Thank you! I am quite impressed by how you pulled yourself out of that spiral," I hear her complimenting my small triumph, the one that seemingly got away from me before I could recognize it. "I know you can do this. Ophelia. We can beat this and you can take control of who you are. It's more than possible."

I feel as though I have been consumed by a thick fog. I've awaken this fatigue yet I couldn't justify its cause. And something's here beneath my chest muscles, sending them into a state of suffocation. I'm missing something. I know it!

She scribbles something on the notebook, before looking up at me again. "Do you see a pattern here? I know she did this a number of times before but when was the last time?"

"I don't know. I can't..."

When? Before Kara?

"I guess... Well, when Andrew came? Yes. That was her when Andrew came into my life." My response surprises me too and I'm mentally connecting the dots just as Jessica is.

She writes some more notes, launching her pen in the air between thoughts. "Very well. So then, let me ask you something. Have you met someone new lately?"

"No!" I lie.

"Are you sure?" she clarifies.

Yet that's not what I'm thinking. Millions of thoughts are flooding my mind right now. I'm drowning in them. What does she want? *No, not Jessica. Her! The woman.* What does she want that I have? Henry! She wants him. Of course! She doesn't want my heart to grow away from him so she jumps in at every small chance I get with someone else. This is what happens when I'm trapped in the dark. It must be.

I suddenly feel my throat narrowing. The air is scarce as I grapple at this realization. A moot point now, but Andrew, was it all real? But the better question is which ones are real and which ones are just fabrications of my vulnerable mind - from all these years of living as either myself or her. All those years? I wonder if she did anything worse than my suspicions. How about everyone I lost?

"Ophelia. Are you still with me?" Jessica's voice penetrates through the veil of photographs and black and white movies swirling around me. I can hear her snapping her fingers.

My eyes open to her speculating face and she tries hard to bring me back from that time entrapment by some words of encouragement. "So that makes sense now, right? That you have a little more clarity. You understand why this is happening now, when Noah was about to become a real figure in your life."

"Noah? I never said anything about him to you?" I tell her, with a tone of reproach.

"Yes, you told me about meeting him, how he makes you feel," she claims, unwary of my confusion.

How? What is happening to me?

"What are you doing? Didn't you see, she was here again? How has it already been half an hour?"

"I don't think that's what happened. In fact, this has been one of your best sessions, in my opinion," she assures. Do you want to tell me more about it though?"

All this, whatever's happening is turning my gut around. There is no sense speaking about it with Jessica. She seems resolved in convincing me that all is fine. But it isn't. She's right about one thing though, that I must claim my life back.

I need to please her so she give can give Henry some sort of guarantee that I will be okay. I did what he asked. "Oh no! I think I just had a moment of confusion. Thank you. That was very comforting, just the realization of it all," I lie.

Her eyes widen, hearing my words and realizing she's done some good. "I'm so glad to hear that. Well, it sounds like we can wrap this up for today," she announces.

She rises up from the chair and waits for me to do the same. I walk up to the door where she meets me with a stiff embrace.

I respond with the same hardy touch, sensing my escape path nearby, "Thanks again!"

And I jump out through the door at the first opportunity. Her faded "you're welcome" barely resonates in the hallway. I am out of here!

.

CHAPTER NINE

The Undoing

Was that her? That was her. Already, I lost some precision towards my objective. I know she got her way again but at least I fought to remain here. The switch didn't take weeks, just less than an hour. I guess that's a good start. I just have to be cautious, more so now. She cannot touch Noah. I will make sure of that.

My phone rings. The dashboard screen confirms that it's Henry. I imagine Jessica calling him, giving her seal of approval for my compliance. If so, I should keep it up. Pop some pills and endure Jessica for an hour twice a week. That should keep him off my back for a while.

"Ophelia?" his voice resounds through the car speakers. "Where are you?"

"Hi! I'm driving straight home, just as you asked!" I answer heartily,

"Good! That's good. When I called the office, they said you had just left." He sounds satisfied. I can hear it in his relaxed breathing, even against the call's static noise.

"Well, like you said, go see Jessica, and go home after," I tell him, mimicking his sweetly deep voice.

He grows amused by my gesture immediately. "Okay, silly!"

I'm curious of his plans for the day. "What about you? What are you doing?"

Silence invades from the other end of the call. Henry seems plagued with uncertainty, even while composed. "Listen. I'll be staying with Landree tonight but first thing tomorrow, I'll be back to check on you. How does that sound?"

The response catches me off guard. How easy could he unleash me like that? Although, I don't mind at all. "Well, that should be fine. Did something happen? You guys okay?" I inquire, as my car pulls in to a stop.

"Everything's fine. She's just having some fake contractions. They call it something hicks, whatever. I thought I'd stay with her, just in case. We're working it out."

"Okay. I'll be fine. You go take care of her," I assure him.

None of us knows what to say next.

"I guess I'll talk to you later?"

"Ok. I'll see you tomorrow," he bids quietly before an urge to keep me on the line dogs at him, "Also...thank you. Thank you for doing this. Thank you for listening to me."

It's a displaced gratitude, for him to tell me that. I should be thankful for his care, not the other way around. And even when we're just connected through the invisible line of cellular technology, his genuine love touches me from afar. I can feel it, gracing my nerves and senses - the one he preserved for me in Marcus' name.

"No, thank you," I insist, my car entering the garage now, "...I'm indebted to you, not the other way around, Henry."

The car engine dies, just as the call ends. I push another button to close the garage door behind me. I jump out of the vehicle, grab my purse, and head inside In my mind, some ideas of how to find Noah arrive swiftly. I don't think I could go another day not doing anything about this ache I'm feeling. I miss him terribly and I've scorned myself enough for throwing him out the way I remembered it. I didn't realize how much I wanted him until he's gone, as the ankle boots left my feet. The cold floor pricks my soles and I gather my pace to the carpeted area in my house.

My goosebumps stir.

Someone else's presence breaks into my awareness. I retreat back to the hallway. My body is now lathered with fear at the thought of my defenseless state, even when help is outside. No. It can't be. It's not Andrew. Not her either. Did Henry lie? Was he just checking on my word, making sure I'd do as asked?

I eye a displaced broom, leaning on the wall across from me. Adelpha must have forgotten to return it to the supply closet. I'm glad she didn't, as I pick it up and knighted it as my next saving grace. For Christ sake! Why does this keep happening to me? Who the hell is here? I suddenly regret my objections against Henry's idea of security cameras inside the house. At least they could detect intruders. The men outside, that was our middle ground instead.

It's not Andrew. It's not Andrew. It's not Andrew. It's not...

"Ophelia! It's me," a voice materializes from my back, interrupting the roaring litanies in my head.

Good Lord!

I couldn't turn around, frozen from disbelief at the exclamations I'm beginning to hear. Yet my mind is in a state of conflict - doubts, hopes, fear, joy, you name it. It can hardly believe this reality, an urge of refusal mustered from all previous heartaches. The uptick of caution pesters my thoughts, telling me not to accept this as true. I'm being deceived again.

"Sorry, I let myself in while you were gone." A cloudburst is sweeping me up in the air now. "It's me, turn around please. It's me, it's Noah." And the millions of blissful butterflies flutter inside my abdomen. My heart is drumming viciously against my chest. I wish this isn't make believe.

I turn around, every inch that I cover is a yelp of anticipation from my starving body. I'm met by his slim smile and eyes burning with desire. He looks back at me, his godly physique fences what is truly inside him. And I wish, if just for today, that it is a heart full of reciprocation towards the totality of emotions infusing in my bloodstream. They all starve for him.

I just want Noah, his caress, and his touch. He's all I see, the pure magic in his being and not just a representation of the life I want to escape to. I don't look for someone else when I see him, not even Henry.

I release the broom, along with my inhibitions. "Hi," comes my greeting, feeling pained underneath this burden of longing.

"Sorry," he says with his candied voice, as I'm reeled in closer, step after step. "I had to go through the back door to avoid Adelpha. I let myself in."

Forget how your day went with Jessica. Forget how easily he was able to break in the house with all of Henry's people lurking in the margins. Forget her.

Not for long, I'm near him, skin to skin. I'm close enough for my famished pulsation to be heard against his chest. I touch his arms, his face, and I feel his beating heart on my palm. This is real. He's here and I'm not imagining it. He came back for me and that is more than enough to merit living another day.

"You're okay. I'm so glad. I was getting worried about you," my body already fastened tightly under his strong but tender arms, "I came here many times," he adds, voice troubled. "But everyone's just trying to kick me out."

Instantly, I pull away to inquire. "They? Who's they?"

"You know, Adelpha. The guys. But it doesn't matter now," he replies, his mouth calling my attention. "Come here," he commands once more, with eyes that have swiftly uncloaked my soul to the brink of surrender.

Back in his arms, I feel home. I Inhale his scent again, breathing life into my own lungs. He deposits a quick kiss on my hair and as an immediate reaction, the thirst crawls up my throat. A day and a half to be specific, is the length of time I got to spend with him - from first meeting to separation. Even as the weeks spread out to divide us, I feel like I've known him for a lifetime. He's familiar to me and my aching senses recognized his earlier absence, promptly at his arrival. Though, I have no inkling of who he truly is.

"I miss you," I tell him childishly, almost embarrassed at the statement. My gaze creeps up to his neck, up to his handsome face that was nurtured by the sunshine. "I'm sorry about how it went down. I was just too afraid. I'm not used to that kindness, your tenderness." I apologize, as if I remember what happened.

His smile stretches underneath the striking pair of cheekbones, gape seizing mine. "I feel the same way, I miss you terribly." His hands move to my face. "It's crazy but I really do."

"I don't know what to say," I tell him in my childish tenor. "Thank you for coming back even when I went berserk? Does that sound like an apology?" I await his approval.

He tilts down to level with my face, with tightened lips that's tucking his amusement inside of it.

"What? What are you..." A finger seals my mouth, interrupting my queries. "But, tell me how you got..." His lips meet mine this time, finally terminating my voice into a tiny moan.

The afternoon stops as his warm velvet kiss oils my mouth with tenderness. I close my eyes, with hands gliding over the silk of his skin. I reach his palms. Locked under my jaw, I join his touch, even as his kiss remains unanswered by my brutal desire. I don't move so I can taste this idyllic sense of chaos from us two, while the world pauses in its favor.

"Oh!" He pulls his uneasy expression away from mine. "Is it okay?"

I smile back, still clutching his hands underneath my palms. His brown eyes float along the bronze on his perfect face.

"Sorry. Too soon again?" he asks, with an unforgiving grin.

He's wrong. This is where I abandon the mocking voices in my head and their generous injustice. I let go of his hands, so I can pull his head to me, to my hungry mouth. I can feel his body jolt in surprise but the kiss is welcome from his equally famished aperture. I unleash my passionate intrusion, until I find my tongue's affinity to his. Every moment preceding this has become one with the distant past, while the future stretches farther away from us two. This is now, for which nothing else matters.

I taste the connection, the wild yearning that blossomed between our time apart. His lips are electric and their movement leaves a trail of cold air down my spine. I feel his hands run through my hair, down my back, and into the curves of my delicate waist. I feel a pull, an ardent strength to ease my climb up his torso. With legs adhered around his strong core, we move through the hallway, and to the sofa in the receiving room. Our making out remains uninterrupted, except for a quick instance when he gently lays me flat on the furniture. He leans down again, to revel in the fire that's burning from within me. I yank him closer, so I can feel his warm body soothe my heart. Slowly, his fingers crawl underneath my shirt, just as I gently lift his up to spare no garment. He jerks. A thought stops him in his tracks. It must have been an urge to release me from his spell.

"Wait," removing his hands from my navel, he becomes tensed. "I think we should take it slow. Do things right this time," he reasons, straightening himself.

I listen to his words as I nurse the abrupt stop to this emotional implosion. The sudden entrapment of both our yearnings pains me. It affects him the same way too. I see him scowl at the incomplete agenda down his pants that he himself halted. Why now when I'm finally letting go of the bondage from my past?

"Okay. Of course. Sounds like a plan," my voice trembling in dissatisfaction. I bring myself to a sitting posture, eyeing him and his tortured expression.

"Sorry," he apologizes, hands adjusting my blouse. "I want us to go through things normal people do when they like each other," he adds, defending his actions.

Yeah, like making love, which you objected to.

"Like go on dates and stuff?" I ask, feeling his arm around my shoulder. "So, that means you like me?" My face tilts under his.

He shakes his head, entertained by my question. His breathing is still climbing down, to recover what has been undone between us two. "Duh? I wouldn't be here and chase after someone I've only known for a minute," he jokes. "Silly girl."

I feel a loving flick on my nose and I look up to his sexy wink. "But why? I am the archetype of crazy. You've seen that first-hand," I ask.

"Well I guess that makes me crazy too," he dismisses

And that is enough to throw any disbelief where it's inaudible. I trust his words as my senses nod in agreement. We're just sitting down now, my mind nudging loudly for me to say something, anything to distract me from the sudden stoppage of libido we're both still nursing ourselves from.

"Oh! B.T.W." It's him, barreling through the silence. "Here's the key I stole. Giving you now before I forget."

The single key dangles under his grip, dirt lodging within its pleats. It's been hidden underneath the flowerpot by the back door. I may have told him about it before but I have no recollection. I don't even want to think about how he evaded Henry's men. He seems to have training of some kind.

"No. Keep it," I respond, gently pushing it back to him. "And BTW?"

"What? You don't know what that means?" The movements in his chest dissolve into a chuckle. "It's 'by the way'," he clarifies, fingers writing invisible quotation marks in the air. "That's what it is!"

"Okay? Sorry that I don't know that. I've been living under a rock I guess."

He laughs even more. "Well, a nice rock that is!"

I feel a moist smack on my cheek and the endearing kiss overwhelms me, more than any lascivious link I have to him.

"You're cute," I hear him say, as he looks around. "It's different here now."

I cross my arms, realizing the same. "Yeah, it is. So, what should we do today? Let's get out of here," I ask, giving him a suggestive wink to change the subject.

His face lights up, teasingly mimicking The Thinker statue. "Well, we could go somewhere but then I don't wanna try and kiss you again on our date, only to find myself being kicked out of your house."

"Oh, stop it!" I reply with a loving anger, slightly punching him at the arm and pretending that I remember that happening.

As a response, he entraps my fist and kisses it once, maybe twice. I find myself stretching my smile to its painful limits. It seems so easy with him. His company gifts me with a sense of liberation from who I was and how people think I should be.

"Do we still need to take precautions? Like from Henry and Adelpha?" he asks, interrupting my musing.

"You met Henry?" I ask urgently, my gaze inquisitive. "When?"

"Long story but yes, with Adelpha." His hand finds its way to my cheek, and with his thumb, he caresses one side of my face. "Don't worry. There was no brawl or anything. But..."

He grows silent.

Slightly feeling irritated by the buildup of anticipation, I glower. "But what?"

I eye him shaking his head, smile still visible on his face. "Well, I was going to say that the message was clear to stay away, that I wasn't welcomed here."

"Yuck! I'm sorry," I tell him.

"Don't worry about it. The only welcome I care about is from you," he says, grinning from ear to ear.

I answer with a beam, virtually seeing hearts in both my eyes. "Well, I showed you how welcomed you are, didn't I?"

We both sit there laughing and the stroke of his fingers on my back still electrocutes me with pins and needles.

"Henry's not coming home tonight," is my announcement after recovering from the emotional upheaval.

He seems surprised. "Really? How about tomorrow?"

"I don't know yet. Probably in the morning, to check on me. Also, I have to go to a shrink to make him happy."

"Okay." A forced smile appears on his face, right after hearing what I said. "We can work with that type of schedule," he remarks, with eyes dissolving into wonder and ignoring the hint of my mental condition.

I feel my chest melt into a pool of regret. Is it too soon to tell him what happens behind my life's smokescreen? He doesn't seem to mind.

He marvels at my pensive state. "You're quiet all of a sudden," he wonders, body now leaning forward to face me, hands clasped together, and elbows on his thighs. "Why? Tell me what's bothering you?" He is sensitive to my profound breathing and slowly envelops me within his tender embrace.

"I just feel like this isn't true. Are you not bothered the slightest to know that I am seeing a therapist? Like I must be crazy, right? This is your chance to go before it's too late," a reply is marshalled by what little courage I have left.

"You mean before I get in too deep?" He laughs. "Honey, that ship has sailed."

Uncertainty flurries from deep within me. There must be a take-away. Is he after my money? What are his intentions? Nobody just likes someone without anything back, especially me. He's seen my crazy, first-hand. There must be something way more valuable he could gain from my company. It shouldn't be this easy. No one comes around and stays for the dark ending. Only Henry is fit to do that.

"Hey. Stop that," he interrupts. "I know what you're thinking. Don't!"

His eyes find mine, to solidify the rule of his charms. How easy is that to feel bewitched, this sweet punishment he imposes? The impending surrender comes next from my mouth. "Okay. But are we gonna go on this date soon? Cuz I'm kinda starving."

Laughter inundates the room. My heart is content and his, full of glee. For now. I glance at our surroundings - the setting of two careless hearts fluttering side by side. I hope to God that these feelings are genuinely reciprocated, and that this is real, whatever this may be. Through my eyes, the walls seem vibrant from the overpowering elation flowing out of my body. This sprinkle of magic, I don't want it to end.

He jumps up from the sitting position, and right away offering a hand out. "Thought you'd never ask!"

CHAPTER TEN

Fighting For The Honor Of My Grief

Two blocks away from my house now and the distance between Noah and I seems vast. The cab driver offers no form of distraction from the conversations floating in my mind, and that may be okay right now. He assured me that things will get better soon and even if I refuse to believe him, I actually do.

"Here we are," the driver announces - his only other statement besides asking where we're headed.

I swipe my card on the pad behind the front seat. The transaction seems quick and in no time, he is handing me my receipt. We both exchange our "thank yous" and I let myself out of the vehicle.

There would have been constant worries about disappointing Henry with my actions but those thoughts feel weightless at this point. I know he means well but I really would like to take my life back. It seems no better time than now.

The door pushes open before I could turn the knob. Henry meets me with a concerned look. He says no word as he leads me inside, and to the kitchen.

"Oh, there you are, dear!" That's Adelpha turning over a pancake, next to a stack of already cooked ones. "How was your night?" she asks, just for the sake of asking. I can hear her giggle to herself when she returns to her task.

I sense Henry watching me as I set the brown paper bag on the marble counter. His question comes next. "Where have you been?" Although he's calm, frustration is foaming at the edge of his words.

"For this," is my response as I snatch the bag of baked goods for maximum effect. "I went to Anne's. Woke up craving for raisin bagels."

I seem to have convinced him of my subtle alibi, while he inspects the bag. But that's just a false hope. He knows. With the amount of surveillance on me, it's hard not to. My only upper hand is that his people are not allowed to intervene in my life, unless the situation becomes dangerous. They must not think Noah is.

He takes one bagel out to eat. "Wow. Not bad," he mutters, getting Adelpha's attention. Meanwhile, I find myself sitting on the bar stool, thinking about how much I already miss Noah. "Have some of this, Adelpha," he offers her some bread in the background as the world around me is swept into a dream.

I remember the warm rush of breathing on my neck just hours ago. There was no urgent call from the blossoming morning, except for the sunrise commanding my attention through the open window. Mt. Rainier rose above the constant cloud shield. I could be anywhere in the world but there I was, in the arms of Noah, while the crisp six am breeze touched opportunely on my face. Watching his seamless exterior move, was discerningly unbearable. I hurt even in the idle parts of my body. My gaze could have been murderous. It was difficult to collect my emotions, along with my saliva.

"My pancake is better than this store food. Right, Ophelia?" Adelpha's underhanded rejection to the bagel Henry offered arrives without effort.

I hear the chaos again - the hustle and bustle outside, the onions sizzling in the pan, the crackle from the artificial fireplace, and Henry's voice, raced with obvious dissatisfaction.

"Maybe next time, you might wanna call me so I know you're alright," he scolds, delivering an icy piece of reality that I'm meant to eat for breakfast instead.

My actual life is groping at his heels for recognition. But I don't want to go back to these monotonous mornings. I want to run away, to somewhere Noah and I can be free from his overbearing care and the residuals of Andrew's dark narrative.

He takes his place on the stool next to mine, focused on Adelpha's approaching exit. I sigh to rid myself of the irritation that's been building up. "Sorry, I didn't know I still need to," I snap at him in a weak voice, feeling powerless at the same time. He's right. My decisions must remain calculated.

He chews the last piece of his bagel, and finds a napkin to wipe his mouth with, taking his time to respond. Maybe he doesn't want to have this conversation in front of her.

"Alright, kids! I take some pancakes for the boys. Eat the rest," says Adelpha. She walks past us with a smile, and waves her free hand to announce her departure, that has long been awaited by Henry.

He abandons his seat to give her a hug. "See you tomorrow then, Moma." Adelpha responds to the gratitude with a maternal kiss on his cheek.

I wave back at her. "Thank you, Adelpha."

He follows her to the door. I feel a stab of guilt in my chest. I hate sneaking out and lying to Henry. I couldn't even look at him as he shuffles back to the marble island. I watch him open cupboards and drawers to find plates and utensils. He tries to busy himself with the pancakes and omelets, his back to mine. Next, he takes out a white mug and pours coffee in it. Colombian brew, I gather. He maintains his silence that is almost an accusatory statement to how penitentiary this living arrangement is starting to feel.

I focus on last night. It's already been a few weeks and every time I'm with him, I give birth to a fresh type of self-discipline, to hold myself back from all the imaginative things my mind proposes. How much strength I squandered just trying to refrain from touching him, should have depleted all my energy. I just want to be his, to be high on this form of drug that I wouldn't mind exploiting. I can't wait to see him again. My mounting smile is hard to hide at the thought of his. When Henry finally turns to bring me my breakfast, he catches my quick giggle.

"What are you smiling about?"

"Nothing," is my quick retort. I regard him in the eye before I continue. "How's Landree?"

He hesitates for a split second, certain of my motives. I've been trying to avoid the elephant in the room. "She's okay now. Just needs the bed rest but..." He pauses to take a deep breath, and allow the weight of his next words to fall from his mouth. "...But where were you really? Last night? This morning?"

This time, he adjusts his elbow on the counter, making sure he gets a full view of the reaction from my face, once I stumble through my lies. The familiar sound of unease begins to climb. I know an argument will soon follow - the same tune, the same ending.

"Did you want me to answer that for you?" he probes again. A hint of fury lands on the counter, as he slams his palms on to it, in the minute following the gap of conversation. The action appears unnatural, as this tough exterior and heated expression doesn't suit him.

"Is it an argument you're looking for? Cuz I really don't feel like it." I settle for a deflection.

"You saw him, didn't you?" He thrusts an undisputable answer in the form of a question. "Last night? And all the other nights before that?"

I feel peeved. Maybe it's for a defensive cause. Maybe I'm just tired of his questions. My emotions swell in anger. I no longer have control of it.

"What is it to you anyway? Blah blah blah, for my safety, blah blah blah." My hands in the air, are now stiff in rage. "Just let me be, Henry!"

I push the stool back with my bottom, so hard I could hear it crash on the wooden flooring. With haste, I abandon the kitchen area, half-eaten bagel in one hand. It is better this way. I don't want to fight anymore. I aim for the hallway, wherever he isn't. Yet I feel him behind me, getting closer and closer. I sense a hand on my arm, cold and irate. He's trapped me in his clutch.

"You listen to me, Ophelia," he orders, squeezing my elbow, enough to stop my childish trudging. "You have no idea who he is. You just had an episode. Remember? I'm only looking out for you. For him."

"Oh! And you do? You know him?" I quarrel back, turning to face his frustrated appearance. "You had him investigated? Followed? What did you find? I know you feel guilty that you didn't do the same with Andrew? You're overcompensating. Well, guess what? It's too late now. The damage has been done. I will fight you when it comes to him. He's different from Andrew and I know you can see that!" With hands crossed now, I await his response while catching my breath from the marathon of words spattering out of me.

"You absolutely have no idea what you're talking about." His head is shaking, face crumpled in repulsion. "You need to calm down and listen to me. Please. One time," he begs, signaling his index finger at me.

I roll my eyes at him but of course, at his whim, I'm able to keep my emotions at bay. "Well what do you want me to do? You want me to take my meds, I would do that. You want me go see Jessica? I will do that for you too, as much as I dislike her. But what about me? Have you asked me what I want? I need a new life where I don't feel like I'm just tagging along behind you and Landree. Now, do you understand what I mean? I want my freedom."

His expression softens as my face mirrors the heartache reviving inside of me.

"I finally want something outside of you. I just want to feel desired, that I am someone's first choice," I add, with tears forming creeks down my face.

And as an anticipated reaction, he comes closer and wipes my waterworks off with his own hands. Although the gesture appears warm, his eyes maintain an apparent sternness that is unmoved by my sobs. I realize that there is nothing I could do to change his mind. There seems to be no compromise when it comes to Noah.

When the household sounds finally recover its pause, there's Henry's footsteps edging away from the frigid affection he leaves me with. He has no regard for my feelings and the more I cry, the more he shields himself from the emotional panhandling. I am no more than a responsibility, a responsibility that is etched on Marcus' headstone. Until he sees a way to break those shackles, or at the very least realize that his life is not bound to his demise, I'm trapped. Not him, who is already pained by this obligation, nor Landree, who has gone to many great places with Henry, except for where she wants to be. None of us are yet to feel free.

"I can't let you do what you ask," he speaks when finally reaching the door. "You already feel that way when you don't even know the guy? Do you know what he does for a living? Where he's from? Who his friends are? Nothing."

In silence I look up to him, his valid argument piercing my mind with realization. The mere fact that I know Noah for only that short amount of time, and shared a bed with him before finding out his life story, surely is a cause for concern. What he can't understand is how easy it is to forget about my sometimes-wise mind when it comes to that man. Being with him is a taste of sweet liberty from my life of incarcerations. How many times do I have to repeat myself?

"Exactly! You don't know anything. So, stay away from him," he concludes his argument, his commanding voice fading into the windy morning through the half-opened door.

Then he's gone, out to the world where the wife he has yet to marry awaits his return. Instead of feeling uncertain, everything is clear to me. Henry's words found no place in my thoughts to discourage Noah away from my life. If I become blinded by this mind-numbing bliss, so be it.

"Well, you look like you just got hit by a train," an unsettling voice swings from behind me.

I turn around to find her, wearing the same thing she wore the last time I saw her before I was 'away'.

"It seems like things have changed since I've been gone," she adds, finding the water pitcher from the fridge.

I move towards her, to the counter where my medication spreads for attention. "Where have you been?" I ask her while managing to open the top of my Saturday pack. She watches me as I toss the contents into my hands.

"I've been here, just waiting for your return." Pills in my mouth now. "You weren't careful enough to let your past self be you again," she cautions, tugging along a cryptic message.

I wait for the medications to enter my throat before responding. She seems to know more about the few weeks that I lost. She always has. "I know that now. But what happened?"

"You hurt him. You hurt the guy yet he's still there, still on your side."

The thought of harming Henry is gut-wrenching. By my own hands most of all, is unforgivable. I would never do such a thing.

"I have nothing to say to that. I don't know. I don't remember," I reply.

"Yeah you could pretend to." Her hands scour the bag of bagels. "But at the very least, listen to him. He only has your best interest in mind."

It's frustrating, whatever she's doing. It doesn't make me feel good if she continues to chastise me and mock what I did when I wasn't me.

"What do you want, Kara? And you're one to talk. You could have stopped her but you let it happen," I argue back, placing some blame on her part.

"Huh! You know I can't do that," she quickly replies. "That Noah dude though, I'm with Henry on this one. Seems like bad news."

"It's time for you to go now," I tell her, while she continues to fiddle with the bagel in her hands.

Her presence that I once wanted while in the precipice of self-destruction, is now no longer. She is a property of my past, one with Henry at the undertow. She rose from the wasteland where, while in his tutelage, Andrew hauled me to. They all belong there, a distant memory that deserves no reprieve.

CHAPTER ELEVEN

On Nights I'm A Tourist In My Own Body

Auburn foliage drift mid-air as activities surge around me. Akin to the spring flurries, people visit in droves to get a picture among the changing leaves here in Green Lake. Certainly, I'm captivated by the spectacle but never more than that man below the wide steps, in his wetsuit on the paddle board.

I wave at him. "Babe! It's time."

My call is promptly answered by a wink. It's almost a shot to the heart, a hard one to recover from. He adjusts his direction and makes his way to me.

Never once in the past as an idle bystander, did it even occur to me that I would be partaking in any sport. But Noah has always tested my adrenaline limits ever since. Last week we rock climbed. Before that, I somehow found myself above Lake Washington, towed by a boat below us. And it's only October.

Henry hasn't missed a visit, hasn't failed to remind me about my medications, but stopped asking for my daily whereabouts. I don't know where in our argument he found defeat but the fighting stopped the last time we talked about Noah. His trail of suspicion towards him has gone cold as well. Either he's trusting of my decision-making skills these days, or just pre-occupied by Landree's critical pregnancy. He didn't even bother asking about my unexploited visits with Jessica. He's slowly keeping his distance, just as he was when Andrew first came in the picture. Henry seems to be trying his best at letting me go, except for the legal part, as usual.

In the midst of that changing tide, I've slowly reclaimed my life and this existence that once got the better of me. I'm discovering new things, seeing this old city with foreign eyes.

"You're so beautiful," he says as he secures the board over his car.

His smile appears after he shuts the trunk. He moves closer to me and I prepare my arms for his warm embrace. But the sweet surprise comes from his hungry lips. He kisses me, long enough for the world to watch. The feel of his arms around my hips is ecstasy. I now realize that there is still something in me that can be restored. Noah showed me that, without obliging to pain and sacrifice. To this kind of happiness, I am simply a novice.

"Hi!" he laughs when we're finally through with our loving display. He opens the passenger door, where I happen to be standing by. "Here you go, my queen."

After fastening my seat belt and shutting my door, he runs quickly to the steering wheel. In no time, we are backing out of the parking lot and on to the main street.

"How'd you get here, babe?" He manages a question, even while intent on the busy road ahead.

"I called Uber," is my reply, while mindlessly fixing my hair.

"Oh! Wonder how Henry would feel about that," he remarks.

Our giggles follow. He certainly would die when he finds out.

"So where are you taking me tonight?" I ask him.

The statement provokes some excitement from his lips and he takes a second, while at the stop sign, to glance at me with a big grin. I feel him pinch my cheek gently before attending to the street again. "We can't be late. We have a reservation," he reveals.

It is apparent, the pride in his voice when he said it. I'm a little bit caught off guard myself. How this spur-of-the-moment person actually planned something as elaborate as making reservations? To his defense though, these dates were all well thought of.

"Wow! Reservations? Who are you and what happened to my —" I catch myself before the word 'boyfriend' rolls out of my tongue. "— to the old Noah."

He's still focused on the road but his free hand makes its way to my back and over my nape. Then, from the corner of my eye, I see him mouth words that are still audible beneath the roar or the Harley bikes behind us. "You did. You happened," a casual retort that is already triggering the voltage down my spine, escapes his mouth. *I happened to him* - no matter how much this thought is probed in my brain, it still feels like a wild dream.

That subtle vibration inside the console is doing it again, probably the third time now since we left Green Lake. I can't help but wonder if he's oblivious to the small but repetitive distraction, or that he's ignoring it. Here comes the 4th! He's jumpy now and his eyes adjust to speculate at a thought, though his gaze remains fixed ahead. Jealousy, like tiny biters and crawlers up my chest, has heeded the alarm bells from my brain. *Is it another woman? Oh, hell no!*

"Someone must really want to talk to you," comes my refined way of asking *who the fuck is calling you over and over.* I've filtered all the other profanities linked with the irritation.

There's a second-long freeze from his body language, and the process of finding an appropriate response becomes apparent in his expression. A wrinkle appears on his forehead as he steals a look towards my inquisitive form before responding. "It's work. I traded my overtime tonight to someone and now he's out sick."

My lips form a pout, having heard his answer. It could be that I am not satisfied with what he said or that he'll choose work over spending time with me. "Must be a really big plane they're making," I comment.

We reach a stop light at red but he decides to shift the car to park before turning to face me. "Don't worry, love, I won't come in today." His hand is on my chin now. "There's no way I'm working tonight. Boeing can suck it!"

I trap any sign of relief within the ball of my cheeks. I'm afraid to give in too easily. Perhaps, I'm too embarrassed to admit that I was wrong, that my suspicion was unfounded.

"I see that big smile coming," he teases before leaning forward to claim my lips yet again. And in an instant, I withdraw the cagy agenda from my thoughts. His kiss can do just that. Seconds into it, he pulls away, still clasping my lower lip between his teeth. I laugh hard with my restrained mouth at his funny eye expressions. He continues his silly display. I feel a single tear roll down my cheek from having to keep my giggles within my stomach this whole time. Minutes pass, I hear car horns assaulting us from the angry drivers behind. The light has been green for a while now, and when we finally return to the world outside of ours, it's red again. We must now deal with everybody else who missed the go signal because we couldn't keep our hands to ourselves.

One last raging honk comes from the woman directly from the back. "Asshole!" she sends her displeasure forward, with a matching middle finger through the driver's side window.

Noah is still laughing, paying no mind to the traffic offense we had just committed. "See what your jealousy does?"

"No," I make a fake angry face. "I was never jealous."

We chuckle together. This time, Noah is slightly attending to the traffic light ahead. An unfamiliar voice bursts in, cackling along with us. It's hard to recall when the red Porsche pulled up next to Noah, and judging from his amused reaction, he's not one we should be wary of.

"What's up?" Noah calls out to him, as he presses a button to roll his window all the way down. I'm not sure if he's annoyed by the intrusion or just being friendly.

I study him. Caucasian, probably mid-fifties, corporate job judging from his suit, and perhaps an easy-going personality.

"You've pissed off half the block there, son," he remarks. "Drove around to see what the fuss is about."

"Sorry about that, Sir." Noah pauses to regard me, then continues. "It's my girlfriend's fault here!"

I feel a squeeze in my frozen hand while Noah awaits the man's response. "Well, I see why that is. Lovely lady there," he replies, after catching a glimpse of me.

I think they're both anticipating a reaction from me but all I can muster is a smile. I'm still fixed on 'girlfriend' and how I was labeled as such.

"Well, better get to it now before another repeat of that road rage," becomes his subtle reminder to attend to the traffic light, as it shifts to green.

"Thank you," Noah responds, stepping on the gas.

"Stay in love, kids!" The stranger's words jaunt out through the heavy rumbles of car engines around us. Noah's declaration toggles at the strings in my chest, while we drive away to our destination. I'm his girlfriend he said and he didn't dispute the thought of us loving each other. What if that was all for show? I would hate to fall back into the ground he lifted me up from. Then I realize, all I have to do is ask. It's never hard to do that with him. I'm going to!

Lord help me!

"Sure is nice to be your girlfriend," I joke nervously.

He grins before steering the car into a busy parking lot, the valet attendant waving at him ahead. *Well, is he going to say something or what?*

"Evening, Sir. Welcome to Las Margaritas!"

I watch Noah slide out of the vehicle, completely leaving me unanswered. My car door opens and a different valet attendant leads me out. I scan my eyes for him without success.

"Well, it sure is nice to be your boyfriend too." I jump up as he emerges from behind me. "Now, let me take my girlfriend to dinner." He rescues my hand and we head for the entrance.

I turn mute. *Don't play me like this.*

The table he reserved has the view of Lake Washington. He attends to the waiter as he always does in all our dates, while I gape at the beauty of the twinkling city across the water. Here we are in plain clothes, equally unprepared for this upscale dining experience.

"I could have gone home so I can look more decent than this," I say, while inspecting my outfit.

"What's wrong with our clothes?" he wonders playfully. "Who's gonna notice?"

Then I realize, it wouldn't matter. The curtains have been pulled halfway around us for some privacy. I feel a little bit better.

I wink at him. "You've done well, Mister."

"Anything for the love of my life."

The words feel like feathers drifting through my senses, yet the weight of their meaning is the emotional eruption I've waited this whole time. Why do I cave easily to this indirect declaration of love? I keep my eyes fixed on the multitude of utensils spread on the table. I am slightly ashamed at my expectations. Perhaps he's just being casual. So, I guess that was just an expression, something that fell out of his mouth without thought. How dare he?

I notice his fingers crawl over mine. They linger there as the silence amplifies my heartbeat.

"Ophie, can you please look at me?" arrives his gentle request.

I couldn't do it. Maybe he heard my silent deliberation. The fear of being denied the love he's been hinting forms a big hollow within my chest.

"Please," he asks again.

Slowly, I meet his eyes and the mystery they bring. He loses his sense of humor. Before me appears a kingly man whose future belongs on a golden throne. He seems stern and I just don't know what to expect.

"I know exactly why you've been weird and I'm sorry."

I nod, questions still lingering in my mind.

He squeezes my hand tighter and continues. "Can I ask you something?"

"Okay?" I hide the intense fireworks in my heart. *Are you kidding me? Please keep going.*

"Hola! How does a round of Mezcal shots sound to the lovebirds?"

I struggle to read his name on the gold-plated badge. Dale, with eyes glinting against the crystal chandelier ahead, seems too polite for his animated front. He is blatantly unaware of his invasion, as his glance bounces between Noah and I, dying for a reaction. I throw a smile at him to save face and immediately, his shoulders recoil.

"Maybe not today, buddy. Thanks," Noah responds, maintaining his hold on me. "But I'll get a Coke no ice please." He tilts his head up to his left and regards our host, whose hands are gingerly clasped together.

He's still oddly quiet while my alternating thoughts momentarily focus on him. The other times, I've been rehearsing what I would say when he confesses his true feelings. Should I squeal? Jump across the table and hug him? What if that's not what he feels and only sees me as less than?

"Ophelia." His prodding voice rejoins the conversation.

I think Dale needs my drink order now, definitely not whatever that Mezcal shit from god knows where.

"Water for now please." *And go now, Dale! Way to ruin the moment.*

"Certainly. I'll get that going right away," he replies, nodding his head in a very inferior fashion before turning his heels.

Noah becomes my focal point again, the main lure of the steady night air against the sparkling structures of Seattle. His face is to me but I am only a transparency within his gape.

"I ordered ahead, as usual. Thought you'd be okay with that too," he announces casually, his sudden dullness killing the forthcoming delight in my heart.

"Okay," I answer coyly, eyes fixed on his now. "You always know what's best."

He looks through my anticipating form and to the beams in the ceiling above, thoughts far beyond reach. He acts as though someone invisible is poking his back, irritated I would say. All versions of excitement are now lost to confusion. It's difficult to read him and I'm not sure if I should blame the waiter or his attention span.

Something looms at the tips of his fingers, I notice it more now. He draws his hand away from mine to retrieve the cause of his concern, from inside his pocket. Though subtle, I can hear a collective gasp from the table to our far left, just as Noah gets up and slides his chair back. With one hand on my lap, I wave them off to signal a false alarm. One cups her mouth from embarrassment, and the other whispers "sorry". He holds out a peace sign with his fingers.

They must have been watching us keenly through the gap in the curtain line. The ambience does boast an air of romance and the clichés of love declarations and proposals. If I didn't know better, my reaction would be more frivolous. Yet I know the root of his distraction comes from the incessant phone calls since this afternoon, which he recently demoted to vibrate. He reveals the black device and sure enough, the blinking screen of urgency screams, even at me. It's definitely not the kind of 'ring' the spectators presumed he'll pull out.

"I'm sorry! I have to get this. Can you excuse me for a moment?" he asks, while I gawk at my own dim reflection on the glass window, fighting my eyes.

I gather that it's more convenient to pretend I didn't hear anything. The same window reveals a moving image of him awaiting my response as I carry on with nursing my internal sobs.

"Ophie," his hand on my shoulder, "I'll be outside for a minute."

This time, his tone is more imposing than one awaiting consent. I nod, refusing to look at him as the voices awaken in my ears. He bolts out without hesitation and I'm left with some residuals of frustration from earlier, when I imagined tonight to be a better version of whatever this is.

I feel like screaming. But the voices in my head beat me to the task. They're here. She's here. The whispers are louder, now-mocking, ruthless. My vision is escaping farther away from me. The table is now out of reach, my fingers barely grazing the white cloth over it. It's as if I'm seeing through a telescope, a peephole from miles away.

"No!" My voice is not my own. It's cold, deep, and gregariously commanding the air passage between my lips. She raises a hand, my muscles unable to control and retract the action.

"I'll have that Mezcal you mentioned please." When she speaks, the sway in my throat is an expertise of hers alone. Dale, unwary of the switch, falls victim to the flirtatious bait. I'm frozen, helpless while I watch myself become someone else. This can't be, a first in a long while. I'm awake and in the brink of losing it. It's starting...

My lids pop open, heavy from what feels like hours of deep sleep, but a mere blink in real time. Noah remains absent from the chair across the table, nothing but a vague indicator of time. How long has it been? I'm afraid to know. Meanwhile, the weird drink is wrapped inside my clutch, only drops left at the bottom of the shot glass. This must be what she had asked for. My tongue tingles from the bites of alcohol in my taste buds but I'm more concerned about the hours I spent while in the void.

"Excuse me, what time is it?" I ask loudly, for anyone to hear amid the scuffle of porcelain plates and trays outside our private den.

Behind the curtain, a shadow breaks away from the flurry. He recognizes my voice and it's Dale. His head swings in the corner, armed with a toothy and lustful grin. "You asked for the time? It's 6:58." A wink follows his reply.

Hell no! Gross!

"Thank you. That's all." I dismiss him. His face falls slightly down his chin. He slips away unnoticed, almost. I'm sorry, but the most I can give him is a big, fat tip. I don't know much about his exchange with her, but I have a pretty good idea what it involved.

6:58 pm. It's only been like 10 minutes since losing myself, 20 at most - not enough time to do some serious damage. I dread the thought of her residuals. Why does she remain? Have I not done enough to distract myself from all the distant yesterdays with her? With Andrew? Over three weeks in the looney bin, that should have sufficed her for a little bit. I almost lost Noah to her crazy antics.

Do you see a pattern here? I know she did this a number of times before but when was the last time?

Somehow, Jessica's words hover in my ear. She didn't make sense then but was she right after all? This woman is torturing me because of Henry. We both love him but she steals my freedom away when I decide that someone else is more worthy of my affection. Andrew. Did she turn him into the monster he came to be, in the hopes of getting Henry back? I don't know. I'm confused. A hammer to my head now, as nothing is making sense. All I know is that I'm shackled to her, dual minds to a body. Trying to solve the mystery is equally scrupulous as remaining in a state of confusion. I just need to be strong for Noah, for us.

Noah returns. His face long from an obvious phone argument, is also my saving grace from my mind's eviction. He didn't see it happen. Thank God. He steps aside to let a family of eight pass by. Another tray of dirty dishes takes up the aisle and he remains there, right by the entryway. His demeanor is off. A clue of frustration prods his brain and impatience replaces his façade.

"Tinga de Pollo and Tacos Al Carbon?"

The server, who is not Dale, has reached the table before Noah could even get through another crowd.

"Thanks. Just in the middle please," I respond, while my eyes loiter in her direction.

The woman sets the hot plates on the table, quietly at first. "Enjoy your meal!" From the corner of my eye, she catches a glimpse of the Coke Noah ordered. The heavily perspired glass probably makes her wonder if I'm being stood up. Then she's gone.

Here he comes, Noah making his way in between the white drapes. Everything around us fades as I watch him move closer. He's done this to me ever since that first day at the restaurant. I just didn't realize it. Even with obvious irritation through his body language and his usually cool demeanor nowhere to be found, my heart still swells at the sight of him. Yes, in spite of it all. By the time he's in front of me, my lungs would be void of oxygen. He's undeniably striking. My chest aches at his perfection, like watching the sun set in the summertime. I can't breathe.

He doesn't resume his original spot. Instead, he stands next to me.

"Ophelia," comes his stern voice.

What had happened in the minutes that I lost? Will he say something about that?

Legs of the empty chair scuff across the wooden floor, as he drags it with grave intention. I adjust my position to face him, watching his body sink down. His commanding stare entraps me, while his hands are successful in their undertaking to find mine. In his eyes, something's steeping, like an imminent goal that must be achieved at once.

"I love you." Our hands are intertwining on my lap. "I have to tell you this now because of what I'm about to ask you."

From his mouth, the words I've been dying to hear for so long, slip out so beautifully. The knots in my chest descend gently towards my aching stomach, as a response to the thirst it finally quenched. Yet the illusion comes to a stop, to a screeching halt. Reason floods my mind, pushing out the quiet serenade brought by his confession. Meanwhile, the butterflies make an abrupt exit and I'm left with no choice but to think rationally. I open my mouth to question him. What does he want? What kind of ordeal is he facing that forced those words out of him?

"No. Please, let me finish, "he exclaims, intercepting the deluge of questions biting at my heels. "Fuck work! Fuck everything else. Come away with me. Let's go somewhere far, where nobody knows us. I know you feel the same way. Just say yes!"

"Why?" I ask, with the only word that escaped the noise in my head.

"What do you mean why? I just said I love you and that's all you're gonna say?" His voice trembles. I hear him chuckle slightly, a standard sarcasm. His grip tightens while I scan my brain for the best possible thing to say next.

"What are we running away from?"

His eyes widen, either from surprise or admission of guilt.. "Forget it." He lets go of my hands while he gathers his next words. I watch him gulp in some saliva as his eyes stare deeply into space. "But to be frank, I know my place when it comes to Henry. I just want you to live for you and not in his terms. Do you know what I mean?"

His bold claim catches me in surprise, provoking an immediate defense to Henry's nobility. The man he speaks of, only cares about my wellbeing and I'm only complacent for that reason. Not once did he ever lay a finger on me and he was always there to save me from harm. I can't let him stain his name like that.

"But I'm not a prisoner. And haven't you noticed? I've been able to do whatever these days. Noah, what am I missing? What are you not telling me?"

"Unbelievable! Didn't you hear anything that I said?" he shouts, letting go of his hold completely. We're both startled by his reaction, to see a hint of anger unfolding from his character. He slumps back into the chair, refusing to look at me. He rubs his wrist in defeat, while I'm trying my hardest to comprehend what's happening before me. Nobody seems to pay attention to our quiet argument now.

He's never been mad before, towards me at least. I don't know how far he goes when he's infuriated. It's only Henry I'm comfortable with, when it comes to situations involving anger.

We both fall silent.

"I'm sorry. It's not you," he whispers moments later, having collected his mood. "A lot of things have been stressing me out these days. It's not your fault," a sigh accompanies his words.

God. I love him, a world different than I do Henry. This kind is emancipating and boundless. I'm in love with this version of myself. My fascination towards this bold existence no longer knows horror. These scars tell their own story but Noah has been the undoing of all that came to be before him. My dark past, the memories of damage, and loss, he obliterated them without prejudice.

One day, I just opened my eyes and became the center of the universe - the bull of his colossal gravity. I realize I am now the woman I envied from afar, engorging in this piece of heaven. Someone loves me and I don't have to fight for my share as I did with the last person. I earned this moment. I deserve a ride into the sunset, to resign from the tug of war against love, and be swept off my feet without compulsion.

So, what am I doing? What did I just do?

"Yes! Of course! I love you too." I lean forward to grab his face and the heavy expression it's nursing. "I'll go with you. Whenever. Wherever."

I kiss him, without caution. Who cares if anyone sees or whether or not it's appropriate in this space and time? His reciprocation screams out loud in the form of his graceful tongue, enrapturing my every human sense. With all my fibers infiltrated with his electricity, a yearning of a more profound kind rouses. He cloaks me tighter in his strong arms, my chest feeling the flames from his scorching body. We continue with our wild spectacle, as if our throats were parched for centuries before this.

He pulls away, and immediately, a blow to my core almost astounds me. It's the hunger wreaking havoc to my soul, the one I've yet to gratify.

"Let's get outta here," he whispers in my ear.

And all the microscopic hair in that vicinity becomes unyielding. I smooth the wrinkles on my shirt but I'm really just trying my hardest to neutralize my body's lethal voltage, caused by our recent encounter. He moves across the table, regards the food for a little bit and tosses two hundred dollar bills next to the perspiring Coca Cola glass. Once I've collected myself and my libido, we are walking out to the exit, his hand on my back leading the way.

A whistle of applause and clapping explodes as we are nearing the check in desk. I look back to find the same group of people from earlier, now finding justification from their prior congratulatory response. I wink back at the lady who gasped at the very beginning, before Noah left with the phone call. An elderly woman from the same table now joins the staring panel. She throws out a double thumbs up sign and mouths "good job". A giggle escapes my throat. She must have been referring to my fine-looking man.

"What was that about?" He finally notices the attention we're receiving, while looking back at the 'thumbs-up lady'.

"Nothing. They saw us earlier. Thought you just proposed," I answer.

Somehow, a naughty thought becomes apparent from his face and I feel as excited as terrified at what might that be. Before I could guess what it is, he turns around to acknowledge the table of spectators. He waves back. And when I feel assured that he's done, he shouts, "Luckiest man in the world!" To which, the whole restaurant erupts in applause and standing ovations.

Warm blood rushes up my cheeks. I'm embarrassed by the attention. To the exit, I drag my feet hurriedly. Noah must still be standing where I was, entertaining the crowd with his successful but fake proposal attempt. Yet I was wrong. I feel a grip on my wrist which stops me in my tracks. It's him, my bogus fiancé, whirling me back into his arms. Like a ballroom dancer, he slides me gracefully, and dips me down to his feet. A kiss follows and the crowd grows more insane.

It's time to head out!

I drag him by our fastened hands. "We gotta go! You're embarrassing me."

He laughs, his usual child-like laughter coming from his belly. "That was fun." And he traps me with his bear hug once more.

"That's enough for one night, Noah!"

A chuckle jumps out of him again. "Okay, okay whatever my girlfriend wants," he says before his eyes wander into the hands of a woman server passing by. "Wait," he breaks his pace. "Isn't that your phone?" He mutters while already walking towards her.

"Wait what? I have my phone with me," I say it without certainty. My fingers scour for it in my cross-body purse. I couldn't find it. That was my phone.

Noah is speaking to the server now, whose eyes have hearts in them. In her body language, a blotch of attraction appears, and she readily hands the device back to him.

"Got your phone back, babe." He returns to my side with so much life and vigor, like a dog retrieving a ball that was thrown far away. I almost forgot he was upset earlier and I have unknowingly ignored how weird he acted before and after that phone call.

"Where was it?" I take the phone back and secure it inside my purse. "I don't remember using it here." I wonder how I left it. I don't recall any moment when I took it out.

"She found it in the bathroom."

In the bathroom? Oh shit! It must have been her.

"But it's okay. Doesn't seem like anything's wrong with it," he assures as we reach the door. "Now let's get back to my apartment and finish what we started." With a sly smile, he holds out a hand.

The evening breeze courses through me like a luxurious silk bath, bringing with it no pain nor a cunning message from my distant past. I stand here as myself, being loved by a man I used to dream in Henry. We are in a different world now, in a parallel existence where our souls only know how to dance to our own melody. To tread in this reality is of exponential significance than the burglary happening in my mind.

And so I take his hand, never intending to let go. Soon we will drive into wonders of this untroubled night, with a love beheld by the spotlight of the rising moon.

CHAPTER TWELVE

Hunger Wounds Incubating In The Heat Of The Moon

I collapse into his bed, back first, after being tossed lovingly by his powerful arms. The drive here was a series of outcries from our bodies' unwillingness to be apart. Not a gentle kiss would suffice. I needed the contact of his skin, the same way my lungs die without air. I am not sure how we made it here, still fully-clothed.

The memory of her appearance and invasion hours ago is now a faint cry in the shadows. I'm still afraid of her return but this moment is reserved for a different emotion.

My heart is frail, laden with an appetite that seeks ravage to my own form. I want him to break me open. He's all that I desire, of eyes blazing with the same longing my soul throbs for.

Right there in the darkness, he kicks his shoes. He begins to crawl up on the bed, to my awaiting body. He is so beautiful, the kind that takes my breath away - a slow and painful suffocation.

"God, you're so beautiful!" he reciprocates my mental commentary, while running the tips of his fingers on my thigh.

I jerk at the action, birthing an ache that I fantasized for so long. His face falls on my neck, his stubble causing a wave of fresh sensations down my loins. My lids instinctively drop, shielding my eyes from the worldly provisions that are non-requisites to the love between us two. Somewhere in the room the burning wood hisses with each crackle, a reminder of the flames sweltering viciously within me. His lips melt into the curve of my neck, down my shoulder, as my breasts swell in pleasure. My bra has been unclasped immediately after being discovered by his exploring hands. I touch his face, his hair, and the crests of his back muscles, stroked tenderly by my anticipating hands.

He eases the cotton shirt off my arms, his grip at the collar. The tease of his skin against my wrist electrocutes my stomach, causing it to roll. With reluctance absent from my quiet whimpers, I offer to him my brokenness.

Smudges of light from outside the window quarrel with the pitch black, only so I could get a glimpse of his honesty. I see passion, raw and unrelenting before his mouth forages for mine all over again. We dance, tongue to tongue, as my lower undergarment drops at my curled toes. He kisses off the sweet dew emanating from all over me - from my chin, down my neck, in-between my breast, and stopping at my navel. My nipples become his plaything, deploying his fingers to remain there with reckless abandon.

When he finally reveals his aim, the delicate spot in-between my limbs, I recoil. Yet nothing stops. His tongue moves on with the task at hand. I look down to find a silhouette of his head, still buried at the center of my being. He remains unmoved by my discomfort and the wheels begin to spin in my head. Terror looms over in an instant. The cold night air thickens, carrying with it a stifling memory of Andrew and the scars he left within that same anatomical vicinity.

Yet something happens amid the subtle confusion. Slowly, I reach a point of carnal awareness that I didn't know I could achieve. Noah is gently nursing my essence back to whole. That seems to be all he wanted to do.

The noise in my brain meets a halt. My fear has been stupefied by the festive sensations that are foreign to my womanhood. The taunting voices gently dissolve into my cries of pleasure that are swimming in the current of his tongue's expertise. Noah has elevated me to a new world, one that leaves no room for insult towards my body's past corruption.

Under the gentle moonrise, outside these four walls, comes a stillness of ecstasy. Here I lay, caving to the love I carry in my voice, the yearning in my wails. I'm high in the precipice of euphoria, unable to endure any more delays. I want him in me, meeting my soul in a heavenly explosion.

He hears my silent appeal, emerging from the pleasure he was gifting me. "Love me, Ophelia! I love you!"

Without delay, I guide him upward. Both our hands, searching for buttons and zippers in his jeans. Somehow, I am to deal with this task as he rolls his arms to undress himself, his shirt flying off his hands. Immediately following that, he confiscates my grasp on his jeans, easily sliding it off his legs, along with his boxers. His eagerness for me soars rigid on his naked body. The definition in his muscles leaves me a stranger to restrain. I pull him forward by the shoulders, towards my anticipating form. He repositions the condom.

After the passing of a few aching seconds, he regards me with tenderness. Those are eyes of a man who wants to conquer me by only the purest of love. I believe it. I believe the profound message in his gape.

"I love you," I whisper to him.

His tender kiss falls on my lips for a few seconds before he rises up to reveal a lustful grin that I welcome. He eases his length in me, mindful of my delicate state. It's wonderful, this mark of propriety, a belongingness to each other's intimacy. I wrap my legs around his back, becoming vulnerable to this sweet dominance. His thrusts are slow at first, instinctively testing the untold capacities of blinding climax. Then as if he's found his mark, he pounds harder and harder. The pressure is delicious, with voltage rummaging through my every sense. Stars circle around my head, wobbly from the orgasmic fireworks shattering in every flesh where his erection glides over. He picks up his pace, pleasure coming out unhurried from his curved mouth. He moans and grunts while I answer with a silent cry of joy.

Noah's grip tightens, burying my hands deep into the bed. My body stiffens, as his, readying ourselves to be hoisted up to a higher form of delight. I reach there first, imploding at the cusp of perfection. My body falls limp in consummation. Straightaway. He follows soon after, prefacing his climax with a limb-breaking and eye-rolling shove. I anticipate his spent body in me as he empties himself into the latex reservoir. I shiver in pleasure.

Here I am, a ruin of his masterpiece. It feels as though every hand that ever touched me before him was criminal. I have been looking at love with blind eyes. Everything before this was wrong. I have been doing it all wrong, even with Henry. At last, my heart is in Noah's hands, thawing from endless winters and finally seeing the blooms of spring. This feels so right.

CHAPTER THIRTEEN

The Choice

His arms drape across my neck, sleep untampered with the breathing of a wind chime. White sheets swaddle the bottom half of his gorgeous body, while my fingers toss around the mold of his strong chest. I lay here, bound by a newfound palate for love. I have never been touched the way he did, never been broken so beautifully. With him, I am a weakling, fluid in his grasp.

Suddenly, I wish for a different beginning than I had. I wish I never met Andrew, didn't waste dragging the years over my back, just so I could be loved the same way I did Henry. If I had a hand with fate, I would have saved my completeness so that I am not this woman laying at the edge of injury. I want to be pure, pristine. But I was to be who I am now - a residual from the fragments caused by the very people who were meant to keep me whole. I don't know how I could reclaim myself from Henry and certainly, no inkling of any extraordinary means to recover what I had lost to Andrew. All these are wishful thoughts, aligned with great impossibility.

I break away from his tender embrace, gently sliding down to keep his slumber undisturbed. It's hard to find any of my garments with everything that's strewn on the floor. Yet somehow, I manage to bring a throw blanket around my bare body. What guy has a throw blanket? The silly thought forces me to trace the outline of his figure in the midst of darkness. My eyes catch the stillness in his form that could be from a million dreams he's lost in. And even in the absence of visual clarity, his magnificence has imposed on me, the same spectacle that my imperfection is undeserving of.

I walk over to the glass window, my body remains veiled within the crocheted wrap. There is a recollection of this scene from a movie, except that reality has lingered for me a while longer. The girl looks down to the city below, frozen from the pause of life and the crisp autumn chill. On the same glass, stained by the moonlight's glimmer, a reflection of her lover fills her heart with content. So is mine. I feel full, my chest unable to seize every hope, dream, and vision of my future with Noah as they all rush in at once. Nothing is of significance ahead of this. Before, I was numb from this malignant infliction that is as liberating as it is smothering. Now I relish in it, like a dog in a pit of mud. Enthralled. Addicted. I don't want this to end. I'm desperate to catch this fleeting moment so I can incarcerate it forever.

Sure enough, my heartfelt musing is disrupted by the slap of reality on the coffee table. My love cloud has retreated back in the shadows of yesterday. I'm no longer floating in it. The precipitations of Noah's romance on my skin has dissolved within my pores, as the hair on my nape stand icy.

Even from a few feet away, the flashing device has Henry's name blaring on vibrate mode. What could he possibly want at this hour?

I scurry towards it and discover that he's been calling way too many times in the hours that passed, forty-three to be exact. I think he's letting up now. Yet I couldn't help but wonder why. He's not his usual self these past few weeks and has been more focused on Landree's pregnancy. His leash on me has been more lenient than it was. Too many voicemails. Too many texts of "where are you?" and the variation of "answer the fucking phone!" It trembles in my hand again, burning for an answer.

"Hello?" I hold up the phone to my ear. "What's up, Henry?"

I gently bring my body to a curl on the plush sofa, as I endure decibels of anger coming out of the device.

"Fuck, Ophie! What the fuck. You can't answer your phone for the life of you?"

With my skin still strewn on the furniture, I mold my mind into my own silence. Henry remains angered. I don't know what to say to him. He's going to ask what I'm up to. Where I am is the very place he once forbade me to be, rosy in post-coital infirmity.

"Open the fucking door!" He blasts again. This time, rendering me confused. What door? "Buzz me in, damn it!"

"Open what door?" I ask him quietly even though I'm almost certain he's downstairs. And with my phone now tucked in between my tilted jawline and shoulder, I dash to find my clothes. "Where are you?"

"I'm here," voice slightly subdued, he reveals. "Noah's apartment."

Shit! I contain my shock but it does little to trap the gasp that left my chest. Noah shifts a little but remains uninterrupted by the reprimand that Henry's tone threatened me with. I need to keep him out of this.

"I'll be right there," I whisper, tiptoeing around his studio apartment. I've donned an AC/DC sweatshirt by now, that I found at the foot of the bed. This is still probably unwashed for some weeks now. But oh, the smell of Noah imbedded in the cloth fibers is hypnotic. The inebriation distracts me from an important task at hand. I want to go back in bed and drown him with my kisses.

Okay now. Where was I?

The call disconnects when I make it at the top of the stairs, after tugging the doorknob to lock his apartment. Henry hasn't said much on the phone before that, except the sound of frosted air from his lungs. From 3E, the television glare has crept through the floorboards and to the hallway. Precious must still be up, worrying about Hazel, whose whiskers have made special appearances at Noah's window on our Chinese take-out nights. I can't be bothered by her social necessity now – what I'm only good for during our stair landing rendezvous. I make slow steps down to the main entrance, as opposed to taking the elevator. This pace will give me time to analyze Henry's resuscitated overprotection towards me. More importantly, how did he know I'm here? How did he know where Noah lives? Yet before I could concoct some sort of mental detective board, I already know the answers. I made it to the ground floor in what felt like a time lapse.

Henry's eyes are scrutinizing my form, from head to toe, as if to look for wounds and scrapes. "You're okay," hands now stroking my shoulders, "I'm glad."

I await the storm's havoc with no argument in my defense. I'm not sure what to make of his suddenly relieved reaction, while my skin nags at my careless decision to go outside without a jacket. Not even a wrap to combat the dawn chill.

"Why wouldn't I be?" I can feel the lines wrinkle on my forehead. "I'm sure you have some kinda idea who I'm with. I'm sure you know he's cool or you would have exiled me to Alaska by now."

"Well of course, why do you think I'm here?" he says coldly.

"How did you find me?" I ask him, while I rub my arms for warmth, pretending I don't already know the answer.

His gaze drops to my thighs, face tightening as a jerk reaction to my inappropriate choice of clothing. He zips down his fleece hoodie and slides it off. "Here. It's too cold out," he orders, wrapping the garment over my back. "You got me all worried, Ophelia."

"I'm not following," I quiz him.

Intuitively, he fishes his cellphone from his back pocket. With the city still asleep, the tapping on his screen could probably be heard from a block away.

"Here." He reveals a message string. "Read it!"

I grab the device from him, watching the haze of my breath as it leaves my trembling mouth. These look like my messages.

"Ophelia, you left me a couple voicemails telling me where you were and to come and get you. That you didn't wanna be around Noah," he's heard saying while I scroll through the texts.

'Where are you?'

'Come get me now!'

'I don't feel safe with this man.'

'Henry! Are you getting this?'

"I didn't know what to think!" Frustration mirrors his voice. He's cracking his fingers now.

"But I don't remember sending you those texts," I tell him.

I sweep my brain and the recollections I have from the night before. As expected, I got hung up on Noah and the time we had together. Him and I, such kindred souls. Our connection is magnetic. I realize that, even as I am standing in front of a guy I have given all my years to. With Henry, I was always chasing fires. My quarrel with him was not with how much love I can give, but in accepting that I wouldn't get any back. Meanwhile Noah, he would burn effortlessly for me. We are a force of gravity that can change the tide. It feels like running towards the ocean and crashing into the waves without being afraid of ever drowning. It is relishing in the magic that blurs out the world around us. All undeniable. All at once. I'm certain of this, even after just a short time.

"Ophelia!" he disturbs me from my obvious musing. "Do you remember anything at all?"

And suddenly, a thought nips at me. That woman had my phone as we were leaving, said she found it in the bathroom. I purse my lips, as I string every bit of information I have that night.

Henry urges for an answer. "What? Tell me what you know!"

"Oh, I guess I left my phone in the bathroom and someone found it. But I never used the ladies room. I must have dropped it on the way in and it got picked up." I say this while still unsure what it means.

"Damn it!" He throws his arms up. "Why take your phone and just leave it behind after texting me? That doesn't make sense at all."

He's right. And how would they know what my security code is?

"Have you been taking your meds?" he asks.

I'm caught off guard. Why the hell would he ask that? "Random question, but yeah!" I lie.

It has probably been weeks since I took my pills. When Noah returned, the nightmares quit me. The ache to sleep stopped troubling my weary mind. I find no use for those at this time.

"You sure about that?" His eyes narrow at me. The suspicion isn't unfounded and knowing that, is something only Henry has the ability to. "I do not take this lightly," he yells, inching closer. "We talked about this."

I feel his warm embrace peel away the frigid layer in my chest. I understand this connection - the one I misconstrued as love. Yet beneath this immense comfort is a voice nagging at me, coercing me to probe the events that occurred up to this moment. He seems like he's starting to look over his shoulders again. I know that the past we left behind still lurks in the shadows. I just couldn't will it to come out so that together we can bury the hatchet. It is elusive, even if it's a part of myself.

"We have to go now," he commands, removing his arms from me. "It's not safe for you anymore," he whispers.

I shake my head, my feet inching away from the curb where he has been standing. I couldn't even imagine a life without Noah. No. It can't be.

He grabs my hand, gently but with forceful intent. "And I mean that with him. You can't be with him anymore. Trust me!"

I can hear the desperation in his voice, even as he's trying to button up his temper that's near eruption. His eyes are imposing, yet I could still see tenderness in them. I trust Henry with my life, always. Yet I think that his worry has outgrown its purpose. Noah poses no danger in my life. This is simply overreaction.

"What are you thinking?" His hold leaves me, tucking his hands into the front pockets of his jeans.

"I just want to be left alone, Henry. Like what you've become so good at this past month." My tone is rising. "Just. Just do your thing and I promise you, I am in good hands."

With all that said, I still feel like Henry has the power to sway me otherwise. I have to leave now before the daybreak could coerce me to join him. I turn around, with no regard for his plea.

"Ophelia Anderson! You better get back here. Time to go home, no more games. You hear me?"

Yet he never leaves his post, doesn't do much to pick up his heavy boots and follow me in. All bark, no bite. Just a few steps more before I could pull the door open, but it swings out urgently. I barely avoided a concussion. What the fuck!

"What's going on here?" It's Noah, hair still unruly from my foraging fingers last night, and eyes half open, raw from disorientation.

"Henry was just leaving," I tell him, as I stomp my way inside the apartment building, leaving alone the two men who bear equal pulls in my life.

"Ophelia!" Henry's scream is muffled by Noah's lackluster reception of his presence.

"Henry," Noah shuffles forward, extending out a hand to him.

"What's up?" They shake hands, with Henry still eyeballing me. His tone is dry, uninterested by this mandatory pleasantry.

I stand by the front door, underneath the awning while the two men remain edgy. The sky begins to drizzle.

"Why don't you come inside? We can talk up there." Noah suggests, voice calm. He looks back where I am and brags for my approval.

I tighten my gaze at him. Does he not realize how awkward that would be? To have us three in there? I shake my head as Henry pops his out from behind Noah's back, trying to regard me with a stern imposition. "Why don't you just stay out of this, man." A note of anger follows. "I just need to talk to Ophie. Is that possible?"

"I have nothing more to say about anything right now, Henry," I yell out at him, raising my arms up to forfeit any opportunity for a conversation.

After which, Henry's attempt to storm towards me gets thwarted by Noah's strong arms. "Sorry, Henry." His grip on his shoulders remain. "Can't let you do that, man." Fight or flight initiates in his body language, his voice edgy.

My chest hollows in astonishment. I wasn't expecting trouble to escalate this way yet here we are, with both men in the brink of a fistfight. "You guys. It's dawn. You're gonna wake everyone up."

My plea falls on deaf ears.

Henry shoves him, nearly knocking Noah over backwards. "I told you to stay out of this, man. This is none of your business."

His lips pull inwards, eyes burning with rage. This has become the brick wall of Henry's patience. He walks over to me as panic paralyzes my legs. I no longer see Henry in front of me. This numbing alarm cloaked around my body, Andrew has been the only one to summon it.

Confusion strikes my judgement and mentally, I have fled to the next town.

"Ophie, it's time to go..."

I feel a hand on my wrist, gentle and protective as the voice that sneaks up to my ears. It's still Henry, my old cavalier lover, with a striking sense of warmth intended only for my frail shape. Above the margin of his broad shoulder, Noah's expression is framed by annoyance. His emotions are budding into rage as he sees me, pleading for a stop against his loud intentions to retaliate. He stops mid stride, absorbing the anxiety from my face. I know he hears my telepathic begging. He slips out from my view as I refocus my senses back into Henry's inconceivable ramblings.

"...just please come with me. We can talk about this at home."

Noah's arm dangles around my shoulders. He drifted stealthily out of my senses, only to awaken the goosebumps on my skin. My body swells, erupting into a cradle of pride. At last, I stand on a pedestal of declaration, to be claimed as a partner. I am here as Noah's other half. The message is roared loudly into Henry's irritated expression, and well into the morning that is about to break. I am in the forefront of Noah's affection and I feel it passionately when he goes on to wrap his hand around the curve of my waist.

This body is no longer a phantom that crumbles at the touch of light. I am not lurking in the corner, chasing after Henry's affection when he could only mangle some pity out of that heart of his. Hell, I wasn't even second best in his eyes. I am just the bonds around his feet that he must lug around wherever he goes, as some sort of payment he owes to Marcus. It is only right to choose this over following Henry.

"Look, man," Henry is speaking to Noah now, releasing his hold on me. "I really don't want any trouble here. Let me just talk to Ophie back at the house." His voice falls to a calm while pleading to my eyes.

Noah swallows a big lump in his throat. He nods at him in forced compliance and tends to the ground, playing pronation and supination with his feet.

"Henry, please. For the hundredth time, please go home," I tell him with eyes closed, wielding the tension on my forehead. My teeth have clenched at the action.

"Unbelievable," Henry mutters, shaking his head to disapprove. I watch him retreat to the street, that is now slowly picking up pace with both early risers and stragglers from the night before. He's never one to push too much once he's told no. Daytime has already covered ground, east of the apartment building. Yet Henry's shrinking figure is able to evade it. He dissolves into the dark side of the city, towards his car. He's always been a man of a few words and a mute in simmering fury. His screeching tires is more telling of his emotions than the arguments he could ever mouth.

I search for Noah's hand, feeling the rough textile of his denim jacket on the pad of my fingers. A few seconds later, he ends my scavenging inside the warmth of his grip. Henry's icy stare thaws into the windshield of his car as he drives by us. From his fleeting gaze, I gather his serious intention of putting me in the place where he wants me to be. Of course, such plan will never involve forceful hands but I know he'll be back soon enough with just the right bait.

It should hit me like a ton of bricks, to watch him leave with our issues still hot on the grill. Yet, I feel fine letting him go that way. Noah's other hand remains bound in the space between my hip and rib cage. I lay my cheek on his chest, his beating heart reminding me of a love that is bursting from mine. With Noah, it was never just slipping and falling. It was I, crashing to the concrete ground, headfirst.

"Well, how's that for the morning after?" he announces with a giggle behind his teeth, cutting off my dramatic anecdote that brought me this sense of freedom. Freedom, rolling off my mind as I test the waves sweeping through me when I say it. I don't know if this is what everyone else talks about. The books I read don't say much either. I just feel as though I could put one foot in front of the other without the shackles weighing me down.

Henry and I, there is always this chain that has us both tethered on each of its end. Yet forever is a long time to chase the wind that kept on lugging him away.

The last bit of dawn has already melted into the sunlight and I endure in the most overwhelming of all realizations. I have a new lease in life after Noah held the door open and led me out of that dark prison. He saw my broken bones and with it, he built a monument out of his love. I have finally withdrawn my hat from Henry's rat race. There's never been a time in my entire life when I was more certain than I am now. I want to be with Noah despite of and specially for his beautiful enigma.

I turn to him, hands numb from the trace of autumn chill. His eyes reveal my reflection, in a daze and all kinds of rosy.

"What?" he asks lovingly, golden cheeks swell atop his jaws. "What do you have cooking in that brain of yours, babe?"

"I love you," the words escape my lips. Air has mugged my chest of the weight that has been there since I first felt and denied it.

"Oh my Ophie." Noah's woeful face inches closer to mine, "You know how I feel about you too, if it isn't already obvious." The tenderness in his voice could exterminate any lingering doubt in my mind about its validity. I almost got distracted from what I really wanted to say. His hands cup my face, while his towering stature leans down to my small frame. He opens his mouth to continue. "I wouldn't be here with you, you know if it…" but I interrupt him, my fingers flat on his lips.

"Noah, please let me finish. I need to say this," I plead fondly. He edges back a few steps while tucking my hands in his grip. He nods at me to carry on. "I don't care about your past that, by the way, I don't know much of..." He chuckles lightly. "But I have a past too." And it's far from pretty according to Henry. I feel my eyes dampen slightly at the thought of what I've been through, of being here with him and how it happened so effortlessly. "But that's how I feel. And I know you love me too, without me doing all kinds of crazy stuff so you could love me back." He doesn't say any more, beyond the pinned smile on his face. "What I'm trying to say is that if the offer still stands, I'd like to go away with you. Let's never come back."

Out of the blue, the street goes silent. My heartbeats and his, are the only sounds reverberating in this peace besides his sudden aloofness.

"Now would be the time to say something," I tell him under shaky breath.

Still, he remains tongue-tied, as if he heard an insult rather than a verbal affirmation of my wild love. And before I could voice my frustration, he yanks me back in his arms with sweet urgency. I feel my lips overcome with uninhabited yearning once he locks his over mine. My waist tingles from his tight hold and I slowly crash into his strong body, my arms around his back.

We kiss and kiss until the morning returned in motion. We kiss some more; even as curious eyes pass us by. The moment is perfect, fond with emotions gushing out of us. His love is tender except for this part of his chest that remains caged. I feel its coldness tapping my heart with questions. A subtle recognition tugs at me now and I pray to the gods that it isn't another dungeon nestled safely within his core, for which I'm bound to fail at invading. Yes, much like Henry's.

CHAPTER FOURTEEN

Yelapa

Whistling and bellowing, the ocean breaks through my feet, as if the noise and sensation could fix the retaliation in my belly. My fingers are buried in the golden sand, hair tousling in the sweet salty breeze. Loving him feels quite like this freedom. There's no warning to our dangerous electricity, as I bathe in its shock. Him and I, we relish in this magic that blurs out the world around us. All undeniable. All at once.

I turn to scan for his location. "I'll get us some drinks," he told me fifteen minutes ago.

I find him, in a sea of tourists by the food stand. He looks animated, speaking to an elderly vendor whose sign reads, "Cocos Frescos." Even from afar, he is too enthralling for words. I'm sure the sexy women in the next line over can say the same. A little bit of jealousy rises up with my saliva. He senses my longing eyes, even with the bustle between us. His arrival rarely earns a cold shoulder, a company that rears the spawn of femme fatales like yours truly. I very much despise the legion of women, hanging on to his coattails.

"Hey, baby!" He yells out, making a single wave towards me, also sending the women's gazes in the same direction.

I feel stunned by the many eyes fixed on me now but I blow him a kiss anyway. He plays along by seizing the imaginary pucker, and pounding it to his chest.

Right here facing the open water, nothing seems more fitting as this parallel. Perhaps I'm always enticed by the depths of everything, to enigmatic pulls. It's exhilarating more than it scares me. Maybe I have this dark affinity to beautiful things that tend to bounce away from me. The chase is innate in my blood. I am an expert at it. With Noah wanting me back, it seemed to have required the reshaping of my bones and rewiring my brain out of the adrenaline rush that is always growling steady, awaiting the green light to run after another unrequited love. That is precisely what is wrong with me. I 've been waiting for the other shoe to drop, and I surely made it happen.

Let's talk about that, my mornings. Someone always calls. He always leaves. The beach has been his place of safety, taking his conversations there. It's almost as if he's making certain that I am not within hearing range. Is it about work? Another woman? We've been here for two weeks in this Mexican paradise named Yelapa and I hate myself for spoiling this dreamlike reality of Noah and I, alone together.

More lively colored rafts arrive to shore, filled with zealous tourists taxied from the mainland of Puerto Vallarta. Led by men who are covered under improvised face masks, they wrestle against the strong tide to make a safety foot on the island. Additional gargantuan yachts moor on the horizon, awaiting passengers bob in and out of the clear blue waves. The lines of shaded beach chairs gather the attention of sunburned bodies drenched in salt beads.

Behind them is an open concept and homestyle restaurant, boarded by a giant hut. At the moment, it's being flocked by hungry bellies and scores of paid entertainments. The iguana guy has been the most popular, hopping from table to table as quickly as sliding peso bills inside his pocket. Conversations grow abuzz, from either the standing crowd at the al fresco bar with drinks in their grips, or the diners on yellow Corona chairs hunching over seafood platters at the eatery.

Everyone boasts varying levels of excitement, origins, and skin colors. The crescent shore, on the other hand, is teeming with frolickers but their undertakings are nearly monotonous. The gamut of which are sunbathers, camera-clad couples, and young children building castles while adult companions float on colorful kayaks.

A face comes to view. The sudden recognition extracts my insides to hollow. Panic arrives, maiming my poised demeanor. They disappear as swiftly as their arrival, those eyes that have been detected by a fleeting memory of horror.

"What's the matter?" Noah asks, walking into the sketched fright across my face.

I can't tell him. How could I make sense of what I saw?

"You have an audience." I point to the group of college females who are pining over him. They are a good distraction. "Fan club?" My voice only offers a subdued sarcasm and maybe jealousy, but there's no way he'll miss the message.

He hands me a whole coconut with a spiraled straw. "Jealous?" he asks, eyeing the women with a side glance. "Babe," he flirts. "There is no competition."

My eyes roll back at the verbal accolade, as if it didn't just stir the critters in my stomach. I could say that I have become jaded to the sweet talking. Damn Noah for spurring a new heart out of the old, obliterated one.

In the era of Henry and Andrew, my nights were spent forgetting and remembering, of beating senseless a love that I myself resurrected. I never thought I would get to this point of finding myself perching so high up in the clouds. I have loved before and even if I deny it, there are craters in places that beheld the shattering of my heart, and the fleeing of my mind from my head. I am beyond repair but Noah walked in and offered his himself to whatever's left in me that could love him back. I am inadequate but he makes me feel enough.

I sense his body behind me, arm swathing my back. I let my spine shrink back to his chest, while he breathes harmoniously on my neck. "Why thank you for the compliment," I say to him, as I begin to twist my head to his face. My lips are puckered up, awaiting his sweet response. Noah kisses me gently, yet my tongue tastes a sense of determination from him, a gushing of needs that we must tame in public. For now.

"Love you, my Ophie," he whispers, delivering an ache in my chest that is enough to drive away the lingering fear from moments ago.

I take a sip of my drink before responding. "Love you more."

"Any good?" he asks, as he maneuvers his body to my side.

"Hmmm. It's not bad. Kinda strong."

He falls flat on the ground, arms tucked behind his head. His wide, boyish grin is infectious. I find myself smiling at the sight of his unguarded indulgence. "Well, my point exactly. Gotta get you drunk like those wild girls at spring break." Seawater runs across his body, washing over his broad shoulders before receding back to the wild Pacific. I shoot a glance at Noah, my lips curled in pretend annoyance, as he bites his in reply. He seems quite amused by my reaction, and his eyes have sunk underneath their lids from laughing too hard. "Come here, you beautiful woman!"

He pulls me down to him, seizing my mouth captive inside his. With our passion still unspoiled, my world becomes a spindle of every raw emotion enfolding around me. I pull back, unable to defy my brain while it harasses the tendrils that are guarding my sanity.

Fuck! I gotta tell him!

"What's the matter, babe?" he immediately grows concerned.

I feel the lines form on my forehead and the drums begin to roll inside my chest, awaiting a violent emotional outburst. Feverish blood runs up my face, heating my cheeks and rendering the tropical sun weaker on my skin.

"I know you've been sneaking out and talking to someone every morning since we got here."

My hushed response is a surprise, even to myself. I was sure to be in near explosion and this disturbance is cracking my ribs. Yet I manage to escape who I was, to become who Noah deserves. I have successfully controlled my anger. Yes!

Noah rises calmly from the golden sand, just as the sea climbs up to his chin. He wipes the moisture off his neck with a small towel, next to my woven bag. "Oh. How come you didn't mention it earlier?" he asks. He doesn't seem to be caught off guard by my statement, much less alarmed about the ace in my hands. He smiles at me as he licks his lips. "That's some good water," he distracts.

"Are you hiding something from me?" I couldn't wait for any build up or when Noah finally acknowledges my discomfort. This is different. He's different. I don't want to taint whatever we have with my own paranoia.

The wave of grim swoops through his expression. He turns serious. "What's going on, Ophie? Why do you say that?" I watch his fingers crawl towards my lap until I welcome them warmly in my palms.

"I'm sorry, I don't mean to be so obsessive," comes my reply, through the rustling of coconut trees. I watch his eyes hang on to my every word with immense tenderness. "It's just that, there's this churning in my gut every time I push something in, rather than tell you." My lungs begin to heave, coping with the lack of air, even as I sit here among its abundance.

"It's okay. You can tell me." Noah releases his hand only to trap it again in his grip.

I take a deep breath, finding solace in the waves that are tossing over the anchored boats along the coastline. I can feel it, his care, and his deep regard for my safety. As a matter of fact, that's how the world looks at Ophie, this maiden in distress who is in constant need of a savior. There is a quiet warning in the universe that has my name written in shiny, bold letters. I am a grenade. Noah perceived his new role when he met me. The anguish in my heart was calling out to him as a wailing child who is lost in the woods. He knew it, even after crashing into my steel front.

But I don't want to be that girl anymore. She was already on her way out when Noah came in the front door. There is an overwhelming sense of hunger in me to be his equal. I want the strength that others have to walk side by side a man in his caliber. Somehow, I'm drawn to the good and I guess it became my obligation to tread towards the path of virtue after having been touched by something so sacred as his hands. Noah affects me that way, all too consuming.

"But yeah," I sniffle. "The last few mornings, you've been so shifty when it came to your phone calls. Like you've been hiding it from me. I don't know." I shake my head. "Just tell me I'm wrong."

He clears his throat before an obvious attempt to speak. "Babe, I'm sorry. I didn't even think much of it. It's the family business and they've just hit a little bit of a snag. I have been in contact with the manager to deal with it." His other hand is now scaling the curves of my back, until he reaches my hair to caress it. I remain in silence but my body stiffens in unease. "All I was doing was making sure I don't interrupt your sleep so I've been taking their calls outside. Time zones are different between vendors. That's why I'm on the phone at odd hours. I didn't wanna ruin our vacation in any way. Is that what's been worrying you?" He cups my chin. "Trust me," his voice chipper now," it's just a load of crap. I'm sorry that I had to take that with me here."

"So, no other woman, slash secret wife and kids then?" I ask him in a sulky tone, my eyes rolling back in playful disdain.

He bursts out in laughter. The elderly couple next to our cabana peeks out from their shade to inspect our loud display. I laugh with him too, realizing how silly I was. That's low of me to even fabricate the thought.

Noah turns to me. "Of course not!" Slowly, he reels me in closer but I would have been pulled by the same gravity anyway, and crash into his sweet body at some point. "Babe," he whispers, melting me under the heat of his stare. "Don't get me wrong when I say this but a man would not go through the trouble of being here. Under our rather unconventional circumstances..." He winks before continuing. "Unless they're trying to swindle you for money, or they're complete psychopaths. We both know I'm none of those. You feel me?"

I act contemplative, "Hmmm." But get distracted by the ocean spraying on his face. I squeal.

"Shit!" he cries, wiping the brine off his forehead. "I'll get you one of these days."

And here we are again. Him and I, we are at the mercy of this whirlpool that's forged in both love and chaos.

"There's just so many things I don't know about you and definitely much more I haven't told you about me."

The thought aches a little bit and its tugging quietly at Noah, who instantly leaves his deep musing to tend to me. His forehead touches mine, holding my body strong but gently.

"We have a lot of time for that now," he whispers, giving my soul something real to hold on to.

My eyes are saying what my mouth couldn't, this awareness of being truly loved by someone I never thought would exist in this lifetime. With the breeze singing in tune with the sea, Noah feeds me with a wild softness that is the perfect meal to my constant hunger. His kiss always spurs an innocent eruption in my chest, as if it has become unable to hold happiness in multitudes.

Even as the music made by our lips and tongues is near conclusion, he never ends abruptly. There's a unique melody to his kiss when he wishes to pull away. It first awaits my permission before doing so, never leaving me still starving and parched. He always loves me even in parting. It is something nobody has ever made me feel before.

"You know my heart and that is enough for me," he reassures, voice crawling towards all my nerve-endings, nodding at every fiber of my body that has ever doubted our fire. And that gaze he gives, has slowly clung to an almost vivid recognition, as if my past has seen the same eyes. There is a sense of acquaintance with those words. I've heard them before too, dug deep from a grave of forgets.

"Is this crazy? I could have sworn that I already met you before," I tell him, believing it from the unconscious parts of my heart.

He doesn't say a word, just a slim grin under the glow of his golden cheeks. And I don't know if it is in acknowledgement to the remote possibility, or from our victory against the laws of attraction. I will take either one.

But Noah is not enough of a diversion anymore. I can't ignore what I saw. It's calling me, the enticement of finding out.

"I'll be right back."

CHAPTER FIFTEEN

My Mind And The Bog Where It Lays At Night

"Ophelia? Stay with me senorita! We're almost there. Paco! Dame mas gauze por favor."

Two figures move about behind the haze, my vision eager to plant some clarity and failing. We're trapped inside a departing vehicle, as the ambulance sirens add to the conundrum. I find it hard to break the mist, silhouettes growing their distance from my eyes, like turning a telescope out of focus. The voices come from afar, even when they are near. I lose my sound in the effort to scream. It pains me, staring at the empty space where Noah should have been to hold my hand, and tell me it's going to be okay. Instead, I'm alone again as if my body is a disservice to the men who came upon it, namely Henry, Andrew, and now Noah.

An innocent sting makes it known on my forearm, carrying a burn to my muscle that will put me to sleep, soon enough. I am knee deep into forgetting, with hands pulling the end of a swollen sac that carries the echoes of my memories. Yet it keeps getting yanked away. There is no breakthrough, or a needle to burst it.

I feel weightless in the cold embrace of the gurney straps and I think the medicine is working its best. We reach a stop. The curtains are now drawn in front of my vision, slowly receding my eyes back into the darkness. My body wobbles and flails at the pushing and pulling beneath the stream of foreign tongues, in their urgent feat to save me. Somewhere in-between the noise, a familiar warmth thrusts through the surface.

"Is she alive? Tell me! English? Do you speak English?"

It's Noah. He's here after all. His voice is shaken, wrestling the barricade of people around me.

"Ophelia! It's me. Can you hear me?" When he finally gets close, he traps my hand in his fist, still cold, still quivering. A soft kiss arrives on my forehead that my skin will never be numb from. "I'm sorry, babe. I'm so sorry. This is all my fault."

"It's okay. But what happened?" I manage to mouth the words.

"God, I thought I lost you again!" His arms spread over my limp body, as tears land on my neck. He's bawling, crying like a child from relief. There are bodies in white, flocking to my side and brushing Noah away from me.

"Dejala. La tenemos que llevar a emergencia," a female voice tells him.

"She said we have to take her to the emergency for assessment. You can stay here and we'll keep you posted," the other guy turns to him and offers some reassurance in the language he could understand.

I still don't know why I'm here. Why can't I remember?

The gurney rolls away, now racing along the hall. All these burgeoning thoughts have slowly surrendered to the quiet. But that's okay because I'm tired,. My mind is falling into the cradle of sleep.

****

The sun swarms into my window through its glistening spears, twisting along the threads of my sheets. This is my next indication of consciousness. It doesn't take long for me to realize where I am. Thanks to the IV bag floating over my head. I've spent too many times in the last year waking up in hospitals with no memory of how I got there. Here comes the nurse, entering into my muddled state. This headache almost obscured her coming. I still feel sedated, body laced with pharmaceutical poison that is supposed to treat what is ailing me.

"You're up! That's good," she waltzes in, donning a white scrub suit.

"Well, my name is Alicia. How's your Spanish?"

"Terrible," I reply.

She chuckles. "Well, me too! Born and raised in Boston, baby. But don't get me wrong, this is my favorite residency." Her accent already hints her linguistic origin, even before affirming it. "So, Ophelia," pulling the rolling stool from under the computer desk, she says. "I'm your attending physician and you are here in San Javier General." She scans the loose pages of my patient file. "What can you remember from yesterday?"

Yesterday?

"Are we still in Puerto Vallarta?" I ask.

She smiles big, a compulsory staple to her bedside manners. Her thin eyes disappear under the round of her pink cheeks. She is a rather arresting beauty, Korean descent perhaps. "Yes, we are. But let's stay on track here please," she presses on gently.

"Uhmm," I pause for a moment. "Nothing much, just getting strapped inside the ambulance and that's it."

But the calm is my disguise. Deep inside I'm ravaging through scraps of my memory, unhinged by the lack of answers. Did she come back, the other me? Did I lunge into the point of no return at her command? It's eating me up now, the fear and anxious questions that I cannot ask her.

"Am I gonna be okay? Why was I sedated?" The real question is whether or not the demon entered me again. It has been a long while.

"I am positive that you will be," she assures. "Tell me how you feel right now?"

"Why do I feel woozy? Was I drugged?"

And where is Noah? Why isn't he here?

"Mrs. Anderson, you have suffered a brain injury. In other words…"

"Concussion," I interrupt. My years in animal medicine have given me a broad knowledge in the field itself. I was, after all, a doctor who has fallen from grace.

"Very well. Anyway, I assume that would be from the plane crash." Plane crash? "Or anything within your vicinity that was dislocated by the incident. At the hand-off from the ambulance, they reported that you were complaining of a terrible headache. Ten out of ten they said. We did some testing and then gave you some pretty strong opiates for the pain. You had some nausea treatment too last night," she concludes.

My jaws drop. "I don't remember being on a plane." What the real fuck?

"No, no. A seaplane. Yesterday, it crashed into Yelapa's shoreline. You were at the beach, were you not?"

"Yes, I was."

How could I forget? I was with Noah. Oh my God! Noah!

Immediately, my body tenses. I'm fighting against the worst possibilities, even as I remember him coming through to see me yesterday.

"You are really lucky. You should know that. I can't say the same for those people on the plane. I mean other than whatever fell on your head, you're gonna come out of this with no more than a scratch." Her voice sounds medicinal. Reassuring.

I know the prognosis. I'm not worried about that. I just need to know what happened to my Noah.

"…so in the next few days, no straining, alright? Take it easy. Not too much electronic stimulation. I have prescribed anti-nausea for your episodes. You tolerated Oxycodone well but perhaps Norco during recovery would be less potent. Let your brain bounce back —"

"I beg your pardon, Doc," I say, disrupting a scroll's length of medical advice from her hospital folder.

She stops, not seeming to mind my rude interjection. Her demeanor is receptive. "What is it?"

"I was with someone yesterday. I need to know if he's okay," I ask her, worry detected in my voice.

"Yes, Noah. He was here all night actually. Slept right there," she responds, pointing to the unmade cot next to the window. Pillows and sheets are still bent around, perhaps from tossing and turning. "Ran into him in the hallway this morning. Said was gonna pick up something to eat. Great help with your info and all other relevant details of your travel insurance too."

Damn! He was here all along, never left my side.

I pull my face back up to her, hoping my expression is of gratitude. Her eyes glimmer. "Lucky woman, that you are!"

Not her too. But I confront the irritation away.

She moves her attention to the wireless phone in her white coat pocket. The vibration clings to the metal part of her stethoscope. Its noise is hard to ignore.

"This must be him now." She answers the call, "Que pasa Sofia? Dime. Que?" There's now a furrow between her brows, signaling confusion. "There's a man outside, insisting to come in. He said he's family," she whispers, taping the phone to her chest in the meantime.

"Why does he have to ask permission? Wasn't he just here?" I'm puzzled.

She slides her phone back to her ear. "No es Noah? Entonces, qual es su nombre? Estas segura?"

"Everything okay, Doc?" Her ailment of confusion is infecting me too.

"They said his name is Henry. Henry Anderson."

Shit!

She comforts me with her protective tone, sensing my anxiety. "We don't have to take visitors now. You're near discharge anyway. Do you know him? Brother?"

"Yes, I do. You're gonna have to let him in," is my half-hearted response. "He's my husband."

Her eyes plummet to the cup of her orbital bones. She steels herself but her gasp has found a way to leave her chest. She must be mentally pursuing a more judgmental response, having learned that I am with a man while still married to another. I'll be ready for it, eardrums anticipating any word of disgust from her mouth.

Yet she doesn't say anything. She didn't have to. The look of judgment and the betrayal of her own assumptions astound her. Instead, she shifts her attention to the caller. I assume she'd be giving them the green light to let him in.

"Si, es su esposo. No me preguntes ahorita. Te explico despues."

Then, she swings towards the computer, engrossed by my medical history once more.

"We're separated, you know. In case you're wondering," I reveal, my tone defensive.

Her eyes are fixed at the edge of the monitor that is opposite me. "We don't worry about those details," she replies, smile scaling up the to the dimples on her face. Her fingers are drumming the keyboard.

We both know she's lying.

"I thought your Spanish is weak. Sounds like you've acclimated pretty well," I joke, driving away the tension in the hot air.

She laughs but I can tell of its forced origin. "Why thank you," she nods, voice elated. "I do try."

A short minute passes. There is a knock on the half-opened door. We both inspect the man, soaring just inches down the doorsill. He is pale, robbed of sleep and peace of mind. The grey sweatshirt bulks over his average build. His whole form is a seeping vision of a neglected man, but his care and tenderness for me will always be a staple. It's undeniable, no matter how much anger rattles his calm bearings. He walks over cautiously, waving a hand at Dr. Hong.

"Mr. Anderson? I'm Dr. Hong," she greets. A formal civility comes forward from her scrub pocket.

Henry receives the handshake politely. "Yes, nice to meet you." He glances over to me before shifting his focus back to the doctor.

"Well, despite the very unfortunate circumstances," she pauses to regard me with a slim grin. Henry follows her gaze, ogling with an air of let-down and pity towards my apologetic expression. "She'll be okay. I'll get the nurse to wrap up and we'll get you guys outta here and back to the States in no time."

"Sounds great. Thank you," he replies.

"Very well. I'll leave you two now." She taps his shoulder, exiting to the double doors.

Her pace meets a sudden stop, swinging her body back to face us. "And Ophelia. Nice to meet you."

"Likewise!"

Henry reaches my bedside, behind him is the doctor's blurry white figure, vanishing in real time. It's just us now, or me rather, likely to be trapped inside a tornado of Henry's kind naggings.

His embrace catches me off guard. Tight. Warm. It's almost sedating, this feeling of melting into his loving fold. "Thank God! You're alright! Got on the red eye as soon as Noah called."

Noah called him?

Instantly, I release myself from his clutches, my arms stretching out against the firm of his chest. "What? He called you? Noah?"

He nods.

"Why? You guys okay now?"

"That's not important," he dismisses, shaking his head as he sets the large paper bag on the side table.

"You always tell me that. About everything! I need to know what's going on?" The touch of sunlight browses my angry face.

"He did the right thing by telling me," he replies, fingers testing the cot where Noah spent the night. Allegedly. "The alternative would have been far worse. And when Adelpha told me you had taken off with your passport and a suitcase, what was I supposed to think? I'd have to send the authorities for him. Did you want that to happen instead?" He eyes the bandage on my right temple. An agitated expression follows. "I did what you said. My guys eased up on you. I told them to keep their distance from you and Noah. Remember, the freedom you begged of me? And what do you do? You leave. And here in Mexico of all goddam places! What else is next? Your dead body from the morgue? Is that what you want me to find next?"

My eyes relieve themselves of the irritation, sinking down at him with a softer gaze this time. Henry sits on the cot, strewn with white sheets and remnants of Noah's skin. Then I realize something. They share far more than the space in that bed. Their elusiveness and their touch that seems fleeting, are indispensable in the character of both men I gave my heart to. "Obviously not," comes my reply. "Is he okay? Where is he?"

His sigh echoes through the white room. "He's fine."

"That's a relief."

"Ophie, you should know that you're not gonna see him again." His fingers interlock with each other above his trembling lap. The soles of his Adidas Stan Smiths are tapping on the tiled floor. I observe him, awaiting some sort of reprisal against what he just said, or maybe an explanation.

I don't believe it. Noah is now a permanent adhesion to my soul. It recognized him, even before I did. I know I've said it about Henry, loving a man so perilously. However, there is a distinction between that and what Noah and I have. It's more than the attraction to each other's skin. He gives me a sense of belonging, in places I was never welcomed before.

"Why would you drive him away? You saw how happy I was. But you refuse to sign off on the divorce." I pause, tossing my hands up in exasperation. "Henry," my voice is low now. "I appreciate you holding out for me. But you can't be doing that for every man who comes into my life." Though, I'm really hoping Noah would be the last. I'm beginning to feel the weight in both corners of my eyes, just as the lump in my throat is readying itself to pull a cord.

"Ophie," he calls out again, his tone defiant. "It's called protecting you and this argument is getting fucking old!"

"Bullshit!" My rage has been fueled by the pain of Noah's absence. "I know we had a rough go at first but things are different now. I have changed." I mean that.

He smirks, just enough to hide the irritation. He's biting his lips now, willing his mouth to speak but doesn't.

I continue the spews of anger, "This is crossing the line!" But rather than penetrate him, it's dissolving quietly into the calmness of his demeanor. "Protecting me from who? Who's after my life this time? You told me he's gone. Andrew's not here anymore. My eyes widen as I allow a looming breakdown to float to the surface. "Or is it just you? Your sick fixation of being my hero?" Even I know there's no truth to these hurtful words but I am wedged inside my own fury. The worst things to say are spilling out of me.

He grows weary, breathing faster than normal. His leg shakes have picked up pace, heavy emotions unraveling on his face.

"Oh, look at me. I'm Henry. The hero," I add, tone chockfull of ridicule.

"That's enough!" He stands and points at me. "That's enough. I've had it with this shit." Still, he manages to conceal half of his anger inside his fists. His tone is raised but still muffled in comparison to my own. "I'm protecting you from everything. Get it? Every damn thing that could possibly harm you. Including yourself."

I'm completely still now, not because I'm afraid of Henry. He's rarely angered by anything and the least I could do is give him the platform to express it when he does. Maybe then, I'll get some clarity to his odd motivations.

His hands collapse to his sides. They make a brief patting sound before his mouth opens again. "Do you think this is easy for me? How can I blame a dead person for entrusting me with another life? Your life." He crosses his arms over his chest before continuing. "Of course I'm grateful for Marcus. He gave me a new lease in life and my debt can only be paid by keeping you safe till the end."

"And how many times do I have to tell you that this is not a forever job. You can't always protect me. Marrying someone you don't love? How do you make yourself do that?" My response has finally pricked the thin bag that held my tears and sullen emotions. The cork has been unplugged and hysteria busts out of me. "But it could have been anybody else's heart, Henry! That wasn't up to him. It just happened.

You were on the list and it was his organ. He couldn't have made that decision when he was alive. It was luck. Coincidence," I tell him as I sink further into frustration.

I suddenly weep for my old ghost that escaped to the blur, savagely warring against oblivion. I stand in front of a past that has been ungenerous with my memories and yet it keeps haunting me with things I cannot touch.

He picks half of my body from the cry-soiled bed and sits it upright. "I care for you. It is my job. I want to do this. Landree, she gives me the life I need, an escape to the normal. You can understand that. It's a necessity," he tells me, thumbing a stray moisture off my cheek. "I care for her just as much."

"I do. I understand," I reply. "But you can't live with this guilt. It does not belong to you."

"But it does. Someday, you'll understand this. I'm not Marcus but I know his mind. What he would have wanted. This is it," he discloses. A profound sigh leaves his chest. "Marrying you at the courthouse all those years ago, it was the right thing to do. I don't regret it."

I throw myself to his waiting arms, flooding his shoulder with tears from all the uncertainties. I think he would have loved me completely. If only he could figure out how to fix my brokenness. I know Marcus by some vivid fragments in my head. The car crash has returned to my memories, or at least the pain of enduring it. It may not be much but they carried an inkling to how much he cares for me.

I pull away, gazing at his bloodshot eyes. "I'm scared."

His emotions incite a sluggish headshake and a face full of apprehension. "I know," he musters. I fear so many things in this moment. Losing Noah. The uncertainty of my future. The weight of Henry's worries. And something else. Something my mind couldn't reach. They're all terrifying.

I observe him move around the bed towards the paper bag that he had brought in earlier, determined to abandon the heated conversation unresolved.

He shuffles some items out of it, pulling a bowl of food and ginger ale to start. Then, comes the Cheetos, and hunger waters my mouth right away. I didn't realize how famished I was until the sight of food.

He turns his head back to me, with a quiet display of affection in the form of a wide grin. "Got your comfort food. Adelpha said you like these things nowadays. Don't know if that's the right kind of pasta though." He chuckles, adding, "And Noah left you a voicemail. He asked that you have a listen when we get back. He lost your phone when everything went down. I'll get you a new one when we're back stateside."

The room flourishes into silence as the incident comes back to me in small fragments. My mind tries its hardest to piece them together. Such burden feels nothing, just incomparable to the desertion digging its way inside of me, where Noah's touch has gained residence for a while.

CHAPTER SIXTEEN

Loneliness Is A Leech, Wearing Love's Skin

He clears his throat in a restrained fashion. Once. Maybe twice before speaking. "Hey, it's me," voice pierced with forlorn anticipation, he readies his emotional assault.

Shock is futile. I already know the ending to this call. He's gone. Henry released the grenade at my feet and I was momentarily thrown into the wind.

"Anyway, I'm sorry I have to say goodbye like this but I've been thinking about stuff. A lot actually." He laughs but the strain in his voice is a cry of reluctance. "I think it's time that I go. Please don't blame Henry for this. It was my decision. It's better for you. Safer." Safer? It sounds a lot like Henry has a hand in this, even if he denies it. "Yeah, this is it. I know it's crazy but I have a feeling that we're gonna see each other again someday. We always do. Okay? You take care of yourself." I hear his tongue click, launching the background in complete silence right after. "I love you. Remember that. Always have, always will." And a whirling sound takes over.

"To save the message, press pound."

By God, I did. I listened to it over and over for the last 7 months, memorizing the words, remembering the pauses, and sighs in-between each sentence.

'Always have, always will', feels a lot like a riddle in plain words. They affect me as a promise with years on its back, deeply rooted but unremembered. I don't recall bending our pinkies together and making this pact, just that my heart recognizes the words even before I came upon them. He didn't have to say it. The way he held me and the way the world felt in its place right after, is more than enough to fill my future with hope.

I kept skimming through the pages, in many different ways just so I could find an answer that isn't there. If he blames himself for the plane crash in Yelapa, it's a fucking accident! What he said at the end, 'We always do', as if we've already met before. The thought has tortured me since.

Henry remains mum about it, even when I ask him if he has any idea where he'd be. His phone has been disconnected and when I went to visit him at his apartment, another tenant was already moving in. I went to his place of work, showed pictures around the parking lot in desperation. All I got were headshakes and evasions, like I was a beggar searching for spare change. I might as well be. There was never a Noah Green . How quickly the world has forgotten.

In his absence, my days belong only to Jessica and our therapy sessions that are all too confusing, especially when she urges me to forget but also remember. In-between that, my search for Noah yields a dead end. There were days that I wished I can put his face on a milk carton. Anything, just to bring him back.

Landree had a miscarriage, which explained Henry's tolerance of Noah during those months. He was distracted but still came to get me in Mexico. I think he would have done the same even if we're not married. Now they're expecting again and I have to be on my best behavior if I wish not to blame myself for another failed pregnancy.

Noah. He's a ghost, an elusive character and that didn't stop me from giving him my all, from putting my trust in every pocket of his skin. I never knew him, yet I do. He's a stranger but also my home. The sense of luxury my spirit feels when he's around, seems to have been tethered from a past beyond our first meeting. It felt a lot like our souls have met in a different lifetime.

Our kisses were familiar, a well-rehearsed recital of two hearts festering in love. From the beginning, our bodies melted together like it was meant to. Our cracked ends fitting the crevice of the other, making a banquet to our endless starvation.

I miss him.

I know these words have touched the gods of superlatives, sitting overused as I prostitute myself to the violent stabbing. This, before my heart goes into the woodchipper for another hour of obliteration, just so I could snort another hit of his memory. But it won't be for long now. They must be depleting now, the stragglers of his scent stuck on my neck, along with the cloud of dust he left behind.

They're almost gone.

Or were we just two people needing shelter and warmth from the winter? Me, from my atrocious link to Andrew, and him, from the caller he's been evading this whole time. Stones can make fire too.

"Looks like we're loading up soon," Henry announces from the driver's seat.

Landree and her 2-month-old belly slopes quietly next to him. She looks farther along than she is. The ferry horn wails with the charcoal–feathered pigeons, over by the docks. Some form a line on the drift woods. Tapping his fingers on the leather steering wheel, Henry sighs with apprehension at the thought of going back to Whidbey. Marcus' passing sent us both away for reasons beyond my memory's reach, along with my utter resentment towards everyone, who in one way or another, has been linked to that place.

Our marriage was hidden under the caveat of survival and protection. We made it through together, with the little scraps of cash we took with us. Whatever I have now is because of Henry and the gift of his heirloom many years later. He made it clear that he wouldn't sign the divorce papers, and Landree remains at his side in spite of.

Maybe her and I are the same, even if I didn't want to admit it before.

The two of us yearn for that love, thrive on the connection we couldn't find in anybody else. That is why she's still here, even if Henry can't or won't marry her. The situation is so fucked up in whichever angle the world looks at it.

"We have to go to the executor's office. They're gonna read the will there but there's someplace I wanna stop by first," Henry says, as he drives up the platform to the ferry.

I don't know what to expect. Do I cry at the sight of my mother's hearse, even when I can't find a hole in my chest equating to her absence? What about my father? He came to see me at the hospital in Seattle. Henry seems to be less edgy when mentioning his name.

The sun has already risen and found its place behind the snow-capped mountains, highlighting the ill-reputed land across the water. I am anxious too, going back to the town where I grew up but was never my home.

****

The twenty-minute ride across the Puget Sound felt to be of a brazen cause, even in its calmness. I feel like I am a warrior, in a journey to no man's land, and suiting up for battle against an unknown adversary.

Here we are, at a quiet bend in the road, veiled by a curtain of thick fog and dense forest. This place is bowing to us in bare silence, as though our return has been long awaited. The engine dies at the grassy shoulder; the car's bumper, just a foot against the pole that is holding upright a traffic signage.

Don't Drink and Drive

In loving memory of

Marcus Davis and Kara Mason

The freight train has crashed to the core of my body. It's visceral, this measure of loss that can no longer be misidentified as anything other than Marcus' death.

"You don't have to get out if you don't want to," Henry tells us, as he slides away.

He reaches in for a hat that has been sitting on the dashboard. It has the emblem of a red wolf and an embroidered line underneath it. Coupeville High, it reads. I watch him walk up to the metal plaque, kicking off dead leaves with his tan boots along the way. He taps the sign, making notice of his hand over my brother's name. His body lingers there, either by prayer or mental conversation to the people who lost their lives here. He sets the hat at the foot of the steel post.

"Do you not even care?" Landree's face darts from the side of the front seat. I can't tell if she's being sly or genuine. "I mean look at him? This will always be his prison. You are his prison. Have some sense of pity." A scowl forms on her expression. "After all he's done for you. Why couldn't you just let him be happy." Her voice grows angry now.

"Landree, I don't wanna fight with you. I'm tired."

She sighs, hearing my response. A war rose from inside of me when we arrived here, and Landree, as her usual stony character, is waging another one. My body is naturally repulsed by her. Landree's lips pout in reflection but doesn't respond anymore. She yanks her look away and back to the windshield, where Henry can be seen in a marring stillness. In my defense to her, he is the one who will never grant me a divorce. That's just his distorted idea of keeping me under his protection, to still have me at the other end of his leash and think that he'll never break his promise to Marcus this way.

What comes next is a feeling of disorder as the call to lay my feet on the ground where my brother perished, can no longer be silenced. I hear voices in my head that once were washed away by parts screaming Noah's name. They're urging me to feel again and dig up the wreckage that I've hid beyond skin deep.

I have to get out.

The chill in the air is arousing shadows of memories from my youth, that have long abandoned me. I am outside of the car now, eyes flared to the spectacle of death that has taken away the only person who's been family to me, or at least what has been told by Henry.

Today's drizzle could be next of kin to the one falling angrily on that fateful night. The line of Douglas firs has made an appearance in some of my fleeting recollections. Maybe I know more than what my mind leads on, that the memories are now vehemently pushing their way through from atmosphere of forgets. Some rest in waiting to be picked out by necessity. Or maybe, I just don't want to find them.

"Refusing to remember does not undo the past, what you did, what you didn't. You can erase it from your mind but it doesn't mean it didn't happen," Jessica told me. She said that, as if escaping from the truth was a deed I could accomplish unaided.

I feel an arm drape around my shoulders, realizing my eyes are staked deep into the letters of my brother's name. It's Henry of course, trying to tap me away from this harrowing state.

"You're okay," drifts his saintly voice of reassurance.

I nod, as a false guise of whatever has been ignited in the purlieu of my bosom. Tears hang on to the wrinkles along my eyeline, helplessly searching for reprieve against falling. Yet the leak in the floodgates is imminent. They're bursting now as I lose my balance on the ground. The crunching of a mound made from dead leaves breaks my descent. I feel my buttocks wet from the ongoing precipitation of the grey sky that was just clear at our arrival. I wail for the memories that were robbed from me, and Henry is still right here, locking me into his embrace. I spy a faint view of Landree through the windshield, shaking her head and jaded from the many times I've done this to receive Henry's attention. Tears too, are running down her cheeks.

"I know you miss him, even if you can't remember," he tells me in his soft voice, while stroking the back of my head.

My retort comes in a soaring course of upset. He seems so sure of my memory. Yet all I see are doors to nowhere, and a nameless scream, whirling against the bright moss that are wrapped around the tree trunks. I feel more ashamed about the fact that I have forgotten. And forgetting is just too cruel, in all the ways I could deface the memory of my brother's short existence.

CHAPTER SEVENTEEN

Things Unremembered

The winding roads prolonged our trail back to town, after a call to Henry's phone informed us that the reading of the will has been moved to tomorrow. It would be right after the burial. Here we are at last, trudging off highway 20 to merge into Terry Street. Some things return to me, the houses that are no longer here, ghosts of all the dogs I walked for ten bucks, and the barren fields where new real estate has been erected. The rich prairies, along the outskirts of downtown have also endured the island's economic shift. I smell the sea, its fresh and pungent scent playing inside my nostrils. But that's all they'll ever be, memories that Henry gave me to nurture until I can reach out to them myself.

The car veers left, merging into Front Street.

"I guess we're here?" Landree comments. The sound of her chewing gum resumes right after.

Obsolete buildings stand, the ghostly atmosphere embodying their dilapidated state. Vibrant colored architectures link along a sloped platform of land mass atop the bay. Maroon, chartreuse, and dated construction that rose from time-stained wood, they would rather belong to a quaint painting of this seaside frontage. Their only culpability? It's forgetting about my existence the same way I did to them.

Bodies scramble around the soft grey sand. I watch them from afar through the sluggish moving vehicle. They are hoarding either buckets or plastic bags to deposit their oyster and clam harvests. The sound is returning for the high tide, claiming back a long stretch of seaweed covered beach. Hovering above is the Coupeville wharf.

I recognize things but not people, as I reach back to the flurry of a faceless crowd during the 4th of July. I can paint them by memory but never the conversations I made, and the smiles flashing at me. I could have fallen in love once before and I would run into him as a stranger these days. Here, I protect my skeleton from breaking, while incapable of grasping the meat that once shared its space.

My illness has been exacerbated again, this madness I have for Noah. I can't feign indifference towards it, even while I'm far away from the city. I miss the feeling of home, but there was never a place I can call as such before he came.

It's almost noon and I realize that time goes by slow yet also fast when you're navigating aimlessly in its hands. Henry foots the break, after parallel parking along a small lodge, sitting on the hill that overlooks the water. I have no clue what we're doing here, which is a testament to how much I give a damn. The only thing I look forward to in a new place, is the thin possibility that I might find Noah. Here is no exemption.

Henry turns to me, as Landree scours to disconnect the seatbelt. "Ophie, please stay in the car and —"

"Babe, can you pop the trunk?" she interrupts.

"No, it's okay. I can get our luggage," he replies while Landree's door flings open. "Honey, I can get the door for you!"

I find him taking her hand in no time, leaving his door unclosed and prompting the passing pick-up truck to honk.

"I'm pregnant, not cripple," she remarks when finally able to slide her small belly out.

Henry waves at the inconvenienced driver, before shutting his side of the car to clear the small back-up behind the truck.

I can hear their subtle commotion behind me, their movements concealed by the trunk lid.

"What time will you be back then?" she whispers.

"We'll have lunch with them, so maybe like a couple of hours?" Henry responds. "Just down the street though. I can be back right away or before that if you need something."

I may have heard a quick kiss somewhere in-between the unloading of our carry-on cases and the scuffling of paper bags. My stomach pits right away, in my ache to touch Noah and do the same with him. I know it was real and perfect, even when I was not worthy of his love. It didn't deserve to end the way it did. With him, I reached a pure consciousness that I never did before. I even wished for him to father my child, but I know that's impossible. I don't have the physiological nor the anatomical prowess to carry a baby, not anymore.

Henry rolls away with our baggage, pushing them up the ramp to the check-in desk. I wish he could do the same to the load I'm carrying.

"Do you wanna just come up in case we take long?" That's Landree, perching her head through the open passenger side window. "We can order food here." Her tone is caring, sister-like even when we are just sister wives.

"Thanks, but I'm not hungry." The thought makes me chuckle, to which she creases her forehead.

"What's funny?" she asks, the inflection in her voice is of both intrigue and annoyance.

"Oh nothing, I just thought of something," I act resigned, demeanor aloof. "But yeah thanks. I'm alright here."

She shrugs. "Okay." I watch her pull her face out. "Suit yourself."

She walks off and disappear into the entrance. Our relationship has been "stable", as she describes it herself. I am a permanent fixture in Henry's life and she has finally learned to accept that in a sweetly sinister way. I have also reached an understanding of her intentions, even if we bicker from time to time. Noah was probably the truce to our years' long battle. It was really spirit-shattering to think about what I have done to win Henry back, while tiptoeing in the midst of Andrew's shadows. I wish I have the power to steer back the time.

I stare at my cellphone, the same one that hasn't seen any activity besides the calls from Henry and Adelpha.

"Welcome home!" I watch Kara slide inside the car. My hairs rise from their pores and a chill runs immediately down my spine. How did she find me?

"What are you doing here?" I ask her, while I look within the periphery for Henry's return.

"Relax, nobody can see me," she assures, pressing down the stiffness on my shoulders. "Did you miss me? I haven't seen you. There's much to talk about."

She sounds animated, apart from her other distinctive traits. It was a mother figure who came to me at the cabin on Andrew's "purge" weekends. Today, seems to be a normal company.

"What are you doing here? You can't be here!"

She plays with her hair, eyeing the phone in my hand, and ignoring the fever in my question. "He might call you know. But do you really want to find out what he says? Are you ready for it?"

A voice breaks in. It's Jessica's, reminding me of our last conversation.

She's not real. None of them are. The second you wield that thought in your mind, you have control over them.

It's times like this when I am unable to draw the line on the sand. Is she in my world or am I in hers?

"So, do you wanna grab lunch? There's a lot we need to catch up on."

I close my eyes as she mouths a surge of words that are almost inconceivable.

You're not real. You're not real. I'm not here.

"Same old spot where we always go? Oh, the one down the stre—"

The glass wall is sliding in slowly between us, her sound is muffled now as I distract myself with the still darkness. Echoes of outside conversations and footsteps take over her presence. I hear the Puget Sound once again, seagulls cawing against the breeze.

"Ophie? Are you okay?"

My eyes dart open to Henry. A concerned look is unabashed on his face while deep breaths escape me.

"Good grief!" Confusion accompanies his words. "You're sweating like crazy. Why didn't you open the window or start the car back up? I left you the keys."

The handle clicks, as he opens the car from my side. The fresh air spreads over my boiling skin.

"You can't be sweating like this in the middle of spring. Do you have a fever?" He touches my forehead.

"No. I think I just fell asleep," I reply, not knowing whether what I said was true.

"I see that. You must have been really tired."

Returning here has proven to be too draining of a task. Seeing the crash site where Marcus died should allow memories to crawl back in, but I know nothing more than what I already do. Kara's appearance was a surprise.

"Well, it's time." he announces, looking at his Apple watch. "I'll be there. We can always leave, okay? If it gets too uncomfortable."

"Okay," my answer is a whisper. "I have to do this. Maybe it'll help me. "

"I think it will. I've been trying to shield you from this but it will be good for you to meet them. I wouldn't put you in a situation if there's even a slight chance that it's not safe for you," he adds, fixing the wrinkles around his collar.

"I know that, Henry," I tell him mockingly as I roll my eyes.

We walk for five long minutes in the loud beating of the quiet.

Now, I stand here, awaiting Henry's cue, outside Front Street Grill. The air smells of a valiant mission, cold in its pursuit to hand me the years that I lost. The view of the cove and its snow-capped mountains in the background, provides a calming sense of amnesty to whatever this town has done to my mind, as well as my own failings towards it.

Here he comes, ahead of an older gentleman whose body has been swathed beneath layers of leather and plaid on this spring day. Henry smiles and even without saying a word, he's telling me that his loyalty is pledged only to me. I know I'm safe with him in our midst.

I hear their footsteps as my gaze bounces between them. The man pushes a grin. Wrinkle lines appear on his cheeks. Both his hands are tucked inside the front pocket of his light-colored jeans.

They meet a stop, Henry just a couple feet away from where I stand.

"Hello, Ophelia." The man waves.

Henry shifts his position, taking his place next to me. "Ophie," gesturing to him, "This is Mr. Davis, your —"

"Father," I interrupt, while offering him a handshake. The man stares at it for a second before reciprocating.

His hand feels clammy and the discomfort from this initial encounter is eating up the space between us.

"Yes, your dad," Henry continues. "I'll give you guys a minute," he announces, while eyeing my father. Then he turns to me in a look of reassurance. "I'll just be inside, okay?" he whispers.

I smile back at him before he takes small steps towards the restaurant.

"Thank you," my father tells him, tapping his back in passing.

"My God! Look at you. So beautiful," he declares, taking a step closer to me. "I'd like to give you a hug if I may."

I bob my head and he wastes no time reeling me inside his embrace. He smells of a musk made from blonde wood and cotton. There isn't any rush of emotions that would have drowned me, having reunited with my father. Maybe it's coming but I'm not ready to keel over just yet. "I can't believe you're back here again. There are so many things I wanna catch up on. Things I need to apologize for."

I pull away, ignited by burning questions that have swam up the surface. "Like what? What do you need to apologize for?" My voice remains calm, even in assertion.

He clears his throat, buying rare seconds to align the words he needs to tell me. I watch his eyes, slowly layered in red tints. I see he's becoming upset.

"Like for instance, I was never there for you while you're still living with your mom in Minnesota." He scoots a foot away, leaning back on the wooden railing, but his gaze never leaves me.

Yes. I heard that before. From what I can understand, she neglected me and left me to fend for myself, when a mother's love would have tended to my raw wounds. That seems to be what Henry's been alluding to and it aligns with my gut instincts.

"It's okay. Saves us both the pain if it was really that bad. I don't remember anyway," I reply, forcing relief in my voice.

"What you've been through, I haven't been able to forgive myself. I failed as a father to protect you," he tells me, shaking his head in disgust.

I glance at him, who's already staggering from the heavy precipitation in his eyes. "Well, I turned out alright," arrives my false reply.

My grin reaches him, as I make light to the dense weight he's been carrying all these years. He laughs too, wiping his face with a handkerchief he pulled out from his back pocket.

"I'm sorry but I gotta ask. What do you know about me? What do you remember?"

His questions stun me, not because I suddenly recall everything. This wave of emptiness arrives in my chest, as the water flows into the shore. There is nothing real or true that I can hold on to when it comes to my family. Marcus is gone. My mom, it sounds like she abandoned me, even while I was still living under her roof. My dad is a stranger, though his presence has brought a growing familiarity to being a Davis.

"I saw your pictures. Everything I know, I learned it from Henry," I answer. "But I gotta be honest with you, I didn't care to come here. I had no reason to. I felt like I had to stay away. That's why I never took your visits." Henry's face comes to view from afar, standing on the other side of the glass entrance. He waves at me. His vigilant eyes are hard to miss. "That man right there inside the restaurant—" I pause to regard him, "—he's been my only family."

"Ophie, I know that," voice trembling, he tells me. "And I am so grateful for Henry every single day. He's sacrificed a lot of his life and time to take care of you. To put you out of harm's way." His tears are rolling steady again, hands landing on my shoulders against his better judgment. "I'm sorry." He retracts them immediately, feeling my body recoil at the unsolicited affection. "I didn't mean to do that. I just miss you. I miss my daughter."

"That's okay. I understand. And yes, you're right, I owe him my life." I whisper, maintaining a steel and rather emotionless front. A thought slides forward, an identity cloaked with a gigantic question mark. "What you said, about missing me, I'm sorry. I just can't..."

"No. No. No." He comes closer, shaking his head, and wanting to show tenderness but couldn't. He pulls his hands back, the same ones that were compelled to hold my face and dry off the tears breaking free. "Don't say or feel anything because you have to. I know it's hard to make sense of things that happened to you. You don't remember them, for one. I just wanna let you know that I'm here. I've been here."

I could stand here reminiscing over a blank canvas and still, nothing would ever be painted. I feel my father's pain while unable to comprehend my own. I knew about his attempts to speak to me and Henry never failed to first ask what I want, before deciding together. It was always a no for me and he would respect that, even if he had the power to make decisions on our behalf. He can do so legally.

I never knew to what extent my memories can reach, if I really try to. If only I could open myself up to Jessica, maybe then I can reclaim what rightfully belongs to me. I just don't want to. Something in me rebels at the idea. It's my past, something's there that is the tiller of my own destruction. I suspect, almost with complete certainty. Why else would Henry go to the trouble of marrying someone he didn't love? Why wouldn't he divorce me? Why does he feel the need to make sure he remains the only person who can make decisions, when my mind impales me? Marcus must have said something in his death bed, a warning that I have chosen to bury.

Then I ask myself, if it is really possible to miss something I never knew. Because I do. I miss myself even if I'm not sure she is worth missing.

"Who am I?" I ask my father, who's dumbfounded by the load of that question.

He smiles, thoughts seemingly gathered towards the innocence of who I may have been. His chest relaxes.

"Wow," he says in a vulnerable tone. "Where do I begin?" He gulps a mouthful of air before uncertainty forms around his mouth. "You are my Ophie. Sweet. Smart. Stubborn. Determined. I look at you and I still see my little girl." A loving smile appears on his expression. I can tell that it's sincere. "I don't know what more to say," he adds, while shaking his head. His glance departs from me and to the water. "You love animals too. How could I forget?"

His reply is void of any purpose but for the moment, it seems enough.

A group of people pass us by, interrupting his next words. We both nod at them as they wave to us in greeting. I expected our reunion to be intense, with me disgorging harsh accusations. This is a far cry from that. Even though I do not easily adhere to his warmth, I feel relaxed around him. Henry seems to trust my father and I have no reason to invalidate that.

"There's so much to tell, so many great things even after your mom and I separated."

"I see," is my response.

"But everything happened so fast. I was out of the country on business. Next thing I knew, your brother's gone and so were your memories," he recounts in a somber tone, adding, "Then you just took off with Henry and married the boy. He told me it was important, that it was Marcus' last wish. I mean, I was surprised. I didn't know you were dating, let alone elope with him. I always thought you'd marry..." He stops there, as if trying to omit the unraveling of further information.

I become intrigued, curious. "Marry who?"

He sighs, his tongue gathering answers to cover up the truth he never meant to share. "I always thought you'd marry someone else. Someone you'd meet in college, or at work. It was just unexpected, though very likely to happen because he was your brother's good friend. I guess."

"He's a great man," I disclose, meaning every word.

He smiles and continues, "I agree but the way it happened then, it was hard to understand. Why you would just take off, leaving your family after such tragedy. But you were already eighteen, a consenting adult. There was nothing I could do."

I remember that night like a child's first recollection, waking up to my brother's bedside. His lifeless body, already covered under a white sheet. Henry stood behind me, forehead bandaged. There was nothing to look back to, just a white board missing its scribblings. They all just left me, my brain's hard drive was completely erased. Henry was my only salvation, and together we began to write our future, even when it didn't turn out the way I wanted to.

"Nobody knew you couldn't remember anything after that. Everything had to seem like you just had to leave because of the trauma," he reveals. There is some truth to what he said. "You looked at me but I was already a stranger in your eyes. I mean you weren't even in the car with him. I didn't understand. I still don't." He's becoming frustrated, trying to make sense of our shared dilemma. His body shifts, facing me now. "I couldn't win that battle but I see it may have been the best thing that ever happened to you. You've made it far away from that hell I left you with. Thanks to Henry."

"I'm sorry." Even I am surprised by the words leaving my mouth. Yet I feel genuinely sad for him. Hearing his pain, sensing its depth, there's no way to make it up. Maybe this is our consolation, to see the magnificence of our scars, and accept the gift of starting anew.

"Oh, honey! It's not your fault," he assures me as we both endure a hurricane of emotions.

I beam at my father, even with a face damp with tears, after having carried the weight of our first meeting. I am okay with getting to know him, learning myself from him.

We don't hug again, at least that is it for now. After all, you don't throw a fish into the aquarium without water from its old home. This will be slow and not without consequence. Instead, we allow the breeze to reach us in places where scars are yet to form. Most wounds are just that, hidden in plain sight.

There's a lot more to be told. He was careful not to speak about my mom with an ill-tongue. In fact, he spoke only a little about her.

"Are you ready to meet your sister?" he breaks my reverie.

I give him a sign of approval, to which he smiles. Our body language is that of a child, still learning to navigate the new world underneath the soles of our feet. He lost me to the years that passed, and I in turn, lost him to oblivion. I can tell he is unable to gauge my thoughts, whether or not he should put a paternal arm around my shoulder to lead me inside.

"After you," he gestures.

I nod, making my way towards the wooden counter.

"How many?" The dark-haired woman asks, still looking down to the shuffle of menus.

"We have company by the balcony. Under Davis?"

Her eyes shoot up. My father becomes her source of curiosity. She misses the sight of me, by just an inch into her blind spot. "Oh, hi, Mr. Davis! That's right. Henry's already down there." Her voice sounds lively but also forced.

"Thank you, Breann," he tells her.

I follow quietly, about to make our way into the maze of crowded tables when a hand graces the fold of my right elbow.

"Ophelia?"

It's her, voice almost leveled to a scream. I hear her behind us, scuffling around the barricade of chairs to get around me. A man looks over to inspect the commotion, before scooping an omelet from his plate. He was startled by her. The restaurant carries on with the rush, with many little conversations fumigating the air.

"Oh my God! It's you!" She screams, eyes enlarged in shock. "Damn," she whispers, wiping her hands on the front of her black apron. "I can't believe it."

I look over to my father, asking for answers, searching for clarity. He gapes back at me, the confusion vivid in my eyes. He moves closer too, sensing the need to safeguard his daughter. He's been suiting up for this, many years in the making.

Meanwhile, the woman stands in awe, glancing back and forth between us. She awaits an answer, at least a greeting back.

"Honey, it's Bree," he mutters behind my hair. "Our old neighbor. Remember what I said?"

Nobody knows.

I collect myself, slowly ambulating towards her with a plan already in motion.

"Oh my God! Bree?" I bring my arms around her shoulders. "I had to do a double take."

She releases herself from my hold, and beams at me from ear to ear. "Shit! I guess you're back from whatever hole you came from," she comments, inspecting me from head to toe. "Your dad said you've been travelling. But I saw you on the news with that politics guy. Got me all confused. You look the same as you did before. No signs of aging huh?"

"Don't be silly," I reply, as I begin to play with her dark locks. "Hmm... Something's different," I inquire. "Must be the hair? I never remembered you to be a brunette."

She giggles, faint lines form over her forehead. "No, I've always just dyed it."

"I remember!" Then I wink, sensing the ease she has with me. If I make a mistake now, it'll be less suspicious.

"Oh," a trace of sadness comes over her. She reaches for my hand. "You must be here for your mom. I'm so sorry for your loss." Her eyes float towards my father, nodding at him in condolences as well.

"Thank you. We're just dealing with it the best we could," I tell her. Though, I wonder if she notices my eyes and the lack of mourning in them.

"Well, I don't wanna keep you but whenever you're up for it, we should get together. Get the gang back before you leave," she says, half distracted by the restaurant staff waving at her.

I force a smile.

"...and then you tell me why you didn't marry the jock. Or the lawyer politician? I don't see a ring on that finger," she rambles on.

"I did marry the jock," I divulge.

I wonder if she's referring to Henry. Speaking of the devil though, he's making his way over to us. He eyes a concern at me and I know exactly why. I don't think Bree heard me, she is quite attentive to Henry's arrival.

"Everything okay here?" he asks, turning his attention to my old friend. "Hello again, Bree."

Bree's eyes flutter. "Hello back, Henry."

I notice a flirtatious tone in her response and I would have been irritated in the past. Henry wraps an arm around me, dusting off some cherry blossoms from my head.

"Oh." She cups her mouth, having connected the dots. "You're together."

Henry laughs and so does my father, who is keeping a small distance away from this pretentious spectacle. Which jock did she think I married?

A young man rushes over to her, urgency in his voice. "We need you in the kitchen. The big party, they wanna add a couple more people and change up the orders."

"Okay thanks, Ken. I'll be right there." She sends him off before attending to us again. "This place would crumble without me." I see her eyes roll in annoyance.

"I'm sure you make your parents proud," my father tells her. "Send them my regards, okay?"

"Thank you, Mr. Davis. I will surely tell them that," she replies. "Anyway, as I was saying," she slurs, eyes promptly detaching from my father and rushing back to mine. "I have to go but I'm serious about hanging out. Between this place and the kids, I gotta blow off some steam." She combs the inside of her apron pocket. A pen and paper emerge and she begins to write something. "Here's my number. Please call me, okay?"

I take the piece of paper and slide it down my shoulder bag. She gives me a hug before slipping away.

"Really good to see you, Ophie."

I grin back.

"You too, buddy," turning to face Henry.

"Later," he replies with a side wave.

Then, she nods at my father, "Mr. Davis?"

"Thank you, Breann. Always good to see you," is his send-off.

And off she scurries to the concerned expressions of her kitchen staff.

Henry shifts to face me, subtly massaging the kinks along my shoulder blade. "Let's go?"

I look up, taking lethargic steps forward. My eyes are scanning for familiar faces, smiles that might provoke my memories.

Nothing.

We are approaching the round table with Henry matching my pace, and my father following along behind us. A woman stands up, demeanor welcoming. She has dark locks, short, and curly. Her olive skin is magnificent under the shade. She must be my stepmom, with the years aging her kindly. A companion has her back to us, engrossed with the large menu in front of her. This must be her.

"She's here," my stepmom can be heard telling the other.

She browses up, but I miss her face by the brief motion. All because a napkin falls from her lap. She sinks to the floor and picks it up. The chair pushes out in the same motion. Finally, she rises from her seat and turns around in what seems like an aching minute. I see the wisps of her long curly hair float gracefully in the air, before revealing the person behind them.

My heart meets a screeching stoppage. What the fucking hell?

I squeeze Henry's hands, half needing moral support, and the other is out of anger. He knew her the whole time.

"I'm sorry," he whispers.

My dad finds his place next to my stepmom. "Ophie this is Mabel, my wife," he announces.

I can't seem to pull my gaze away from the younger woman, who maintains a nervous smile.

"Oh dear!" She shuffles her way to me.

"Honey, wait!" My father becomes alarmed. But it's too late. I am already trapped inside her tight embrace. He had no time to let her know that she must tread slowly when it comes to physical contact with me. I can still feel Henry's presence among us, giving just enough space for this reunion, but never abandoning me.

"I hope you remember me. I have missed you. I know you would have," she says behind my shoulders, sobbing gently. Her voice is so tender, obliging a light feeling from within me. She pulls away and inspects me, brushing off stray tendrils away from my eyes. "You have grown to be a lovely woman."

I offer a polite smile, still eyeing the girl behind her. "Thank you. Nice to meet you," I add, bobbing my head.

Then, she slips back into the arms of my father, giving me a full view of the younger woman that I have already met in the past. I couldn't just forget a face.

"I'm Harlow." She moves closer to give me an awkward embrace, before a quick release. "Your sister."

"Why didn't you tell me who you were when you came with Adelpha?" I ask her. My place in the hierarchy as the older sister is palpable in my tone.

"It was my idea. Just not a good time then to let you know who she was," Henry defends her, his voice entering from behind me. I give him a quick and expressionless glance, before attending to my sister again.

I was in awe of her beauty when she came in quietly that night. Her role was Adelpha's help but I'm sure now that she was just there to visit, to see what became of me. The truth is, she lost two siblings that night, Marcus to the car crash, and me to its aftermath.

"Shall we sit?" My father breaks the uncomfortable silence.

He pulls a chair for Mabel before taking the spot next to her. Henry readily makes two available for Harlow and myself, next to each other. He moves around and claims the seat adjacent to Mabel.

"I just wanted to see how you were," Harlow mutters quietly. Some inaudible conversation is taking place at Henry's side of the table. "My dad never told me what happened. Though, I asked for many years. I was young when you both left but I remember how you just vanished one day after the accident," she explains. Her nerves are palpable. "You would take me to dog sit Uncle Stan's golden doodle after school..." I can sense my father discerning our interaction, even from the corner of my eyes. I'm sure he's waited for this moment all these years. "...Hmm. What was his name again? I'm trying to remember."

"Archie!" Mabel interrupts from across the table.

"Oh that's right! Archie. He was such a good dog," Harlow brags, before taking a sip of her already diluted Coke. She must still be eighteen years old, ripe from her youth but still raw to the future that awaits her. I hope her cards are better than mine.

They all laugh in amusement about something someone said. I don't know but I missed it. I just giggle along, clutching my chest and the emptiness that is burrowing deeper beneath it. I don't belong in their world anymore. This makes missing Noah all the more incessant.

"Ready to order, everyone?" Mabel asks, loud enough to lure heads from the next table.

"Everything is on the house, courtesy of the owner," the waiter tells us.

"Nice!"

"Sweet."

"Glad we know the owner."

"Good looking out Bree."

Somewhere in the buzzing sounds of conversations around me, I hear my mind depart from them myself. They are near yet far away. I feel hollow but also harassed by the things that I couldn't remember. Even if my elbows are brushing against tangible people such as my family, I still feel alone.

CHAPTER EIGHTEEN

Drinking From A Different Bottle Of The Same Poison

"She was a great spirit, revered by the town for her charitable causes. Her heart though concealed…"

In this sea of mourning black, bereavement is yet to triumph in its efforts to hold me hostage. I have no feelings towards this woman, whose portrait is front and center at the church altar.

"I remember it like it was yesterday, when Mrs. Davis was behind me at the cash register. I was barely getting out of an abusive relationship. I barely had a dollar to my name. Then there she was like an angel."

Brown hair flows clumsily over the notches on her face. She was smiling, never showing teeth. There is chaos, even madness, just hovering over her impression. She emits a striking formality and elusive calmness, that is ready to bust out of the seams at any given moment. That ogle is the only indication that I once belonged to her. We share the same almond-shaped eyes. Hers stare deeply into what seemed like the abyss, and I wonder if mine does the same.

I don't know if she was loved by many or just a significant name to the census, judging from the many people in attendance here. Businesswoman was her moniker but a blur is more fitting. The eulogies are different, but they tell the same story of a woman who was kind but solitary.

I don't deserve to sit in the front pew and it doesn't have any right to claim me either. Here, I am an alien in this foreign land, feeling violated from the many hands that touched my body, sympathizing a loss that I already endured way before this. Most of them know me by title and distant relatives stand frozen, after seeing a face from the dead.

My feet are getting blistered, having been on my high heels for a long time to usher people at the funeral of the mother I didn't know. My father has been by my side, coaching me with names at every fresh footstep.

"That is your Aunt Carol."

"Cousin Jean, your old playmate."

"Family friend, Jay."

And I play along, as if time returned to pay back the memories it robbed from me.

I feel my sister's hand over mine, with Mabel next to her. My father is just returning to his seat, fresh from the killing fields, also known as podium, after speaking kindly about the woman he ended up leaving, Henry is always just nearby, with a pregnant Landree in tow. She is on her best behavior, at least for now. I would have loved to be around when Bree saw her with my so-called husband. I don't know her anymore but I would think she's readying her barrage of questions for when we get together.

The choir is singing Andrea Bocelli's Time to Say Goodbye, the same one playing in the background during Marcus' private funeral. Henry was also by my side then, still frail from his condition, and contending with the bittersweet news that his fresh heart was harvested from the demise of his close friend. I have no recollection of my parents being around, let alone his new family.

The priest is now signaling something to my father, launching a group of men wearing black suits to the altar. I watch them maneuver the casket, preparing for the procession back to the hearse. On cue, they lift my mother's remains out of the stand, walking it along the red aisle. Her body passes by me with a gust of cold disremembering.

I wonder if there is enough space in her coffin, between her and all the things she has yet to return to me. Part of my memories were consigned to her safekeeping, and I wish I had taken it back before they're buried with her forever.

"Are you okay?" Harlow consoles, her hand caressing my back.

What a parody, my younger sister consoling my heart from the grief that isn't there. I haven't been able to process the revelation of her existence, that we once crossed paths and didn't even know we share the same half-blood cursing through our veins. There will be more to talk about in the coming days.

"Yes. Thank you," I respond, stroking her arm.

Everything is happening so fast, almost at lightning speed. Sleep was terrible last night. Aside from sharing a wall with Henry and Landree, I have been plagued with thoughts of Marcus. I couldn't shake off the picture of my father, inconsolable after dinner. I was at a safe distance from him and Henry, but I already have an inkling to the bulky weight their conversation held. Harlow was standing next to me by the car, also beset with emotions wielded from the loss of our brother. We both watch Henry unbutton his shirt, low enough to expose a long mark down the length of his chest. The vertical scar was adorned by thick knobs of keloid, the passageway where Marcus would have entered to be resurrected in Henry's body. For a while, I refused to scrutinize the events leading up to the heart transplant, that my brother is still here, still living in the flesh of the man I married. In a sense I was protecting myself from the pain but, coming back here, there's nowhere to escape. The validity of that disaster spreads wide enough to encapsulate me entirely, and my mind's insinuations that I have some responsibility for my brother's death, is stifling.

So far, my mornings are still intact, with complete recollections of the last 24 hours. I just don't know for how long. How long until I watch my body helpless again, being auctioned off to the next winning persona? The voices returned last night, the same way they did after Noah took me out the first time, and before opening my eyes to a bare room at the looney bin weeks later. I'm tired of ingesting poison, in the form of those pills, but they keep me in line. And if that was the last time I'll ever see Noah, I hope I can buy the kind to help me forget about him too.

The music stops abruptly, after the conductor makes a motion with his wand. All fall silent, except for the melody in people's footsteps. Cautious strides pour out slowly from the church. I can hear the shuffles behind me, as the priest nods his psychic words of sympathy before carrying on. Same as the pallbearers, briefly parking their gape at me, either feeling bad or curious to see this fresh face from their past. I have been drowning in attention. None of them I truly need.

"It's time to go," Harlow whispers, coaching me to leave as she carries her hollow weight up from the pew.

Mabel is already gone. I am now alone with just my sister, and the ghosts of people's whispers. It is loud in this silence, from the voices of my mother percolating in our midst. Yes, voices that are teasing me with answers she's unwilling to give. Yet I have no right to accuse her of leaving with unfinished business, when I had all the time to confront her while she was still alive. Why is it that when I'm finally ready, it's too late?

"You've been really quiet," Harlow voices her observation, walking side by side with me towards the wide cobblestone exit.

"I guess I don't know how else to be." I shrug, feeling the carpet's friction against the soles of my shoes. It's the most truth I've ever told anyone since coming back.

"I understand," she mutters.

From the corner of my eye, I watch her gaze jump between me and the crowd outside the door. She hasn't yet tested all the ways to console me. Harlow's indecisive, body language awkward. She has been betrayed by everything she knew about me. There is nothing to re-learn here, just a whole new world to discover. When she looks at me, I can tell that she sees nothing more than a stranger.

We're moving past the circles, made by people in hushed conversations. All are waiting to embark on the convoy to the cemetery. I'm glad they're engrossed in each other's speeches, unaware of my company among them. Their inquiries, either mental or vocal have been so difficult to tame.

"Where have you been?"

"Ophelia, is that you?"

"I'm sorry, this must be hard for you, knowing you haven't been home in a while."

"I saw you on the news with Andrew. How is the young Congressman?"

And the latter makes me cringe, remembering my association to him. I stood side by side with Andrew during the elections, being photographed underneath an exquisitely designed suit to hide the feral attacks on my skin. To think I was willing to marry the same monster who gutted me, was really a grave desperation when Henry left to run after Landree. He took advantage of my vulnerability and sent me to prison after promising me a home.

In some ways, I haven't forgiven Henry. He displaced me from the life I was used to, though I have forgotten, only to desert me. His actions now have been a sign of utter restitution after what he has done, but two things remain true. He couldn't love me the way a man would to a woman, yet he wouldn't leave me, even for Landree.

A thought prods at me. When Noah first came to the house, he saw the newspaper clippings and articles about Andrew's victorious election. It was all over the news, the youngest member of Congress. I watch the features over and over until I bled. He's gone and I have escaped from his clutches. Noah assured me then that Andrew's gone, as if he was watching my life story in the sidelines. I can't help but think that he knew me before I knew him.

"I wanna say something," Harlow turns to face me, the afternoon wind blowing her curly locks. "I have been wanting to see you for a while. Desperate to talk to you. That I forced Henry to tell me where you were . He came here a lot," she reveals.

"Thank you," I reply, confused by my inappropriate answer.

My hands are now in the safekeeping of hers, our hold feeling moist. "But that's not it. Don't you remember us? At the trail? We knew you were staying at your cabin. I just wanted to catch you for a few minutes, in any way I could."

My heart stops. Why didn't I remember her then? I met her way before I thought I did. "You lost your dog."

I can see the tears welling up her eyes, awaiting a nudge to start falling. "Yes," she whispers, trembling. "I meant to just watch you from afar, to see what you look like now but then..."

"Andrew found you guys instead," I finish the sentence for her.

"Yes! But then I didn't know how to act. I was hoping that when you look at me, you would recognize your sister but you didn't."

"You know why," I tell her.

"Trust me! I do." The tone of despair is tangible in her voice. "I was hoping for a miracle."

"I wish you had said something. Things could have been different." What a regret not knowing her sooner. I think I would have been spared from any more damage from Andrew. But it's unfair, to put that responsibility on her and Mabel.

"Believe me, I tried but when I saw you," she cries out. "I felt you didn't deserve to be pulled back to the life you had already forgotten. Plus, with Andrew you seemed really happy. And the guy appeared to have really taken good care of you. I mean that's what you needed after everything. After Marcus."

I will spare her the gory details about Andrew, even though I want so much to tell her everything. I needed her to console me the way Henry didn't, that my suffering was warranted. Nobody could have made up that inferno I went through. But now is not the time and if I were to really move forward, there's no point in sharing that with her.

"It's okay," I assure her. "We're okay now." I pull her into an embrace, retaliating against the draft of discomfort between us. She is, after all, my sister; a prized piece from both my past and future.

"Hey guys!" Henry comes up to intrude our delicate moment. "Sorry but we have to go soon. Are you riding with us, Ophie?"

Landree stands behind him, smiling to greet Harlow.

"Uhmm..."I pause to regard my sister.

Somehow, Henry understands how crucial it is for me to be with Harlow even during this odd circumstance. "Or you can ride with her," he says, giving the permission that I wasn't aware I asked.

"Thank you," I whisper.

In turn, he pats my shoulder. "Stay close."

He walks away, with no feedback from Landree except for the quick glances we exchanged.

"Whatever happened to you two?" Harlow asks, as she begins to take steps towards the parked car.

The church lot has been emptied, no one else here is left mourning, but the sun's high noon glow.

Landree coming in the picture, that's what happened to us. But also, there may be a part of me he just can't accept enough to love. I don't know what it is but it would explain why he never stopped caring, even after he left me for her.

"You don't have to answer that," comes an interruption to my profound deliberation. She must have sensed the distress in my body language "Just know that even with the arrangement you have, that man cares for you and…" She hesitates for a second. "It's crazy sometimes. He really deserves Marcus' heart."

"Thank you. I know," I respond quietly.

We reach a white Range Rover and Harlow can be heard scuffling her tiny clutch for the key, or the clicker. "Even in the smallest purse, these suckers are hard to find. Wait up, sis."

I grin a little, amused by her dynamic character in the simplest of situations. Henry's car is parked behind us, engine already running. I acknowledge his presence by a wave. Hordes of automobiles are parading behind the hearse. There's a group of Harley riders merging in.

"Fuck!" That's still my sister, already plagued by impatience in her pursuit of the key. "Oh, I hope it's not in the car."

Among all the vehicles passing by, one catches my attention. A shiny, black Silverado is driving auspiciously at the edge of the crowd, closing in on the sidewalk. Its window is open, and a man drives even slower than the rest. The driver stops at just the right moment to catch a glimpse of me, away from the sunshine's loud glare. I too, steal a glance from him and would soon recognize the person at the wheel. He presses a smile, the way a devil would smirk after having risen from hell. I turn to Henry, his face clear behind the windshield, with a confirming scowl. Andrew is back.

"Found it! Let's go!" Harlow squeals, finally realizing where she had placed the car keys.

My mother's interment is close to conclusion and I feel quite uneasy standing above her open grave. I keep looking over my shoulders to see if Andrew has made his way near me. So far, not yet. Flowers have been tossed above the coffin as the priest reads scriptures from the Bible. I wish to just jump in there with her. Bury me too because it may be the only way to escape from Andrew, but thoughts of Noah stand in objection. There is still something to live for.

Without much noise, the hole is filling up with dirt. The workers in t-shirt and jeans are gently diminishing the mound of soil next to the grave. Everyone is starting to leave from the ceremony, even before the coffin is completely obscured, and the ground leveled back up. Now would be the time to say a prayer, leave a parting message. What do I even say to a mother who never was? The brick wall always rises up higher, every time I entertain thoughts of her. Was she great with me? Did she take me to school? Helped me build my dreams? Even just for a short while? I guess I could ask my father. Henry has been so tight-lipped when it comes to the late Mrs. Davis.

"I'm sorry for your loss," the voice reaches me, sliding cold down my spine. I know this moment was coming but he couldn't just wait when the burial is over. My mother's casket is still lying warm on the ground.

I turn to him, the spirit of fight or flight immediately possessing me. He is his usual handsome self, and a little bit more dignified in appearance, now that he is in government office. His camel sport coat floats cohesively with his eyes. He must be boiling in there with this unusual spring heat. Andrew's hair is lighter and his freckles have grown in number, as they do during the warmer months. He displays a buttoned-up grin with his mouth, that I once thought only knew tenderness. Somewhere within the bowels of admiration, fear has struck me in the harshest way possible. I don't remember the last time I saw him, only that I nearly died at every stroke of his hands. I make a sidestep, keeping a secure distance from his vile flesh.

"What are you doing here?" I ask in a furious tone, briefly looking back to see who hasn't left the cemetery.

Landree is standing under the shade of a western hemlock, fanning herself with the funeral program. Her gape is far towards Henry, who's speaking to an elderly couple. The woman appears well dressed, in a sense that nobody would in this part of Washington state. She dons a charcoal, two-piece ensemble. Her skirt is well structured to her thin frame, and her hands are adhered under the gentleman's hold. Meanwhile, he dangles his suit jacket over one shoulder, leaving only a white undershirt and slim pair of tailored pants exposed. I figured some big political names would be here. Of course, everyone's friends with everybody, and we all would just end up in an unlikely reunion in Coupeville. I can't expect Noah to show up next. He's not from around here. God, I don't even fucking know where he's from.

"It's okay. Henry knows I'm not here for trouble," he says calmly. Although, I can hear the snide tone he's trying to control. "I just wanna pay my respects to your mom. I'd be here even if I didn't want to. You know what I mean."

Yup. I forgot to mention that Andrew's father and mine have a long history. That's what I've been told. I'm sure his family has some sort of resentment towards me when they found out their son was never able to wed a married woman. The only way for Henry to sign the divorce papers was in his death, in his own blood. Yes, I was suited up to be a politician's wife and I pretended to oblige the role. Imagine the panic they must have felt, when I disappeared before the elections. I was a great face for a while. Surprisingly, the opposing party never mentioned anything about me. Maybe I was too uninteresting. Maybe it was hush money. We all know now how it ended. He won, appealing to the voters with his Native American ethnicity, in this so-called era of trendy racism and bigotry.

It could have worked with Andrew. Something just stirred him, in the moments when I finally found the courage to try and love a man apart from Henry.

"I guess it's good for your image," I sneer back, crossing my arms around my chest as I frown at him.

"It has nothing to do with that. But I'm quite surprised you're here. Did you finally remember stuff about your mom?" He tucks his hands in his coat pockets, as if preparing for an interesting revelation.

I bite my lower lip, sensing my racing heart underneath a fortified chest. I'm almost paralyzed by terror, but I couldn't allow him to see me in a frail state.

I refuse to respond.

He shoots a look at Landree's direction, before returning his gaze to me. "How do you feel about that?"

"What do you think?" I roll my eyes, despise obvious in my tone.

He chuckles as he plants a foot forward. "I guess you don't care now. Heard you moved on." Andrew twists his head, so we're face to face. "Or tried to," he mocks, drawing invisible quotes with his fingers.

It is obvious that he's taunting me and my lungs are suddenly enduring a hunger for air.

"Tell me," he whispers, drawing his face closer to mine, just inches away in fact. "Did he leave because he can't fit all of you in his single body?"

"Fuck you, Andrew!" I scream at him, loud enough for the men who are shoveling to hear our dispute.

They stop for a few minutes to regard Andrew but then go about their business again.

"Is this what you came here for? To insult me. Haven't you done enough?" I ask him, feeling my palms numbing up.

"And you think you're innocent? You know I did nothing. I stand by that. But you tell Henry and my family that I beat you up?" He becomes livid,

233

pointing a finger at me. "I never laid a hand on you and deep inside that head of yours, you know I'm right."

I shrug, sensing the receptacle of my patience about to tilt over.

"You almost ruined me, Ophie. The things that you said I did, I don't know how you could sleep at night. Damaging my character. The only mistake I ever made was loving you."

He notices my grin as drops of perspiration appear on his temples. Love me? His was a demented version of it.

He shakes his head in frustration, feeling defeated that he hasn't been able to penetrate my strong barricade.

"Are you done, Andrew?" I ask, staring him dead in the eye.

"I know why Noah left too. He probably got tired of wondering which Ophelia he's gonna wake up to in the morning," he whispers again, trying to slight me even more.

"You don't know him! None of you do," I reply with rage. My gaze shifts to the grave, that is now completely covered up. I need to tame myself. But how should I feel, after finding out he's still keeping tabs on me?

"But I know you." He points his finger at my head. "There's many yous in there and none of them are worth keeping. Henry can't even love you, more than just to repay you for your brother's heart. He can't stomach this madness but he's stuck. You know exactly why."

I feel my body shuddering, vibrating towards an imminent explosion. Only Landree would give him information about Noah. I know they keep in contact. I wouldn't expect any less from her.

"So, this is what we're doing," I comment, backing away from his monstrous stature. I do it, only so he could take a good look at the Ophelia he never knew. I am not crawling back in the corner anymore. "To insult me and make me feel like garbage in front of my mother's grave?" I watch him shake his head, expression mocking. I steel myself as my next words leave my thoughts. "Or do you need a fix only I can satisfy? Don't think I have forgotten!"

He becomes more appalled, inching closer to launch his strong grip over my shoulders, but thought better of it the last minute. "Don't pretend that you care about your mom." He's fuming now, almost spitting out the words he says. "You didn't know her, to give her the time of day," he adds. "You're here because you got nothing better to do with your damn life. Everyone who comes ends up running. They're terrified! Why do you think Noah left?"

And just like that, he got me.

"You fucking asshole! Get the fuck outta here! You. Crazy. Lunatic!" I'm in his charges again. My emotions are always susceptible to his authority.

Many eyes have been sent to our direction now, including Henry's. I notice him watching, deciding if he should save me. Landree meets my scowl.

"It's true. And let me tell you again that there's only one crazy person in this space. I'm looking at her right now."

I do not move, feet glued to the ground. It's inducing tremors to my body. I must retrieve my anger. I won't let him control me. We embark on a glowering contest for a good minute, anticipating a white flag from the other. I won't do it. Then he drums his left foot against the weeds, nerves palpable. I hear knuckles cracking as big lumps fall down his throat. I got him too!

"What's the matter? Too many people?" I break the quiet tension. "Here's you denying what you did but a little taunt from me gets you all boiled up. What do you wanna do? Rip my PUSSY apart like the last time?" I smirk as his eyeballs nearly pop out of their sockets. I don't think he's seen my defiance, ever.

"You're crazy," he yells, twirling a finger next to his head. "Coming here was a mistake. I wanted you to rectify everything. To tell me that you lied to them. But I just can't reason with a lunatic. You're long gone. You have been for a while now. I don't play your psycho games." He stops to carry our attention to Henry. We both look at him but he doesn't notice. "I'm not him."

His words are plagiarized straight from Landree's script. I've heard this from her before, trying to back me in the corner, so I'd lose it. He's deflecting. People do that when they can't admit guilt.

"You should leave," I order calmly, thrusting my uninhabited emotions back inside my rib cage. My fury is building up even more. I feel like I could take a life with it. He wins if I do. I can't let him.

He takes a few steps back to collect himself, pulling a white cloth from his back pocket to wipe his sweat. A deep sigh comes before opening his mouth. "In the end, I feel bad. I really do. Because I could have been that person who would give you the world." If I didn't know better, I would have fallen for this sham. "I really tried to be. And you know, that isn't the saddest part. Because after everything, I will move on and Henry is on his way there. But you, what about you?"

His words were meant to bully, a threat to feed me to the wolves under a rather absolute credibility. Many times, my neck has been enfolded in-between the quiet force of his hands. I know better than to accept the bluff beneath his breath.

I look up to find his hurried departure, the growing distance shrinking his form. He passes a nod at Landree, making his way into the conversation between the well-dressed cameos. I watch my father arrive at the same assembly, with Henry understanding that it's time to leave. He shakes hands with Andrew, while Henry taps his shoulder. They both shoot a quick glance to my direction - heads bobbing, mouths dancing.

I feel severely deceived by Henry. Of all people.

Anger crashes in my margins. The world spins. The ground underneath my soles shakes without compassion. Its intensity mimics aftershocks. My throat closes shut, flesh numb from the face down. Henry and Landree smile fondly when they finally find each other, uncaring of the confusion and betrayal thundering inside my chest cavity.

Mabel is absent from the pleasantries in the now empty lot. Far ahead, near a marble mausoleum, Harlow is sitting inside her car, subconsciously separating herself from the tidal clash between the present and my unremembered past.

I march along, feet heavy from the unused retribution I saved for the woman who stole my old love. The passage of my shoes has softened up the firmness of the dry grass. I stop, needing to cut my fury into tiny pieces. I'm afraid of what this rage might do but the heat of my anger further incinerates every ounce of my humanity.

My vision is changing, with the edges of my sight taken over by black shadows. Make no mistake though, it's still hot on the pursuit of my target.

"Ready?" Henry asks when I reach them, his words falling on deaf ears as I turn to Landree.

I glare. Her eyes become laced with panic. I know she sees it, a deeper rage beneath my irritation. That is not a wrong guess. She takes a step back, spotting my finger that is moving towards her face.

"You told Andrew," comes my deep and trembling voice. I almost don't recognize it as my own. I take a breath, scooping air from my belly before continuing. "Really low even for you, Landree!"

From the corner of my eye, I see my father, walking away in conversation with Andrew's parents, heedless of the implosion brewing within his daughter. I know Andrew is watching this scene. Good.

Henry jumps in the middle, slicing the tension between Landree and I.

On one end, she shudders at her fear of my retaliation, and on my half, a pure and salacious hunger is pitting against my chest.

"What has gotten into you, Ophelia? Jesus!" Henry screams.

I, realizing that madness has started to poach below my pores, slowly recoil the rage back in my clutches.

"Ask your woman," I reply, without sharing an inkling to the typhoon that is bouncing off the walls of my body.

He gives Landree a look, the kind that would force the truth out of her. But I don't want any part of this, especially now that Andrew has decided to join the circus. Before she could open her mouth to state her case, my body has already catapulted itself towards the parking lot.

"Ophelia!"

I hear bodies scrambling in place, calling out my name, and asking where I'm headed. None of them run after me, thinking that I may just be getting inside Harlow's car. But I continue to dash away, passing the horrified face of my sister.

CHAPTER NINETEEN

Pictures Percolating

There is no stopping this course, as my now bare feet scorch against the hot ground. Finally, the meadows greet my arrival with wild crunching sounds. I pick up speed. My lungs feel thin, sacrificing strength so I could survive past this plight. Voices from inside me are reaching out to the world, grappling against implosion, if only to be heard. They are getting louder and louder. The bomb is ticking and tocking in both my ears, while my whole form shakes and jolts. I need to be far away from Andrew, from Landree, from everybody.

Minute objects prick my soles but I will continue to race towards the unknown finish line, where answers might be found. My mind is flickering, dancing in the space between remembering and forgetting, until images begin to nourish my vision.

I see a little girl, maybe seven years old, inside this house. The walls are white, lined with gawking strangers. I smell coffee, a strong chicory brew. The girl is naked, her back to me, getting patted down by a woman. There is a whip in her hand and everyone chants when she lifts it up. The girl cries without a sound, just obese tears falling down from the red blindfold. Her thin lips tremble as the whip triumphs on her back. A pinkish welt forms immediately. The woman raises her voice to speak an unrecognizable language, while the girl stares at her hand, as if she can see beneath the eye covering. Everyone in the group kneels around her. Next, four men, between the ages of 40 and 60, rises up from their respective velvet chairs, also in color red. Just as the girl, the men are naked, erections soar below alcohol and hair-engorged bellies.

My skin freezes, fur raising up in unadulterated fear. The girl must have felt the same way too. A boy raids in, breaking their sacred circle. He is a younger version of a familiar face at twelve.

"Leave her alone!" he chokes the words.

Both love and pain overcome him at the sight of the little girl. Relief gathers in my chest at his arrival. I know she's safe now. He's here now.

The woman looks to the civilian guards, eyeing a silent order to take the boy away. They slowly plod against the horde of faceless people in white.

"My dad will know about this! You're evil. All of you are!"

I can still hear his scream as the chanting voices drown out his protest. He continues to plow in, until finally reaching the girl. There is a towel in his hand and he immediately envelopes the girl underneath it, before he embraces her. The woman with the whip lets him, knowing that help is near to remove him soon enough. The little girl connects to a sense of familiarity, even underneath the blindfold. She instantly crashes her vulnerable body against him. She begins to sob. Her stone shell has been broken off and the warrior becomes a girl again, in the arms of the one who loves her.

Yet the reunion is brief, as the guards tackle him. The girl screams, now quivering in fright. The boy battles back, flimsy hands landing like cotton on the guard's muscular chest.

"Listen to them, Marcus," the woman tells him in stern command, while the guards drag him away. "If you don't want me to tell Henry's parents too."

I scan the room back for the girl. There she is, still heaving with anger yet courage is resuming on her face. She stands still, eyes drifting to the corner of darkness, the one that will rob her of her innocence and humanity.

My feet have found a reason for stoppage. A fallen log nearly baited my leg to a face plant but I saw it in the last second. I have been running for a while, body defying limited strength. My insides are twisting, like on the verge of being gutted completely. There is a gag reflex beating loudly inside of me. It's the only thing I hear now. I don't think I can hang on to it much longer.

Here it comes.

As if a string has been pulled from my throat, the vomit reservoir opens from the blunt force throbbing at my diaphragm. I tilt my head down, drawing strength from an old oak trunk. There on the ground, repulsion that was sparked by my vision, leaves my entrails. It keeps going, fatiguing my back as abhorrence creeps over my spine. I was the girl clothed in bare skin, spread out as a meal for the hungry men and women with slant beliefs.

The vomiting stops but not the reverberating cries I have drawn out from my stomach. I collapse down to the hardened mud, right next to the puddle of memories that my mind finally set free. My face is soaked from perspiration and tears. I feel sick. I crave for a knife to peel off my skin, the parts that have been diseased by pedophilic hands. But that would mean obliterating all that I am or was.

I fix my head up, to a break between the thick forest, a hole to the blue sky, and an entrance for the noise to rush in. The wilderness sings in freedom, with critters large and small going about their business as usual. In the subtle whipping, I feel lost in abounding silence, that is a blanket to my weary soul.

It is happening again - my mind separating from its whole, body drifting away from its parts that could touch the world. I'm farther now, away from myself. I'm looking through a keyhole, to another Ophelia lying mercifully in the middle of nowhere. She's graced by only the portions of the sun that are allowed into the deep woods.

On other days, I would have fought it, the prostitution of my body for another mind to take. I watch them, the two other clones of me waiting in line for a turn in my vessel, before I finally exit to the oblivion. I have not been awake for much of the switches until today.

I welcome the nothingness and the numb that is my refuge. I want this now, to escape this realm without leaving my body. Let another pilot my mind until it is their turn to grow tired of the battle.

Now I understand why I forced myself to forget, burying memories of my youth down to the deepest exile. I would have to perish to cleanse myself anew and forgetting is as close to dying as I can get.

And how dare Henry! How dare he bring me back here?

April 24, 2003

She lurks from behind the mist and darkness, pushing herself against the trappings of Douglas firs, one trunk after another. The rain has stopped, but not the residual precipitation soaking the leaves and branches above her. She dreaded her destination but here she is, just some feet away from a grim scene unraveling before her. The victory party down the street still rages. She realizes how quick she ran back when she heard the metal clatter and tire screeches.

Surrendering to the hunger for air would be instinctual, after the life or death marathon that brought her here. But she saves that for a rather apparent reason. She's going to need all the energy, including her will to live, after discovering what had happened.

The pick-up truck, or what's left of it, lays upside down on the dark road, that is illuminated by a single light post. There's blood everywhere, spilling on the ground as if a bear or mountain lion has just been foraging in the area.

"Ophelia, is it? We're sending help now. Hang in there, sweetie."

And the line goes dead after she thumbs the 'end' button, phone slipping off her hand, depleted of its purpose.

She gets closer to the vehicular carnage and find a familiar face, grunting beneath the glass fragments. Half his body remains inside the overturned truck. Other than that, it is piercing in the quiet. The air blasts an eerie silence, as death comes to collect two fresh souls. It would meet its quota for the night.

The man struggles for a word. He notices her presence, and even in his demolished state, his concern for her is more than evident. Love creeps boisterously along the thin line of death and survival, towards her susceptible form.

"Don't come any closer," he coughs up. "You can't see me like this. Trust me. Just go!" He screams at her in a thin and suffocated voice.

She defies the request at first. But there in the corner of her eye, a bed of long brown hair splays out beneath the eruption of brain matter, from a crater on the girl's head. She stands frozen, unable to grasp this reality that is being understood by her thoughts, already blistering in overdrive. She scours the scene bravely one last time, to notice that the girl's other leg is nowhere to be found. Her arms are spread on the concrete, as if embracing it as a last resort. Everything else around is a sheet of red gore, still flowing from bodies that have long been cold. She doesn't know yet, that the other boy who loves her, is still in the vehicle. He's going to live, by way of nothing less than a miracle.

The moment engulfs her like a tornado, as she moves closer to the man. Then, a million seconds crash into her, awaiting a decision. Shock and fear waves to be noticed as well. Too many emotions stand before her, crowding the space meant only for oxygen. They all reach out for her hand and she undauntingly absorbs them all, unbarricaded and vulnerable. She weeps, then convulses, cries some more, and finally breaks down with her knees scraping the wet pavement.

The man's eyes submit to its fate, as sirens scour for a purpose. It was monumental, the way he left before the noise comes pouring in.

The atmosphere whistles back to life, after the silence became a gateway between the living and dead. She inches away slowly, enduring the many whispers and cries in her head.

And then she's gone, obeying the voice in her midst that told her to leave. She turns around, the light bars flashing behind her, as the distance expands. She finds herself back in the woods, alone in the freezing storm. The fresh rain makes her scent, soil quaking at her feet. Damp brushes swallow her legs, while the noise of disaster reverberates louder across the forest.

She keeps going.

In haste.

In fear.

The ambulance has arrived, more squad cars, and a chopper roaring overhead. Many voices saturate the air - lungs breathing, and pounding hearts that are not from the bodies she wishes to hear them from.

Finally, a cloud of smoke diffuses up ahead, maiming her senses. And instead of escaping, she runs towards it like a miner finding gold. The dense tree line ends at the other edge of the forest, to a darker street bend. She's here now, legs shaking and weary. An apparent graveyard sleeps quietly across the street. It wasn't smoke, just a cold veil of fog that seduced her to come. It welcomes her now, embracing the shock off her body. The wind sings to her, melody cajoling her thoughts to release everything it contains. She opens her arms wide for the enticement, realizing what it had just offered.

This is an escape, the land of forgets. She's certain of it now, even as the other side of the woods stirs in both shock and urgency. This pain she carried across the trees, the one she picked up from the crash, that she stacked over the hell that was her childhood, it will be her death. This is the better option. By now, her great love is turning over every inch of this town, searching for her.

She's ready at last, to seize the chance that presented with an expiry date. She is going to take it. With eyes closed, her dirty fingers clutch over the wet ground. She descends, inhaling the last batch of air she would have to breathe as herself. Then, she lets it all go out in a deafening cry, releasing her anger to the world that has treated her unfairly all these years.

Her memories.

Her self.

Everything.

The force could have unearthed old pains that were once engraved in fossil rocks. They're from those who came here before, to be reborn the same way. Silence is the only thing that is heard.

Her eyes fling open, the slate before her now clean. Everything seems how it should be until a screeching sound bursts through the stillness. It's coming from a clunky Jeep Renegade. The driver's door opens and slams with resolve. Footsteps hurry around the vehicle. Brown eyes widen upon finding her.

"Ophie!"

He brings himself down and reels her in for an embrace, tight and almost suffocating.

"It's alright, I'm here now, baby," he tells her with sincere consolation, kissing the top of her head.

Later, he would find out that a stranger now inhabits the space between his arms, where once was love's home. She had come here in this place meant to intern memories, where broken minds go to die.

The birds call for a statement of triumph, in the moments after the reunion. Another one has been taken.

She didn't have a choice, forget it all or spend this lifetime nursing a demon that would hold her responsible for what happened to Marcus. This, without knowing that the same monster would later lay underneath her bed each night, handing her pieces of damaged flesh, until she finally remembers how much it hurts. Slowly. Definitely.

CHAPTER TWENTY

In The Thick Of The Blur

I stir, with the smell of fresh laundry detergent percolating in our midst. Eyes open to the late sunshine, stretched in-between the shadows of my flat sheet. A peculiar stillness indigenous only to this place, has come to be acknowledged. About a minute or two is spent by my mind, orienting back to consciousness. Firstly, how long have I been in bed? And mostly, where am I? Not to mention the litter of memories I came upon some time ago. I need to hold on to them before they disappear again.

Somehow, I am already sure of the answer before I asked the question. They weren't just dreams. Dreams don't come with stains of familiarity aiming at you to be recognized. What I saw were lines connecting the dots. They were snapshots arranged in no particular order, from the many yesterdays that haven't found a proper home in my thoughts.

The next time I blink, they've already been forgotten, slipping like grease in the gaps between my fingers.

I catch a sharp whiff of chlorine bleach. Must be coming from the same vicinity as the laundry, even when it smells like I sprayed some on me the night before.

"Morning, sunshine," greets Harlow, carting away the last few littered memories I was trying to hold on to.

"What happened?" I ask her, still fazed by the break in my timeline and worried about what I may have done.

She drops at my bedside, the mattress sinking to mold her form. "You were so upset yesterday," she sighs. "You were overfatigued, they said. Henry ran after you and then he found you passed out by the old trails."

Okay, I recall that. "Anything else?" I ask her as I sit up to regard my surroundings. Dirty white paint covers the weathered walls, where football memorabilia are artistically mounted along. The cottage is rustic, inviting, and safe.

"That's it. I mean you were in and out of sleep. You asked if you could stay with me while you rest so Henry brought you here."

"So, I just stayed in bed the whole time?"

"Uh-huh," she nods with a blunt smile.

What a relief! I was still me before I closed my eyes and when I opened them.

"Thank you," I tell her. "I know you have so many questions, why I ran away from Andrew yesterday. What happened to Henry and I. What I remember and what I don't. One day, we'll be able to sit down and figure it out."

Immediately, she hurls herself into my chest, enfolding me in her arms. "What are sisters for," she whispers behind my hair. "I'm glad you're back with us."

"Me too, "I reply. "Me too."

She skips up to face me. "But first, breakfast!"

But her boisterous appeal is reduced by the distracting smell of bleach once again. I can smell it in my hands.

"What's wrong?" She notices.

I hold my teeth together, unable to figure out what's bothering me besides the obvious odor.

"Bleach?" I finally ask her.

"Oh!" comes her response. She begins to cup her mouth and slowly giggle. "Uhmm. Mom went overboard with the cleaning. It's just been a while since someone stayed here."

"Oh wow! Like how long?" I wonder loudly as I scan the place again, now on my feet. That explains the bleach smell that I now gather is from the bathroom. I love what they've done to this place, an overflow of rustic presence, that is a far cry from the main house and its style. I can see their main residence through the window, as my dad emerges from the back door. A black garbage bag hangs down his clutch.

I feel a little bit lightheaded from having just gotten out of bed, but I am more apprehensive at how much comfort I feel being here.

"Uhmm...since you left," she reveals with reluctance.

I stop in front of an old painting, right away impounding my awe from it after hearing what she said. "Me? I was here?" I'm flabbergasted.

I turn to her. She stands with calm bearings, while fiddling her fingers. "I'm not sure if I'm allowed to tell you yet. I'm sorry," she says nervously.

My body finds itself next to her, comforting her while I urge the truth from her mouth. "It's okay. I can take it." She welcomes the feel of my skin on her shoulder.

"Well, this was where you stayed when you didn't wanna be at your house. I mean at least that's what I remember. This was all yours." She points to the display wall. "Everything here. Dad didn't change it."

She can tell that I'm eyeing a particular corner where a red jersey has been hung. The name Davis sits above a large number thirteen.

"And those? I played football?"

"Nope! But Marcus did."

Of course! The hat that Henry left at the crash site, it was his. He played alongside him. In high school? Or college?

"Gosh, we would have had an NFL player for a brother right now. Henry too, but he turned down any promising offers right after. Right after..." Something pauses her thoughts. She's being cautious with me but there's no need.

I think I've been carrying all the remorse in the world that another tiny drop on my back would be no thing. She can say, 'right after the crash'. Yes, the crash that might as well have had me at the wheel. I would have propelled Marcus' death regardless. I am almost certain that I put him there.

"I'm sorry," she apologizes, looking past me and to the French door. "I didn't mean to tell her."

I'm confused. "Tell who, Harlow?"

"It's okay. I was going to," arrives the familiar voice of comfort.

Henry walks in, sluggishly. He nods at me before tapping a tender hand at Harlow's shoulder. I look at that face and a flood of reminders come over me, like how lucky the world is to allow such pure soul to inhabit its space. His selfless hands have always been ready to lend to me at any given hour. On the flipside, a trace of anger awakens in my chest. I don't know what to make of it.

"Can you give us a minute?" he asks my sister. "Your mom said breakfast is about done."

And with haste, Harlow leaves the cottage. It's just us now, with his footsteps shrinking the space between us.

"Hey," he greets, grabbing my whole form into his embrace. "You're okay. Nothing happened, if that's what you're worried about."

Hearing him makes me want to be buried alive, with all the shame resurfacing up from the stone floor beneath us. They're here to collect me now. Gently, my hands push his affection away. I stare at him and all the genuine care rising from his pores. Henry threw his dreams away just so he can fight for a girl's redemption, a girl he didn't even love. I know that now.

"I'll tell you what you wanna know," he speaks. "It's exhausting. This always looking over our shoulders. This worrying. All the lying. I think we're far away from that now. You're mom's gone. They're gone, people looking for you. You deserve to know." He pauses, to swallow an obstruction in his throat. "But just give me time to figure out a better way to tell you." His voice trails, a resonance of his pain.

Yet I waste no second. "Is it true? You gave up football for me?"

He seems unwilling to keep his new promise, that even now he still worries about how I'll react. His body just towers over me, looking into space, catching my imminent outburst.

"Answer me, Henry," I scream at him, hands on my sides rolling into fists. I'm not convinced. He remains quiet as anger forms over my wet eyes. "Please don't lie to me. Stop lying! You just said a moment ago that you're gonna tell me."

"Ophie, of course not."

And somehow, my yelps and bawls have finally struck a chord in him. He marches towards the corner where memories of broken football dreams hung beautifully to taunt him.

"What, Henry? You know I'm right!" I prod again.

I break his shield. He turns back to me, feeling scorned by his own emotions boiling at the chest. "I said fucking no!" His voice climbs but just enough to send me a statement. "It's me, okay? I can't play. People expected me to play again, with my new heart. But how could I?"

I watch him fall to the cushioned bench by the window, face hardened before burying them inside his hands. The next time he looks at me is a version of Henry I don't see too often, frail and overcome with emotions. His face is red and so are his eyes. "The truth is I couldn't play anymore. I can't live with myself, relishing in a new life at his expense. It was our dream, both of us playing for the NFL, and we did it. Or at least we almost did."

"So, you pretended to pursue a veterinary degree with me? You made yourself love me, even if you didn't? I know you just wanted to keep me safe. But was I worth throwing your dreams for? I didn't think so," I argue.

He holds his palm up to my face. "Just stop right there, Ophie! I regret nothing. All that I did for you, I wanted to." His eyes turn red even more. "Of course, I care for you, both of you. For Christ sake! I moved here with you guys when your parents divorced. Minnesota was hell. For all of us. I'm glad your dad realized it before it was too late. My parents never did. They died with their hands tied to those people. Now all I have is their money, dirty money. Sick bastards!"

Those people? He's lost in tangents.

"Henry," I want to console him but his eagerness to finally share, is a strong wall. I couldn't penetrate.

I make my way to his direction, intending to sit quietly next to him. There, his hand crawls to mine, still giving me love when he's the one who needs it now the most.

"Ophie, sometimes I envy you for not remembering. What we went through as kids—" he pauses. "Was just beyond words, for you most of all." A deep breath follows. "Even moving here, the nightmares followed us. We couldn't escape it. I wish I could forget but wherever I go, is a reminder of what we lost, us three."

I couldn't even begin to comprehend. It's hard to feel loss, to miss something I never remembered. In some ways, I feel like I was spared from the grisly plight that may have been the same thing that forced me to forget. It seems that the only thing I'm supposed to do now is continue to trust him. I lay my head on his shoulder, and in return, he palms my cheek with fondness. That's enough questions for now.

"I'm always here for you," he declares. Hearing it momentarily takes my breath away. "But you were also a reminder of everything that I am trying to run away from. A reminder of what I lost. When Landree came, I saw an escape route. I fell in love with her because she gave me a way out. I know it's shitty. She deserves better." He sniffles. "But then we saw what happened that one time I let my guard down. When I thought I could take a break from watching over you."

I take an obvious guess. "Andrew?"

He nods and I wonder if he is finally going to believe my accusations towards the man. "Because after a while, when you were seen on TV with him, they found you."

Definitely did not expect that but it explains why he suddenly cared enough to free me from Andrew's clutches. Yet after all, he stayed with Landree, or rather, she let him back in.

"They?" I ask, confused, but as soon as he senses my fresh curiosity, he shakes his head. Was it a slip up or another episode of 'it's-best-that-I-didn't-know?' I already know it's the latter. "Right. Need to know basis only. Give you time to tell me," I add, with an aggressiveness that's hard to dilute with humor.

I pull away from him, to nurse a thought that aches within. "Henry, I'm not well and we both know it's much more than my lost memories."

He squeezes my hand tighter, wanting to console me and at the same time, ashamed that his mind is in agreement with my words. His stillness is sympathizing, but there's no room for any of that when entertaining what's rational. It's only a matter of time before I'm gone again. Who knows? It might mean for good this time. It was never an "if", it was always "when" this becomes permanent. All the more, this longing to set him free feels so strong. He must get out of this prison.

"Can I ask one thing of you but please don't be mad?" arises my request.

He looks at me. "What is it?"

"Will you think about signing the divorce papers? For real this time?"

I sense retaliation. Incoming. His mouth stays shut, though ears are open.

"Just hear me out. I think it's time to let me go. Now that I'm getting to know my dad, I'd like to stay here. I know you trust him. He can carry on with the task that Marcus left you with."

"I'm afraid I can't do that. You just don't understand," is his stern reply.

"I'd like to know more. Why?" I grow insistent.

He gapes into space, sighing in-between head shakes but I can tell that he'll give in.

"He loves you, more than I even realized and when he…"

"Loved!" He's taken aback by my interruption. "Remember, 'loved'. All in the past. We're talking about someone who's dead."

Yet as I'm saying that, guilt comes slinking in, grazing through my neck and ready to suffocate on order.

I watch him lace his hands together and anchor it over his thigh. He seems uneasy, like there's so much more he wants to say. He alludes to this constant mystery hovering over his life, nothing less than in Henry's true fashion. He twists his neck to my direction, coaxing me to pay attention to him as I hop glances between the black magpie in the courtyard outside, and his sullen expression.

"Did you know he was ready to give up his only shot at making it to the

NFL for you?" he says, with his tongue spiteful at the revelation, voice laced with tremendous pain. He's still mourning, grieving for his dear friend and his own promising future that he buried with him.

He said it over and over - it was his fault. Was it really? He was drinking. They both were. He said Marcus didn't want to but he made him. The Colts just drafted him hours before. There was a party and then he was dead.

"Your mom. She was wanting to see you, said she's planning to settle here. Second chance, she said. She ran away from that life. Your brother was too worried cuz he was leaving soon, right after the draft. Mr. Davis was always away. Who was gonna look after you?" he recounts.

My shoulders collapse, and not nearly to bear the weight of his statement. I'm gravely astounded at the fact that I feel Marcus' apprehension of my mother come alive in the voice of someone else. I should be more curious, dig deeper but I can't. I won't. There is something stained inside my core that is preventing me from needing to know, and every living cell in my body obeys it.

I shrug a little before entertaining the urge to find out what happened. "And what about you? What happened to football?"

"You just won't let up, huh?" He chuckles nervously. "Well, I'm not as noble as you think I am. I didn't give up football on my own accord. Are you forgetting about my heart condition? Right after high school was when I got diagnosed. That was a lucky break, your brother's heart."

Oh my God! I feel like a total asshole, springing the football thing at him. Of course, he had a heart condition. Of course, he could no longer play. And even with his new organ, I get why he refuses to try again. His life completely changed and he already had me to look after. He couldn't just rob my brother's dreams right off his grave. It's a twisted way of thinking but a mindset that I fully understand.

"So it'll be the same answer every time. It's a no."

Oh, that's right. We're still circling around the subject of divorce. The one that he revolts like stale meat. What he doesn't understand is I'm not willing to give up so easily. I'm sorry to Marcus but his promise is expiring soon. If I'll never see Noah again, then at least I did something to contribute to Henry's liberty and happiness.

"You don't get a second shot at life only to punish yourself for it. My brother didn't give you his heart to let it beat for someone else. I don't deserve it."

"No!" His voice comes out deep, halted by the strings of self-control, or it would have been a scream. Henry is so great at that.

"Will you think about it? I beg of you."

Yet there is no sort of reaction from him, at least to go on with. He has dismissed the thought, long before I asked. And his silence is very difficult to read even when he's holding my hand.

The next time he speaks, we would have already flipped the pages to something else.

"I went through the reading of the will by myself. I just want to get it over with while you get better from yesterday." His tone is now calm and always believable.

The reading of the will just really means hearing what I have been able to freeload from the mother that I didn't know. I'm glad I wasn't there. I imagine an old and balding lawyer with round eyeglasses, reading the will in monotone. How boring would that have been?

"What did you find out?" I ask, as I release my hand from his, to straighten the wrinkles on my striped pajamas. A message from my cellphone becomes a brief distraction.

"Well, nothing much to it. A quarter of her properties have been donated to the city. You have the rest," he replies, seemingly convinced that I have forgotten about everything we argued about.

"Well, am I rich?" I laugh, as I bounce off the couch and head for the bathroom.

I hear a snicker from behind me. He's a little cautious with hiding his amusement. But I would never miss it, a chance to see him a little less fastened than his usual self.

"I can show you your bank account," he yells out from the living area, where I left him.

My reflection appears calm and unsuspecting of any butchery happening at the edges of my mind. A smile is even present to make it look convincing. I use it as a believable armor against what is slowly brewing at the foot of this reality.

"What's yours is mine, baby!" I wink at him as I briefly pop my head out of the bathroom door.

Laughter echoes across the room, gently crashing into mine here in this small space. The truth is, he doesn't need my money. What he shares with me, I am more than capable of surviving multiple lifetimes, if at all possible. Maybe I don't have a true understanding of how lucky I have been when it comes to that, because I just can't care about the things that won't fulfill me in my death bed.

"What are you up to today?" He asks, the way he always does over breakfast.

I'm not sure if he's okay with my plan but he'll send the cavalry if it means he has to let me go against his will.

He'll hear the truth anyway. "I'm gonna see Bree today."

Then comes silence, an unbounded suspense before his reply. I poke my head out again to see his reaction and find an emotionless man gazing out to the window. I can't read him, as all the other times.

"Okay. Have fun," he says quietly.

My jaw drops, wondering what's the catch. He notices me before his lids fling over his eyes, reading a text message. He's being nonchalant. This is just too easy.

"Get ready and have breakfast," he orders at my frozen form. I'm simply awaiting a screaming battle but I don't think the circumstance will oblige. It's busying itself with something more important, perhaps a phone call. "Ophie!" he re-asserts before I scurry back to the restroom. He's a little distracted but I should take advantage.

CHAPTER TWENTY-ONE

Coming Out Of The Woodworks

I watch my family, and Henry, waving at me by the porch as though I'm the daughter leaving to college for the first time. He fits in so perfectly in that dynamic. For the longest time, I have tried to satisfy this ache to have him in my life, at all cost, against any barricade. It is something born in me, this space meant only for him. I just couldn't betray it by letting him go. I feel like I have misunderstood this pull, as something else other than being my brother. I believe he made a mistake too, thinking he could love me as I am. We shall repair that now. We can. We must.

This is someone's car, backing out of my father's driveway. I'm in it, feeling a slight sense of emancipation from the filtered world they created around me, especially Henry. Questions are eagerly crawling out from the dirt they were buried under. What about Andrew? I'm still reeling from his return. I feel I should keep looking over my shoulders, as long as he's in the same mile radius. Henry appears uninterested in talking about him.

Who are "they"?

What did my mother ever do to Marcus?

And Noah, where has he been?

Why haven't I wondered about this before?

And why does it feel like I can easily answer my own questions.

Right now, I am patriot with no country, or even a godless worshipper. This is me floating down the river, searching for someone to blame for not remembering. I still feel lost. Nothing has changed. No validation of belonging feels like home. I've been looking for an evil with a human face but I might have found it at last, staring back at me right in front of the rear-view mirror.

About fifteen minutes in, I see an accumulation of cars at the downtown crossing. Something must be going on. I think Bree was clever enough to get together outside of town. Somewhere else, her presence would not be on a professional capacity. She will just be Bree, having fun, and maybe a wild time. However, that doesn't fix this traffic problem here in Coupeville.

Banners and streamers embellish the quaint town center, crisscrossing above already narrow lanes. Vendor-lined streets have amassed quite a bit of eager pockets and in return, closing many roads to motor traffic. The weather is just perfect, with a full sun on display, and an awkward spring chill if you're not under a light coat. My speedometer runs boringly at ten miles per hour as countless footsteps pass by me, twice as fast. Nobody seems to be in a great deal of hurry but me. Two cars up, are police officers under bright orange vests, directing the flow. They match the detour signs beneath the light post.

It's my time to cross now. My leisurely acceleration gives me a chance to see the water on my right. The tide is high and many sailboats and rafts sit afloat the Sound. It is as lively there as it is on land. I notice a big sign hovering over the wharf entrance: 'Whidbey Sail Fest'. I wonder if Andrew stayed long enough to take part. I don't see any reason to.

Passing the detour is proving to be more sluggish than the main roads, with the festivities reaching along the alfalfa fields. There are buckets of tulips in different colors, while vendors wave to be noticed. I see stacks of hay with the invisible cameo of reeking animal manure. Even veggies and fruits have their own mini stands. Every farm fare is present yet irrelevant to my day.

I'm slowing down even more and the crowd to my left is drawing my attention. People appear to be handing out clip boards for signatures.

Let's see what the signs say.

I squint my eyes to make it out. Looks like some kind of petition to improve the public library. Sounds like a good cause, if I care.

Not long enough, I see a shadow of an animal on the ground. Luckily, my body reacts before my mind could align to it. I feel my back bounce against the seat, immediately after slamming the brakes to the floor.

Good God!

My screeching tires are still echoing across the rolling hills, after everyone else scrambles in panic. My heart is pounding now. I can hear it in my head. I sure hope I did not just run over a dog. A woman dashes toward the hood of my car, screaming out a name. Meanwhile, I nervously change my gear to park, and get out of my vehicle in haste.

I go around and along my footsteps is a quick prayer. Please don't make me an animal murderer.

There she is, hovering over a furry creature that is crouched on the pavement. On her shivering wrists, dangles part of a severed leash. She cries. The dog's tail suddenly wags and I feel my spirit being lifted away from damnation.

She looks up to me, visibly upset. Wet blue eyes stare back in surprising gratitude, even when I nearly killed her beloved pet.

"I'm sorry! I almost caused you to crash," she tells me.

"Oh," I reply, almost speechless. "I thought I wasn't paying attention."

"No, on the contrary, you were. The dog got away from the leash. Ran off from the other side," says an older male bystander, wearing a wide straw hat.

I look up to find the woman staring at me, forgetting the terrifying ordeal that just happened to her dog. She tilts her head to one side, forcing recognition in her brain. "Do I know you? I swear I saw you —"

My phone rings, invading the solemn astonishment in my body. The woman knows me but I'm afraid to ask how. I scour my pocket and find that it's Bree calling.

"Hey," I answer.

"Girl, forgot to tell you that it's gonna be busy today." She already sounds a bit tipsy.

That didn't take long enough.

"Too late for that. I'm stuck and I almost ran over a dog. But be there as soon as I can," I reveal calmly.

"Oh shit! Are you okay? Is it?" Her high pitch freely escapes my phone for everyone else to hear.

I assure her. "Everything's cool. I'll be there soon."

"Okay! See you real soon. I'm sorry!" Her apology lacks sincerity.

The call ends with someone scurrying from behind me, as I tuck my phone inside my back pocket.

"Babe, what happened?" he inquires with palpable patience, quite like Henry's.

But that voice, every hair on my body jolts up, slowly sustaining a colossal shock after my system finally registers it.

It can't be!

"The leash broke or something, but the lady stopped at just the right moment," she narrates, voice still quivering. "It's okay, baby. You're okay,".

The dog whimpers in the background, while I'm trying to connect the dots of this broken picture behind me. I sense him lowering his body to the ground, to pick up the edgy dog into his arms.

"It's okay, Daddy's here," he consoles, as the dog cries some more.

Noah is here, or his married doppelganger. I wish for the latter. It's wasn't easy to miss her ring finger. I notice those things these days for some odd reasons. Undeniably, that is his voice. It's the bottom line we're going to run into.

Conversations about the almost crash thrive within the flurry of activities. I hear them but the turmoil in my mind is louder. Every will inside of me is coaching me to run away. This is the only method to remedy this reality, this promised future collapsing before my eyes. I may not be able to recover from this.

How dare he retreat back to my past, where he knows I will never go looking for him? How clever!

"Miss?" I feel a tap on my shoulder. It's his. And I wonder if Noah already recognizes my form - where my bones curve and where his touch can be wildly felt. Not there, at the spot of his hand.

I turn around in a slothful pace. Every second is painful.

His eyes stretch vertically, signifying a heightened sense of disbelief, more than any acknowledgement of my presence before him. An o forms in the middle of his neutral smile. I scan him from head to toe. The markings on his arms are gone. Not even scars and residuals unless he went through an impeccable and costly cosmetic procedure. He dresses differently than he did when he was with me. More formal. It appears as though he put on a little bit of weight as well, judging from his freshly rounded face.

"No way!" He finally puts his shock into words, but quietly so only I could hear.

The woman walks to my side, having noticed our tensed interaction. "Pardon our rudeness," she apologizes, while elbowing Noah. She stretches out a hand, while the other cradles a fawn Pomeranian. "I'm

Stella by the way. And this is my husband, Dylan." She makes a side glance at him, schooling his manners.

Dylan, such a far cry from his alias back in Seattle, from when our love was really just a foray of his boredom. I now gather. The need to be by myself is enticing more than the time I first heard his voice, after a very long while.

"Dylan now, huh?" I couldn't help myself.

He smirks before responding. "So, you recognize me now?" His tone is disdainful, maybe even some hint of anger lurking around the periphery.

The nerve! His question provokes more internal inquiries from me. What does he mean? Did he think I hit my head and wiped out every memory of him? How could he think it's that easy?

I take his hand, clammy and unfriendly skin feigning innocence. They no longer felt like the one that stirred a deep love in me, some long months ago.

"Why wouldn't I?" That's my reply in the most cynical tone I could dribble out.

"Wait? You two know each other? How?" She becomes curious.

"Yeah, Dylan! How do we know each other?" The furrow in my brows is an indicator of my angry meter.

I gape at Noah and his whole aura of many alterations since we last saw each other. The confirmation of a previous meeting is there on full display with his eerie stare. What isn't, is the love, an all-consuming, and deeply rooted connection that felt like centuries old. It is absent now, along with the mystery shrouding his whole form. What remains is just a searing indifference from him, almost like he's furious at me. It's as if Noah died and came back as this brand-new Dylan. It might as well be true in every sense of the word.

"We all grew up in town," he finally musters.

"That's great, honey!" She claps her hands in excitement. For two seconds she attends to the dog and realizes right away the impoliteness of the distraction. "Sorry, just so glad my baby is okay. Well, why don't you join us for lunch? We're on our way to the docks," she invites, before shooting a glance at Dylan. She faces me again. "Uhmm..." Her voice drops, entertaining an uncertainty. She doesn't know my name.

"Ophelia," Noah's incarnation quickly breaks the awkward silence.

"Right. I'm sorry. My name is Ophelia."

"Like I said, I think I've seen you before. You look very familiar." She eyes me with scrutiny.

I shake my head. "I'm a common face."

She laughs and then shrugs, giving up her fleeting suspicion of my identity. But I couldn't help the curiosity she planted in me. How did she see my face? Not Noah's phone? He knows better than to keep my photos for his wife to see.

"So, what do you say?" Stella prods again. "Will you join us?"

I turn my gaze at Noah, who has surprisingly remained calm this whole time. There is no retaliation in his expression.

"I'm afraid I'm gonna pass for now. I 'm actually meeting someone in Freeland," I reply, with grave emphasis towards her waiting form. "But thank you very much."

"Are you sure?" Noah asks. He sounds relieved.

"Next time then?" she adds. "Dylan can just get in touch with you."

"Sure, Dylan knows where I live," I reply, giving Noah a side glance. "He has my number. Unless he changed it."

I think of an exit strategy while I look back to the traffic behind my car. "I think I'm causing a back-up now," I tell them.

Thank you, God!

"Okay. Get in touch though. Please." Not long after, she traps me inside her embrace, the dog sandwiched between us.

Please make it stop.

I pull away to see Noah's beat expression, the one he was so good at masking earlier. Good! I thought he was a robot for a second.

"See you later, Ophie," he bids, while backing away from our huddled form. Afterwards, the festivities and its bustle return to baseline, even though I'm still navigating this cloud around me, or rather I'm floating in it.

In my car, I'm slowly re-orienting myself back to today, the 21st of May. Okay, I think I got that correct. I'm here still, as myself. Everything happened so fast but I managed to move my car to the side of the road and only half-remember our farewell, before retrieving some crucial information across the street. A whirlwind swept through this part of town and brought in an unsuspecting dog, half of its owner, and more importantly my one true love, or at least I thought he was. I'm beginning to believe the curse that Andrew placed on me yesterday. I'll be all alone. I'll die the same way. Not only did I discover he's been in my hometown this whole time, he's also married.

FUCKING MARRIED, for the people in the back.

Somewhere in the midst of all that, I heard her ask Noah where their daughter was. The knife had already stabbed me at that point. It was just a matter of which way to twist it to.

Seeing him again would have meant all of my Christmases coming at once, but the circumstances were different. He knows me and doesn't deny that at least. I'm connecting all the dots now, including the reason why he's been so secretive and making phone calls behind my back, towards the end of our relationship (if you can even call it that).

I feel like I'm at square one again, uncertainties crashing into me in waves from a stormy sea. I have disregarded a lot of rational signs because I loved him and damn it, I still do. There's no way to know how to deal with this new information. The thought is grappling, sending me back to a darker version of Ophelia. I should feel sick that I'm rather inclined to gut his mind and see what's in there. I need to know why he would take the time to light a fire in me, only so I could burn. How could he? He's got a family here.

Yet how we met was a lie of course. No, we didn't grow up together but what if there's some truth to that? Was he the jock Bree was alluding to? Perhaps we were together as young kids but I disappeared after the accident. He may have been looking for me this whole time.

They found you after you were in the local news, at the time of Andrew's political race.

Was it him? The one Henry has been protecting me from even when all efforts were in vain? He found me anyway. Henry was so engrossed in Landree's pregnancy debacle that he almost didn't care about us getting (back) together.

Noah's been here, hiding right under my nose and I know Henry would possess such a knowledge about his whereabouts. He claims he's protecting me. Is it from this horrific reality? I can't let him know I'm on to him, or he'll thwart my plans to find out more. The piece of paper is still in my hand. I wanted to keep it at first and thought better of it, then changed my mind again.

Earlier, I felt an ache of desperation as I watched Noah and his wife walk hand in hand into the afternoon mirage. Underneath their feet are broken chards of his empty promises to me, lying helpless and mute.

"Always have, always will."

My ass!

If anything, I deserve an explanation, the simplified version of the truth. He owes me that, even just the "why."

So after they left, I crossed my trembling fingers and the busy street, in the hopes of finding information about Noah. If there's a chance his name was on that clipboard, I'll take it. At first, she regarded me from head to toe, the middle-aged lady with greying locks and black-trimmed, round specs. Before she could interrogate me, I told her I'm from the Davis clan and she seemingly appeared less suspicious. For what it's worth, that should help me get what I want from around here. She handed me the clipboard as I deliberately scanned for Noah's name under Dylan. In the background, her spiel about the library and its expansion floated behind the invisible wall in front of me. Her voice is muffled, as I slowly write my name while memorizing the address of a certain Dylan Mason, just five lines above the blank space.

I'm back here in the car, clutching the key to finding Noah but completely fearful of what else I might discover between shovels. It's as if I'm certain that I have buried something here and sifting the soil while looking for a few answers, might reveal a plethora of dark truths that were meant to stay hidden.

I'm utterly terrified. Of what? I don't know. The same goes for the why.

I have got to go now. Bree has been blowing up my phone to its death and I still haven't decided whether or not I should come clean to her.

CHAPTER TWENTY-TWO

Frederick

What the fuck is that!

A brief knocking startles me, before I realize it's from the passenger side. I look up to inspect and see a hand waving at me, inviting me out. I usually don't entertain strangers banging at my car but what the heck! The street is full and some vendors are already awaiting the next development of this scene. My previous encounter with Noah placed me in their radars.

I push the door out, this time not in the same haste as an hour ago. The gentleman meets me in front of the vehicle, all rugged but also formal. I have a sense he's not from around here, a visitor or a transplant. His sling bag is noticeably thick of documents, and it catches my attention even before his facial expression.

Hi, I'm Fred," he greets nervously. His clammy hand confirms it.

"Ophelia," I answer pointblank, my attention caught by his unforced charm.

"I know," he reveals.

What in the world! Who is this fellow? I should be surprised but my body hasn't recovered from the shock it has stockpiled earlier on. I'm still on top of the summit, on this mountain peak of disbelief, distress, and all kinds of confusion.

"Let me guess," I tell him, in my tone of disinterest. My arms are slowly crossing against my chest as I fearlessly regard him with this empty confidence. "You grew up with me too, right? Did we date?"

I begin to laugh, lips still pursed with tension.

"No, hardly. I know of you from my dad," he whispers.

"Okay?"

"Listen," he adds, while pulling something from the front pocket of his bag. "Here is my card and credentials. I write for the Seattle times but I'm actually working on something on the side."

I accept the card, just a minimally-thought of design on low cost paper material. It reads Frederick Kirkland, reporter. The Seattle Times emblem hovers boldly above it. Behind the card is a wider and laminated document. His journalist credential is revealed with a picture ID, after I slide it to view. It's him undeniably, the same eye features beneath a thick pair of corrective lenses. The same nervous smile was also caught on this photograph, revealing just a glimpse of his pearly white teeth.

"You don't waste time," I say, while returning the items to him.

"I have some experience, speaking with the others. I know I have to present myself from a place of trust. Considering what happened to all of you."

Huh? I'm more lost than enlightened. The "others"? What do you mean others?

What happened to us?

I have a feeling this has nothing to do with my quiet warfare real life, whichever one that might be. Other angles remain suspects: Marcus' death, my mother, Andrew, and even Henry.

"It's okay." He comes closer. "I know this may have brought back some of your most painful years but I need your help closing this chapter. Send everyone else responsible behind bars. If not for me, at least for my dad."

"I'm confused," I say to him. "Nothing you're saying makes sense or relates to me."

"I'll tell you everything you need to know." His tone opens up a new level of certainty that he was too bashful to show earlier. "In exchange for your personal account. A statement."

I don't know what to do, say, nor feel. On one part, he could just be this serial killer luring women out of the crowd before doing the deed. Documents can be falsified and that is a fact. Yet the flip side of that, his genuine goal, or even just his mere curiosity affects me as a willing recipient. Somehow, we're in the same lane of unknowing, both contending for knowledge and parching for the truth. Mine would be for my whole life that was lost in one night of trauma, along with Noah. His could be for something entirely different. Here is someone who seems willing to give me answers while everyone else tiptoes around me like I'm this broken glass.

"Okay." My words are meant to convince both him and I. It's going to be alright. I'll be fine.

****

"This is Ophelia Anderson, previously Davis of the Minnesota clan - founders of The Disciples of Light..."

That's Fred, speaking to his recorder, across the table, inside this quaint café. We're a few miles out of town and my trail should be cold by now, just as this coffee I have ignored for the last fifteen minutes. In the background is a buzzing sound of retired people making small talk and killing their purposeless time with each other. I'm in this mental space, far away from the reporter gibberish across the table. Fred is setting up our interview.

A lot of things should have flooded my mind on the way here but it was rather the opposite, as if it knew I had to be in a clear state to receive what I'm about to find out from this stranger.

"How did you find me?" The question just spurred out of my cup of anticipation.

"I put up feelers around town. They call me if a name comes up," he replies, rather willingly. "I've been here since I read about your mother's death. Just waiting for you to turn up."

Fred's response is brimming with confidence and credibility, even in the realm outside of knowing him. Is this a reporter or a charisma thing? I'm almost left with no choice but to believe what he said.

"How'd you know who to look for?" I probe again.

He smirks a little bit before replying. "I didn't know I'd be answering the questions."

I laugh with hesitation.

He continues, "But I spoke with your mother a few weeks before she passed. She gave me a lot of information, including the state you're going to be in."

My forehead wrinkles.

"Ophelia, I know you don't remember. I know that when Marcus died everything suddenly became new to you."

I open my mouth for a second but I'm processing this revelation in my head, in the fastest pace my permeable brain could.

"Why still talk to me then? I'm useless," I tell him, as I gather the edges of my napkin into a ball.

"It's a long shot, I know, but I feel like I have to," he says quietly. "Your mind is gone but everything else is still there. Your body revolts the same way to the things you feared before, yet no longer remember. When I said the Minnesota and the cult, I saw it. You're scared. I've seen this before in others."

That's it!

"I'm not your experiment. This is a waste of my time and yours," I tell him angrily, as I wave the server to bring me the bill for my stale coffee and untouched croissant.

"Wait!" He springs himself across the table, hand over mine. "Please," he implores again, with his harshly humane gaze.

I decide to sit back down on the fawn-colored chair and release my hand from his grip.

"You better give me a good reason why I should stay," I whisper in anger.

I watch him take his seat in the calmest demeanor, noticing the server now in close proximity to our table. He first attends to her conversation before sending her away. She takes a quick glance to my direction and then leaves.

"I'm sorry. I'm just desperate to find out what you know about your mother and her comrades. Let me re-focus this conversation from a different angle." He rectifies the situation before sipping his coffee.

I give him my piercing eyes. "Keep me listening then."

He shifts his posture, even rolling his shoulders to relax. He realizes the recorder is still off and hurries to press the red button. His wrists remain on the table, knuckles cracking simultaneously. He takes a deep breath and then looks at me in what appears to be a graceful pain.

"My mother was also from Minnesota." His introduction brings in a lump in his throat that he's obliged to swallow quickly before he continues. "She was in the same Disciples clan as your mother."

My mother?

"I mean, to put it out clearly, they were in the cult together. You and your brother were raised there. I mean, we were kind of in the same situation. Your dad left your mom and she joined after. I don't think Mr. Davis was aware of what was going on at first, not until you guys ran off. Years later, my mother kind of watched her life slip away and knew she had to get out. She asked my dad for help. They were already divorced long before I was even born and he had custody of me. Court ruled that she wasn't mentally capable of taking care of a child."

Cult? It's sillier than it sounds.

"Anyway, she fled and sought help from my dad. She committed suicide later on, just like your mother. My dad didn't know right away that she was with the Disciples. He thought she was just addicted to drugs." He shifts, possibly allowing the pain of her mother's memory to roll off without being felt. "After her death, my dad went digging and digging until he uncovered something he wasn't supposed to, information about the clan. Including what they did to her. All the abuses, especially to the children born into it. It was horrific. They drive them to their deaths. He had all the information to make something big out of this one. National news. I guess a small-town sheriff had a lot of credibility. He had old Disciple members behind him, politicians. Then he was killed by a wildly mysterious car accident. The case is still open but cold."

Hearing what he said, I remember something that is drawn out from a distant and almost unreachable memory.

"Henry Anderson, my husband. Was he in it?"

"As a matter of fact, all three of you were. But he wouldn't give me the time of day, even warned me not to get close to you. I understand the fear of speaking but the dangers of keeping quiet is just as bad."

Henry! My God!

How does this guy know so much? But what if it's a trap? What if he's the one Henry has been protecting me from all this time?

"I'm sorry. I just need your help. I think they killed my dad. It's a long shot, proving what they did to him but if we could just light a fire in their tail. All the horrific things they did to former members. To you. To Marcus. What if somehow when enough people speak out, we could place them under a microscope? They're still out there, doing the same things they've been doing for years.

"Do you even know how you sound right now?" I interject, feeling the uneasiness blow through my core.

I can't take it, this overdrive of information short-circuiting past the proper channels, to be comprehended by my unequipped mind. Am I in a movie? Is this a sick prank? First, Noah, and then this cult story - they all seem too far-reaching. But are they?

Through the corner of my eye, I see a glimpse of his disconcerted expression, even shaking his head at one point or another.

"I can't do much if you don't believe me. But just think about it? Why would I know so much about you? I can lend you my dad's journals, his recordings, including the ones from your mother when he spoke to her and when I did. These are insider information. You were pretty much under the radar until you started dating the politician..."

They found you after you were on national television with Andrew.

There it is again, schooling my senses on the authenticity of Henry's warnings. Should I be cautious of this Fred character? Though he seems trustworthy, I have yet to validate his intentions.

"My mother. She's the ringleader in all these? Is this what you're trying to tell me?"

Through the barrage of doubts he's been receiving from me, I see a spark of hope flicker in his eyes. He must be glad he's finally piqued my interest, or that I took the bait - whichever is the real story here.

He clears his throat in a restrained fashion before answering my question. "Well, sort-of. She was the leader's main partner. In fact, they were married, only in cult ceremony of course. You have a step-dad by way of the Disciple law."

This is becoming more and more like a tangled mess. I feel better off just hanging on to a blank sheet than holding memories of this unsubtle disarray. It's too much. I'm dizzy from all the revelations floating above these murky waters. Beneath them is a trap, ready to drown me in confusion. I can't grasp anything, these words, and the suspicions screaming from the back of my head, like how he found me so quickly when I have been under the dome of Henry's protection all these years.

"Aren't you gonna ask me more about your mom? I mean, besides her role in all these. You spent your younger years with the Disciples and to be more forward with you, those are the information I need," he adds, with a little bit more urgency in his tone.

Now I'm back in this defensive state, against his penetrating manner of inquiry. The compassion that almost bewildered me at first glance, is now lost. Here is a man on the cusp of hopelessness, following crumbs no matter how stale they may be. Who knows how long, but I've been his shining idea of hope and he's doing everything in his meager power to make sure I stay that way. I'm sorry for the death of his father but I am not responsible for avenging his name against these cult people. My mother is already rotting in her grave and whether or not she did horrific things in her lifetime, her sentence has been paid. As a matter of fact, she rode the bullet train on the way there by committing suicide. Yes, I knew about it, even when the town was almost paid to keep quiet about the details of her passing.

The idea of a stepdad sounds bogus. I would have met him by now but I wish him well if there's truth to that.

All these are just ricochets of my past from which the music is abrasive, bland, and uninteresting. There is no point to lingering here. My faith in Noah and I's love have been destroyed by a certain Dylan, drifting by unsuspectingly. That doesn't mean that I have stopped enduring this mental torture surrounding his disappearance and resurfacing.

"I told you before and I'm telling you again. I don't know. No memory! I have nothing to give you." I push my seat back to stand abruptly, meaning to leave the way I was supposed to earlier. The anger in my voice has recoiled back to our table after scattering across the dining hall. I see heads turning, from the corner of my eye. "This is a waste of my time," I raise my voice, as I rifle through the contents of my small purse. I pull out a twenty-dollar bill and toss it next to the coffee cup.

I watch his stern gaze thawing in the midst of my refined outburst. He remains seated, frustration collecting inside his joined fists that are trembling on the white linen.

"You're lying," he addresses my denial, calm and firm. His gape is still latched on to mine. "You know what happened, why your brother brought you here..." The elusive gurgle in his tone, I caught that pretty quickly. He's trying to coerce me into telling him while his body retaliates against his own fear. Of what exactly, I can't be sure. "I can guarantee that, Ophelia! You know but you're scared to admit it."

I release my scarf from the back of the chair, while letting his words bounce off my rigid front, like splashes of harmless moisture.

"Come on! I need your help. I need you," I hear him say, while the soles of my feet are enduring all the anxieties I've collected from the beginning of our meeting. I walk slow towards the door.

Despair and obsession are both taking turns carrying his voice towards my locked ears.

"Maybe remembering it all will fix you!" He yells, when I finally grab the doorknob, that is just a few steps from the table.

Fix me? That went past my slim filter. Who the hell does he think he is, telling me that I need to be repaired? He has no idea what he's talking about! And with every effort going against what I'm about to do, I still turn my head in response to his passive taunting. I let it linger there, just above my shoulder. He notices my frown and brazenly gets himself up to come for me.

When he's finally close, the air of his sigh brushes my neck, warmly but with discomfort. He moves his face behind my hair and begins to whisper.

"You know what I mean. All the pills. The crazy house. Doctors telling you that you have a mental problem. What was it? Multiple personality disorder? Seeing things, hearing things? People? While everyone around you is pretending that all is fine. They're not willing to tell you what's really going on or what happened when you were young." His voice rings with confidence and with it, is an aggressive undertone. "Meanwhile here I am, ready to help you so we both could find the end to our sufferings."

"Fuck you!" I reply, clutching the knob harder. My livid presence has been refused by his almost expert reaction. Has he taunted enough people during his time in reporting, that he seems connivingly unfazed by me, by himself? "Write about that!"

"You're welcome," he says while taking a step back, smirk forming at the edges of his lips. He raises both his hands before continuing. "Suit yourself. You know how to get a hold of me now when you're ready. When you finally want to get out of this prison."

I pull the door open, unable to take any more of this mind games. The skin down my back clenches as I bear the cold assault of the late afternoon breeze.

"And Ophelia?" He calls out, in what seems like a closing statement.

I oblige him one last time.

"When everything comes crashing down on us, we turn to our thoughts to help us shut out the world. To keep us safe from memories of trauma. But the mind is a dangerous place. Don't let yourself be trapped in there forever."

And I finally saunter out of the café, with his voice still jabbing my neck without mercy. The evening is coming sooner than usual, sensing the sunlight's pretense of being innocent, even when it isn't.

Maybe he is right. In some ways, I feel an upheaval budding steadily from within me. Yes, as if I'm preparing for an eruption of sorts that belongs to either discovery or further oblivion.

The rest are just products of an imaginative thought, quite like Frederick's. In the midst of all this, I know I am my only reprieve.

CHAPTER TWENTY-THREE

Following Stale Crumbs

The rain here pays no homage to the authority of seasons. It is spring yet the ground is soaking in precipitation and the smell of damp mulch. I only had two hours of sleep, away from my spookily comfortable bed at my father's home. On the way to finally see Bree last night, I found myself here instead. I was running down the clock in this dirt road off the main highway. This was last night and I'm still here, making notice of the heavy fir branches stooping down with their water baggage.

I found a spot in front of a small shed and I've been parked here since. Tracings of a campfire lie next to it, with the tip of an ax still buried inside a log. There are red cups filling past the rim of a garbage can, and some strewn along the sidelines. The wooden bench has sustained the mild storm decently, much better than me. I was not equipped for a freezing and thunderous stake out. Though, my dad's extremely furnished car did not disappoint. I was able to find a small fleece blanket and a canvas jacket for warmth. I would have been an immediate alarm, had anybody decided to come this way. Yet there has been no sign of life outside the porch.

I'm struck by an old but also unfamiliar feeling of being detached from the world. I have no grip on anything. My strange encounter with the reporter yesterday is all but a distant nightmare. His accusations are unfounded but an upsurge of fear soaks my bearings as I say that. What if they were true? Yes, I have forgotten everything before his tragedy but we haven't been able to explain the gaps in my memory following that, and why neither Jessica nor Henry won't approve of my friendship with Kara.

He's getting to me. Fred's manipulations have found a way to lodge inside my skin and perplex my already muddled reality. He's lying. I'm sure of it now. Henry has been protecting me from him, all this time. I should call him and Bree. They're probably worried sick by now but I can't find a way to. My phone is dead, along with its navigation system.

And in the next minute, two bouncing animals suddenly emerge from the hood of my car.

Holy hell!

I take a few seconds to make them out from beneath the wet windshield, before I catch a glimpse of the two dogs play fighting over a slender wooden stick. One has the other end in its bite and the bigger retriever chases it. Both tails are wagging, both enjoying their short but unrelenting taste of freedom.

"Louie! Rusty!" A woman's voice escapes the small crack of the screen door.

The golden retrievers heed her call and prance to the porch. An older woman emerges, feet on the tan, fabric top doormat. Her pink curlers are a very bright contrast to the earthy surroundings. She wears a white robe over a standard pinstripe pajama. She fixes her attention to her pets, both self-sufficiently scratching their paws on the yellow towel she laid out for them. I become rather impressed by their abilities to clean themselves that I failed to notice her serious ogle.

I didn't realize she saw me but I have no problem waving at her. This is what I came here for anyway, to get some clarity, answers that I wouldn't find by staying in the shadows.

She continues to stare while I find the zipper handle to my dad's oversize coat. Once I'm bundled up, I pull the handle to spread the door open. I immediately get clouted by both dogs. They continue to sniff my thighs as I make my way to the skeptical expression of the woman.

"Hi there!" she greets, sunnily. It's a welcomed surprise, the way she shifts her face from mistrusting to warm. I notice her medium complexion immediately, skin still taut and smooth, even in her age. Her face is framed by short curly locks. Not sure if they're natural, judging from the remaining curlers above her head. Wrinkles are gracefully drawn on the sides of her eyes and some on her chin. I am in awe of her whole appearance, seemingly peppered with wisdom rather than age. I won't doubt that she's older than she appears.

"Sit!" She orders the obedient animals. "Sorry about them. Too friendly sometimes," she adds, while petting the dogs that are now composed beside her. There is a trace of serenity kindred to her raspy tone, that is an absolute enticement of home.

"Good morning, Ma'am," I respond, extending out a greeting to her friendly form. It takes me a minute to figure out what to say until I decide on the obvious. "I'm a friend of Dylan." But what I really wanted to tell her is that I am looking for Noah, my old lover who ditched me at a hospital in Mexico. I'm here for answers.

Meanwhile, she browses my face, down to my damp shoes, grip persisting over my hand. She must have found something affable in my whole form because I notice her body roll back by some cognizance.

"But of course," she says with pure tenderness. "Why don't you come in?"

I'm taken aback by her immediate kindness, to a stranger no less. "Huh? Are you sure?"

"Of course! Aren't you here for the annual memorial? The return address is here but his house is five minutes away."

I'm confused but decide to go along. "Yes. The memorial," as I slowly cross the threshold towards the unknown.

We reach the foyer. An antique mirror captures our faces as she's trying to say something. It's held by a golden metal frame that has sustained some scratches from its years.

"Give me a minute and I'll get him over here. Who should I say is looking for him?"

"Gosh! I'm sorry. My name is Ophelia. How rude of me." I turn to her, my apologetic face now painted on the mirror's reflection.

"It's okay, dear," she assures, tapping my stiff shoulder. "And I am her grandma. Call me Vita."

She ushers me into what I assume would be the receiving room, our footsteps echoing through the wide halls. Then, we reach an elevated space at the end of the corridor.

"Make yourself comfortable while I give Dylan a buzz. Would you like some refreshments?" Her eyes drizzle in radiance while speaking. This kindness is surely wanted after a night alone.

"I think I'm okay for now. Thank you," is my reply.

"Okay, I'll be back in a jiffy!"

I laugh and also feel bewildered by her spirit as I note her animated footwork leaving me. She seems to be someone I would want to speak to about anything, a woman with many thrilling stories to tell in her lifetime.

Now that I'm all alone, I take notice of the home's interior, not to mention its jarring stillness. I felt that walking in. The thought draws goosebumps along my shoulders with speculations on how many people perished here. Uninhabited thoughts, these are needed distractions from my looming meeting with Noah. I wonder if she resides here alone.

All the walls are equally in an outdated shade of cream. Large and colorful oil paintings were seemingly from a grave attempt to revive the style lost in its weathered years. The soles of my feet remain glued to the golden oak flooring as I scan the remainder of this restored bungalow. The moldings below are an exact color match. And the smell, that chalky scent has been my acquaintance since being welcomed in.

I draw my attention to the wide steps, three to be exact, and I allow my footsteps to wander towards that direction. The low platform as I now gather, houses a living space above it. I'm in here now, pleasantly astonished by the wide glass window, and the unobstructed view of Mount Baker it offers. I even notice a dull reflection of my gaping mouth.

Just, wow!

I linger there, longer than I expected.

This waiting, not knowing what Vita's doing at this moment, is opening up my body for anxiety's callous delight. What is taking so long? It has been about twenty minutes. I have become a bit tired of standing, and need the couch to take away my exhaustion. I take a couple of steps towards it and allow my bottom to fall down the soft trenches of its foam. Looking around, I finally realize how wide this furniture expands to, almost the length of the wall. The chocolate colored cross-sectional forms an L, with the shorter end flushed against the scenic window.

Picture frames decorate the walls here, through and through. Magazines scatter above the leather ottoman, at the center of the room. Ahead of me, is a flat screen television, maybe 80 inches in size. Below it, crates of toys and stray Lego pieces still litter on the floor. Half-consumed water and soda bottles rest on the narrow window ledge, all cloaked in condensation. Throw blankets are tousled next to stacks of pillows. They're stored in one corner of the room, all riddled with sleep and familial joy.

I imagine the many days and nights spent here by the love of my life, with the other ones he chose to love him back. I am not one of them. The sinkhole has swallowed me up again, of this grief that seems rooted from forever ago, even when we just spent months together. I can't pretend that I don't know who those toys belong to either. I pray to whatever god is willing to listen. Give me another dose of amnesia after today. I'm already certain. There's no starting over after all this.

The portrait of Noah with his wife, I can't believe I missed it when first walking in. I was more engrossed by the aged oak beams, running across the vaulted ceiling. Shall I inspect it closer? Of course, I will. After all, I am a glutton for punishment.

There is my love, such unbearable bliss igniting all over his face. He is holding her close, the woman whose name I have already forgotten, and a baby fresh from the womb. Another photograph of him receives my eerie attention. It is posted in the same size frame as the first. He appears scruffier here but in a refined sense of sultry. Noah sits above the hood of a vintage Mustang, face looking far beyond the camera lens.

I miss them a lot, the notches above his perfect jaws. The sensation is digging a pit in my gut, a slow but excruciating excavation. I have memorized the impression of his stubble on my hands. The cross tattoo still lives on his neck in this photo. The V on his collar dips low to his impeccably carved chest, the same spot where he loved and then unloved me. I feel his skin melt into mine once more. This is the version of Noah I remember.

Unfortunately for me, it was just a phase in Dylan's life that I loved and succumbed to. Quickly. Dangerously. It's mind boggling, how he got rid of the tattoos very fast. Most of all, how menacing he's been able to create a storyline and presented it to me as the very reality I hung on to for a while. Henry was spot-on with this one. I should have listened.

To my right is another photograph wall, a time and weather-beaten corner. This is a little more out of date than Noah's special shrine. The sepia prints are smaller and are mounted to the wall by wooden tacks, probably placed there by amateur hands. Some edges are torn and a few are stained by some dried-off moisture. The lower photos are mostly wrinkled Polaroids but the faces remain recognizable. I scan them with intention, making notice of Vita's solo shot in her younger years. The rest of them have one element in common, football players.

And then I freeze, eyes succumbing to a mental burden. I identify the icy smile of my own brother. It's really him. His remote gape is indebted to a deeper emotional cargo, that probably belongs to me. He's gone but he still lives here, in Vita's home of all places. A rush of speculations reaches my thoughts but I'm not done unearthing this minefield of information.

One. Two. Three. Four. Five. Six—

Eight pictures, I spot eight pictures of my brother with Henry in it, both flaunting the same pose in all of them. Football was their shared victory, at least on the surface. It's not too far-fetched to assume they were both in leadership, both in the frontlines with the trophies. But what are these pictures doing here? There's a connection I'm not seeing. I keep wondering what I'm missing. What is it?

The gods hear my prayer. I steer my eyes. The most illuminating discovery arrives. Noah.

Of course. What else could it be?

He's there too with everyone else. Their jerseys match the hat Henry left at the crash site a few days back. My dead brother, Henry, and my lost lover were once kept in a pleat of the same past.

I let the revelation froth through the incumbency of a dangerous shock. It's looming, like a gun to my head, but the adrenaline from this unearthing is the violent rudder that has become unstoppable.

I widen my search, taking me to the bottom half of the collage. Polaroid prints occupy its surface. They're coaxing my attention. The first one is of Noah again, arousing some deep electricity from my veins. It never fails. My old lover, already in arresting candor, even while still trapped in the innocence of youth. His eyes glimmer in inebriation, love struck for this girl behind the ranunculus bouquet. I inspect them one by one, curious of her and what she might look like. Maybe it's the same woman he married. There's this one of her facing the camera at last. I notice the dark pixie hair immediately, so young, and so relaxed. Her dimples adorn the boundaries of her detached smile. I'd die for the freedom in her laughter, but not the prison in her eyes. Once upon a time, she was me.

I am her!

I read the notes at the bottom of the instant prints. 'Always have, always will'. The ink has bled through the pores of the paper, and the penmanship was a futile attempt at cursive writing. But it's beautiful, everything about them. The photographs tell a story of a boy, a girl, a sincere but inexperienced love, and their faith that nothing will ever change what they have.

She has a similar depth to her laughter, the way I was with Noah. That undiluted elation, they belong to me. She is me, the younger version of myself.

Noah and Ophelia forever, how could I bury that into the deep ruts of my mind? Why did I forget the only love that deserves to be remembered?

"I thought you'd marry the jock." Bree was referring to him, not Henry.

It's him, Noah, also known as Dylan. He has been able to untangle this protective knit outside myself after Henry, a feat that Andrew didn't even come close enough to taste. It is remarkable, even near impossible, the way my heart and body recognized its old and only throne. Months ago, I fell too hard, too quick. But all of that was really just a rejoining and restoring of throbbing pieces, that are awaiting rebirth. We have already met in the past, in a lifetime that was stolen from me. I'm stunned by the unraveling of this. If I was as madly in love with him before as now, it all makes perfect sense. But his old face has yet to return and be remembered. I love Noah but I hate him as Dylan.

I continue to trace the rows of memories like dots. The face of a friend stops me in my tracks. Two young girls wasting away in enjoyment. I can hear their laughter while balancing on the floating driftwood, hand in hand. The rest of the shots were of them two, down to the bottom. I spot a few taken at a beach during low tide, both with buckets of clam harvests. The last one, they were on a grassy field. Kara was in the widest grin I've seen her display, locking my feet up on her shoulders. My arms were spread while above her, awaiting the shot, embracing the moment. Perhaps I already knew that we will never get it back.

Maybe relief, it's what my mind is screaming after finding out that the people around me, have always been there. Yet there's also this wrenching vulnerability aching to be heard because I just found out that I've been manipulated to eat up what they fed.

"I always wondered when you'll come back so I can tell you that it's not your fault, what happened to Marcus and Kara. I know you blame yourself," that's the sound of Vita's voice behind me.

I turn around to see her expression and the recognizable tenderness remains domestic in her gaze. All the while, a battle ensues from deep within me - between disbelief and confusion.

"Blame myself for what? What about Kara?" I ask her, as my confusion causes her to recoil, dropping a black leaflet to the floor.

I pick it up to give her, but the words magnetize my attention before I could.

The Annual Bonfire

In loving memory of Kara Mason & Marcus Davis

Always in our hearts...

I don't need to read the rest. I failed to detect the connection at first.

"Kara's gone? She was with Marcus?" I mumble to myself as answers fill some of the blank spaces in my mind. Without question, we are talking about Kara, whom I just saw days ago.

It was her name after my brother's, on the road sign. My best friend, she died with him that night. But I just saw her. Although sparingly, her presence has been irrefutable throughout the years.

"Sweetie." She comes to my aid, enveloping my shoulder in her embrace.

We find ourselves on the couch, my eyes welling with tears as she continues to console my horrified profile. This knowing and discovering, has collected the stronghold around me. I have lost the strength to prop myself back up again.

"It's okay, my dear. I'm here for you." She tucks a bunch of flyaway strands to the back of my ear, while oxygen is being ruthlessly impounded from my lungs. My body vibrates at its own retaliation not to cry. "Dylan may think otherwise. Just give him time," she adds.

So, he blames me for Kara's death. He wanted to avenge her by making me fall for him, intending to pull the rug from underneath me once I'm in deep. What was she to him? Just doesn't make sense.

I tug away from her hold so I can face this warm façade. Right then, the edges of her tight grin melts immediately to a frown. She sees it in my expression, this feeling lost in understanding, drifting between spaces of time that are out of chronology. She sees my pain and perhaps she has an inkling of its profundity.

"What happened? I don't understand. Do you know what happened to me? So Kara and..."

Vita interrupts my rantings, sliding her gentle hands underneath my trembling elbows.

"It's okay," she consoles. "I'll tell you what I can."

I shuffle my form, planting my heavy feet deep into the floorboards, legs spread to support my elbows. I bury my face inside my hands, praying for the darkness to shed some light.

"Kara was my granddaughter," she reveals.

I'm dazed. Is that an acceptable reaction? I tilt my neck to discern any possibility of a lie from her face, but I'm met with utter transparency.

"Kara was Noah's sister," Vita confirms, accompanied by a suspenseful music pulling her hoarse voice in every direction. I'm the only one who can hear it.

You mean Dylan's sister?

I don't know why I'm blown away by the shock at the obvious. Why else would her photos be all over the house?

"Why were they all in the car? Henry? I mean why would my brother drive away when he's had a lot to drink?" I shrug, trying to understand the logic of their decision. "I mean, nobody even tried to stop him?" Every word, I lay them all in haste, urging her unguarded body language to speak only the truth.

I watch her, patiently awaiting the calmness to soothe my emotions. We link gazes as her fingers stroke the greys and blacks in her hair. The curlers are gone now, and all that's left of this woman in front of me is the impression of a polished family matriarch, for whom I feel a great deal of trust.

She sniffles before answering my question. "You were missing. I don't know but nobody had seen you all night." She shakes her head, arms spread out in resignation. "They thought you were at home but he —" She stops, sensing that her words must tiptoe around my explosive eggshells. She's referring to Noah. I know.

I cock my head up to his photograph behind us, the one I'm eagerly familiar with. "You mean him?"

She nods. "Yes, him. He couldn't get a hold of you. They were celebrating that night, all of them. Marcus made it to the NFL, like we all knew he would. They were all here, out back," she recounts, pointing to the wide glass window. "Henry too. Drinking, even when I wasn't agreeable to it. Having fun. Laughing. Like what kids do. They realized they hadn't seen you in a while, thought you were just somewhere in the house. They called my grandkid too. Maybe you went with him. You two, you two..." She pauses, running a thumb down my cheek. "You were inseparable. Two peas in a pod. But he didn't know where you went, not even in his room. You were still there before he went with his dad to pick up yours from the airport."

And there I am, grasping at invisible wisps of memories. But nothing. There's nothing to find.

"Are any of these juggling your memory?" She asks with kind reverence.

I shake my head, not a sound.

"I'm sorry, dear. I didn't want to believe it when Henry told me. We already lost a great deal after Marcus and Kara. Then you. I mean, how could that be? You just lost them all." She blows her nose against the Kleenex that miraculously found its way inside her grasp. "I always knew I'd see you again. But not this way. Not when you still don't remember. I want you to rush back here and look for me, return to your great love, mourn your brother and your friend as your old self."

Great love? Before yesterday, I would have believed it.

"I'm afraid...I'm certain that's never going to happen." My reply is with grave acceptance to this truth. I pull my gaze up to her solemn appearance, whose grimace is a caution to a looming breakdown. "This is me now," I add. The old Polaroid with Noah and I, comes back to my attention. What I would do to turn back the time.

Once again, our space nurtures the silence. There's so many things I want to ask but I suddenly forget how to form a question.

"What's on your mind, dear?" She pats my shoulder.

"A lot," I tell her the truth.

She cocks an eyebrow, patiently anticipating my words.

"Well for starters —" I pause, cultivating her interest even more, "— I don't get Noah's motivations. Up until yesterday, I thought I knew him. All those months ago, I can't believe he played me."

"He did? He knew where you were this whole time? Noah found you?" She mumbles on. "Told you where to look for me?" She seems uneasy.

"Yeah," I reply. "And then he left. I didn't know he'd be here all along. Running into him yesterday —"

"Yesterday?" She asks, tone doubtful. You saw him? That's impossible."

"I wouldn't put it past him," comes my argument. "I saw him in town. Henry brought me back for my mother's funeral and I ran into him yesterday." I watch her process my words, at times mumbling to herself for a better understanding, eyes glued to the floor. "With his wife," I add.

A sense of understanding lands on her expression, replacing her dropped jaws. "Oh. That can be explained."

I shrug in response. "It's alright. It doesn't change the circumstance." I notice her, fixing her attention on me while I do the same to Noah's family portrait.

"But! Ophie," she interrupts. A flight of alarm widens her eyes. "You don't understand. About Noah."

I shake both my head and hand on her face, dismissing this irrelevant explanation. In the end, he's still married. "It's really alright," I say, adding, "I just wanna forget about it. I'd rather find out what I don't know."

She nods, face remains baffled. But she understands, more than she shows.

"So, they all looked for me? I was nowhere to be found?"

I watch her nod, expression making certain that whatever she says next, will have my full attention. "Had I known then, I would have asked other people to look for you and not allow some drunk twenty-something year old boys to operate a car. I was already asleep."

"They eventually found me, but how?" I probe, dying to know the series of events that lead me back here.

I hear a deep sigh, but I don't turn to look. It seems like she's uprooting the heavier portions of her memory from her thoughts. "You called hours later but it didn't sound good," she continues, planting more seeds of suspense in my chest. "Your mom had just moved here from Minnesota and I guess you decided to see her. Marcus didn't know. Said you ran off from her house. Something happened. I don't know." She shakes her head, grasping at the thought. "I heard you were scared. I don't even wanna know why. You were running away. You only called to say goodbye."

"And of course, there was nothing that could have stopped him from getting in that car, and rescuing his sister. It didn't matter how many drinks he'd had. And of course, Henry would be right there with him at any cost," I'm telling her while asking, mind stupefied by the lengths Marcus and Henry took to get to me, in spite of the dangers. Henry has continued to do so, without fail.

"Yes," she confirms, leaning closer to me. "Your brother loved you so much." Her voice becomes hopeful as she says it. "Your lives as children were horrific. I cannot even fathom the thought, how he was able to muster all that love from the darkness. So, when Henry told us about what Marcus wanted, how he had made sure Henry knew to take you away if anything happens to him, we respected his wishes."

"And Kara? You never told me how she got in the car?" I ask, excruciatingly spotting the plot holes to this narrative.

"Kara?" She yanks her body away from me, as if surprised by my question. "I'm sorry, dear…" She touches my shoulder. "We're still having a hard time even after all these years, just imagining how she felt before it happened. All the confusion. The pain…" She begins to sob and the tremor in her voice, they're already an indication to the struggle, the torture. Losing someone, losing them like that, I've been there, even if I can no longer remember. "She had been sleeping on the truck bed. It was dark. They didn't know when they drove it. We all found out right after. She had quite a few to drink. That's what the autopsy revealed."

I am to blame. I knew it. No matter the reason, I put them all there. It was just as good as me driving the vehicle.

"But it was no one's fault. Not even yours," she assures.

Is it, really? Did Vita mean to say she never felt any anger towards me? Even a little bit. Even for a while? It would have been reasonable to. It would have been human.

"What is she doing here, Grandma?" Noah's voice disrupts the thin film of silence around Vita and I, sending us both to our feet. The weight of his footsteps ricochets across the room. It's furious and undeserving of my relief.

"Dylan." She regards him before uttering another name. "Henry? You're here."

Unlike Dylan, Henry's demeanor is calm but distracted. He appears worried but they're not meant for me. Fingers beating the screen of his phone, he's typing a thousand words per minute. "Hi Vita!" He waves at her before sliding his phone inside his back pocket. His tone is detached.

They both dissolve in the background as Noah stands unmoved by my presence. And I mean that in the coldest way possible. Yes, those eyes were once thawed warm enough to tell everyone of a great love, a love we once had. But it isn't there, or maybe it never was. Even the way he stands and the manner in which the edges of his eyes sag to his cheekbones, they're not Noah's. In some ways, I know it's him but nothing about this man reminds me of our electrifying affinity to each other. This is just a repository of his likeness, steered by a nonentity who calls himself Dylan.

His lips ripple against each other, simmering in indifference. They weren't the ones I tasted, not the ones that demolished my soul beautifully. But what about our past? Those photographs? Did it change when Kara died, even when I still believe in my heart that she didn't. Why pretend to love me again those months ago? Did he not have anything better to do with his life?

I have been made a fool.

I move towards Noah. Henry mimics my actions from behind him, his eyes guarding both Noah and I. He's intuitively certain of what I'm about to do next.

"Oh my God!" I hear Vita scuffle from behind me but dares not to make skin contact.

I turn livid, cheeks scalding in rising temper as I feel my ribs crowd my chest. Henry's strong arms have made their way around me.

"What are you doing, Ophelia?" He screams, as he breaks me away from Noah's flushing face.

"Asshole! You said you love me and then I find out that you're married?" My shouts are aimed at Noah, while I thrash inside Henry's tight hold, like a fish out of water. I needed to get a piece of him, show him an inkling of how it is to be duped the way he did me. "Have you no shame? At least in the memory of my brother's death. What kind of a friend does that to his sister? Might as well spit on his grave!"

Henry drags me to the couch, carefully but with force. I bounce off the cushion as I catch a side glance of Vita, visibly upset at the rumpus happening in her own home. We've been down this road before, Henry and I. He's always been the neutralizing element to my scalding temper. But who's counting?

My eyes never leave Noah. He's there where he has been since he came in, rubbing the part of his face where I slapped him. He hardens his look on me. Who knows what's going on inside that head? Months ago, I was naïve to think that I did.

"You need to calm down. Listen to me!" Henry releases his reprimand.

I blink, and the second I lost was enough time for Henry to pin me to the couch. I'm lying on my back, discerning Henry's clenched teeth and fraught expression. My mind has been too sluggish to realize my own frenzied outburst happening right under my nose. The loud beating in my heart has muffled their conversations. I only hear ringing in my ears. Their lips move, nodding in dialogue but there is no sound. I see my body brawl back, my mouth moving to scream as if I have been separated from myself. Here I am, a silent spectator amid the chaos, from whichever plane of existence this is.

"I need an explanation! I deserve that from you!" And in another swift second, I recognize my words again, everything at once. There is a strain in my throat, from the shouting it has endured. "Anything? Whatever! Just tell me!"

For a moment, I hear a stranger in my own voice. It sounds deep in urgency, with an ear-splitting terror that expertly warred against a similar danger some years ago. The blur is slowly subsiding as I finally sustain an eminent disbelief against what is happening. Henry seems a little bit more trusting, enough to loosen his force and bring me to a sitting position. Vita's shudders appear as a spooky dance with her steady wails. I know they're not meant to express fear but of commiseration towards what has become of the little girl she used to know.

"Alright! This is bullshit," Noah shifts from his ungenerous responses. He's finally speaking out. I recognize some reminders of his old self within the thunderous accent, parts that I know and have been attuned to when we were together. Yet swirling along its rough stream, is an echo, an immense loathing towards me. "Where the fuck is he?"

Where's who?

"Not another word!" Vita shouts a firm directive. She points a finger at Noah, all dignified as the highest of the pecking order. Her command was not of abuse but of an important purpose that is not yet known to me. "This is not for you to explain." Her words force him to retreat back, but not without retaliation.

Momentarily, he inspects his phone and throws it to the display cabinet, barely maiming the furniture.

Henry grows uncomfortable again, bearing some fluctuations in his sitting position next to me. "Come on, man. Calm the hell down."

Noah doesn't listen, throwing an intense glare to my direction.

"Suit yourself," Henry settles. He throws his hand up to concede, sensing that Noah will just do everything else but.

Who is this man? He's not the one I met at the café in Seattle, doesn't even seem like the boy I was in the photo with.

"Why are we playing games with this woman?" Noah asks, voice trodden by hopelessness and eyes searching for answers to materialize.

Then in her maternal tenderness, Vita takes careful steps toward her grandson. Even before she could reach out to console him, Noah's face softens. We both watch it happen, Henry and I. It almost astounds us. Their relationship has a likeness to conformity but this one is out of love.

"Have a little understanding. We have to wait. Okay?" Her voice has a fluidity that brings calmness to whoever gets to hear it. It's gingerly but also yielding respect. She strokes his thick tresses, this small statured woman consoling a man towering over her. He allows her, half his body leaning sideways against the white column. "She's been through enough," she adds.

"And we haven't?" Noah argues, head shaking, look piercing. He pulls farther away from her.

Hello? I'm right here. You guys can talk to my face.

That'll be his last words before taking off towards the rain, his spirit as remote as it was when he first walked in.

Vita does nothing to stop him while Henry sits in silence next to me, inspecting his phone again while spinning it between his thumb and index finger.

The lost pieces to this giant puzzle have inundated me but I just can't find the strength to place them where they should be kept. Shock has devoured my ability to comprehend and no amount of pinching my arm could release me from its charges. It seems like it.

"I'm gonna get some fresh air," I announce, partly asking Henry's permission.

But I don't wait for a nod. Instead, I push myself up from the couch, briefly bowing at Vita's sullen expression on my way out. Henry has no protest.

The brittle forest air does little to enliven the flatline that's pinned to my torso. I'm holding on to this nothingness. This state of being forsaken by every emotion, as if I no longer deserve to feel. I've carried the numb from all the revelations and brought it out here, hoping for a Good Samaritan to free me from this cage.

Noah leaves. I watch him drive off to the main highway as an enigma. It's almost unbelievable to think that was the same person who once made me feel alive. He couldn't leave fast enough at the sight of me.

"Let's go home. There's stuff I gotta deal with." Henry's voice comes cruising in with the fresh wind surge.

He catches my pleading gaze and he knows immediately that his gentle touch is compulsory. I inch away, not wanting to infect him with the horror rattling my insides.

"I deserve to know the truth. You need to tell me. We've come to a point where the choice is no longer yours," I tell him quietly.

I watch him shake his head, forcing a smile, while staring at the fresh tire tracks left by Noah's car.

"That's all I wanna do now. I told you yesterday," he replies.

"Of course," my voice cynical, "But why am I still getting the run-around? What happened to being honest from now on? What is the price for your truth?"

He exhales, blowing the hair strays above his forehead. "He wanted to be the one to tell you. I owe him that," he replies.

"Who?" I'm puzzled but also interested.

"Noah."

I laugh, a nervous giggle that sends me floor bound on the porch steps. "Tell me you're kidding?" He wanted to tell me? Man, can't even look at me without wanting to vomit. He's disgusted by my presence, screamed more in his actions rather than words. He could have just told me everything back in Seattle but he wanted to draw it out to be able to plant the knife, and await the right moment to push it deeper.

"Just trust me on this one, okay?" His voice returns to the warmth, hands drawing lines on my shoulder, as he hovers my seated form.

I lean on his leg, just a simple resignation to his genuine devotion for me. He slips his palm down my cheeks. It lingers there, this tenderness protruding from a place of aversion. We know without words, this unspoken promise that we will always have each other's back.

"Where's Landree?" I ask him. Not that I miss her but not having her around is out of the ordinary, especially now that she's pregnant.

He sighs, seemingly releasing some deep-rooted tension. He's been doing that a lot lately. "That's the thing. She left and I haven't been able to figure out where she went. I'm trying to find out where she could be."

"Oh, why? Did you get into a fight?" That explains a lot of his mental interference today.

"Well, after you got upset at the funeral, she left first and then she sent me a text telling me she's gone. I know she's not home in the city. I checked last night."

What the fuck!

"What she say?" I become curious.

He lowers himself next to me, slanting his head to show off his blatant confusion. "Not sure if you wanna know."

"Tell me."

He bites his lower lip, adding, "She was scared you were gonna do something. After Andrew came back. Now that we have a baby on the way, she didn't know what to do. She doesn't believe me when I said you weren't gonna hurt her."

"And what do you think?" I ask him, while cracking my knuckles to draw out the uneasiness.

He eyes me for a long while, my face still tilted to him. He's seemingly trying to say the right thing but doesn't know how. "Are you kidding me? You wouldn't. I know you."

But does he really?

"Hard-headed?" He jokes. A nod follows. "Yup! Always worries me, especially on days when she leaves her phone to die and doesn't come home? Right on the money. Barging into a stranger's house? Uh-huh!"

I plant my elbows on my thighs so my hands can cradle my already weary neck.

His lips are slowly forming a ripple, making light of this dire situation, as always. "Yeah! My Ophie would do that. But hurt my future child? Never."

We both laugh. I wish I could say they're no longer there, all the knotted pieces of confusion and betrayal waiting to be unwound. If only there's a way to harvest all the answers I need from everyone. If only I can comprehend their motives. If only I can remember.

"Henry?" I ask him while my eyes narrow at the beads of rain falling.

He takes my hand, standing me up as I pat the dried pine needles off my buttocks with the other.

He looks at me delicately before replying. "What's that?"

"Have you known about the memorial?" My question surprises him. I know because I notice him cupping the back of his neck. He's uncomfortable, thrown off guard.

And without further thought, he acknowledges it. "Yeah," Henry's reply is soft and sullen, drawn from a tragedy that took the life of the people he cared about, but spared his own. "I attend every year."

This would have been the moment I would lash out at him, blame him for not allowing me to participate all those years. Yet I understand why he did it. Though in its very deceitful manner, his decisions have mostly just been in my best interest. Say he did tell me about it, I wouldn't dare set foot here. I have cultivated a firm abhorrence towards this place.

Perhaps it takes a while to mourn when it is the mind that dies.

Why Henry all of a sudden decided to bring me back to where we fled from, adds to the mountain of question marks heaping on my shoulders. Deep down inside my core, remains a bone I've yet to pick with him.

"I wanna go back there. I feel like I need to." I reveal to him, this passing but urgent thought.

"Okay, we can go now. Let's just say goodbye to Vita first," he replies, certain of exactly where I need to be.

Henry turns around to head back in. He picks up his stride but breaks his footsteps halfway to the door. I know he saw it, the reluctance on my expression. He does a smooth one-eighty to reveal a face filled with empathy. His forehead wrinkles, making his way back where I'm standing.

"You wanna go alone," comes his certainty.

CHAPTER TWENTY-FOUR

Where Everything Was Lost, Where Everything Returns

I'm stunned by Henry's ability to set aside the domineering parts of himself and allow me to go alone. I knew for sure he would have not wanted me out of his sight, after my recent disappearing stunt.

Yet I'm back here with just myself, forcing away my body's protective rebellion that has shielded me from the pain, when I was here the first time. I come now with a little more courage but also a lot more offshoots of this fear, stalking me at all angles. The unexpected sunny day seems like a good omen.

Take my car. Gas is full. That should get you by. Bring my cellphone while I get yours recharged. Call me when you get home, okay?

Henry's parting words are echoing through the open window.

You have cash? Got your wallet?

Deep inside, I laugh. My money will outlive me, much more now that Marcus' share inheritance was also gifted to my name. It was never an issue even then. Henry made sure of that. I can't imagine what that woman did for a living but it didn't seem like her life of solitude was a reflection of her wealth. She was a mother but nobody regarded her as such.

Yet even when my mind shouldn't have the faculties to welcome any more thoughts, I think of the person whose absence continues to instigate an immortal famine deep in my gut. Noah, where do I begin with you? Somehow though, I already know what I'm going to do next. I love him so much. It kills me, this gut twisting, blade-searing, chest-piercing infliction. I need to see him one last time before I squander away all that I feel for him. Just as he wanted. I don't think I have a choice on the matter.

It astounds me, just the thought of giving up. I never imagined it, to consider quieting down this ravaging hunger to be with him, just so he could be free. Maybe I'm capable of being noble. Maybe I still have a shot at redemption, after everything that I did, including the ones I know nothing of.

I push out the car door halfway, before hearing another message come through from a guy named Derek. I wanted to read them, even steal Noah's new number from his contact list but I fought the urge to. I just couldn't help but see the texts on the cellphone banner as it comes, how he hasn't heard from Landree either and that they'll get the cops involved by tomorrow.

Henry said she fled after our fight, in absolute fear of me. She was sure I was going to do something to hurt her. Did I? Oh God, I hope not. I wouldn't do that to Henry. I never have. What about the smell of bleach? Okay, that's reaching now. This is not a movie.

Calm down, Ophelia.

In my quiet resolve, I rush to shut the phone off and leave it there in the console.

The ground underneath my soles injects a shot of voltage up my spine. I immediately scour for an emotional cradle, as I see the sign again, bearing the name of my brother and my best friend. I failed heavily at putting the puzzle pieces together earlier on. I walk towards it, with fresh eyes and an uncloaked heart. It was better not succumbing to it then, this sensation of being gutted and torn apart into a multitude of emotions that is unfitting for a single person to endure. Yet here I am, unequipped but ready to bear them. The saddest thing most of all, is that I was the one who handed them to the palms of death. It was I who killed them. I didn't deserve Vita's sympathy, not even a little bit.

I begin to trace my unremembered steps to the center of the road, hearing a quiet sound to be deciphered - a whispered caw of a baby crow. The smell of blistered tires comes to me, as well as the metallic putrefaction from the blood swamp, that has long been washed and dried. I imagine their cries. Was it immediate or was it a sluggish partaking of death? Bile rises up my throat. It is sickening, gruesome, whatever happened here. Somehow, I'm certain of that, as if I was here.

I was here.

I couldn't imagine what Henry went through, waking up in the hospital and realizing he was the only one who made it out of that truck. I understand now, his innate and unrelenting obligation to keep me under his protection. Always. Maybe it was the only way to shut it off, the trauma and gore. Maybe it was his desperate resort to wash away the guilt of being alive. After all, he wouldn't be here without Marcus' heart.

In the end, we all perished in this place. My memory was robbed here, as was Henry's peace. While Noah, well, he took the brunt of it all. He either had to continue loving me or honor the death of his sister and my brother. He couldn't have both. We know now which one he chose.

"Watch it, lady!"

A violent air nips my earlobes, thrusting me to the side of the road. I watch the car swerve about fifty feet away from where I'm standing. The driver's hand lingers on the car horn, painfully received by my ear drums. I didn't realize I have been stuck in the middle of this death road, as if subconsciously, I wanted it to take me too.

"Sorry!" I wave an apologetic hand, to which the passenger proudly displays a middle finger, before vanishing into the curve.

I take a deep breath. A vision pounces in. I'm alone again, back in Vita's house.

"Let's see it," that's Marcus' voice perforating through the other side of the wall. In some unexplainable way, I recognize it even when I have forgotten how it sounded. I peek my head across the hallway. There they are, in the same room where I found the photographs, sitting on old and musky furniture. The walls are dark, surroundings loitered by young but hopeful college boys having a good time. Red Solo cups are scattered in every table space imaginable. Two girls dangle over the dark brown ottoman. The one with a short blonde hair has her stomach over it while the other, more slender girl, has her elbows buried in the cushion. A magazine, whose name I can't decipher, consumes her. None of them, I could recognize.

My brother's athletic form extends the length of the velvet couch. It is in an eye-shocking citrus color. He's sitting up, gathering his attention towards the red box in his hand. A Colts hat sits above his dark and curly locks, that are covering some parts of his forlorn eyes. This should be a happy occasion, after being picked up by an NFL team but there is a stain of brooding in his expression, a sense of bitter sweetness. With the pillows behind him contouring to the shape of his back, he flips open the box.

"What do you think?" Noah asks, his voice penetrating untouched portions of my heart in one fell swoop.

My nerves suddenly devour me from the inside, organs realizing what's happening before I could draw awareness to it.

"It's my Nana's but I already had it resized," he adds.

I scrutinize him, the love of my life enfolded within the perfection of his youth. His eyes, they're telling of the depth, of this profound love he has for me, or at least who I used to be. There in his skin, the golden effervescence of the man I would have spent every lifetime with.

No wonder it was immediate, our connection and the ease to be with each other. My body and heart didn't need to depend on a mind that, for years, has been running adrift. I have a separate capacity within myself to know without recognizing that my Noah has found me again.

He wanted to seek my hand in marriage. What a life it would have been, if not for the circumstance that was placed in our paths right after.

It was a beautiful love story, if only the ending was the same.

I find him next to my brother. He pulls the ring from the box and holds it up to the light. "If she doesn't say yes to this then I don't know what will."

"Damn, that ring is as big as your ego!" Henry interrupts, footsteps causing a wave of amusement from the rest of the unnamed faces. He yanks the box from Marcus. "You sure you wanna give away your sister to this guy?" He points to Noah, who's face is teeming with delight.

I've never seen Henry like this. Relaxed. Untroubled. The years has yet to pile on the limits of his laughter. Something tells me that it's happening soon.

I see my brother smile, head shaking as he confiscates the jewelry from Henry. "Well, as much as I hate to admit it, I've never seen my Ophie so happy with this one." He taps Noah's back afterwards.

They both bump fists before Noah gives him an awkward embrace. An eruption of applauses and hoorays cause the room to tremor a little bit.

"Oh! Young love!" The blonde-haired girl cries.

"No time wasted, man! Didn't she just turn eighteen?" says another.

"Well, everything's set for tonight. Right?" Henry asks the group. He's met with nods and a dozen thumb ups. "What else do we need, man?" His face changes, now focused on Noah and on the task.

"Well, my dad and I are gonna pick up Mr. Davis from the airport," Noah responds. "So everyone, don't get too drunk and make sure my Ophie is where she should be."

"I can pick up my dad, you know. If it helps," Marcus tells him before taking a sip from the plastic cup.

"Nah, man! You should be here. Keep everyone in line, you know," Noah replies. "Wait, where's my bride-to-be anyway?"

"Easy, she hasn't said yes yet!" Henry jokes. He laughs some more while dodging the flying pillows that Noah is sending his direction.

"You're making me nervous, dude. Stop that!" Noah says, as he closes the jewelry box.

"Kara and her should be here soon. They just went to get their prom dresses from the town," someone else comments.

They didn't know that I'm already here, listening to their well-devised plan. I drove myself after making a hasty decision to see my mother this morning. Soon I'll be reminded of its repercussions. My body and its decrepit condition will collectively stand in protest against Noah's grand gesture.

Cheers!

To Marcus Davis, Indianapolis Colts newest running back!

Woo-hoo!!

To Ophie and Noah!

I hear their residual chatters as I find myself walking away. My body splits while crossing the threshold through the back door. I'm me again inside my own but Ophie too, the younger me running outside in haste.

I follow her, finding ourselves inside a baby blue Volkswagen Beetle. She buries her head inside her hands, leaning down on the steering wheel. I watch her back heave and finally, her cries are felt inside me. I'm familiar with them, the tears soaking her skin. I know of their origin, the hurt and damage rooted from a deep pain and self-hatred. She loves

Noah, more than she ever thought she could. He's there inside the delicate faculties of her heart that were made for the kind of love that extends beyond her years. She didn't think anybody would look at her, to accept her wounds and tame the demons lurking from her past the way he does. Her ragged pieces seem unsuitable and unworthy of Noah's pure hands.

That is why she wants to run away, to seize some sort of clarity. Because of what she is and the kind of life that reared her, she felt like she didn't deserve to envision a future with Noah. This morning was a confirmation that she finally reached this sort of darkness that nobody could pull her out from.

She will say no to him but she couldn't bear the thought of hurting the one person she cared so much. Evading is the least sharp of all these swords. She has to leave, get as far away as she could from this place, from her soul's massacre this morning. She will call Marcus when she makes it far. They wouldn't be able to find her. They'd be all passed out drunk by nightfall and she'll be free from what transpired this morning.

The picture whirls again as a shudder by the change of scenery. After surviving the blur, I have resumed the visit to this old memory that I have kept hidden and forgotten since I recovered them some days ago.

It's hell to be here once before. Now this pain is setting my skin ablaze, invoking a sheer terror that matches the little girl's whimpers. The guards just removed Marcus and Henry, as the girl's naked outline is being ushered forcefully to the back of this make-shift altar. Eyes follow her, the ones lurking inside the sea of red hoods. Their gazes trace every inch of her innocence, both in worship and in malice. The chants grow louder, where once spread apart from every corner of the complex.

In a small dark room, foreign hands are carefully setting her quivering body down on the four-poster bed. Her quarrel is not with them but against the woman in pursuit of her soul.

She has arrived, her wicked cape sweeping the dust on the wooden floor.

"Ophie," she says, lovingly. "Remember what I said? It is important that we do this. I told you. You're gonna be okay. Just close your eyes and it'll be over soon." Her voice is soft, tucking away the sinister intent prowling in the midst.

I watch my own effigy clench her teeth, hands gripping tightly the sheets beneath her. She knows it's coming, the torture that has been rehearsed against her will, night by night. Most of the time, it's just whatever she finds at home, and some days when she's unlucky, a metal fork.

I remember her thoughts, the way she wondered if the pain would cease once the bleeding stops. I wish I could tell her the obvious, that her worst foes are the things her eyes wouldn't see and unreachable by her hands. I want to tell her now, to suit up because the future is not as promising either. Things are going to get worse from here.

The phantom moves swiftly through the dim, pushing the girl's body down in urgency. She's lying now, face up to the pitch black. I let out a shriek, at the same time she does. We know what's happening, the object of choice arriving promptly along her insides. Unwelcomed hands are steered through the entryway between her legs. She winces, holding her breath as she anticipates the agony to gouge her flesh. Then it encounters a halt, this exploitation. Whispers befall in the moment, between the woman and another pair of ogling eyes. His wide teeth sheen in the night, vile and hungry to witness this sodomy up close.

Then, prompted by the man's approval, she moves about from within her. I feel it again, the thick metal awakening the brokenness in her cervix. She is reminded of the fact that nothing has healed yet, while the object's jagged edges shred their way up and down. There's moisture now. The bleeding has commenced. Her pace is picking up but her silence is more brutal than the act.

The girl, why doesn't she struggle? I want her to war against this severe brutality.

Shout!

Scream!

Kick!

Spit!

Anything, to give her a fighting chance but she doesn't.

I know, little girl, I know. There is no point to. It's either this or the beating.

Even in the pitch black, I can see her tears collecting at the edge of her eyes, but she doesn't make a sound, not even a movement. The only motion in her body is the one steeping from her waist down. The shoves are harder, more solid than the last. I try to mute the ache but there was no way to. It's here scorching my purity, this flaming barbwire and a feeling unanimous to hers.

Of course, I distinguish it. This is the ruthless imprint of her mother's hands that I already met while I was her. I commiserate with her suffering that is almost impossible to describe, besides telling those who listen. I'll say how it is a lot like watching your own death.

"Faster," orders the man behind the sheer drapes.

It's discernable, his hands stirring down his pants, urgently fiddling inside the open zipper. She does as told, collecting energy in her grip to achieve the maximum force in her thrusts. The little girl grimaces quietly, a loud scream is visible even in her silence. Her body bounces off the bed, needing to liberate the spare blow that exceeds beyond the strength of her juvenile physique. I am aware of this stupefying violence, in the hands of my own mother no less. The woman's weapon continues to scrap her raw internals, with the throbs making their way up her stomach.

The man's moans are heard like howls, ending the woman's thrusts in an instant. He seems to have relieved himself of the poison lingering in his inhumanity. He dismisses himself out of the room. Soon she follows his exit, barren of any maternal concern for the child that once relied on the sole protection of her womb. She'll wash her hands with his, gracefully distancing themselves from the slaughter.

It will be just as she does to me at home. The memories of my night times are told not by the fairy tales that would have carefully tucked my tender body into bed. They are of cold female hands, slithering up my skin, and intruding my innocence. Yes, that fleeting innocence I would have lovingly surrendered to the one deserving of it.

It will be just as he does with all the other little girls in this god-forsaken community.

There's a crack in the door, calling forth the thin beam of light from outside. It crawls over the girl's wasted body, shining a spotlight on one half of her face. Her blank stare is a mirror of the horror that will continue to haunt her, long after it leaves. Her eyes narrow, sore in agony from a spirit that's severely broken.

I hear her thoughts, painfully asking herself the same question, as I have done the same all these years.

Have I been praying to the wrong god?

Her despairing calls to her mother, they become mine. I scream passionately, in the hopes that our collective voices are heard by the right people who could save us. What a pointless endeavor, to undo the past as if my bellows could wield such impossible feat.

Why did Henry think that her funeral deserves my presence?

The landscape flicks.

Suddenly.

Wistfully.

My shouts have ceased, deadened by the ache of that memory and this vision materializing before my eyes.

"Kara!" I call out to her as she crosses the empty road.

Urgency mars her form, arms signaling me to move away.

"Oh my God!" I tell her when she finally comes near me. My arms cloak her with all the cries of I miss yous, and this newfound hurt after relearning her fate.

She shoves me hard, away from her stiff and unwelcoming body. I can tell she is furious, disgusted even. There's an undulation between her pursed lips, signaling fear more than anger. She's different today, more youthful even with her aged torment.

"Go!" She orders. "Go back to your car now."

I still couldn't comprehend this insistence. She must really hate the sight of me. This is where she lives now, the very place that robbed us all of everything. She's reminding me, that it's my fault. I am responsible for all the blood that seeped here in this very ground.

I look up to her again, still screaming. This time, silence takes over the space where her voice should have been heard. I see her face, mouth frenzied and limbs panic stricken. Her apparition is thinning now, dissipating along with the sound of her voice. Until finally she's gone, as a smoke cleared away by the wind.

"My Ophie," a man walks over in calm authority.

A face comes to view, this stranger ripened by horizontal age lines. Parts of his forehead appear red, the kind that comes before the sunburn. His hair is long, strands resting on his shoulders. The blue in his eyes is vivid, my reflection drowning in its depth. He would have looked handsome, if I didn't know better. Behind him, is a blurred glimpse of a red, worn down pick-up truck. His tan leather jacket is torn at the collar. They smell musky, when we finally stand inches apart. He towers over me, about six feet in height, gaze violently reaching my confused form.

"You look just like your mother nowadays," he comments, pulling me into his perfumed embrace. I freeze, heart still in terror as my mind rearranges its broken pieces. "You still smell the same, my dear."

There's a croak in his voice, throat impaired by apparent cigarette smoking. He's imposing, even in his softness and I couldn't help but notice his wandering hand. It's slowly gracing the edge of my breast. I pull away, but he limits the distance between our bodies. He sees my scowl as I look up, schooling him of his actions while remaining helpless.

Vehicles ceased their passing, suspiciously since he came. There are just birds, murders of crows flying blindly by.

He pulls his face forward, down to mine. I don't know why, I truly don't. I'm not chained to the ground yet my feet couldn't move. The hairs on my skin are protesting in fury, battling against this ominous ending. He's closing in, eyes glued to mine. But my voice of retaliation remains caged somewhere. He has this power, this wizard strength that I seem to obey against my will. Yes, it is as if I was born to this subjection.

But something happens. The shards align. Ends fitting along my memory. Those eyes, I've seen them hiding cowardly in the darkness the very first time. He was always there watching, on nights when my mother indulged in the gluttonous partaking of my own flesh. Why? Because they follow a code, the one that says only women can touch children until they turn eighteen.

It's him, the king for whom my useless mother was a willing servant.

I gasp, not able to bear the shouts within, from a horrific form of remembering. He becomes distracted, allowing me to slip away from his grip. "Ophelia," he calls my name, soft and without necessity. I sprint away, knowing that even the wrecked parts of myself deserve to be saved.

To my car, that's where I'm going. My trembling hands are digging into the pits of my pockets, scouring for the key. I'm mapping it in my head now, how I could get help. Maybe start the car first to somewhere safe, then get to my phone. Call Henry? Then 911?

I momentarily turn my head, to see him walk leisurely, not even giving himself a fighting chance. Why is he not trying to catch me?

The passenger door is wide open. I crash into it while nursing my memory's betrayal. I could have sworn I closed and locked it. All the while, I indulge in this faint sensation, as a ruthless reminder from the hours of no rest and food. My pockets are empty. No sign of any key or hope of escaping this.

"Stop! Stay right there, Owen!" I snarl at him with my palm against his face, spitting out a name that I have guarded for so long.

"So, you remember me after all," he scorns, voice unnerving yet every bit of serene. "Looking for this?" Around his index finger, dangles Henry's key chain and half my lifeline. He smiles, exposing some specks of silver along his teeth. And the terror from it reaches my pores.

No! How could I leave my keys and my phone turned off? What am I supposed to do?

Okay, Ophelia, think!

"My money looks good on you," he sneers. How could someone so composed stir chaos in every surface of my body?

He comes closer, boldly approaching as if I won't retaliate.

"You can have it. Won't do you any good though," his voice is bragging.

I don't need to look hard to comprehend what he means. My front tires have been slashed to deflation. It's been revealed in horror by my rousing eyes.

"Now, where were we?" he asks, his grip sneaking up my arm, fingers clawing at my skin.

A swell of panic rattles my insides. I could vomit on the spot. How long could I run before I get tired? Before someone finally drives by to save me? My fingers are frozen at the joints, just as my numbing feet. The landscape grows more sinister in the silence. My heartbeats have been amplified, jumping up and down against my ribcage for all the wilderness to hear.

His stare threatens, inspecting me from head to toe, as a meal he's about to devour. Andrew's eyes looked much like his, in this particular second. This kind of ogle is a warning to heed, only seen in moments when death is about to trap me at the ankles. My next thought arrives, ordering my feet to scuffle away, far from this position before it gets dire. I'm going to run, flee with a certainty that my life depends on it.

Hurry now!

I zip by my car, feeling the soles of my feet melt into the foam of my tennis shoes. The weight of my body from this urgency is absorbed with each of my sprints, painful but relieving.

Still running.

Even the wind knows how grim these seconds passing have been. I don't feel it, not even on my cheeks. I want to look back but I'm afraid to. All I hear are loud thumps of his boots hitting the ground, hardly scurrying in chase of me. My body begins to feel flimsy as I carry on, in-between rows of endless forests and grey pavements. There is no clue how far I've darted from him, just a pair of lungs dwindling down to hyperventilation. I pray for a miracle, or any sign of a saving grace.

I need Henry to sense this peril. He should realize that I haven't checked in with him as instructed. He'll worry. He has to!

Car! Car ahead!

I see it, a red Camry heading this way. I run faster towards the other end of the old carriage road, while throwing my arms up.

"Help! Help!" I call out, my remaining strength dumped into this dire task.

Yet, as if I haven't had enough bad lucks today, the car slows down, then turns into a private road. That's why it was decelerating before it could even cross over. It was never meant to find me, not even a glimpse of this human figure frantically jumping up and down.

No.

A jerk is felt at my wrist. He pulls me back, with great force that I wince from the discomfort of my arm twisting. "I wouldn't do that," he warns. To which I battle immediately, from what little energy I have left.

He caught up too quickly. Okay, gotta do something. Gotta do it fast. What do I do? What do I do?

I kick his crotch, hard in intention but frail in outcome. His strength catches me off guard, still firm on his stance, with one hand contending with my yanks. His grip is able to trap my leg before it could land on target. Then it arrives without pity like a hard gavel to the ground. I ignore the abrupt cracks on my femur upon impact.

"Let me go!" I yell at him, my rebellion not meeting anything but his calmness. Both his arms are sparring with me now, as I continue to grab whatever I could – his shirt, hair, arm, or leg.

I'm failing at every form of attack, not meeting the number he's already made on me.

He finds my hair, roots burning at his brutal pull. Immediately, blood rushes up my tilted head, as I brace for what's to come. With a clump of my hair still in his grasp, he drags me without mercy while on my knees.

319

The concrete's jagged edges are scraping my skin raw, even with my jeans on. It burns and cuts, both sensations felt side by side but I close my eyes and cage my cries.

"There now, Ophelia. See, if you would have been nicer, it wouldn't be like this," he murmurs, while loosening my hair from his hand, probably fatigued by my dead weight.

The friction stops, as does his footsteps. His deep and labored breaths emerge from the quiet sloshes of the trees around. The rigid hold turns into a soft touch, as the back of his hand grazes my cheek. Then, he runs his fingers down my hair, ever so gently. And if I wasn't looking, this feels like love, a sweet yearning.

This is it, another Hail Mary from the sky. If I could just bring myself to injure him, enough to give me a head start. I'll bolt away, to that hidden road where the car went. I'll figure it out from then, cross that bridge when I get there, literally.

Okay. Okay. I got this.

"Fuck!" he groans as he nurses the fresh blow to his crotch. But that's it. He doesn't say much. His agony is stifled, not meaning to expose the rest of his vulnerabilities. This time around, my strike lands with precision. His face whorls, lips bent onto each other in agony. His bottom crashes on the ground, ducking his head as his long silky hair spreads like a curtain across his face. I watch his arm wrap along his sides, maneuvering something from behind him - his pain perhaps. It doesn't matter now. I get myself up, and all efforts of flight fortifies my legs. It's now or never.

"Somebody help!" my shout echoes along the empty road. "Help! Help!" I feel it, my voice forcing against the thin band across my throat, like a warning of its limits. It hurts. It strains, as if I may never be able to wield a sound ever again.

I make it to the edge of the carriage road, succumbing to a severe exhaustion. It's becoming clear to me how much strength I lost, how close I am to giving up. He's not far behind me. I know this. But if I could just take one more step, then another but there's nothing left in my energy chamber.

"Ophelia?" His voice, once again, is a reminder of my fierce drive to live. "Don't make me do this," he adds, hindering my next steps by the sound of a gun cocking.

Damn it!

Air feels like thorns in my lungs, my head light. I turn around, half-deciding whether I should just let him end me. Maybe he'll put me out of my misery. I'm crumbling at the edges now, slowly making my way to the cold ground. I manage to keep half of my body erect, searching for its weight. Sitting down is the best I could do.

The silver weapon sits stiff in his clutch. It's aimed at me, awaiting to drive a bullet into my flesh. He treads closer, with a cut on his cheek. A small creek of blood has dried up beneath it. At least my efforts weren't completely in vain. Yet even in the height of peril, I manage to look at the harmony in his footsteps and the sheer calmness of his gape. I know it's a false sense of belief, but his familiarity exudes a perception that he might be here to save me instead. And I'm also certain that I'm otherwise wrong for thinking that.

Quietly, he taps the barrel on my skull, knees to my face. His blue jeans reek of bonfire and the suffocating strength of some cologne. The latter is more pungent.

"I've been waiting so long for this moment," he tells me, as if I was a lover he once lost. There isn't an inkling of a gruesome plan but I know better.

I close my eyes, not intending to quarrel with him, but making home of the idea that this may be the last of my days.

"Ask me how many times I tried to get to you," he adds, placing a palm on my cheek, with a voice that mirrors the tenderness of the morning tide. At the same time, it plants a certain panic beneath my skin but something's delaying the horror, at least for now. All I feel is this heavy numbness, a cold weight over my face that's forcing my eyes to open. He swallows his spit grudgingly before speaking again. "Thousands," he reveals. "But Henry's always there. He's got all these people from the city keeping watch of you. Kid's got a lot of friends from high places, let me tell ya!" he chuckles in arrogance. "You acted like you didn't even know me. Like the time before that. Or were you just pretending?" His eyes narrow, almost awaiting my reply. "And you know that army boy? He's been a pill!"

What? Who? Andrew?

"...sticking his nose where he has no business in. Being a damn hero for you. Even in Mexico," he adds. "He already got in my way once when I figured out where you lived. Thanks to your politician friend."

Army boy. Army boy. Who the fuck is he talking about? Mexico! Noah?

Henry said that when he let his guard down, that seeing me on the news with Andrew led "them" back to my direction. It was him. But what is this pursuit for? Money? He could have taken all that back from my mother, if what Fred said was right. Retribution? For running away? And Mexico? I thought there was a plane crash. He was there too?

"Tsk. tsk," he shakes his head, a smirk stretching to one side of his face. "Gotta give it to that guy though? What's his name again? I mean, still hanging around even when you're already with that Andrew person."

Noah. Of course! Wait, Noah was in the army? He was around before I met him again? Why would he lie? Why would they all lie?

He looks far away, as if tugging certain memories that were trapped in the wind. Both his shoulders fall, gaze returning to me. "How's Henry these days? "How's my nephew?"

Nephew?

He gloats in the revelation, showing off a familial immunity against Henry's iron fist. He thinks he would never hurt him, even with everything he's done. I would hate to learn that he's right.

"Ungrateful son of a bitch." His words are searing but the voice cradling them lingers in the stillness, reposed. The warning of any danger dissolves in his unruffled demeanor. And to be honest, that scares me more than any rage he could ever throw at me. "Took him in when his parents died and ran off when he got access to their money." His head tilts to level with mine before something lands in his thoughts.

There is a moment when he forgets the part he plays in this confrontation. The gun leaves my head. He relaxes. We both notice it, the open window that would have sent me back to my escape. But he returns to advantage, with the weapon back to my temple, before I could make any decision.

"Why do you hate me so much, Ophie?" he asks, voice falling. There's an air of sadness gripping it. Even I know the answer to this question. Though, it's a moot fact now.

"I could have given you everything but you chose those other men. Henry. Andrew. Army boy." He gestures his free hand up and down while recounting the familiar faces in his head. "I'm sorry about Marcus though," he adds, sounding regretful. Anyone else would have believed it. "He was always so protective of you, dear sister. Him and Henry."

The sound of my brother's name steers a knife into my chest, cleaving the flesh in-between my ribs through my back. I killed him. The guilt chases me everywhere I go, even in the long stretch of not remembering at all. And this man right here is equally guilty of the same sin. What he did to me. What I allowed him to do that day.

"What do you want?" I finally ask him, voice rasped by fear and fatigue.

And what answers is the sheer terror growing from my pores when he laughs. The monster that was concealed beneath the false guise of his softness, jumps out at me. His eyes darken with vile thoughts before he opens his mouth. "See, you're just like your mom. Even after I give you everything. You still find a way to want something else. Did you know what she took from me?"

And did you know what you took from me? And my mother, I am nothing like her.

"Did you know she left me for you and Marcus? You ungrateful spawns! Next thing I find out, I'm broke and she had people come after my friends."

Friends? You mean the cult people? Say it like it is!

"She took my power. Everything. Couldn't even set foot in that town again. It's still her fortress until now." He grits his teeth, as if to rid some tension off his body. "Caught up to her though. Caught up to you. Remember? Our first reunion in Coupeville?"

Urgently, I sense whispers and ogles from eyes hiding behind the tree trunks. They're all here to supply a memory that once broke out from hiding days ago. Its quick to invade my thoughts. The chants grow louder, eyes narrowing. They're calling my name, uttering my mother's too. Her betrayal emerges from the fog, coaxing me to accept her forgiveness. And when I do, this man crawls out from the shadows, wanting to take me and conquering that horrific goal. My mother, she only stood there watching the barbarity through my eyes. I couldn't make anything out of her gape. Is she numb to my pain? Or does she feel it? Is she biting her tongue from screaming because this is the final cost of her freedom. And perhaps, ours. Mine. Marcus'. Henry's. But we now know it was all for a defeat. I lost my brother that same night, as was Noah's love that was my only chance of redemption.

I don't want to remember any more of this. Please! Make it stop!.

Owen's face draws closer to mine, displeasure still boiling in his expression. And something out of courage forces me to look at him, when I would have sent my stare back to the ground. He becomes furious at my steeled front.

"Say something!" he shouts, tilting my chin up to him. "Answer me, damn it!" He grips the edge of my face tighter. "We could have been good together. You. Me. Your mother. How I've missed you. I want you, Ophelia. There was no getting rid of you from my mind."

"Pull the fucking trigger! You sick bastard. What are you waiting for?" I demand and beg at the same time. Submitting bravely to my fate. I want this all to end.

"Not yet," his sinister reply comes, a sneer climbing at his mouth. There is a gruesome objective cooking inside of him. I just know.

And it lands. The blow reaches me, arriving on my skull. It's incredible, the force it brought to my senses as I taste the dirt in my mouth. I'm down on the asphalt, lying molten on the pavement while still intact.

"There. Before you make a run for it again," he murmurs, his voice so far away even when near.

I'm tired. This is a fight I could never win. I must let go of my grip on this world. I have been stained by its desolation, like a pitiful whore being shunned by all the beds I try to get into.

I don't deserve Noah. I never have.

I chose Henry in the beginning because I was sure he would understand my pain. It was just us from the start, us three. Marcus, Henry, and myself, we all fell in the same trench and found a way to get out of it together. Henry knows to leave it untouched and undisturbed, the hollow inside of me. Noah would have to spend his life trying to make me complete, and that would have been an existence of disappointments. I love him, always have and always will. That was our promise and I've held up my end so I can save him from any more misery. And underneath all that, this man and my mother left my soul branded with corruption. I was reminded of that once again, the day Noah was supposed to seek my hand in marriage. There was no way to clean myself off from the exploitation, no matter how much fumigating is done to my body. And I just cannot bring myself to return to Noah as a foul corpse. That is the reason why I left that day.

The haze finally reaches me. It's steady, drawing my eyelids down, and sending me to the darkness where I've always felt tethered to.

CHAPTER TWENTY-FIVE

An Eye For An Eye

"Ophelia! Wake up!"

I toss around to sense my doppelganger speaking to me in the pitch black. She looks different, in front of the only sliver of light slipping through. This version of me appears to be sure of herself with a head held high, and a pace too determined. Her motivation to survive is more aggressive than mine ever could.

I bring myself up to a sitting position. I know I'm here, somewhere in my thoughts where she resides.

"If that was me, I would have fought the crap out of him," she scolds, with a furrow at her brows and arms crossed against her chest. "But you haven't let me in for some time now. You don't let me fight our battles anymore." Her voice is more stretched, sultry, but also dangerous.

We only meet in passing during switches. Her true presence hasn't been this palpable until now. Henry is sure she came after Marcus' death, that somehow, I was prompted to seek an ally within myself. At this point, it's hard to be certain. The outside world calls it an illness, merely a way to survive. Jessica made that clear to me. Yet, how could they force me to trust their idea of what's real and isn't, when it is only I who gets to live them?

"You need to fight if you wanna live!" She insists, pointing a finger at me. "Don't forget what he did, what he made your mother do."

"But…" I try to mouth something in protest, but her insistence spoils my efforts.

"What are you waiting for? Go!"

I don't want to. Here seems safe, far away, and most of all, unreachable by anyone who wishes me harm. Perhaps by the force of some divine gesture, it'll soon be my home. While that is enticing, an ache ripples through my viscera. It devours me, the pressure incarcerating my chest from this utter void named after Noah. That would be enough to submit myself back to this gigantic funnel, that will carry my passage back to the world I was momentarily forced out of.

I come to it, the wake state as my head throbs in obvious agony. Some higher power has clearly decided my fate before I could. I'm in motion, body dragging parallel to the rough ground. The weeds rush against my back, blunt rocks scraping it. He has my hands, trapped inside his grip. I have no sense of time nor direction, only of this terrifying motive - he's getting ready to kill me.

Surely, he could try his hand at obliterating and tearing my flesh. But to send me to my death? Well, it has already been done a long time ago. What she did, what they both did, my life was obtunded by it.

His heavy footwork is chucking dirt over my face, some shifting to the inner edges of my eyes. I force them open while awakening a swell of nausea from my stomach. There is vomit now, just a little bit, but also enough to simulate a drowning sensation. The pool lingers in my mouth before I shove it back down my throat, all slime and putrid.

Disgusting.

I'm still drifting at the bottom of the lush forest and thick shrubs. Only a small gap between the woods offers a fleeting picture of the blue sky. Then, it's gone before I could even blink back the ire in my vision. It is dim again, us two shielded by a giant fort of grand old trees soaring high. I hear the sways and creaks from the touch of wind floating in. It's starting to get cooler under the wide shade, especially after catching the scent of his ominous intentions.

We stop. He rests my flimsy body over a hill of leaves. Here we are, me looking up to an old malignant disease of my past, while he primes his claws for invasion.

"I have waited years to taste you again, Ophelia. No lie. Something about you," he says quietly, depositing the gun back to his side holster. "You made me chase you for so many years. It was hard to get to you, but not impossible. I was sure Henry would take you somewhere far away. But Seattle? The boy thought he was clever, hiding nearby because that would be the last place I'd look. It would have worked though, but thanks to your T.V. stint with that Andrew kid. Not very wise."

He descends, jacket slipping off in coincidence. My eyes float between his and the clothing article, now resting over a thin log. I wanted to be slaughtered fast, like how my muscles won't even have time to prepare for their impending rigor mortis. Truthfully, I know what's going to happen next. And an even worse admission? I won't protest. I've been hardwired for dark offerings such as this, as if my mother had long planted a switch inside my skull, that only either of them can control. I was taught to simply lay there, that pain from penetration is but a foreign language.

'Your head must be trained to be resilient, Ophelia, and intelligent. You must be able to translate that foreign message into one that you can understand within yourself. For instance, you have the power to interpret this hurt as something you don't have to feel, once it hits you. This is how strong women are made, my dear. You'll thank me one day.'

That's what she said. My mother was teaching words of wisdom to my tender brain as she violated me. Behind her was always this very same man, coaching her what to do or say, and awaiting years to be able to breach me. The Disciples of Light, their men can never touch children. On the flip side, once she turns eighteen, every woman is free game. As a child, I believed her, imagining that Wonder Woman became a hero in the same manner. Somehow, all of us in the camp were educated that way.

That's why I swallowed my cries. That's why I remained mum. And that was why I forced myself to forget.

So many strewn memories. Here. There. All have been anticipating the day I pick them up and remember them. Today seems to be prophesied for just that.

"Hmmm, you smell so lovely," he mumbles as he dips his head down the chill of my neck. My arms are spread wide over the soft loam, held down by an invisible fear. His nose continues to rub my skin. My body is trapped in-between his stride, erection prodding at my navel. His fingernails are black, housing months-long grime in their folds. I watch them crawl down my chest, maneuvering the buttons of a blouse that I don't recall putting on. By this time, my chest has been completely unwrapped and vulnerable to his ravenous appetite.

His head disappears from my direct view, descending back down to my neck. I feel lips and then a blade-like sensation from his tongue, sucking and tasting the brine off my pores. There is nothing beneath him but a cold, repulsed maiden, satiating the hunger from his groin. His dense hair hangs over my chest as he goes at it. One hand is greedily sliding down my woman, missing before finding the unwelcoming entryway of his fingers' target. He grumbles and moans incoherent words, as accompaniments to the slithers and rough pulls inside me. My body feels betrayed by my easy surrender, and nothing speaks more of its retaliation than being reminded of his callused digits, igniting friction in my flesh like sandpaper.

The repetition of agony down the lower half of my figure has picked up speed, while he makes brutal purpose of his other hand. My breasts are laden with fear, sustaining the pain of each nipple tug. His teeth have sunk deeper into my neck and rather than summoning pleasure, my body has recoiled further into its defenses. I'm fighting his multiple assaults by simply unfeeling.

"Cum, darling! Cum. Show me what you couldn't the first time!' He exclaims, as his fingers slash in and out of my vagina.

The first time, as if such memory deserves tender sentiments. It's already too late for my mind to pull back its curtains.

They enter, visions that pay homage to a certain savagery, as this moment. The invisible lightning bolt strikes, arousing more feelings of disgust and trauma that I once sent to eternal sleep. They are awake, viciously reminding me of the hours leading up to the very first time I was broken into as a woman.

The almond eyes that had always been void of emotions, were burdened with fear, even pain. The sight of my mother was frozen in panic, it was clear to me even when she stood the wrong side up. I lay on my back, head hanging off the edge of the bed. I tried but couldn't ignore the merciless flaying beneath me, from arms pulling my skin in every direction, head and hands taking turns conquering my chest, and adult sex. His organ was hungry to foray into an alleged virgin territory between my legs. It was as though an earthquake tremored the room.

It was a long stretch of time. I lost count. I remember thinking if that was my final test of strength, if this was what my mother's brutal training prepared me for. That day was an inhumane partaking of men in cult power and I was the dead animal at the altar.

They sought me years after I thought I was safe in Coupeville, away from the painful memory of my childhood. Marcus didn't know I was there the morning he left me forever. I couldn't figure out a way to tell him. He'd be furious. He warned me not see her, that it was a dangerous curiosity. Yet there I was, enduring the repercussions of that hasty decision.

Without words, I begged her to save me. This was her chance for redemption for all the times my tender flesh has been forsaken by her, for the moment she sold my soul to the devil. It would take a miracle but I still prayed for it to come. She failed me, simply because that was the kind of mother I had. And for the longest time, I thought she was all that I deserved.

Watching Noah flaunt that engagement ring and ardor for my name, it was the purest form of torture. How could I accept his love for the rest of my life when I was already tarnished? My body had been infiltrated by filth and malady. He deserved better, not this garbage of a woman. There was no chance for us.

I didn't know that I would lose my brother and best friend in the process of setting Noah free. If I didn't call Marcus to tell him what had happened that day, he wouldn't be looking for me in haste. He wouldn't have driven drunk. They would have left the truck alone, the one where Kara passed out drunk. Everyone else would still be here. Instead, I plagued them with the misfortune meant only for me. It was all too much to handle, the darkness eager to consume. Forgetting was the safest place to be.

A heavy hand lands on my cheek. I hear a clap before the burn registers, also stirring the blow to my head. He eyes me with scorn, angry that I haven't contributed to this sexual predation.

"Ophie, kiss me. You want me. I know," he declares in a pale tone, voice riddled with erotic stimulation. He has already forgotten the fact that he just slapped me.

I am thoroughly disgusted by the suggestion, forcing my head to turn to the side.

"Fuck!" he growls, missing my lips. "Bitch, I gave you a chance." The eyes staring back at me is no longer from the same person I met earlier. This one is more famished, lusting for gore.

What he said and how he said it, reveals some sort of awareness akin to my nights with Andrew, like they are the same person. It worries me now, my inability to distinguish one assailant from the other. Or was it always just Owen, thriving in the eyes of an innocent Andrew? I don't know anymore. What about Mexico? There's a connection here. I remember something, being trapped in the bathroom, quivering from a possible attack. It's true. He was there with that fierce expression, laden with arousal. My mind has been so good at its defenses, the way it erases things I'm meant to forget.

The anticipated attack comes. He yanks my linen pants down, just enough for the elastic waist band to sit above my knees. My underwear goes next, stopped just above my lowered pants. He stands up, pulling away to disrobe the lower half of his body. I hear a belt buckle flailing urgently against its own metal part. The next thing I see is his aged and wrinkled penis, dangling loud and hard in the silence of the forest.

Many chances have been offered in the passing minutes to fight back, especially while I'm free of his hold. I'm frozen. This is the dilemma. He's detached from his gun but my thoughts and body aren't connecting. Maybe there isn't anything left in myself to war with.

His face is a blur among the rough tree shafts, an irrelevant sight beneath the pair of birds nesting on the lush branches. They don't care about this sickening sight, blind to everything else but their objective. My eyes follow a train of large ants, making their way out of the gigantic roots to my right. Everything else becomes of interest against the growls of this feral monster, edging towards my defenseless shape. They crawl along the soil, gracefully passing outlines of shoes and boots, over piles of patterned stones, and beneath green shoots of fresh plant life.

Wait. What?

Owen clears his throat while I nurse this critical shock running down my spine. I'm not convinced of what I saw, despite my reaction.

"What's the matter? Seen a ghost?" he asks, clasping his erection. He descends slow before opening his mouth once more. "You know what I like about you, Ophelia, compared to the other girls at the camp? You're just so..." he pauses to think, "... quiet and well-behaved. You know exactly what to do." Next, he spreads my trembling legs, ushering crumbs of dirt and decomposing forest into my genitals. Yet I haven't forgotten about the presence I saw just moments ago. "But you deceived me though. You and your mother, lying about your virginity. You should have seen what you've done. You ruined the natural order. You ruined everything. She deserved what she got and you will too!" He's right. I was already with Noah when he came to Coupeville.

I feel his hand caressing my thighs, fingers dancing up towards my labia. I clench my muscles hard to reject him of entry, while evading his face in utter heat. I turn to the pairs of feet that have been strangely undetected until now. My eyes narrow at the sight of them, heart pounding in surprise. I look up, partly relieved that it's them I see.

There is now just gloom in her eyes where once only fear lived. She peers at this horrific sight, similar to what she's been through. She's me, the little girl I failed to save. Next to her is my brother, just watching quietly with sorrow, clutching her hand. Kara's expression is bursting with fright, hand covering the disbelief in her mouth.

"Urghh..." Owen cries in pleasure, rubbing his manhood in monotonous strokes, while his other set of fingers remain in my genitals. The action is done with intense force, as I watch my bottom spring up from the ground in retaliation.

The pain, this lung-collapsing terror is getting harder and harder to ignore. This call is urgent, a looming re-demolition of my body. Yet I can't help but wonder what they're thinking. Why aren't they saying anything? I need to know what they need from me, much more than what I should do for the cries of help aiming knives at my skin.

My eyes sail back to her. Little Ophelia's expression stained with torment rather than the tenderness and divinity of a child in her age. Her hair draws waves of black strands, with ends arrayed fluidly over her collarbones. The black polka dot dress has been cinched tightly over her waist's bony structure, skirt flaring above a mast of thin legs. Thick wool socks slouch woefully over a pair of black flats. Out of all the said vestments, the only thing I remember wearing is that harrowing gaze.

Slimy hands arrest my thighs, shattering against my peaceful interaction with my loved ones. He swings them upwards and against a beastly chest. It has come to this. Why did it come to this?

The world stops. Everything pauses before his stiff penis can slide and extol his dominance.

It enters, the dark room that was prison to the little girl. She's inside it. Her neck and thighs are lathered in purple bruises. There is a bind around her wrist, as she looks out to the crack in the doorway. Two boys are maneuvering the locks on the other side of it. Marcus picks the doorknob with an unwound paper clip. Henry pacifies her cries, comforting her broken spirit. He urges Marcus to hurry before they're caught. They have always made every effort to release me from the cult's incarceration. Henry most of all, has safeguarded me from memories such as this. It would be thankless of me to allow the end of this life without defiance, for which Marcus died to save. It has always been my survival that forced Henry to ignore his own.

A fight stirs. It boils from within me at the last hour, even as I lie helpless.

My lower half is spread wide for his ravenous delight. I'm naked not just for his masturbating purposes. He is going to penetrate me. A prayer would be in vain, a dire but dumb resort. Our last encounter is a fresh memory riddled with slaughter. Somehow, I'm sure of his wretched capacities even when there's so much more to remember about him.

He hovers above me in slow calculated motions, dusting away leaves from my hair. The vision of him glints in and out, showing Andrew's face in-between hazes. I'm starting to believe that I have been wrong about the guy.

"So beautiful," he tells me, as the forest's creeks quiet down in decorum. They either agree to the proclamation or simply stand in complacence. I run my fingers on the ground, finding his discarded shirt and the contents of his pocket. A small compelling voice inspires battle through my ears. The wind rushes in our space as the squall of fresh hope lands in my hand. Meanwhile, his heavy respirations mark a new opportunity. I have a chance. I know I do!

They're gone, all three of them, but the shadows of their presence linger in the loud urges inside my head. It was mostly her, the little me. I didn't think I could disappoint her more than I already did. She didn't rival against the deep wounds of her young cult life, just so I could forget about her courage. I have failed her, neglecting what it took to stand brave while crippled.

Minutes pass but it hasn't arrived, his penile assault. Instead, he tosses himself above me. Spent lips fall on my neck, mustering kisses to cover up his impotence. He's gone limp and I am swept by both comedy and hopefulness in this very moment.

"Ophelia! Are you here?" A faint voice resounds along the boundaries of the woods, with a burning worry.

I'm well-acquainted by its comfort and relief even from afar. Henry. He's here! He knows where I'd be. I could always count on him for my rescue.

"Make a sound! I'm coming!"

There it is again, growing louder and moving within proximity. All the while, Owen remains drowned in his feeble masculinity on top of me, clutching various parts of my body to stimulate a fresh craving within himself. His mumblings and grumbles are gullibly muffling the pressing steps approaching us. He always thought I wasn't going to fight back and he was mostly right. They've had a stronghold in my mind, him and my mother. It has been hard to battle against this certain jurisdiction that makes me falter at their will.

I grip it harder in my hands away from his view, the blue pen I found earlier from his jean pocket. The transient thought of little Ophelia is gently allowing an onslaught of courage to rush in my chest. This is my chance at redemption. For me. For us.

"Urghhhh! You psycho bitch!" He cries in agony, startling the birds and insects within our margins.

He rolls to my side, left ear now bleeding. I rush to pull my panties and pants up before standing, ignoring their soiled state from Owen's recent gonadal implosion. He remains there on the ground, naked body still reeling in this surprise attack. A cyclone of fury engulfs me, quickly breaking the spell they once cast on my child body - the one that made me vulnerable to him and my mother's sexual orders. My will to live and this recharging adrenaline rise up in rank, ready to be expelled into a dire vengeance.

He's howling in the background, forgetting to retaliate against me. He clutches one side of his face with both hands, grimacing in disbelief. Then he tries to kick me with his thick legs but the pain in his ear calls his full attention again.

"Fuck!" He growls at me.

I watch him begin to comb the ground for his gun but with luck now on my side, I eye it next to my foot. We both see it at the same time but only one of us will get a hand on it. A smirk grows beneath my embattled face while he jerks back. I expect him to wriggle away like an injured snake but he doesn't. The fear for his life has mustered him a newfound immunity to pain. And as the chilling scene in the movies when the severely wounded antagonist is impenetrable to stabs and gun shots, he brings himself up in all his naked glory.

Oh no!

I hurry and take the handgun with all my might, and fling it away into the deep brush. Slithers and hisses are heard for a short time, as the weapon makes its way down into seclusion. Immediately, the weight of his body wrestles me back to the ground, arms chained firmly around my shoulders.

"Don't make a sound or else," he whispers, his dense build slumped over my back. He knows we have company.

Or else what?

And before I could make something out this frustration, I see black.

"Arghhhh! Damn it!" His distressed cries go reverberating off the pines and firs, loud enough to pierce through their foliage.

He wails again, both in agony and defeat, the way he truly deserves. In-between my fist, the pen remains. Blood and flesh drip down from its pointed tip, staining my tremored hand. I hold no remorse for what I did while this compelling need to tend to my anguished shape is hard to silence. There's hardly any time to waste.

Owen's generous gripes and exclamations from the fresh harm I inflicted is growing in distance. My bare feet are sorely taking pricks from the forest floor, as well as brash slaps on my face from twigs along this unchartered part of the woods. It's been minutes now from when I started racing towards Henry's voice. The urgency has brushed some parts of my thoughts clear, so I could make sense of what just happened.

There was a struggle, an evasion of his strikes. His punches landed on the dirt. Next thing I remember, our brawl was spooling on the ground. We rolled until I came out on top of him, my knees locking down on his neck as if we had equal power. I don't know how I was able to. I siphoned all the energy from the tiniest pools in my body towards the surface of my skin. Perhaps, desperation or survival? Whatever it was, it blinded me with anger. I was intent on revenging as I charged the pen towards his eyeball. The repeated action drilled blood and epithelium, oozing out of his eye.

I couldn't stop. It was hard to. I felt stronger with each stab, my body fortified. The fury I put out returned to me twice as much. It gave me a sense of liberation from the demons that have made a home out of me since I was a child. All the while, giving birth to a new litter of them nearby. I kept wounding and assaulting, hoping to make proud of the little girl who bears my name, who suffered in vain. Truthfully, it was an inherent hunger that I wished was satisfied by standing up against my mother instead. It's already too late for that.

I stopped, not because I was tired but of what I saw. It gave him a window to clash back, shoving me away. My head almost landed on a large rock but I was able to evade it. It was her. I have forgotten what she likes to be called but she seemed pleased. In those moments, I have morphed into her protege. I almost lost me there and the transformation would have been permanent, had I given in to this maiming wrath. That's why she woke me up. She needed me here. She wants me to fight because I'm her only ticket back into this plane, back to rule my mind.

Today is just not enough to avenge everyone I've lost because of Owen and my mother. Marcus. Kara. Henry. Me. They are the root of this quarrel.

"Ophelia!" Henry's voice calls once more. I'm getting closer to where he is. I look back to see if she followed me and feel relieved that she hasn't. No sign of Owen either.

I reach a small clearing, a glimpse of the road almost within reach. The sirens lead the way for more. Years ago, they were in this very same place, to collect bodies that have been sacrificed for my survival. I can hear them. Flashes of red and blue appear in and out of the breaks between the tree line. I keep running, not meaning to stop unless I'm certain that Henry is at the finish line. The breeze of safety graces my skin, alerting my body of its severely frail shape.

I'm here. I'm finally here.

"Help! Help!" All but broken whispers leave my mouth. I lost my voice to the scuffle.

But at last, I see people. A lot of them behind this figure running faster than the rest. The sun shines high above him, showing only a moving silhouette sprinting my direction. Then gently, he reveals himself from the distortion.

"Wait, let me talk to her first," he tells the throng of people behind him.

Both shock and confusion are taking turns leaking the air from my lungs, ogling at him. He said he didn't care. I could have sworn he would push me off the cliff at the slimmest chance. What the fuck is he doing here?

I catch a sight of my father among the uniformed crowd. He covers up his worry with his hat, while Mabel consoles him. All pause, as the man takes careful steps my direction, distracting me from the fact that Henry and Harlow are nowhere to be found. Some groups disperse to the forest, possibly to alert Henry that I have been found, or rather I found them. The rest hurry back to the road with a purpose.

"Hey," he calls to me softly, hands held up in a neutral fashion. "You're okay. You're okay. I'm here." The tremble in his demeanor is hard to conceal.

I narrow my gaze, making sure it is truly concern in his expression. His skin is gold again, cheeks no longer gruff in loathing towards me. Some parts of his neck tattoo peer above his collar. This smile forming down his mouth, is incompatible to his intensely penetrating stare. His eyes seem haunted by the war he left behind, or the one right in front of him.

"It's me. Babe. It's me," he assures, finding his protective grip around my wrists.

I know that voice, its dips and ascents dance in congruence to my heartbeats. It's happening right in this very moment. The feel of his skin against mine, I concede to its prevailing current. His presence alone could command both my life and death. This is my Noah. Undeniably. Irrevocably.

He wears his full camouflage gear in masterful charm. Even in grave danger, there will always be a loud vindication of how much I love him. I watch his army green boots move, obliterating the remaining space between us. N. Mason, the sewn patch reads on one side of his chest. He's real, not just a version nor a dark shadow of the man I met at the old house. I understand now, the failed connection that I tried to revive when meeting Dylan. It was only meant for us, Noah and I. They're two different people.

"I'm sorry. I've been deployed this whole time. I couldn't get back fast enough. Henry called and told me everything yesterday," he whispers, gloom leaching in his voice. He lifts my face up at the chin, inspecting my battle wounds as I do his. There's a power of utter brokenness in his expression, that is not in any hurry to be dismissed. "What has he done to you?" comes his angered question. "God! I'd kill that son of a bitch." I believe him as his rage begs to be freed. He runs his hands along my hair, down to my shoulders, and my back. He craves to hold me in his arms, back in the safety of his love. But he first needs permission from my body. His fear is palpable, afraid to touch my segments that would possibly deny him the chance to feel. What he doesn't know is that the space he left next to me remains molded to his shape.

I crash my aching body into his, giving him the nod to do the same. It can only be explained in a few words, the fitting of lost parts, and our separate heats colliding into a consuming blaze. I'm sure this happens every time we find each other. It is enough for me to forget that I still feel betrayed by him, leaving without saying goodbye.

"Uhmm... I'm sorry for the way I left. It... It killed me, not being able to say goodbye. I thought it was for the best." I continue to melt within the safety of his military gear, while he stammers in speech, trying to mend the disloyalty he sensed from me. The smell of fireworks breaches my nostrils, escaping the threads of his apparel. Soot and dust remain uncleansed from his neck, I feel them as I caress him lovingly. They all remind me of the plight we both endured to get here. All the answers seem enough, even when there's still a mob questions awaiting them

Yet there's so much I want to tell him, things I want to find out. They all flood my thoughts while I hug him tighter. Then my world comes to a thunderous stop. It's abrupt and unkind. My energy is funneling out of my membranes. All my systems are overloading into one another. I sense a stoppage in my veins and arteries.

"Ophelia! No! No! Stay with me," Noah grows alarmed.

I become this floating lasso inside Noah's cradle, being reminded of my recent feat, while lacking sleep and food. The light bulb in my head flourishes brighter as I become duller. I have been hit in the head, clawed at the genitals, and thrown into the forest floor among other things. Adrenaline is retreating back into its home base. I have forgotten that it always operates on borrowed time. I fight hard against this airy feeling, keeping my eyes fixed on Noah, who's been screaming for help. I notice more heads crowding my view of the sky, mouths opening, and fingers pointing. I can't close my eyes just yet. I'm afraid that he'll leave again.

"Why didn't you get the medics right away? Damn it, Noah!" The voice is audible among the sea of murmurs. It belongs to Henry. I recognize his heavy footsteps immediately upon arrival. "Over here! She's fainting." I imagine him waving at the ambulance people, pressing on them to hurry.

"Oh my God! Dad! We saw him. He's there in the woods. I'm worried of what he might have done," Harlow cries, while stroking my hand.

"Ophelia. Stay with us, okay. Don't you leave me!" I can sense his pain and desperation. I wish I could just tell him that I'll be okay. It's just fatigue. My worry is better warranted. I don't want him to disappear on me again. This is what I wish to beg of him but even that seems hard to. "She was fine, man. She ran this way." He's probably explaining to Henry what happened here before he came.

"Hey you. Hang in there for me, okay?" Henry's touch is icy but also brimming with relief, voice soft and soothing. I welcome it on my face full of gratitude, even though he's now a haze. Noah's reasoning has been obviously ignored.

I don't think I can hold on much longer. My vision has been eager to draw the curtains for some time now. I'm too weak for this battle. Surrendering is the only choice left.

So there in the heart of disarray, the wind bends the sky to darkness. Night falls upon me, loosening my grip on consciousness.

"We got you, babe. I'm here. We're here." It's Noah's voice, seemingly delivered across a narrow tunnel. I seize its echo before the imminent disconnect.

CHAPTER TWENTY-SIX

The Coast Is Clear, Isn't It?

"What the actual fuck? Are you crazy? You've seen what happened. She's better off with me around." It's Henry's voice boiling in argument. His quiet nature excites and scares me at the same time. His anger leaves a lot to unleash, the few instances of them, I mean. "And that fucking Owen, how the fuck does he always get away? All the people we pay to protect her. Damn fucking useless."

It's strange how much repulsion and distance are laid between him and Owen, as if they aren't related by blood. I remember how he seemed so sure that Henry would not hurt him for that very reason. But I have all the faith in the world in this man whom I've known since he was a boy. He couldn't love me the way I wanted to but I'm certain that he will do anything to protect me. I know he took care of him, one way or another. Yet I'm still afraid to ask.

"Well, all those years that I stayed back on your order you couldn't even guarantee her safety. He found her cuz you let her go with that Andrew character in the beginning. Exposing her like that, man. On national television? Does that juggle your memory a little? I trusted you when you said you had a handle on it. But why? Why bring her back here? All the shit you did to keep her away from here. What were you thinking?" Noah. He's here. What a relief, to hear the sound of his voice. It's easy to ignore the revelation that he's been around this whole time, just standing by in the periphery, awaiting my need of him.

"Do you realize that I'm only human? I was responsible for her safety. How do you think I felt when I failed? Man, I replay that in my head over and over. She still thinks that it was Andrew this whole time. That attack, walking in that room," comes Henry's sullen response. His regret is felt in my bones.

At will, I know I could get my eyes to open, but I refuse to disrupt this conversation. Henry has been withholding a lot from me throughout the years. It's cruel but he stands by the justification of my safety. There is no difficulty deducing the fact that I'm in the hospital. My wrist is wrapped tight underneath a bandage tape. A needle or two rest without pain on parts of my arm. The subsequent machine beeps have been entrancing, forming a remedial harmony. I'm alive, no matter the circumstance and my Noah remains at my bedside this time around. Besides the distinct coupling of life and death that has been taunting me in this space, I feel wildly relieved.

"I was there too! Remember? He got away," Noah responds as his footsteps arrive at the edge of my bed. "And even after that, you left her alone in her house while you ran along with Landree. I don't care if she had protection. I can't believe I allowed you to make that judgement. We couldn't even fucking call the authorities because you were afraid they'll ask her questions, throw her in a spiral once she remembers the cult. You were worried about what happens when they ask her about the details of Marcus' death. You didn't want them to dig up our past but she would have been safer if we did this the right way."

"Well, I guess after today it's not a choice anymore. Cops are involved now," Henry says with a hint of sarcasm before drawing attention to his own anger. "And stop being so righteous. Mexico was on you! I told you to stay here but you never listened," he growls. "They got him there alright, but he's back. Today, that's the same man. That bastard we're supposed to protect her from. I lead her right back to him. I already beat myself up for it. Will you give me a fuckin' break?"

The room grows quiet from both their impending outbursts. I hear a crunching at my bedside from a small package being opened. A mastication follows. It's Noah. I know. I've memorized all of his rhythmic actions, even the simple fact that he's chewing a gum. I'm not certain if this knowledge is from when we got back together or from our beautiful but dark past.

Henry clears his throat. I hear his body sink down to the couch across the hospital bed, picking up a magazine, and randomly flipping pages to break the sharp tension between the two. Yet, he tosses it back to the center table and mumbles to himself before regarding Noah again. "I know this isn't just about Owen. I know that Andrew thing, you're still pissed about it. I mean we already discussed that, didn't we? I didn't want her to have any exposure to her past."

Noah can be heard disgorging a sarcastic laugh in return. "Except for you, right?"

"Oh come on! I know I made a mistake, okay?" Henry defends. "The last thing she needs is for us to be fighting."

Noah takes a deep breath, hands scouring for something at my bedside. He finds my hand, lovingly squeezing it to my heart's content. "You know how difficult that was for me?" he tells him. "I already wanted to die when you told me you were taking her away, after your accident with Marcus. After you got his heart. After my sister died." His words ache and at the same time causes my heart to nurture a subtle repulsion towards Henry, for what he has done to tear us apart. But I'm no innocent. I had a hand in that, even when I only remember some parts. I ran away from his proposal, didn't I? "She was right there next to you, looking at me as if we didn't just talk about spending our whole lives together. She didn't wanna leave your side and you loved that, didn't you?"

"The fuck you talkin' about?" Henry replies, voice small though teeming with furious defense. "Marcus wanted that. He made me promise before he left."

"And I respected your decision," Noah debates. He lets go of my hand to clutch the bed railings. "But more than that, I saw the way you looked at her even back then. Wasted no time marrying her. But you left her vulnerable for that bastard Owen because you couldn't love her the way she needed to be loved. That was my job. I did that all those years and I could have done better had she stayed with me. I will take all of her, even the broken parts that you couldn't stomach." Henry grunts in the background. "Deep inside you know that. And Andrew was right. Whatever sick, twisted shit you have going on in your head, to think that you could keep Ophie on a leash while you fuck Landree. Dude, you're still married to the woman."

Henry seems lost for words at this unleashing of resentment, old and new. My bed tremors, absorbing the wrath that has escaped Noah's hand. He's not even done yet.

"I'd kill to be in your place. I don't know why you let her fall over and over? You didn't even have the decency to let me know when you were tired, that you wanted Landree. I would have been on the next flight to get to her. You let her suffer, man!"

Henry battles back, "You don't know what you're talking about, Noah. You don't understand my point."

"Then make me!"

Henry withdraws, not wanting to say more. He doesn't appear willing to explain himself further. I wonder the same. I wish he could shed some light to it.

"If anything, I thought we were friends and you know how I feel about her. I didn't have to tell you. Everyone fucking knows! I bought the ring first, remember? I have done nothing but obey because Marcus said this and that." A sigh follows his outburst, but it isn't an indication of retreat. "I'm tired of this bullshit. He's dead for fuck's sake! That first call should have been me. Isn't it proof enough? I return and she still chose me, even if she couldn't remember. She will choose me again, no matter how many times you take her away from me."

Noah spits the gum, his teeth and tongue making slurping noises right after. There's still nothing from Henry's side of the room and that is to be expected. He's always the one to wait for the strain to settle down.

"I shouldn't have left her. I should have stayed in Mexico and stopped you from telling her another lie. Paid people to lie too, about some plane crash when we both know Owen tried to hurt her. I'm tired of the lies." That's Noah's voice, rage defeated by Henry's brave composure. "In the end, your explanation is owed to her. I just hope you grow some balls and tell her the truth."

I hear footsteps, commencing from where I sensed Henry to be seated. For a moment, I thought there's going to be a brawl but they should know better. The walking ends at the bottom of my bed as the cushion caves in to a fresh weight besides my own.

Henry is now seated here, across where Noah is. "Maybe you're right," he begins to speak. "But more importantly, what was I supposed to do? You would have done the same thing if you were in my place." He sniffles while adjusting his bearings. "I stayed married to her because I needed to continue making decisions on her behalf when she loses herself again. You haven't seen the worst of it. So, forgive me for lying to her so I can make sure she doesn't spiral into a God knows what." His tone is capped with ceasefire but I can tell from the subtle trembles when he speaks, that his patience is also hanging on the edge.

"And I couldn't? Be the person that she marries and make those same decisions for her? Well, I wasn't given a chance to prove that I can handle it, was I?" Noah makes a smart remark. "And you're wrong. I know she's not perfect even from the start. I love her more after finding out. She didn't hide anything from me. You thought wrong."

Henry lets out a deep sigh in retort, ignoring the stark reaction from him. "And I don't think you have the right to discount what I have done for her. I was with her since we were children, when we were at the camp. Out of everyone, I am the only person who understands, really understands. That life, we both ran away from it together. We are still running away from it up to this day. Of course, I love her. But I understand why you don't see that."

Noah gets up, pulling the weight of his anger with him. "But that's just it, Henry. You love her because you needed to. I have done so much more and not because I felt obligated. I know you care for her. You would die for her. I'd give that to you but I don't think you love her the way that she deserves. You look at her as some kind of cracked glass. The truth is, you only know how to keep her safe and the only thing that she has ever given you is the reason to. Otherwise, you wouldn't have left her for Landree. No matter the cost. No matter what's missing. I would have stayed away if things were different."

My eyelids fling open, met by a thin blur in my vision. Still, Henry's expression is obvious through the veil. He's struck by regret and also solemnity. He doesn't need to prove it though, I know he cares for me. The fluorescent lighting is piercing my eyes as I recover their clarity. Along with that, a weight on my skull materializes, as does the agony all over my body. I feel it in my woman most of all. There's a tray of food on a metal cart. It reminds me of my famished state. It's parked near the visitor's sofa ahead of a side table, where a few vases of tulips and pink carnations sit to obstruct my view of the outside world.

"I didn't think that we'd come to this, man," is his reply, uttered by a mouth filled with a nous of pain. He stares at Noah, who from the corner of my eye is lost in far thoughts. "I admit it. I fucked up before, many times. It was a mistake bringing her here too. I was thinking now that her mom's gone, maybe everything else that she inflicted will disappear. She has a family here and I just wanted her to get to know them. I didn't think that Owen would get past our people again. I mean, I thought I made sure of it. I was dumb enough to forget why we even left in the first place."

" I'm just telling you what I should have a long time ago. I'm tired of nodding my head every time you or Marcus, or Dylan asks something of me," Noah asserts. "I love this woman in the way that you just can't."

The power and vindication in those words have anointed my spirits back to life. I have felt Noah's love but to affirm it to Henry of all people, ignites a larger flame deep inside my center. It has always been us, after tragedy's ingenuity of bringing us together. This is real, both founded and foisted into misfortune but has survived all of it.

I love you too, Noah.

"We're cool. Besides her, all these are just stupid crap between us," he adds. "I guess I just... I need to tell you that. I was never given a chance. I can't talk to my twin brother about this. Dylan hasn't forgiven himself for letting you guys go that night. He's still pissed."

You think?!

"It hasn't subsided after all these years." Noah's expression has been drowned in his hand gestures, that has been whipping across his face while he speaks. He's edgy and smudged with grief. "What I'm trying to say is that, you're not the only one who lost somebody that night. Kara. She had two brothers and both failed to get her out of danger. Marcus was my friend too. And you wanna know something? Somewhere in the midst of that craziness, I still felt some sort of hope that things will be okay afterwards because I had Ophelia. I didn't expect that she'd be taken away from me too."

"I don't know. I don't know what to say," Henry voices his apprehension. He shakes his head almost violently.

"Don't worry about it," Noah's reply, though short, is enough to pacify his friend's discomfort.

Though he may be great at being composed during disputes, Henry would certainly rather walk away than fight back. A grin forms at one side of his mouth meant for the only other conscious person in this room, followed by a flash in his eyes. He notices me, unsure of how long I have been quietly an audience to their intense exchange. Noah jumps in front of my view, immediately draping his shoulders over the bed railings.

"Hi there! You're awake," Henry greets me, coming out of his seated position. I find him standing next to Noah shortly after.

I force a smile at them as well as some sort of ocular focus. With my eyesight barely managing to see, the pounding in my head is getting worse. Even the light blue curtains behind them seem like a visual assault. I'm convinced that the drugs they gave me was only good at manifesting the side effects, rather than take the pain away.

"You heard all that?" Noah asks, nervous.

He's met by my nod. "I heard everything," I tell him.

And as if it was rehearsed, they look at each other, manner succinct. They both make blaming faces before turning to me to plead their case.

"What exactly did you hear?"

"I can explain."

"It's the truth"

"Well talk about it."

"Stop it, man, let me say something first."

The room becomes an instant auction, with mouths tattling too fast to comprehend. Both want my attention. Both need to be heard first. I stare at the white walls ahead of me to regain focus. There's another seating area next to the door, a chair in maple wood with an auburn tweed cushion that holds a backpack. I assume it's Noah's, judging from the military markings. The dull painting above it catches my attention, anything to distract me from the shouting frenzy in the sideline. The art portrays a scene at a beach. There's the strokes of blue waves, golden sand, and bright hues of green around the margin to represent the dune grass. It's mounted by a gold frame that is thinner than usual. I'm noticing more of similar paintings around the room, but not enough to pull me away from the dizzying argument they're both having. The beeping sound in my right ear has shattered my sound barrier. I'm hearing them again in normal volume, shouting and pointing fingers.

"This is all your fault, Noah," Henry yells.

"Me?" Noah throws his hands up to assert his innocence. "Why?"

"Come on! We're supposed to tell her together. Not this way!"

"Stop!" I hold a palm up. "Stop it! Both of you."

The effort almost yanked off the IV needle from my forearm. I ease myself up. Noah is quick to come to my assistance, but I jerk at the mere concern. He is mindful of my reaction, giving himself a few seconds before touching me again. He has one hand on my shoulder and the other supporting my back. I have forgotten how my skin remains on the defense from Owen's forceful strokes.

"I'm okay. Thanks." I acknowledge his tenderness, patting his wrist.

The action enlivens my rather dehydrated veins, much more than the medical fluids hosed to my body. It recognizes him, reminding me of how much I have yearned to feel him again, this whole time we were apart.

"I miss you," I read the soundless oration from his lips.

I could die from the weight of those words, from the instant bewilderment spilling across my chest. How I have missed him too. How quickly my wounds have been silenced momentarily.

Henry rolls his eyes without hesitation. "So," he opens his speech with a rather displeased tone before checking on my welfare, "how do you feel?" he asks, crossing his arms over his chest. "Where does it hurt?"

I shake my head. "Not much. I mean my head is pounding a bit." I lie. It hurts a lot.

"Okay. Are you hungry? I can get you something different than this hospital food." He adds, pointing to the cart.

"Hmmm. Nah. I'm good for now. What time is it? Is today still today?" I ask either of them. My voice sounds rough, having passed through the raw tissues in my throat.

They nod in chorus. It's palpable from their faces of uncertainty that they are carefully treading this conversation. They couldn't just say, you kicked butt today, Ophelia. Great job! Kudos. Considering how disastrous the situation was, I understand.

The truth is, I still hear his voice taunting me in accord with the ringing in my ears. I'll be afraid to be alone, even just for a minute. From here on out, every crowd I'm in would toil at the possibility of his presence. The darkness will manifest his face and my mother's. They will crawl out of hiding from under the bed, once I close my eyes. Nightmares will plague my sleep even worse than it did with Andrew. I'd have to fortify my walls against their memories, while fighting off the other me who refuses to remain idle in my mind. She has been eager for the permanence of this body. She's equal parts friend and foe. There's Kara too and then my brother. That's too many demons than my prayers can surmount.

No wonder why it was easier to become another person. How dare I question myself, when forgetting was the best thing I did to save me from all this pain. I can no longer blame Henry for making sure the memories stay that way.

"Mmmm... Is he?" comes my question to whoever is brave enough to reply. Not my first thought but he's a newly-resuscitated and lingering horror upon mention.

They look at each other again, this time in search for a silent nudge. Henry submits to it first.

"He's been taken care of," Henry says with firm assurance, no sighs nor side glances.

"Yeah! After they find him a new ear and eyeball," Noah plows with an icebreaker. His tone is leaking with sarcasm but also nerves.

Henry couldn't help but sneer, slightly elbowing Noah to scold him of the joke. They act like kids, one minute bickering to their anger's content, and the next making puns with each other.

The level of this trauma has been misconstrued by all of us. I am gradually enraged and confused by the realization. Because the last 48 hours have been forced beyond its tensile strength in order to fit the memories and secrets I've uncovered, more than a decade worth. I am not equipped to accept them at once, and the manner in which I received them was as brutal as the origin.

"Also…" Noah recaptures my attention while my fingers romp over the white sheets. "I meant to say that you can ask me anything and I'll tell you what I know."

"Just because I heard you guys?" I challenge him.

He denies, expression surprised by the subtle assault. "No, not at all!" He runs his hand through my fingers, trapping them in his fist.

I want to see how Henry takes it, this derision. His arms return to his chest. He doesn't look at me. The floor becomes the only direct witness to his guilt. He should be. Just because he took good care of me, doesn't mean lying is excused. Noah too! He went along for the ride. None of them are free of fault.

"I'm sorry. I meant to tell you but the circumstance, I didn't wanna make it worse." Noah asserts. "I wouldn't do anything to hurt you. I promise. I care about you so much even before. If you only know," he adds.

"Yeah, I remember," arrives my crucial revelation.

Noah squeezes my hand tighter.

Henry looks up in surprise, the display of gloom still radiates all over his face. "You what?"

"Us, me and Noah. Marcus. Kara. My mother. The cult. A lot of it." My eyes fix on Noah, whose face is disfigured by a multitude of emotions coming over him all at once.

"That's good, baby, that's really good," he says to me, voice shaking. Noah engulfs me in his tight embrace. "Wow! I don't believe it. I could cry, baby!" he mumbles further from behind my ear.

Henry is right there, at the center of my vision. He grimaces from the mixture of pain, anger, and disappointment that have come out from hiding. I know he would rather keep me from my past.

Noah pulls away so I could see his profound glee and I realize that he has misunderstood what I said. "I meant I remember a lot but not everything," I tell him.

"Oh!" He purses his lips, unable to say anything more.

This injury has reached new heights, and I must confront them head on, even when Henry seems unwilling to narrate. He is too protective of me and he's pained at the thought of old memories returning. He knows what happened, even the details.

"I only have one question for the both of you," I say.

The men ahead of me stand a little taller in attention, wondering what they'll soon hear.

"Why? Why lie to me? Why help me forget rather than remember?" They had no right to dictate my motivations but somehow, I already know their answers. I just wanted to hear them.

I can put two and two together. By the day's end, I'd have a timeline of what happened to me based on these new memories that have resurfaced. Owen wanted me out of vengeance towards my dead mother. But I also know it's more than that. For years he's been harboring a sick addiction to me and I almost succumbed to it today. He needed her money too, that she allegedly stole from him or the whole cult. How she was able to flee is still beyond me. At present, I inherited the bulk of it. Marcus came after me the night of his accident, regardless of his condition because I told him I was running away. I couldn't accept Noah's proposal after being victimized by Owen and his men that same day. Kara was simply an unfortunately an innocent fatality.

I will never know why my mother did what she did but there's no way to ask her now. She summoned enough strength to leave the cult and swindle them out of their dirty fortune. But when Owen caught up to her, she did nothing to stop him from violating me as a newly fledged adult. It seemed like she owed him the chance to touch me at last, when his previous abuses were only carried out by her. Most of all, I couldn't fathom my intention of being quiet all those years, why I didn't make my voice heard, even to Noah. He should have known about my childhood. I couldn't imagine hiding that from him. Or did I tell him?

Yet, would he have accepted me had I revealed to him that I didn't put up a fight? Would he have understood that I deliberately submitted my body to a horde of men and their gluttonous needs? Maybe I was sparing him from the damage more than I did for myself. Maybe he already knows all these.

I notice Noah open his mouth but it is Henry who takes the floor. "It was my decision. My fault. I forced it on everyone. None of them had the chance to object against it," he tells me.

He moves forward as Noah takes a step back to give way for his coming. There is a slight ache when he disconnects from my hand. "I don't know if I misunderstood your brother's last wish but I took it how I took it," Henry continues as he clutches the top of the bed railings. "I just want you to escape from it all. The loss and the inconceivable pain that comes with it. You've seen what it did to you when you finally remembered. I just want you to be okay. I want a great life for you, away from the tragedy. Far from the memories of the Disciples. I didn't care if I was being excessive!" His voice grows more upset.

"And marrying me? That wasn't out of love, was it?" I ask him, almost afraid of what he'll say next.

He is quiet for a few seconds, possibly testing his choice of answers in his head. "I care about you a lot. Come on, we grew up together. With Marcus gone, his job became mine. It was necessary because I felt like you were always gonna need me. I have to be able to protect you and make decisions for you when you can't. I don't know how I could make that even more clear to you."

"And sending me to Jessica was supposed to help with your cause?" My impatience has mustered enough force to float in the surface. His overprotective nature has always irked me in more ways than one.

"She was supposed to help you get better, look forward to the future." I shrug my shoulder before his touch could land on it. "I intended to keep you safe and well, Ophie. It's true, no matter the cost and I would have done that for you even if I didn't receive Marcus' heart."

"Well, if you were supposed to know what's best for me, why didn't you get Noah? Not even when you got tired of the job? You knew from the start how much I love him. Landree came and somehow you just fell apart at the seams. You left me, pushed Andrew to my direction. Who by the way, you allowed to take the blame for Owen's attack. Did your plan ever involve my happiness? You let me forget about Noah. How could you!" To be frank, my rage doesn't completely belong to Henry. I'm mad at everything else, this whole situation, and my past. How did I let the years slip away while being drowned beneath the unknowing?

This whole time I felt like I had nowhere to go, especially when Henry met Landree. It was all just there, my fate with Noah has been adhered to the maze in front of me. I was too much of a coward to face the terror that I allowed my thoughts to bury him with it.

"Ophie, baby," Noah's voice and façade emerge from behind Henry. He stands at the foot of the bed, where Henry was a while ago. I feel his tender caress on my leg, telling me without so many words that he's there for me. At the same time, he possesses a deeper understanding of Henry's intentions more than I could.

Henry turns around, finding his place at the center of the grey sofa bed. He almost seems embarrassed by what he's about to say. "I'm not perfect. It was a time in my life when I was filled with so much confusion. I admit, I didn't handle that very well, leaving you, going with Landree," he replies. "To have Andrew take the blame, I don't deny the amount of wrong in that. But it was between him and making you realize it was Owen this whole time. He came in while he was away." I watch him voluntarily shake his knees while rubbing the back of his neck.

"It's true. I was there." This is Noah speaking now. I look at him and sense the weight of the world heaping on his shoulders. It must be from the memory or the responsibility of telling me the truth at the time when he should have. "When I come home from deployment, I go to where you are just so I could see you. I just have to be at a safe distance for you not to notice me. That was the agreement. It was pathetic but I took what I could get." He throws a fleeting and accusatory glance at Henry before continuing. "I was lucky to have been there when he came in. You didn't remember me helping you. You still didn't when I saw you at the café. I was watching you the whole time you were doing the same to Henry and Landree."

"It was him in Mexico too. I'm sorry we had to make it look like something else." Henry's admission is to be expected now, after the things that I heard. "I mean, it was me who wanted to lie about it. I was hoping you won't have any memory of it, like all the other times. I just couldn't risk driving you to a place of madness, the same one you were after the car wreck. I'm sorry to say but I felt relieved that you just snapped into this permanent escape from reality afterwards. I was the only one you recognized while everything else that happened around us, before and after has seemingly been forgotten. You couldn't bear the pain. I couldn't. Watching you in that state, I thought we were better off dead. I still have nightmares about it. So, forgive me for keeping Noah away from you. I thought he belonged there, to the horrendous past we both escaped from. Why else would you have forgotten about him? Was it really worth risking your stability and mental freedom so you could dig Noah out of that big rubble? You can't pick and choose, Ophelia. You shake a tree for a single fruit, you have to expect that's not all you're gonna pick up from the ground."

"I can't believe you have the nerve to ask me that, Henry," I tell him. "After everything we've been through. Of course, it would have been worth it. You allowed me to go on with a false pretense that I was meant for you and I believed it!"

Noah comes to his defense. "Please don't blame him for everything, babe. I share the fault. I should have come back sooner. I should have been more forceful. I didn't fight hard enough for you. Maybe I was too afraid that you'd reject me if I show myself as someone you once knew and loved. I belonged to the past you ran away from. I was a willing participant too, you know. Henry did everything he could with the money he had and the influence of his parents to keep you safe. I was wrong to blame him. He's only one person against the cult. Truth is, he couldn't tell you about me without reminding you of that fucker. He had to do the same thing with your family, your sister."

"Fighting back was never an option? Against him? My mom? Them?" I pitch the question at Henry, while I gracefully become embattled with lightheadedness.

"Hey. You alright?" Noah senses my discomposure and is quick to push down the bedrails and jump on the space next to me.

"I'll be fine," I reply coldly, awaiting Henry's answer.

I think this is more than just what he did or didn't do. I'm aware of what he went through with me but I feel incredibly challenged by my emotions, of this anger at all the lying and spinning stories.

"Oh come on! You're asking me?" He points to his chest. "Tell me you're kidding!"

Henry paces back and forth, tension-filled hand rubbing his nape again. He rests briefly to look at Noah and continues on.

"Would you stop that, Henry!" My shout startles him.

The effort spent the last of my control as nausea infringes my barricades. I'm brushed by a large swell of it. I could vomit. The strength of this antiseptic smell around us has grown since I ignored it. Henry shuffles forward, face marked by obvious exasperation.

"See how many times he got away? Owen? And your mother, too many connections with friends with old money. That's more power than what I have. We were gonna lose before it starts," He reveals, frowning at the memory of the two big bad wolves of my life. "You said you don't remember, there's that. What about the trial? What if they need you on the stand? How would you handle that? I couldn't let you go through with that. They'll make a fool out of you. Not to mention the exposure to Disciple members on Owen's payroll. I'm sorry that I was more focused on getting you better than throwing you in the lion's den. Does that sound fair to you?"

His idea of getting me better is questionable but I understand his motivations.

The quiet follows his uproar, with us three staring into space. Of course, he's right. He's always right, even when the circumstance appears wrong. I felt the need to question him, to find fault in everything that he did. I wanted someone to blame for what I lost but neither of them deserves it.

Noah holds me closer, more secure. He's half consoling and half imploring for me to find sympathy in Henry's actions. "To be fair," he says. "I don't know if you remember, but I was the one who found you, the night of the accident. I got the call. You hadn't returned, they told me. There was a crash. Henry was hurt. And Marcus, I knew he was gone at that point. Of course, they waited to tell me about Kara when I got home. For good reason. All I'm saying is, that there was a lot of value in what Henry did for you. I was first to see how broken you were, even when you have already lost your memories. He just wanted to save you. We all did. You've been through enough. Maybe that's why I didn't fight as hard I should have. I couldn't offer anything better at that time."

I did, I've endured so many unthinkable situations. It's a wonder why I'm still capable of love. I look at him, and in my eyes is a spirited sense of content. He sees it. He understands in the same capacity as I do. There's no need for words.

A ringing from a mobile phone surges across the unnerving silence. We all look around for its location, and each other. Whose is it? I certainly don't know where mine is. Henry reaches for his back pocket, ending the seconds-long stand-off between us, to figure out who the common ringtone belongs to. He stares at it for a quick second, wrinkling his forehead in the process.

"I gotta get this. Excuse me."

He scurries out to the door in no time. There is a hint of oddity in the manner of his reaction and departure, that is only natural to Henry. I let go of the thought before I'm consumed by the mystery and forget what is more important.

"Was it him? On the phone with you in Mexico. Conversations you didn't want me to hear?" I ask, remembering the mornings he snuck out to make calls or receive them. It only makes sense.

I feel Noah shuffling his body so we're face to face. He clears his throat to feed the stillness, a loving grin floating over his mouth. In every way, a force arrives with his presence as an ordained prescription meant to treat my brokenness. This carnal want is foisted towards my abdomen like a hunger pain. I yearn for his touch as soon as possible.

"Yup," he confirms while cradling my chin with both hands. He detects my brooding look. "Hey, you're safe. Do you trust me when I say that?"

I nod.

Beneath the question comes the strength of a promise, as if he's telling me without saying that we'll never be apart from here on out.

"I'm sorry for everything that happened to you. I'm always here. I will never leave you, not anymore. I'll fight for us. No more waking up in the hospital by yourself. Looking over your shoulders. You're not gonna spend your life chasing love. It's right here in front of you. I'm here."

He flickers back the moisture in his eyes, in the moments before he becomes ruled by emotions. Us two, we sit here as our lungs lurch up and down against the tonnage of sentiments sinking over our bodies. I remain quiet, words unable to fill the space meant to explain this phenomenon.

But he grows troubled, conceivably wondering what I'm thinking. "What's wrong? Is it what I said?"

He tugs me into a sweet embrace, my tearful surrender arriving with care over his shoulder. The flames swaddle my flank as my heart thrashes against its normal beats. The echo of I miss yous is shawled around my neck. I'm afraid to believe the legitimacy of his promise, not because I don't trust him but because I feel that I don't deserve it.

"Shhh. Stop crying please. I hate to see you this way," Noah consoles me. His palm circles around my back, voicing the same message.

I hang on to him, as his strong chest eagerly receives my heaves and sobs. I feel like I'm in the precipice of drowning but I'm reminded that Noah is here now, keeping my head above water.

He brings me back to his face, as mine remains riddled with moisture. "Hey, "he whispers. "I want you, all of you. Everything you can give and couldn't, none of that matters to me. You don't remember but I've said this before. I promise you, nothing can keep us apart anymore. Okay?"

I sniffle before intoning a reply. "Okay."

He smiles, the kind that always turns my gut inside out. "That is, if you let me. If you give me another chance. Will you?"

I let out a nervous laugh, watching this perfect man ask for my approval, I'm not deserving. I should be the one begging for his love. Did he need to ask? Isn't it obvious? I will always fall victim to his arresting lure, as evidenced by my lips, now only a few inches away from his. Surprisingly, it is him who draws in for a kiss, but it is I who places the world around us in conscious abandon.

I cape my arms on his neck, almost to the brink of suffocation. I want him, this maddening and disarming soul who renders my pain forgotten and obsolete. I have missed the grace of his tongue and I relish in the quiet incursion of its flavor.

Always have, always will.

The words soar along my senses, vindicating themselves against my doubts and memories I've yet to remember. His touch frolics all over my skin, as we savor the quiet foray of the drumrolls in our chest. Everything is clear, even in the midst of this distortion. I am unabashed by this appetite, nourished only by his love. His lips retract from mine as it travels down my neck. I feel his fingers sneak inside my hospital gown, finding nothing else besides my raw and wanting skin.

"Oh, shit!" Henry startles himself, finding Noah somewhat on top of me.

Noah jumps off the bed, as I pull my garment over my shoulders.

"Huh," Henry breathes with uneasiness while facing the door. "I was only gone for a minute."

"You can turn around now," I tell him.

He bites his lips when finally able to face us. In his eyes, something grim strikes. It was momentarily distracted by our coital display, when he slipped in unnoticed. From the corner of my vision, I watch Noah smooth kinks and wrinkles on his white textured dress shirt, unaware of the looming information yet to be told.

"What is it, Henry?" His expression is making me weary. My aroused heart has been replaced by a gripping sonata.

"Uhmm," he hesitates, as he buries his hands inside the front pockets of his jeans. "That was your dad with the sheriff people. They want you for questioning at the station."

"Okay? I expected that." I would think they'd be here by now, even before I woke up. Something else is there though, choking his patience. "What's really bugging you?" I press him further.

"I'm not talking about what happened today, Ophelia. It's... They —"

"What, Henry?" The suspense will give me a coronary any moment now.

"They found a body. And you're a person of interest," he finally reveals.

"What?" I hear Noah's loud gasp, while I endure a quiet barrage of my own.

Oh my God! Landree has been missing. The smell of bleach when I woke up? I was livid at her the day before she disappeared. I don't remember, but should I? Maybe it's her. She always takes advantage of my fury. I watch Henry as he focuses at something else. He couldn't even look at me. Of course, he thinks I killed her. There's no doubt. I know I'm not capable of such, but is she?

Henry takes a deep breath before speaking to me again. "I know it's a lot to take but I can —"

"Where'd they find her?" My bold question disrupts his ramblings. I can't imagine how I'd be able to exonerate myself. Would any jury believe me if I tell them, Well, she's me but I'm not really her. If they're already questioning me now, my chances seem too slim.

"Her? What do you mean her? I'm talking about the reporter. The one who's been following you. The same person who's been trying to get me to talk for a while now."

Oh!

"Fred," I whisper to myself.

I can't even feel relieved that it's not Landree. Shock eases its way into my skin, compelling goosebumps down my spine. Fred was relentless, pushy but never deserving of his untimely death. As a matter of fact, he was right about a lot of things, even the ones I knew but denied. I feel some amount of guilt for pushing him away. Maybe I could have prevented it if I brought him along or worked with him. It is obvious to most of us with background about the Disciples of Light, that Owen would be involved. Fred was after all, trying to expose and dismantle their clandestine operations.

"Uh huh. Some people remembered you chatting with him at some café. That was the last time he was seen alive," he adds.

"But. But. I didn't do anything. Was it an accident? Of course, it wasn't if they need my statement," I ask, nervous.

"I know. It was nothing you did. All they told me is that some cyclist found him in a ditch near town, gunshot wound to the head. They think he was murdered. But..." Henry shakes his head, anxiety materializing on his face. "Just too much for you at this time. We have to deal with the aftermath of this Owen shit. Your safety and health..."

And the flood of disordered memories that are gradually finding permanence in my thoughts- let's not forget about that.

I hear him expel a deep sigh as Noah and I turn to each other for emotional support. "We just can't fucking catch a break. Damn it!" Henry seems to have made it to the spout of his own tipping point. He trashes his phone to the tiled floor but the rug saves it from breaking.

"Henry, I really appreciate your concern." I tell him while adjusting the pillows behind me. Noah is quick to my aid. "I know it's gonna be harder to live my life from now on, knowing what I know and remember. After what happened today. But," I turn to face Noah before finishing my sentence. I just want to steal another dose of this humbling reality, breathing close to me. Also, it's my way of affirming his words and holding him to his promise. "But it's different now." Noah beams, grasping my message.

Henry processes my statement as Noah clasps my hand tighter. He finds his way to the bare wall next to the window, and is suddenly interested at what's going on outside.

"Man, I'm not going anywhere," Noah breaks his reverie. "You may not like my ways but we both want what's best for her. Besides, your plate's gonna get even fuller when the baby comes. Of course, once you patch things up with Landree." His jaunty tone is always refreshing but a foot to the mouth at the same time.

God, Noah! Just not the right time.

I elbow him and bite my lower lip, awaiting Henry's expected reaction.

"Sorry," Noah whispers.

That's a sore subject for Henry, for both of us. But in Noah's usual fashion, he always tries to make light of a difficult situation.

"Hmm!" Henry turns back to us. "That's a rub right there."

Both men chuckle together in a synchronized but also distinct mesh of deep and gruff voices. Noah shields his mouth in the fold of his arm, as Henry laughs some more. I don't see the comedy in this but good on them for trying.

The frigid air reveals a cast of my own face, strung by the divinity of love towards both men. I haven't yet exhausted all nine lives from the pit of decay I fell in. Thank goodness.

Not much has been said about the Disciples of Light, but my scars should tell you everything there is to know. People are quick to speak about our horrors of trauma but not what sprouts from their seed, long after they leave us. Some grown-ups are still frightened by the same demons they met as children. Me? They tuck me in bed night by night, and are always in my midst at every waking moment. With cadavers trailing at my heels, it's only a matter of time before the rug is pulled from underneath me again. Maybe for now, it's best to just be happy even if this may not be how it ends.

"Don't forget to call Bree. She turned the whole town over looking for you when you didn't show up," Henry says before vanishing into the threshold, leaving Noah and I to finish what we started.

I guess this is it, the turning of a new leaf and the closing of a severely weathered book. I didn't think that a lifetime's worth of wars, squabbles, mind-wrecks, and blood lettings, could still shuttle me here in the future I once dreamed of.

CHAPTER TWENTY-SEVEN

In Memoriam

It's true, there's always a sense of lawlessness that he provokes inside of me, and I'm suddenly brave in fear of losing him. Noah is sitting across the burning logs with his powerful smile, lauding conquest in the fullness of my soul. He has been my heaven, among the presence of sins. He reminds me that I don't belong inside those wooden boxes, that have since leached in decay. He maintains a stronghold in the living rather than in death.

"Your battle is mine now," he said.

And that is why I fight even if it means fighting myself. Trust that it hasn't been easy. I have dreamless sleeps now though, plenty of them. Perhaps it is the universe's reprieve, knowing that I wake up to and live in a nightmare every day. I think of what people see when they look at me now. They must wonder where I pull it from, this strength. It thrusts me against potent barricades that are preventing me to curve a smile. How I could still love and earn Noah's touch. How my bearings have been soft and easy these days. They're not. Pain and fear, they never die. The years merely stretch a stifling hand over their mouths and silences them, for the time being. That is my mastery after all. How else would I have been able to dump my mind into the safety of forgetting? All this time.

The truth is I feel it all, everything. My prayers have been begging the wrong hands for mercy, as if my demise is my only absolution. But I don't let the world see my shudders and grimaces as the wounds revive on my flesh, especially Noah. Not even when Fred's dead body left a trail of sharp questions that I don't know how to silence.

I don't want to. Not anymore. I don't want to remember what I knew about them.

Dylan becomes irritated by the heat of our ogles. It's clear, even with the bonfire's flames weaving in and out of view. His pout is palpable as darkness eagerly blows the crimson sky away. Waves continue to wash up this ill-fated shore, where parts of my past remain in its custody. Everyone is bundled up inside freezing weather garbs, finding shelter against the breeze behind the lines of beach grass. All our bodies are huddled on canvas folding chairs, driftwoods, or mats. The ocean's aroma diffuses wildly in the air, but I welcome it in my starving lungs.

"... For all their souls will always be remembered in our hearts forever," my father closes the memorial in prayer.

He held my hand in moments when he needed a reminder that Marcus did not die in vain. Noah's parents and grandmother clung to each other the same way at the mention of Kara. The Masons were kind in introducing themselves at the beginning of the service, aware that I have no recollection of them. Yet I felt it, their indifference. There will always be a wall between me and his family. Though thin, it's still a barricade against forgiveness and acceptance to seep in. I don't believe they hate me and if they did, I couldn't blame them either. I've been fighting hard over the past year to absolve myself from Kara's death. I could only imagine what they see and feel at the sight of me. They're in pain, as all of us.

We ached and throbbed for their deaths, for bodies that have long been cold before I could pay them my grief. A decade felt like a lifetime.

I'm coming to terms with Andrew's part in bringing me here, back in Noah's arms. If only it were easy to sway my terrors into believing that he never hurt me. But my mind feuds brutally against the idea. Even if he swears by my trauma as the culprit, it's his voice I remember and his hands laying wounds on my skin. In time, perhaps it's possible. I can only hope.

"Ophelia?" My dad releases me from my reverie. He reaches a hug, making it seem like he'll never see me again. "You deserve to be happy," he adds.

"Sweetie, it's true, you really do," Mabel's nurturing voice comes forward. She pats my shoulder while I remain inside the paternal cocoon. "It's over. It's all over, sweet girl."

Is it? The year that passed, only lobbied enough horror in the face of Owen. I almost forgot that he's still there. Somewhere. He's somewhere in a cell, clawing his fingers at the concrete wall and wishing it was my face. It's hard to study him, his motivations. Just like the woman who gave birth to me. How could a mother be inclined to live with this harrowing infection of abuse? And even in their deaths, I am certain that the stench of their sickness will grow nine more lives.

"Thanks, Dad, Mabel," I reply, feeling the warmth spread across my chest.

A kiss lands on my forehead prior to the emancipation, before my parents pull away. Then, they turn to host the faces awaiting their greetings.

The circle breaks into small conversations, with the younger crowd more eager to meet the banquet table. I watch Landree pull a flannel blanket from her sack, and cloak herself with it. She catches my stare and greets in a peaceful nod. Over the last year, we have remained in this sort of ceasefire. I couldn't find Henry, though he was with his son this afternoon, playing with sandcastles at the shore. He's somewhere and I wish to see him, if only to say goodbye.

"You guys are gonna burn each other alive with those freaking stares!" Harlow teases as she sits on the log next to me, burying her cold Heineken in the sand. "Might as well throw you and Noah into the fire."

"Haha! Stop," I reply, casually shoving her shoulder.

"What? It's true." She brings a deep sigh to life, abetted by the strong howl of the sea breeze. She stares at me with love and some regret. An incursion of her tears follows. "I'm gonna miss you," she sniffles, tapping her index fingers crosswise, underneath the bags of her eyes. "I'm being dramatic but a year flew by so quick. It's not enough."

I smile at her, playing with her dark, curly locks. "I'll be back," I tell her. "Don't worry so much."

We hug for a while before a thought strikes me. I pull back. She becomes puzzled.

"At the cabin, did he know who you guys were?"

"Huh? Who?" She asks, still riddled with confusion.

"Andrew, did he know who you guys were when he picked you up? When you lost your dogs?" I clarify.

"Yeah of course, he set it up. Told us to be careful not to spook you. Very kind too. He knew how sensitive the situation was."

Hearing her say those words, conjures some sort of disappointment. I'm unable to identify the actual reason. I guess I wanted to be right, to be certain that I wasn't making things up. Andrew was hurting me. But there are parts of my body that knew all along. He was not the villain I painted him to be, and for that I'm mad at myself.

"Why do you ask?" she probes further.

I shake my head. "Oh nothing, just curious."

She seems satisfied with my answer, releasing the furrow in her brows. "Okay."

Harlow pours a fist full of Skittles down her mouth, and she chews them while winking at me. Right away, I'm struck with a sense of envy, a fleeting jealousy of her faultlessness. Some people are simply lucky enough to be immune from corruption.

The chatter softens, muffled by the distance that is earned from my footsteps. I have reached the top of the hill, as if the crescent moon is now within my reach. I'll wait here for Noah, who is fetching our stuff back at the house. Down below, the festivity draws to a peak, as the fire grows higher in Marcus and Kara's memory. Laughter escapes through the crisp air, bringing with it the sound of crunching paper on the ground. I pick up the littered item from the soft dirt, cradling it. Staring at what's inside my hand, I'm met by two faces of loss: one of my brother and the other of my best friend. Yet how could I reduce them to just that, when I have become the sum of their purpose? There is hope and hope is still some sort of victory.

"Oh, sorry! Baby Marcus had that in his hand. Must have dropped it on our way up." It's Henry, materializing from the shadows. He points to the memorial flier in my possession and removes it from my hand with care. "I had to bring the baby up for a nap. He's in the car with the nanny. Sorry I missed the rest." He gestures his thumb above his shoulder, aiming at the celebration below us.

"Still can't believe you named him after my brother," I say, moving closer to him.

My words seem to have provoked a profound emotion. I see it on his face. "Hmm. Me neither but enough of that. Where's Noah?"

"He'll be here soon."

A blue puffy jacket swaddles him in this cool spring night, and a burp cloth remains on his shoulder. His eyes are haunted by sleepless nights, but I know he toils out of love and never of obligation. He did the same thing for me all these years, and he'll continue to do so if I'm just not too stubborn to defy it. Henry's life is shrouded in mystery and damage, and we share a big chunk of that horror. Yet through it all, his impaired body has been able to nurse a heart of gold against tragedies, that would have steered everyone else the other way. I will always love him in a special manner, just as I love Noah differently.

"By the way, I have something for you." He leaves his spot immediately to rummage through the things inside his trunk. His car is just steps away, parked under the street light. Soon enough, he returns with a manila envelope.

"Oh," I become I little bit startled, taken aback by his action. He has driven me inside his embrace, the one that always made me feel safe.

"Call me anytime when you need me," he orders sternly, even while we relish in this sweet moment. He releases me and hands the item. "Here you go, a little gift."

His lips find its way on my cheek right after, warm and tender. "You're free. More importantly, the weddings are a go," he says next.

I couldn't contain my shock. Not even the tangible item in my hand could validate the realness of this moment. I am a free woman, his words not mine. But why does it ache? The severing of his protective tie is felt sorely from my chest. I know he'll always be there for me, but the finality of our separation is frightening.

"Are you sure?" I mouth the words before realizing their weight.

He throws a questioning look. I expect it. "What do you mean?" His chuckle approaches. Its riddled with tension. "This is what you've been wanting, isn't it?" There's confusion in his tone, but also some likeness of hope.

"Yes. Of course!" I reply, pulling back the uncertainty from my voice. I shouldn't have said what I said. This is what I had hoped for in a long while. This should make me happy.

Then he retreats back into the night's silver curtain, vanishing before I could process our farewell. I slide the documents out of the packaging, the lamp post making it easy for my eyes to confirm my assumptions. It's a certificate from the state of Washington for the dissolution of our marriage. He did it, finally signed the paper that has since collected both dust and confusion for over a year now.

Thank you, Henry.

But then he returns, back in the closest proximity we've been in a while. He brings his head down to me, eyes screaming with words he refuses to say. I feel his grip on my wrist, so tender and with love. His breath reaches my forehead. It startles me, that I take a step back.

"What's wrong? I ask, tension leaning in beside me. He doesn't say a word, expression desolate. His chest rises to inhale, deep enough to cross his lungs' boundaries. "You're scaring me."

"I'm sorry," he apologizes, almost lacking warmth. I feel his hold grow tighter, as we remain face to face. "I need to say something," he continues, whipping a cold air down my spine. I'm afraid of what I'm going to hear. "You asked me so many —"

"Stop!" I order, retrieving my hand and disrupting his openness. I pull away, maybe a couple of feet from him. "I don't wanna hear it, whatever you're gonna say." Somehow, I know what's about to come out of his mouth. It's too late. It won't matter. "I have to go," I tell him, turning my heels to run without direction.

"Ophelia," he calls out from where he's standing. I stop, refusing to turn around. "I thought you deserve to know some things. Why I left." Hasn't it been obvious? The reason is clearly the mother of his child. "Two things," he continues, as the suddenly quiet night tends to his heavy respirations. "I couldn't protect you and love you at the same time," he reveals, his words pinching the skin on my chest. "With how much I care about you, it makes it incredibly hard to do what I'm supposed to do. And I can't let my guard down." He moves closer, I feel his body behind me. "Look at me. Please." My trembling hands are once again confiscated by him. "Please," he begs some more.

An image of a broken man surfaces, the moment I turn around. I immediately want to console him but decide not to.

"That's why I left, because of the potential damage it could put you in," he adds. I had to be vigilant. Can't let anything cloud my judgment. Not my heart. That was my job. It was never to love you but I did. I fucking did! Much more than I led myself to believe. And it kills me inside. Everyday. Because by leaving, I put you in bigger danger than you would have been if I stayed."

"Henry," I call to him, hoping to give him comfort.

"No please," he says, tone insistent. "Please let me finish." He pauses for my permission. I nod as he swallows a lump in his throat. "Second, I always had this fear. You know, the fact that you can't love me back the way I do. The fact that at any given moment, he will return." Noah, there's no one else he could be talking about. "And he did. I didn't want him to come back but he did. And those times you told me that I was the one you loved, I just didn't wanna believe it. I always felt like one of these days, the rug is gonna be pulled from underneath us. I knew it was a lie. You only said it because you can't remember anyone else apart from me."

"I don't know what to say." I'm stunned. I have always felt some semblance of love from him, but I accepted it as part of survival. I thought he couldn't love me because I'm lacking in many ways, but he was just afraid. He was always afraid of the day when I finally rekindle my love for Noah. Remember is more appropriate to say. It pains me, sensing his regret because all that he feared came to be.

His admission makes me realize the authority of our words, how the ones that never left his mouth would have altered my destiny. I wouldn't be here now. It's also clear to me, how uncertain he's been. He wants me to refute what he said. A part of him wishes that I would object, to tell him that I did love him. It's true. I loved him and I would have died believing that he was the only person I felt it for. I still love him.

"You don't have to. I just wish things were different but I'm not holding you back and I'm not trying to change your mind. We both know who you should be with. Him coming back reminded me of that."

I didn't realize it at first, but I have thrown myself at him. His embrace is protective as usual, skin is warmer than the last time I felt it. Henry's actions finally match with his words.

"I'm sorry," he whispers.

I pull back to regard him, his face still harassed by guilt. "Henry, stop! I am here because of you. You know that. And I wish things were different too. I wish you had said something before but we can't turn back the time anymore. Have you seen me? In the last year most of all? It's because of all the sacrifices you've made." I cup his face at the jaws, his soft skin meeting my cold hands. "I am forever in your debt."

"I'm sorry," he cries out again. His hidden anguish is released with his small tears. "I'm sorry for bringing you back to your mother, and eventually to Owen. I was a fool to believe that it was over when she died. I just wanted us to come here so I can be sure that it's real. What was I thinking? I was the one who broke my own rule, to never again bring you back to our past. I just wanted you to remember the family who loves you here. I just thought... I thought we were free."

"But it all worked out," I try to convince him, pulling away just so I could mean it.

He wraps me again in his embrace without saying another word. We stand there for a long while, in each other's grasp, allowing tears to soak on shoulders that reciprocate in love. I feel sadness but also some release, in knowing how he sees me, much more than a thing to be nurtured.

Shit!

I become startled. A loud honk of a car horn withdraws Henry's embrace, as the white Ford Explorer meets a screeching stop next to us. Out emerges Noah's face from the driver's window, brimming with exhilaration.

"I'm here for the future Mrs. Mason. Have you seen her?"

There's an intoxicating luminescence how his eyes approach their beholder. It's as if Noah certainly could pull every star from its death and revive fallen galaxies from their black hole burials, simply by his gaze. And before I could recognize our separation, Henry is gone. He leaves me with a parting gift that sits heavy on my shoulders. But I'm lucky. I know I am, to have both men love me in varying degrees and reasons.

"I don't know, what does she look like?" I joke back, playing with my ring finger and the heavy jewelry crowning it. The square diamond glistens in the night, awaiting to be praised.

"Well, only the most beautiful woman I've ever seen in my entire life!" He boasts.

"Oh yeah?" I walk closer to him until we're nose to nose. He is entirely mystical and conceivable at the same time, even the darkness agrees. It couldn't help but offer up his perfection back to the light. "Love me?" I ask.

"Yes baby! Always have, always will," comes his undoubted response.

Then we kiss, inside the noose of our fate. In this once familiar landscape now peopled with strangers, my home rests unchanged.

CHAPTER TWENTY-EIGHT

The Past Enters, It Always Does

"Okay, I'll be right back. I gotta take a leak and fill this baby up," he says, releasing himself from the seat belt. I have come to appreciate the stubbles adorning his face. His sensual candor is making my butterflies riot inside my stomach. I blame it on his white linen shirt and his longer locks swaying with the breeze like silk. "How about those sour bear thingies? You like those, right?"

I nod at him, failing to unruffle my arousal. He walks out of the car and into the gas station store, leaving me here to admire the sparkling addition to my ring finger. It's only been a month but it feels like a lifetime has passed since I became his wife. Wife, I still watch my soul leave my body at the sound of it.

We inherited a few skin burns from the brazen sun in this part of the country, having spent our days in the Havasupai wilderness. I'm struck with awe, seeing the motley rock faces and canyon heads through the windshield, though they mean nothing without Noah.

I begin to wonder what became of the world while we were momentarily released from its spindle. It might be worth checking my phone, but I only find his upon opening the glove compartment. It is currently squirming in vibration for who knows how long. I take it out from storage, and see Dylan's name on the screen. Should I answer it? I guess not. Besides, I am still on his naughty list. The vibrating stops, revealing that he has called about thirty-three times.

My heart jerks, mind speculating on what could be of pressing cause. There's still no sign of Noah. I need him to be here to call Dylan back. I'm starting to get worried. Another vibration comes through, a voicemail. My anxiety is creeping up to boil. Did something happen to his parents? Grandma? What if he's calling about mine? Oh god!

I need to look for my phone. I pat my front pockets for it. No sign. Not even inside my jacket. I comb my fingers under the seat, my body wilting to the side by the action. Finally, the device makes it to my grasp. I pull it out and press the screen. It's dead. What if they've been calling my phone until the battery drained.

Shit!

Noah will understand, he has to for what I'm about to do. I take his phone again, this time unlocking it by a six digit code. It's our wedding date. He told me when he changed it. I tap a finger on the voicemail widget, and press the play button before bringing the phone to my ear.

"Hey man! Fuck," It's obviously Dylan. He seems upset, even frantic. "Why aren't you answering your damn phone. Is she close? I need to talk to you but she can't be around for it. Call me!"

A long beep follows the message. The next one plays right away.

"Listen, they were doing some surveillance shit across her mom's old house. Pulled tapes from a year back cuz the husband has been cheating on his wife, and she needed to prove it. Man," he pauses. "Fuck! They saw her. Ophelia. She was here the night before her mom was found dead. Saw her on the tape, man. It was dark but it's her. It doesn't look good. I don't think her mom committed suicide. I think she killed her. She remembers. She doesn't have fucking amnesia. Bitch played us! Now you call me back. Need to know you're safe."

I feel my own body obey its autopilot, clearing Dylan's calls as well as his voicemails at once. Something drags my feet outside and I conform to its survival tactics, realizing the fate of Noah's phone long after it already found a home inside the trash bucket. I sit back here with a fist over the other, weighing the high stakes I might lose with this information. I can't lose. Take everything but him.

The driver's door opens, letting in the taste of tenderness in the face of Noah. "Hey, Babe! Guess who forgot his wallet?"

I force a laugh, convincing him that things are as they should.

"Oh! You gotta charge your phone," he advises, realizing its drained state. "I wonder where mine is. Hope I didn't leave it at camp?" He finds his wallet under the tribal blanket. "Found it!"

"Okay."

LUNA

Her eyes falter back to their own mystique as the weight of my attendance presses further down on her shoulders. I must admit, she's beautiful even with the hardened lines on her face. They are branding scars, burrowed by the claws of evil that she eventually became.

"Ophelia? Honey. What are you doing here? It's not safe," she warns.

For you, it isn't.

"That's not my name," I tell her, tone biting with ire.

Unlike my other partial self, I remember everything that she has done to me, to us. Everything. On the other hand, Ophelia is weak and lack the ferocity to deserve this body and mind. She's right there in the corner of my previous chamber, plagued by another loss and self-abhorrence from this Noah person. Here I am, surfacing from the flood of her limitations, fighting and surviving for the both of us.

I want her to look my way and at least give me a nod of approval, for I have mustered what she couldn't. I'm facing this woman who calls herself her mother, with a goal of retribution. It's time to collect the dues, to pay for what she has done to our body. You see, I could care less about Ophelia's utter pain when she woke up without Noah by her side. Yet her disadvantage is both our failure, and so despite the error of her ways, I'm forced to remain on her side. After all, I'm getting so tired of being repressed in the background when I could have been in the forefront, taking care of business as they should be handled.

Pathetic. This woman is still in the morrow of a rather confusing few days in Mexico. She's still lost, even after months have passed. This is a coward, sinking herself back into the hole of forgets because she'd rather do that than face on old foe. We all know it was Owen, the stench of his grubby beard still lingers on my neck. He took advantage of the opportunity to claim her back into his clutches once more, all while

Noah was merely some feet away.

Ophelia allows them all to play a role in her charade, believing a lie about an airplane accident when she was in fact assaulted. She always wants to forget. This has always been her mastery.

I'm not her though, not some pitiful woman who believes that a great love is the only way to fix her. I'm smart enough to know that the past can never be undone. And the future? Well, that is now in my hands.

"What do you mean, honey? How long have you been standing there?" she inquires again, slipping into a fleece robe.

She stretches a hand to the wall. Light pours in the room as she finds the flip switch, her body moving about in sheer inelegance. She's severely unqualified to sit up on the bed. When I finally blink away the rage in my eyes, the thin woman forces a smile. Ophelia's mother has been enlaced by her defeats against cancer. It's almost unequivocal, the parts of her body where death came to smear. Color has been drained from her skin, face painted by undernourishment. Her lips droop, lacking fight and vigor. Those eyes too, edges of the almond shape yielding to gravity. She has evaded sleep or rather, it has evaded her. She shouldn't look this old. I almost contemplate on leaving her be. She's going to succumb to her disease soon enough but where is the justice in that?

"What are you doing?" she asks as I move closer to the bed. Her voice trembles both in illness and fear. She locks her sight at the object in my fist and there is a momentary shudder in her body afterwards.

I smirk before an answer leaves my mouth. "What I should have done a long time ago."

The breeze falls in through the open window, driving the white drapes to dance in silence against the striped wallpaper. Goosebumps awaken my body hair, the same way it wields on her skin. I observe her. She wraps the robe tighter around her skeleton. I catch a glimpse of the orange pill bottles strewn on her bedside table, chuckling to myself at the thought of her misused life, and how it would meet its end at any moment.

"Ophelia. Stop," she forces a scream, using up all the air in her lungs. The bed catches her tremors. "I'm gonna die soon if that's what you wanna see, but I beg you. Leave now. He's gonna be here any minute. I have a plan. Just leave. Now."

"I said my name is not Ophelia! I told you, didn't I?"

She swallows a lump, a flicker of knowledge landing in her eyes. The woman realizes it, becoming aware of the new person in Ophelia's face. At the same time, she staggers at its unfolding.

"Ophelia?" Her gaze bravely defies mine. "If you can hear me, he's coming. Owen will be here. You know it's not safe. You have to go!"

I arrive at her bedside and partially expect her to scoot up on the bed, farther away from me. It doesn't happen. She's calm, the last of her fears have seemingly been infected by cancer too.

"Ha!" I quip. "She's not here. It's just Luna now."

My hand reaches for hers and she readily relinquishes it in my control. I'm not surprised.

"Please, you have to trust me on this one, Luna. Ophelia would want you to," she pleads again, foisting against my already firm decision.

The gun makes it inside her grip and I drive it up her bony temple. She doesn't flinch, not even at the sound of it cocking.

"See the problem is, this is not Ophelia anymore." I press the barrel farther against her skin but worry fails to rule her. It's almost something to be admired. "And I'm sure as hell not at anyone's bidding. I do what I want and right now this is what I'm supposed to do, cut away the root of Ophelia's suffering."

She mumbles again but failing with her words. "But. He…"

"Shut up! Shut the fuck up. I don't give a shit!" My shouts penetrate through her bearings, more than the gun to her head. "Whatever you say, it won't change a thing. All the horrors you put Ophelia through, this is to be expected. This is how it ends."

I wrap my index finger around hers, forcing it on the trigger. It's time, we're all owed some retribution here. This is for Ophelia, after being forced to a fate worse than death. She is the perpetrator, this very woman, her mother pimp. Maybe this body and mind will finally surrender to my control after all this. Perhaps Ophelia will, once and for all, trust me to take the wheel.

But then, something crashes against the door downstairs. Tire screeches pummel through the dead of night. Headlights flood the long and dark driveway. I see them through the window. Human figures begin to scurry in the shadows.

She wasn't lying.

END

ABOUT THE AUTHOR

Author of contemporary women's fiction and confessional poetry, Elle Bor's emotional adherence to old world, and often antiquated literary works, spurred one facet of her writing style. The other part is steered by a contemporary interpretation of this deeply-rooted language.

An esteemed writer from a small town in the Philippines, her paternal grandfather was instrumental in her passion for the craft. His influence is notable in Elle Bor's equally nostalgic and new age tone, in both poetry and prose.

Having been raised in a family that often refrains from expressing emotions, writing was her only method of healing following the death of her mother 28 years ago.

When not creating, Elle Bor takes advantage of her eclectic book collection. She loves to travel off the beaten path and embark on gastronomic adventures. She also has a severe obsession to crime series, reality shows, fashion, and dogs.

**For details of our other books, or to submit your own manuscript
please visit**

www.green-cat.co